The Sound of Us

The Sound of Us

Sarah Castille

TOR PUBLISHING GROUP · NEW YORK

This is a work of fiction. All of the characters, organizations, and events portrayed in this novel are either products of the author's imagination or are used fictitiously.

THE SOUND OF US

A Bramble Book
Published by Tom Doherty Associates / Tor Publishing Group
120 Broadway
New York, NY 10271

www.torpublishinggroup.com

The Library of Congress Cataloging-in-Publication Data is available upon request.

ISBN 978-1-250-28991-9 (trade paperback)
ISBN 978-1-250-28990-2 (ebook)

Our books may be purchased in bulk for promotional, educational, or business use. Please contact your local bookseller or the Macmillan Corporate and Premium Sales Department at 1-800-221-7945, extension 5442, or by email at MacmillanSpecialMarkets@macmillan.com.

First Edition: 2024

Printed in the United States of America

10 9 8 7 6 5 4 3 2 1

To anyone who has ever fallen in love
with the boy their mother warned them about

The Sound of Us

CHAPTER ONE

"Learning to Fly" by Hills X Hills

SKYE

"I can't do this."

I hesitated on the threshold of the bar, taking in the teeming mass of bodies on the dance floor, the scents of stale beer and deep-fried chicken wings, and the ear-splitting shriek of "Cotton-Eyed Joe" playing over tinny speakers. Bile rose in my throat, bringing with it the taste of the multiple virgin margaritas my best friend Isla had made me drink to "warm up" for the start of a new year at Chicago's Havencrest University. I'd missed the tradition the previous fall when I'd been away on a medical leave of absence and now everything in the room screamed that I didn't belong.

"Yes, you can." Isla grabbed my hand and dragged me through the crowd. Steamworks was a typical college bar decorated in Havencrest's purple and gold, with pictures of sports teams and pennants on the walls and a reclaimed iron bell hanging over the bar. The recreation area consisted of a cramped space along one side where a pool table had been jammed precariously close to the dart board. A raised stage for live music and a generous dance floor took up another corner. I hadn't been to the bar since freshman year, but it still had the same upbeat vibe.

"I didn't drag your sorry ass all the way back from Colorado just to fill the empty room in my apartment," she continued as we zigzagged around the scattered tables and chairs. "You promised you'd help me land my fangirl crush while we try to get your mind off your basketball tryout on Monday and I'm holding you to it. Maybe my fantasy guitar player has a friend . . ."

"I don't have time for hookups." I had to raise my voice so she would hear me over the buzz of the crowd. "I need to stay focused. I have to get back on the team, Iz. I have one chance to get my basketball career back on track. I really shouldn't even be out tonight."

I stumbled after her, still struggling to get used to walking in heels after my accident. I was okay in running shoes, but heels required a whole new level of coordination. Still, I'd been determined to dress up for my first night out in over eighteen months. I'd hidden the scars on my legs under a pair of skinny denim jeans that I'd paired with a new carbon-black lace camisole, big hoop earrings, and lots of bracelets. Instead of my usual ponytail, I'd left my long dark hair loose. Isla said I'd never looked hotter, but I missed my skirts and dresses.

"It's Friday night, party night," Isla pleaded as she squeezed us into the only two empty chairs at the bar. "I need you to dazzle him with your music knowledge or I won't have a shot."

With a head full of dark, bouncy curls, a round cheerful face, and an undying sense of optimism reflected in her wide, caramel-colored eyes, Isla was impossible to resist. She was loud, upbeat, and lived her life without a filter—pretty much the opposite of me. I would never have imagined we'd become besties when we found ourselves assigned to the same dorm room freshman year, but we complemented each other. Isla had a way of unleashing my wild side, and I had a way of keeping her calm.

"I'm not going back on my promise," I assured her. "You want the lead guitarist of the Jethro Tully Band in your bed; I'll do my best to get him for you."

"I need some liquid courage first."

"You had three liquid 'courages' before we came here," I pointed out. "You need to be semi-sober so you don't go all fangirl and make him think you're a groupie who only wants sex."

"I am a groupie who only wants sex," she said. "But he's not going to know that because you're going to lure him in with music talk and then I'll do what I do best."

I hadn't had a chance to really talk music in the eighteen months since my father and I had been hit by a drunk driver while on our way to the airport. Music is my everything—my escape, my solace, medicine for my soul, and the only way I can express emotions too deep and painful to share. Music is my language. It filled the silence in my heart after I found out my father had died in the crash, and for the duration of my recovery, it sustained me.

Isla managed to catch the attention of the blond, tanned bartender by leaning over the bar and shouting, "Broken glass!" He introduced himself as Scott and told us he spent his summers surfing in California. When he added an extra splash of juice and a cherry to my mocktail, Isla gave me a not-too-subtle "he's into you" poke in the ribs. I gave her a discreet "not interested" shake of my head. Aside from the fact that blond surfer dudes weren't my type, and the fact that I had more riding on the tryout than I'd shared with Isla, I wasn't ready for anyone to see my scars.

Isla, of course, didn't take the hint and decided to hype me up. "Skye is in journalism and she's trying out for the basketball team," she said as he handed me the drink with a flourish. "She is also big into music and has hundreds, probably thousands of playlists. She got paid by her boss at the Buttercup Bakery café to make a playlist for the coffee shop—"

"Isla . . ." I didn't want to be having this conversation. It had taken all my effort to mentally prepare myself to return to college after having to take so much time off and give up my hard-earned position on Havencrest's Division II basketball team. I knew Isla wanted to help me get back to normal, but I didn't have the mental or emotional energy for anything other than sports and school.

"I've got tons of playlists." The bartender whipped out his phone like we were in a competition and slid it across the bar. "Take a look."

"Wow." I flipped through his list. "That's . . . quite a collection."

I sipped my drink, hoping he wouldn't want to have a discussion about his musical choices including a cringe playlist called *Boner*.

"Show him yours." Isla gave me a nudge and I grimaced. I loved talking music but I didn't like talking about *my* music. My playlists are intensely personal, a secret peek into my soul and a record of poignant musical memories. They are a way to process strong emotions and express myself using the words of the poets of song.

I gave him an apologetic shrug. "I'm actually in the middle of changing things up, but right now I'm into Angerfist's 'The Depths of Despair.'"

His face paled as he listened to the track, and I called it a win.

Isla shot me a look of exasperation and quickly smoothed over the awkward moment with a smile. "We're here to see the Jethro Tully Band. When are they on?"

"They aren't playing tonight," he said. "Last-minute cancellation. We've got Dante's Inferno instead. They're a great band. Well, they were. They had a few bad gigs over the summer, but we were desperate."

"Sorry, Iz." Guilty relief tempered my sympathy. We could finally go home, and I could find another way to deal with my pre-tryout jitters that didn't involve high heels.

"Just my luck." With a sigh, Isla opened her purse and pulled out her vape.

"If you want to smoke, you'll need to go outside," Scott said. "It's quiet in the back alley." His gaze flicked from me to Isla, letting us know he'd take whoever he could get. "I'm heading out there for my break in about ten minutes if you want some company."

"Sounds good." She tucked the vape away. "We'll see you out there."

I followed Isla past the long lineup for the restroom and down the back hallway, trying hard to disguise the slight limp that warned I'd hit my activity threshold for the day. Six months ago, still deep in depression after the accident, I'd never imagined I'd be able to walk properly, much less be back at university and planning to try out again for the Havencrest Warriors, but I hadn't accounted for Isla. When I told her I wasn't planning to return to Havencrest for my sophomore year, she flew all the way to Denver with a bag full of summer basketball training camp brochures, scholarship applications, and a copy of her lease. She was there for entirely selfish reasons, she said. Her roommate was graduating, and she needed someone to move in who knew about her past and could put up with her particular brand of crazy.

The back door to the alley had been propped open, and we walked outside into the humid, muggy night, where four guys were unloading band equipment from the back of a van in the semi-darkness.

Isla gestured me away from the door and I leaned against the brick wall to take the pressure off my left leg, wishing for fall with its crisp air and the cooling Lake Michigan breeze.

"Why are we here, Iz? We can come back another night when your fangirl crush is playing."

"Because we need to talk about why you told the cute bartender who's into you that you were listening to Angelfire's 'Song of Despair.'"

"The band is Angerfist," I corrected her. "The song is 'The Depths of Despair,' and I came here tonight for you. I'm not ready to date, especially not someone who called his sex playlist *Boner*."

Isla laughed. "He had playlists. You love making playlists . . ."

"I know what you were trying to do, but it's not a good time. Tryouts are on Monday and if I don't get back on the roster . . ." The fear I'd been trying to suppress all day welled up in my chest, stealing my breath away.

"Then you become a journalist," she said firmly. "You didn't just come to Havencrest to play basketball. You came because of their journalism program. Skye, they chose you out of thousands of applicants because you have talent."

"Journalism is my fallback option," I said. "Basketball has been my whole life. It's what my dad and I dreamed about, and now he's gone. I want to honor his memory. I still want to make him proud."

I also needed the full-ride athletic scholarship that came with a place on the team. Between medical bills and the loss of my father's income, my mother could barely make ends meet. My younger brother Jonah had a heart condition and required special care, and I didn't want to add to her burden by telling her that I'd just had a meeting with my student financial advisor and things didn't look good. I'd lost my prestigious internship at the *Chicago Times* when I withdrew to recover from my injuries, and even with my part-time job at the coffee shop on campus, I couldn't pay for another three years at college without financial aid.

"Your dreams are going to come true." Isla pulled out her vape. "I've got a sixth sense about these things."

"Iz . . ." I shook my head. "You promised me you were going to quit. You're a biochem major. You know how bad vaping is for you."

"I just need one hit to get over my disappointment," she said. "It gives me the kind of buzz I can't get from alcohol. And Scott's on his way. It wouldn't be nice to make him vape alone."

"Give it to me." I held out my hand.

"This is the last time. I promise."

"You told me if I saw you vaping again to stop you by any means possible." I lunged for her, and she backed away just as two guys emerged from the van carrying a large amp. Isla stumbled, grabbing my arm and pulling me off-balance. We went down hard, falling against the amp and knocking it to the ground. I rolled off Isla and snaked up beside her to grab the vape from her hand.

A shadow fell across us, and a deep voice resonated in the darkness. "Now, that's loyalty."

CHAPTER TWO

"Sound of Your Voice" by Port Cities

SKYE

Have you ever heard a voice that takes your breath away? I'm talking that deep, heart-melting bass with the low C talent from musical greats like Johnny Cash, Leonard Cohen, and Jim Morrison—a voice that makes the most mundane words sound rich beyond imagining. Silken and sensuous, distinctly seductive, the first time I heard his voice, it vibrated deep into my body and bones.

"I'm so sorry. I didn't mean to . . ." I looked up, my voice trailing off as I fell into the most intense dark eyes I'd ever seen. For a moment I thought Jeff Buckley had come back from the grave to rip my heart out with his haunting cover of "Hallelujah" all over again. The man holding out his hand to me was quite simply my fantasy come to life.

He had features a sculptor would love: angular jaw, high cheekbones, and a strong chin. A vintage The Cure T-shirt molded over a body that radiated raw, lean power, the short sleeves revealing chiseled arms covered in ink. His black Levi's sat low on his hips, held in place by a brown leather belt that matched his Red Wing Heritage Blacksmiths. The way he moved when he held out his hand screamed street-level royalty—the hot dude at the party you would never approach in case you stutter or stammer or stare at your shoes.

"Let me help you up." His warm hand engulfed mine and he pulled me up in one smooth, easy motion, his forearm rippling beneath the ink. Liquid heat flooded my veins, and my body came alive with the most primal of hunger.

He helped Isla to her feet, and she shot me a worried look. "Are you okay?"

"Uh . . ." I nodded, unable to take my eyes off the pure, exquisite masculinity in front of me.

With a snort of laughter, Isla picked up her vape and went to join Scott, who had just walked out into the alley.

"Are you sure you're okay?" My rescuer's voice moved through my body like the beat of a song as he brushed messy strands of his dark brown hair out of his face.

"I'm . . ." Bewitched, bewildered, entranced. I was a down-to-earth, practical person who preferred facts to fiction, reality to fantasy. Never in my life had I met a man who so utterly and completely overwhelmed all my senses.

His lips quirked at the corners, drawing my attention to his soft mouth and straight white teeth. "'Eye of the Tiger'? 'Eye in the Sky'? 'Eye Know'?"

Did he just name "eye" song titles?

"You forgot 'Eyes of A Stranger,' 'Eyes Without a Face,' 'Eye,' and 'Eyes on You.'" The words came out before I could stop them, my competitive streak tweaked by his music-based query.

"She knows her music." A grin spread across his face, taking him from beautiful to breathtaking in a heartbeat.

"So does he." I held out my hand. "I'm Skye."

"Dante." His warm palm pressed against mine, sending a delicious shiver down my spine.

"Are you going to include any 'eye' songs in the playlist you're making in your head tonight?" he asked.

I vaguely remembered mentioning the playlist to Isla when we'd walked into the alley. "You were listening to a private conversation."

"That you were having right outside my van," he interjected. "I couldn't leave without disturbing you, so I was effectively trapped inside with nothing to do but listen."

"If you found yourself inadvertently listening to a private conversation, you should have made some noise, covered your ears, or, here's a thought . . ." I couldn't keep the sarcasm from my tone. "You could have come out of the van, let us know we were disturbing you, and we would have gone back inside."

"But then I wouldn't have heard about the guy with the *Boner* playlist." Dante's voice rippled with laughter. "I wouldn't have known that your tremendous leap for your friend's vape was the result of being a basketball player, and not some kind of secret superhero skill."

My lips quirked at the corners. "How do you know I'm not a superhero?"

"My bad." He held up his hands, palms forward. His fingers were long, slim, and calloused. Musician's hands. "I must have missed the cape."

"Is that your idea of an apology?" My eyes followed the rugged contours of his face, the line of his jaw, the fullness of his lips. *Big mistake.* I could feel my face flush hot, my cheeks burning like I'd spent a day in the sun.

A grin lit his face. "If I really wanted to apologize, I'd send you a playlist of carefully curated songs."

A sliver of pain shot up my leg, warning me I'd been standing still too long, but damned if I was going to walk away when things were getting interesting.

"What would be on this apology playlist?" Creating a playlist is both an art and a form of personal expression. My playlists are inspired by an emotion, an event, or a moment in time. I build on the feeling with songs that not only flow together but whose titles and lyrics express a cohesive story. I desperately wanted to know the stories his playlists would tell.

Dante's eyes glittered with amusement, and he pulled out his phone, scrolling until he landed on something that made his lips quiver. "Which one?"

"Which one?" My voice rose in pitch. "Do you make a habit of pissing people off?"

"I like to be prepared," he said.

"For eavesdropping on private conversations?"

"For riling up a beautiful woman."

My mouth opened and closed again. I'd given up on feeling beautiful a long time ago, and especially after the accident that left my body covered in scars. "You're dragging this out," I said. "First song. And if you even mention Adele, I'm out of here."

His lips twisted in a grin. "'Wrecking Ball.'"

Laughter bubbled up in my chest and came out with an inelegant snort. "Seriously?"

"Seriously."

"That's not really an apology. It's a song about regret."

"I regret overhearing your conversation," he said, his eyes sparkling. "But if you really need to hear the words, I can change it to the 'Apology Song' by The Decemberists."

"That's about a bicycle." My cheeks were sore, and it took me a moment to realize that I hadn't stopped smiling since we met. I looked around for Isla to share the joy, but she was deep in a conversation with Scott.

"He was very sorry he lost it." Dante tipped his head to the side and gave me a teasing smile. "It's not easy to find apology songs that don't deal with heartbreak."

"What else is on your non-apology playlist?" I wanted to know every song. I wanted our conversation to go on until I could figure out why, for the first time in forever, I felt a lightness in my soul.

"'A Little Bit Me, A Little Bit You.'"

"The Monkees?" I liked that his musical tastes varied wildly, so much like mine. "I am not to blame. *You* were the eavesdropper."

"How about Chicago's 'Hard to Say I'm Sorry'? he offered. "Demi Lovato's 'Sorry Not Sorry'?"

"I'll take your pathetic and unsophisticated apology playlist and raise you Madonna's 'Sorry' and OneRepublic's 'Apologize.'" My heart pounded, and I felt a rush of adrenaline like it was Christmas and my birthday and the day I'd been accepted to

Havencrest's prestigious journalism program on a full-ride basketball scholarship all at once.

He staggered back in mock horror. "You reject my apology?"

I smiled. He smiled. Where had he come from? This man who spoke my language in a world I no longer understood.

We spent the next five minutes trying to outdo each other with obscure songs or silly lyrics. He knew more classic rock. I knew pop. He beat me in hardcore but couldn't match my love of jazz. I was vaguely aware of his bandmates behind me, climbing in and out of the van to unload their gear.

"Where does Angerfist feature?" Amusement laced his voice as his smoldering eyes danced over me. "Dutch hardcore or hardstyle beats don't really seem to be your vibe."

"It doesn't feature. I was trying to put out a 'I'm not into you' vibe for a guy who . . ." I glanced over again at Isla and Scott, lowering my voice so they couldn't overhear us. "Wasn't really my type."

"What is your type?"

"Someone who doesn't have Hudson Mohawke's 'Cbat' on repeat as their number one song on their *Boner* playlist."

Dante threw back his head and laughed. "That doesn't really tell me anything except that you like a little variety with your sex."

Burn, cheeks, burn. "A track full of disjointed beats and a repeated sample of squawking is not particularly romantic."

"So, it's romance you want." His eyes dropped to my mouth, and I couldn't help but wonder what it would feel like to kiss those soft lips. "Is that the theme of tonight's playlist?"

"I don't want anything," I said, turning away. Music, I could handle, but not the direction of the conversation. "My theme was about escape. I haven't been to a bar for a long time, and I was feeling a bit overwhelmed."

"First song?"

I could have just walked away in that moment instead of giving this stranger a glimpse into my soul, but he had me under some kind of spell. Not everyone understood the rules of creating the perfect playlist. Nothing is more important than the first song. It establishes the mood or theme and gives a hint of what's coming next.

"Rusted Root's 'Send Me on My Way,'" I blurted out, and then, since I'd broken my own rule about sharing, I let it all go. "Then I was playing around with G Flip's 'GET ME OUTTA HERE,' Dobie Gray's 'Drift Away'—the original and not a cover—The Lost Patrol Band's 'Going Going Going Gone,' and Kanye West's 'Runaway.' Sometimes you just need that literal meaning when you're feeling something big. I try to capture the mood in the moment before it's gone."

"That's what I like about Paul Simon," Dante said. "He's one of my favorite songwriters of all time. You always know what he's talking about. When he says, 'A man walks down the street,' he's just telling a story, and you don't have to get into heated debates or analyze the meaning of each word. It's the kind of music that really resonates with me."

"Like Cat Stevens and Harry Nilsson," I offered.

"Exactly."

We stared at each other in a comfortable shared silence, the sense of being separate together almost as seductive as his sexy smile. I'd never been so attracted to someone's mind that I wanted to give it space. I'd never connected with someone in a way language could not express.

When he finally spoke, my heart skipped a little beat. "What song are you listening to right now?"

I pressed my lips together to stop myself from smiling. I always had a song. My mind wrote my soundtrack as I lived my life.

"Is that your equivalent of a pickup line?"

"Do you want it to be?" His words shimmered in the air between us, sending a rush of white-hot heat through my veins.

Yes. No. I don't know. On the surface, Dante was the kind of guy I fantasized about but could only watch from a distance. Too cool.

Too hip. Too unpredictable for someone like me who had spent their whole life trying to avoid rejection. But underneath . . .

"Coming through," a man said behind me.

I startled, moving a second too late. Something hard and heavy hit me from behind and I stumbled forward. Dante moved unbelievably fast, catching me and pulling me into his chest.

Our eyes met. Locked. Gold flecks glittered in the midnight depths of his gaze, and he palmed the dip in my waist, drawing me closer. We'd barely acknowledged the hum of electricity between us, the sexual tension that had kept us in the alley when we both had other places to be.

"I should get going," I said. "You're on stage soon."

"I've got time." Neither of us moved. After twenty minutes of easy conversation, we'd run out of things to say. But I knew what I felt. Desire. Raw and soul deep.

I don't know what came over me in that moment. Maybe part of me feared I wouldn't make the roster and I'd never see him again. Or maybe for a brief time he'd made me feel alive. I'd never been the kind of woman who made the first move. But then I'd never met anyone like Dante before.

"Skye . . . ?" he whispered like he knew my thoughts, like he could see into my heart. His breath brushed over my lips, sending a flush of heat through my veins that made my body tremble.

I reached up and pulled him down to me, and anything else he had to say was lost the moment our mouths pressed together.

Some great song intros are long and complex, but in Marvin Gaye's "Let's Get It On," three simple notes let you know you're about to be treated to five minutes of soul-deep sensuality. Dante's kiss moved through me like the rhythm of that song. I melted against him, slowly unraveling as he eased my lips apart. His tongue glided along mine, sending a wave of heat rippling over my skin. I knotted my fists in his shirt and pulled him closer. He groaned low and deep in his throat, and then his arms wrapped around me, and for a moment we were one body, not two.

"Dude." The voice behind us was laced with irritation. "Break it up. I need to switch out this amp and we're on in twenty."

Dante froze and pulled away, breaking the spell. For the briefest of moments, I'd forgotten we weren't alone in the darkness, that I wasn't the kind of woman who kissed strangers in dark alleys, that I might very well be leaving and wouldn't be back.

A gust of cold air blew through the alley, and I gave an involuntary shiver. Dante's gaze dropped to my arms.

"You're cold."

"I'll be fine once I get back inside."

"Wait here." He disappeared into the van and returned a few moments later with an oversize black hoodie. It had a stylized bonfire on the front with the words *Dante's Inferno* written across it.

I traced over the embroidered lettering. "It's got a retro look. I like it."

He hesitated, his mouth opening like he wanted to say something. Instead, he held out the hoodie, his voice quiet, controlled. "Hands up."

Without giving it much thought, I obediently raised my arms. Dante carefully pulled the hoodie over my head, blanketing me in warmth, his voice dropping to a sensual rumble. "Good girl."

My brain short-circuited, my face heating to what felt like one thousand degrees, and an unexpected wave of desire pulsed through my veins.

If only he knew.

I'd spent my entire life trying to be a good girl. I'd put aside my love of music and my interest in journalism to join the school basketball team so my father, a former NBA player, could live his dream of playing professionally through me. But it was never enough. I was never enough. I'd never thought that my deepest darkest self might harbor a secret craving. A need that might manifest itself as a rush of white-hot heat, a fire kindled by praise that flamed and licked and begged for more.

Dante tugged the sweatshirt over my head and gently pulled my hair free while I studied the worn, brown leather of his boots. My heart pounded, my traitorous body trembling. I tried to smooth my expression so he wouldn't know he'd pushed a button I didn't even know I had.

When I finally looked up, our gazes met, locked with an intensity that made it difficult to swallow.

"Skye . . ."

I felt everything in that one word . . . how much he wanted me, how badly I wanted him, how deep he saw inside me. It scared the hell out of me.

"Dante!" the same dude shouted from the open doorway. "You've been working that bitch up for over half an hour. Save the groupies for after the show. Christ, how many times are you gonna make us set up without you while you hit up some chick? It's not fair, bruh. We all want to get laid."

How many times?

Dante's face hardened. "Shut the fuck up, Quinn."

The guy who walked into the alley had a broad, craggy face, straight black hair that hid his eyes, and a thick, muscular body. He smirked knowingly as his gaze slid to me. "You've got ten minutes to give him what he's after, honey, or you're gonna have to wait until after the show like all the other girlies he's got lined up for tonight."

I felt a pain in my chest and had to fight back the overwhelming urge to turn and run. Even with my clothes on, I felt naked in the alley, on display for everyone to see.

Idiot. I should have known. Guys that gorgeous thought they could have anyone they wanted. This had been a game to him, and I didn't want to play anymore.

"Iz," I called out. "We need to get going."

Isla took one look at me and turned off her vape. She exchanged numbers with Scott and caught up with me by the door.

"If you want to stay . . ." I began.

"We came together. We leave together," she said. "Also, you look like someone ripped out your heart. I'm not about to let you go home alone."

I couldn't have loved her more.

We made our way back into the bar and wove our way through the crowd. The band had set up and the drummer tapped out a slow beat on stage.

"Well?" Isla asked as she pushed open the front door. "What happened with your hottie?"

"For a few minutes there, I thought he was . . . special. Different. Or maybe the same. We had a lot in common."

She put an arm around my shoulder and gave me a sympathetic squeeze. "At least you've got a good story to tell. 'Isla dragged me to Steamworks for a good time, but all I got was this lousy sweatshirt.'"

I touched the logo embroidered across my chest. Despite the fact I'd misread our encounter, the memory of what could have been was woven into the threads that spelled out his name.

I thought he'd seen me—the real me. But there was no "me" to be seen.

It was the story of my life all over again.

CHAPTER THREE

"Electric Love" by Børns

DANTE

"What the fuck is wrong with you?" I slammed Quinn against the van as soon as we'd finished loading up after the gig. He'd been high on stage, and his addiction was written all over the lines in his thin face, the sunken eyes, and his almost skeletal frame. Worse, he wasn't the only one. Both our lead guitarist and our keyboardist had been messed up. It was yet another disastrous gig after a string of bad performances over the last few months.

"What the fuck is wrong with *you*?" Quinn snickered. "You're always taking the best pussy. Didn't your mother tell you it's nice to share?"

It took every bit of my self-control not to punch his smug face. My mother had been too busy trying to survive my father's abuse to share much life wisdom with me and my little sister, Sasha, but she did try to teach us to keep quiet. Sasha had taken that lesson fully on board and retreated into herself. I'd taken the opposite approach and suffered for it every day.

"She isn't that kind of girl." If I'd been any other man, I would have given in to the urge to punch him, but damned if I would become my dad.

Quinn held up his hand in a warding gesture. "My bad. You clearly haven't fucked her yet. I wouldn't have wasted that opportunity. Did you see that ass?"

I'd seen all of her. She was the kind of woman who drew attention without any effort. My mind flashed back to the moment I'd seen Skye walk into the alley—thick dark hair falling in waves down her back, high smooth cheekbones in a perfectly oval face, jeans that hugged sweet curves and a top that had looked so much like lingerie I'd had to stay in the van until the vivid images of running my hands through the soft material and sliding it off her had passed.

Meeting her in person hadn't helped the situation. I'd fallen into eyes the rich brown-gold of whiskey, arresting and startling at once. I could still remember the feel of her body pressed against mine, the floral scent of her hair, the soft groan she made when she kissed me. But it was our music connection that had hit me the most, as disconcerting as it was intriguing.

"Ignore him. He's just trying to wind you up," Jules said, tucking her drumsticks into the ratty canvas bag slung across her shoulder. Her look was a combination of punk rock and '90s grunge, with a black leather jacket over a ripped tank, torn skinny jeans, and a pair of combat boots that had seen some serious action. Jules had her problems, but substance abuse was no longer one of them.

"He's already wound up," Quinn sneered. "He just didn't have what it took to bring it home."

"At least he could play." Jules turned on him, her pink-streaked bob swinging over her shoulders. "You promised you'd be clean this time."

Quinn's face twisted into a snarl. "I don't have time for this shit. I've got a coupla groupies waiting outside, and *they* appreciate my talents. Who's coming to party?"

"Not this time. I've got a show tonight." I DJ'd the late-night show at Havencrest's independent campus radio station, WJPK, five nights a week from midnight until 2:00 A.M. It was my escape—the only time I could just be me.

Jules turned down the offer as she always did, and we got busy packing up the van. "We need to talk about the band and what's going on." She kept her voice low as I helped her load her drum kit. "We can't do this anymore."

"Do what? Play with half the band barely able to function? I don't think we need to worry about it anymore. The manager wasn't happy, and I'm pretty sure that was our last gig at Steamworks. We already got the axe from three other venues and the next two have canceled based on the rumors. I'm done, Jules. It's over."

"You can't just leave." Jules stared at me, aghast. "What will we do without you?"

"It's my last year at university," I said. "I need to focus on my marks and preparing for the LSAT or I won't get into law school next year. There's nothing I love more than playing live, which is why I've been making the time, but that's my name they're dragging through the mud—my reputation as a musician that's being destroyed. The joy is gone, Jules, and that's everything to me."

Music had been my life when I was young. My mother had been a singer in a band before she met my dad and through her I learned about rock gods like Led Zeppelin, Queen, Jimi Hendrix, and Pink Floyd. She bought me my first guitar when I was five years old, and my grandmother, a professional cellist, gave me my first electric, a black Les Paul, when I was eight. The most important women in my life had given me the gift of music, and even my father couldn't take it away.

"It was just a bad night," she pleaded. "Don't make any final decisions. We can't be a band without a bass player."

"I'm sorry, Jules." I put my bass over my shoulder, adjusting the strap so it sat against my back. I'd discovered the bass after hearing my middle school music teacher play during our annual teachers vs. students Battle of the Bands. He was like the secret hero of each song, steering the band from the shadows and laying down the rhythm of a song. If the lead guitar was the lightning, he was the thunder. I offered to do his yard work in exchange for the lessons my father had refused to pay for, and he gave me his old bass and taught me how to play.

Jules turned on me, hands finding her hips. "What's more important than your music?"

Except for Sasha, nothing had been more important to me than music after my mother died. It was my escape, and after Sasha took her own life, it became my retreat. But when I finally got my life back together, music had to take a back seat to vengeance.

"I'm pursuing my dream of becoming a lawyer." As far as I was concerned, my father was responsible for the deaths of both my mother and sister, and my life goal was to work for the DA's office, where I would be able to make him pay for his crimes.

"What about your talent? What about the fact that you come alive on stage?"

"I haven't truly felt alive since I lost my family, Jules."

At least not until tonight.

I wasn't surprised to see Noah Cornell at his desk when I arrived at the station shortly before midnight. As station manager, Noah lived and breathed WJPK. Within five years of taking over, he had turned the middling station into one of the most popular college radio stations in the country, amplifying voices and issues that are often underrepresented in mainstream media.

When podcasting started to gain in popularity, he added podcasts to the schedule but kept the focus on traditional radio programming. He'd understood what others in the industry hadn't—that radio audience figures remained stable year after year because listeners still wanted the immediate connection and engagement that came only from radio, allowing for a community experience that brought listeners to WJPK from all over the world. He was highly respected in the world of independent radio, and the only other person I'd met who understood music the way I did—at least until I met Skye.

"What's keeping you so late this time?" I walked into Noah's office, careful not to step on the piles of papers, albums, and boxes scattered across the green carpet. Noah was a great station manager, but he was a hoarder of anything to do with music. Band posters. Memorabilia. Vinyl. CDs. 8-track tapes. T-shirts. Buttons. Between the disaster of his office and his retro fashion look, people often underestimated Noah, but he was a card-carrying member of Mensa, the society for certified geniuses. He was also highly intuitive, keenly observant, and he carried more trivia in his head than the best *Jeopardy!* player.

"It's my fault." Nick Chan stuck his head out from behind a pile of boxes. "Noah just bought a vintage Gloria Jones vinyl on eBay, and I made the mistake of asking to hear it after my show. He's been cleaning it for the last hour."

Tall and lanky, with a thatch of black hair, Nick was an economics major who DJ'd the jazz and blues shows at the station. He was a music virtuoso and could play the saxophone, guitar, trumpet, piano, and he'd just learned how to play the trombone. Despite the late hour of my show, he always seemed to be around to help with my sound check, and I'd caught him sleeping on the couch in the lounge a few times when I was done. When I'd mentioned it to Noah, he'd waved it off. He said he wasn't about to raise the issue in case Nick had nowhere else to go.

"You shouldn't have tempted him." I leaned against the doorway. "Does he know we have an accounting test tomorrow?" Nick and I had several classes together, and he always came to sit with me, chatting away as if we were friends, inviting me out for drinks, or to group study sessions at the library. I didn't understand it. We weren't friends. I didn't have time for friends. And yet, Nick was always there, no matter how many times I turned him down.

"Are you guys ready to hear the original version of 'Tainted Love'?" Noah held up the record, one finger in the center to keep it pristine.

"Would you consider trading it for Gloria Gaynor's album *Never Can Say Goodbye*?" Noah's vinyl addiction was worse than mine and it wasn't the only thing we had in common. He'd also wound up busking on the street at the lowest point in his life and had been given a second chance by the then-manager of WJPK. I was eighteen years old when Noah saved me. Devastated by Sasha's death and the truth of my mother's accident, I'd disowned my family and had been living on the street for two years when he offered me the same deal the former station manager had given him—a job at the station, a place to live, and support to finish school and clean up my life.

Noah snorted as he walked over to one of three turntables he had set up in his office. With his shoulder-length straight blond hair, pink shirts, tight black jeans, and silver bolo ties, he looked like he'd stepped straight out of the eighties. "Don't make me laugh. That's almost as bad as the time you tried to convince me to give you Tommy Johnson's 'Alcohol and Jake Blues' in exchange for a first pressing of Bob Dylan's *The Freewheelin' Bob Dylan*."

Nick and I found places to lean—Noah's chairs were always full of junk—and we gave him the courtesy of listening to the title track of his new treasure.

"I heard a scratch." Noah peered down at the spinning record. "I can see it. Goddamn it. That's why it's always better to buy local."

Noah rarely used swear words, so I knew something was wrong, and it was more than a scratch on vintage vinyl. "What's going on?"

He glanced at Nick, the meaning clear. "It's nothing."

Nick took the hint and made his way to the door. "I think I'll head out and spend the night processing the greatness that is Gloria Jones. See you in class."

After he'd gone, Noah sighed. "Things aren't looking good for the station. The university just turned down our annual request for funding. I've been swamped preparing grant applications and making lists of potential donors. I can't eat. I can't sleep. I've been up late every night, sometimes all night, trying to find a way to keep the station going."

I'd noticed Noah had lost weight—his skinny jeans weren't so skinny—and his face had become pale and lined. I'd thought it was too many late nights listening to music and watching his favorite reruns, but Noah didn't lie and the tension in his voice was almost palpable.

"I've heard rumors the new CFO wants to repurpose our space for a revenue-generating business," he continued. "If we can't show we're a viable nonprofit, they'll have an excuse to shut us down."

I stared at him in shock. "Are you serious?"

"Nonprofit isn't good business." Noah shrugged. "I've been going through the books to see where we can cut costs. Things are going to be very tight this year. No new equipment, no free snacks in the lounge, less promo, fewer parties, staff reductions . . . I'll be asking *all* the volunteers"—his gaze cut to me, his meaning clear—"to help take up the slack." He carefully removed the album from the turntable and slid it into its sleeve. "I don't suppose they offer a class on fundraising for nonprofits at Havencrest . . . ?"

"I'll ask around."

There was very little I wouldn't do for Noah. Eight years ago, when I'd gone into a downward spiral after my sister's death, he'd given me a reason to go on living. But that was Noah; he was the kind of guy who picked up strays. When the previous WJPK station manager retired, Noah had bought his run-down house in Forest Glen and filled it with rescues—two cats and three dogs, and later on, me.

"What have you got planned for the show tonight?" He returned to his desk and refilled his cup from the ancient coffee maker beside the window. Noah had a three-pot-a-day habit and was totally unaffected by caffeine. He could drink a triple espresso and fall asleep in two minutes flat.

"I got in some demos from a couple of new indie bands that I want to showcase, then a bit of pirate metal . . ."

"Be careful if you're planning to play Alestorm." Noah knew even the most obscure bands that I dug up for my show. "We got warnings about the language from the higher-ups last time."

"That's the point of pirate metal."

Noah laughed. "How about some baby metal instead?"

"I'm feeling the need for some hardcore catharsis." I hesitated, but the words tumbled out before I could stop them. "I met this girl—"

"You meet a lot of girls."

"She's different," I said. "She knows music the way we do. She knew bands I'd never heard of. She was listening to Angerfist—"

Noah perked up at the name of the fringe band. "Was she wearing a hockey mask and a black hood? Did you hear her metal scream?"

"She was the opposite of an Angerfist stan," I said. "She was . . . fun and sweet and loyal and . . . interesting. I've never had a conversation about music like that with anyone except you."

"So where is this mysterious woman who captured the interest of a man who breaks more hearts than I break coffee cups?" He kept his tone light, but I knew Noah well enough to recognize the hyperfocus of his attention.

"Quinn was messed up at the gig again and said some stuff that scared her away."

His shoulders slumped the tiniest bit. "So that's it? No wedding bells?"

"Christ, Noah. I spent less than half an hour with her. I'll probably never see her again." Damn Noah for making me regret my decision to just let her walk away. He could always do that to me. A question. A word. And suddenly I would realize that what he'd just said was what I'd been thinking or feeling all along.

"So, pirate metal because of a girl?" Noah put his feet up on the desk. I could swear there was a dent in the wood beneath the mass of papers from countless years of refusing to sit up in his chair.

"That and the fact I just found out I have to visit my dad's lawyer to discuss my grandmother's estate." I'd been putting off the meeting just like I'd been putting off reading the correspondence from my grandmother's lawyers that had been piling up for over six months. Not just because I simply didn't have the time or emotional energy, but also because I didn't want to face the reality that the last family member who truly cared for me was gone. "I wouldn't be surprised if my dad shows up and tries to convince me to join the family business again."

"You'd be rolling in cash," Noah pointed out. "More than enough to help out a struggling nonprofit radio station . . ."

"I want to help, Noah, but I don't want that life," I said. "It comes with a price tag I'm not willing to pay." There was no way I would ever join the family real estate business that had been passed on from father to son for four generations. It was all going to end with me—the business, the legacy, the generations of trauma, and the family line.

My father had done something so unforgivable, I'd even changed my last name.

CHAPTER FOUR

"Can I Call You Tonight" by Dayglow

SKYE

"You don't look totally wrecked this morning," Isla said when I walked into the kitchen Monday morning. She'd decorated the small space with brightly colored accents and added a vintage table and chairs to give it a cozy feel.

"Is that meant to be a compliment?" I hadn't been able to sleep properly since the accident. Every time I closed my eyes, I was back in the car, pinned by twisted metal with my father lifeless beside me.

"Considering the dark circles I usually see under your eyes, that would be a yes," she said. "That's a good sign for your tryout today."

"How was your night?" Scott had come over after his shift, somewhere close to midnight, but Isla was alone at the counter, which meant she'd kicked him out at sunrise.

"Nothing to write home about. He put on the *Boner* playlist. You were right that it was a play on 'Bone-her.' He needed Mohawke's 'Cbat' to get his game on, and I don't think anything has turned me off more. Who wants to have sex to the sound of a squeaky door? I couldn't get him out of here fast enough."

Isla wasn't one for sentiment. She didn't like long mornings in bed or lingering hugs, and nothing disgusted her more than people wandering around in their pajamas after 8:00 A.M. She hadn't been that way when we'd first started living together in residence. But a few months into our first year when she was alone in our room, someone broke in and sexually assaulted her. Isla hadn't been able to see her assailant in the dark, so without a description, the police were unable to find him. The university managed to hush it up, paying Isla a nominal amount of money in exchange for her silence on the outrageous basis that she bore some responsibility for leaving the door unlocked.

It was a year before Isla felt comfortable enough to be alone with a man, and then only in her own apartment and only when her roommate was in the next room. Her hookups were never allowed to stay the night, and relationships were strictly off the table.

I grabbed a bagel and popped open a protein shake. Isla was a grazer and didn't like to waste time cooking, but I needed regular meals when I was training to keep up my energy.

"I can't imagine you'd write home about any of your hookups," I said, checking my messages. Isla's family was very religious. They assumed she was still praying every night before bed, going to church on Sunday, and avoiding temptation. They couldn't have been more wrong.

"This is true." She grinned, sliding a clip into her hair to hold back the mass of curls. "They still think I'm going to marry the preacher's son." She waved a hand over her crop top then down over her very mini mini-shorts. "Do I look like I was made to be a preacher's wife?"

"Maybe a very progressive preacher?" I slathered peanut butter on my bagel and added a few slices of banana.

"No such thing."

While Isla filled her lunch bag, I responded to the good luck messages from my mom and little brother. Jonah was a miracle child. My parents had adopted me after being told they couldn't have children, but four years later Jonah was born. My father had been overjoyed, but his dreams of having Jonah follow in his footsteps were quickly dashed when Jonah was diagnosed with a heart condition that prevented him from participating in competitive and contact sports. My father channeled his disappointment by turning up the pressure on me, and the first few years of Jonah's life were some of the most difficult of my childhood.

"Jonah says hello," I said after we'd packed up. "You made a huge impression when you came to visit in summer. He still thinks you're the coolest person he's ever met."

"He's a great kid and very intelligent for a ten-year-old." Isla preened in the mirror before closing the door. "I am pretty cool."

After we were done, we walked through the building and onto the street. Isla, being Isla, had managed to find an apartment only a few blocks from campus in a leafy student-oriented area of the city. It was real estate gold, and I still couldn't believe she'd managed to get it.

"You're very quiet," she said. "You haven't hummed a single song since you got up. I think that's a record. Are you nervous about the tryout this afternoon?"

"I've just got so much riding on this . . ."

"You're going to kick ass," she assured me. "They're going to offer you a place back on the team. I feel it in my bones."

"And if they don't?"

"In the unlikely event that happens, we'll go to the financial aid office and apply for every single scholarship we can find," she said firmly. "I'll also hit up the editor of the Havencrest alumni magazine to see if he has some freelance work. I just hope he's managed to get over our spectacular breakup." She stopped at the corner where our paths diverged. Most of her classes were on the opposite side of the campus to mine. "It involved a pitcher of margaritas being poured over someone's head."

"Not yours I hope."

"Of course not." She patted her curls. "No one would dare ruin this hair."

I was ten minutes from the end of my shift at the Buttercup Bakery Café in the main library when my injured leg began to ache—an irritating response to the cooling weather. It was our busiest time of day so asking for a break wasn't an option. I mentally chided myself for not keeping up with the exercises my physio had given me, but with all the intense training I had to do to recondition for tryouts, the twenty minutes of tiny movements three times a day was not only tedious and inconvenient, but it was also a constant reminder that I still wasn't fully healed.

Gritting my teeth, I limped from the register to the espresso machine to give my co-worker Haley the cups for the latest order. Haley and I had hit it off the moment we were introduced. She was a sophomore, just shy of five foot seven inches tall, with high, sharp cheekbones and a wild mane of curly chestnut-brown hair that fell past her shoulders in a controlled chaos. She was still undecided on a major and spent most of her free time auditioning for bands and performing at open mic nights to try and launch her singing career. Her style was equal parts edgy and bohemian, and she had absolutely no filter—good for her *Hidden Tracks* show at the college radio station; bad for business when she eviscerated rude customers with a few well-chosen words. I was terrified she'd get fired and I'd wind up with no source of entertainment at an otherwise routine job.

"Are you okay?" Haley whispered as she poured milk into the steamer.

"Fine." I retied the strings on my apron, bright white and decorated with yellow buttercups.

"My uncle used to say 'fine' when we asked him about his limp, and it turned out he had bone cancer and they had to amputate."

"My leg is made of titanium," I reminded her. "It's got a half-life of sixty years, so it'll still be around when I'm gone. I'm like my grandpa who had a bad knee and could tell us when a storm was coming."

"Speaking of storms . . ." She lifted her chin ever so slightly in the direction of the till. "Look what just blew in. I'd ride that hurricane in a heartbeat."

I glanced over, my eyes immediately locking on a familiar dark gaze and the breathtaking face of the man whose voice I had been imagining every night before I went to sleep. *Dante.* He was wearing a vintage Twisted Sister T-shirt tucked into worn jeans cinched by a black belt that had thick silver chains hanging off one side. His hair was artfully disheveled, like he'd just rolled out of bed, and his dark eyes glinted when he grinned at me. Everything about him screamed "bad boy," and I felt a tingle in my stomach, followed by a thud in my heart.

"Do you know him?"

Haley laughed. "Everyone knows Dante Romano. He DJs the late-night show at WJPK, our independent campus radio station. *Dante's Darkness* has the highest ratings of any late-night show in Chicago."

"*DJ* Dante? I thought he played in a band."

"He's all over the music scene," she said. "And he's majoring in finance here at Havencrest. I heard he's graduating this year. What a total loss. I tune in to his show when I can't sleep. You should hear his voice. I could get off just listening to him read a shopping list."

"We met on Friday night at Steamworks," I admitted as I helped her prep the orders, straightening the row of paper cups and checking the coffee bean supply to keep my gaze from drifting across the counter. But it was no use. It was as if the strength of his features and the power rippling beneath his muscular frame had magnified until I couldn't ignore him.

Haley's eyes sparkled with interest. "Do tell."

"Isla dragged me out into the alley so she could vape with the bartender, and Dante was there unloading gear with his band. We were talking music when one of the guys said something about Dante always trying to hook up before their gigs. He thought I was a groupie." I grimaced at the memory and the reminder that what I thought had been a special conversation between us had, in fact, just been a standard seduction.

"I'm not surprised," she said. "Dante is a player. My friends at the station say he's with a different woman every night."

I could feel Dante's eyes on me as I added coffee beans to the almost-full dispenser. "Can you take his order? I don't want to talk to him. It's too embarrassing."

"Sorry, babe." Her curls bounced when she shook her head. "My mouth starts going and doesn't stop when I have to deal with the tall, strong, silent types. I can't handle a noise vacuum. I'd chase him away."

With a sigh, I returned to the till and plastered a fake smile on my face. Dante's gaze dropped to my apron, where the word *Buttercup* was printed in big yellow letters across my chest. He looked up and grinned. "What's up, buttercup?"

"My name is Skye; not buttercup, as you know," I said, trying hard not to melt into a puddle at the sound of his voice. "Is this a coincidental meeting? I've never seen you here before."

"I talked to Scott, the Steamworks bartender, after our gig on Friday night," he said. "I might have asked him if he knew anything about the mysterious woman I'd met in the alley. He might have mentioned that she worked here and that she'd made a coffee-bar playlist. I might have been intrigued—"

"By the woman or the playlist?" I couldn't believe he'd made the effort to find me, especially if he had women beating down his door like Haley said.

"Both." He reached over the counter and released a lock of hair that was caught in my collar, sending electricity dancing over my skin.

I huffed out a breath, still uncertain about whether he was here for the challenge or out of genuine interest. "You're listening to it now." I pointed to the speaker in the corner that was playing Van Morrison's "Brown Eyed Girl." I'd convinced my boss to switch up the smooth jazz for something more upbeat because I'd noticed people came to the café to socialize, not study. "I put a little bit of everything in it, from Edward Sharpe and the Magnetic Zeroes to the Eagles, Adele, Tracy Chapman, CCR, Queen . . ." I handed him my phone so he could see the entire playlist. From our brief conversation in the alley, I knew that he'd appreciate it in a way no one else did.

"Jesus." He scrolled through the list. "That's some mix. You've got over three hundred thirty songs on here."

"I wanted my boss to be able to play it all day and not worry about repetition or having to switch from one playlist to another."

"I approve." He smiled. "But there's a song missing."

"What song?"

"ABBA's 'Take a Chance On Me.'"

"ABBA? How old are you?"

"Twenty-three, and they are one of the greatest pop bands of all time."

Laughter burst from my chest before I could stop it. "Seriously?"

"Seriously," he said. "Quinn was being a dick. If he hadn't chased you away, I would have given you my number and then I would have spent the entire weekend waiting for you to call."

"That's very presumptuous. What if I didn't call?"

"You would have called." His voice was strong, confident, daring me to deny the connection we'd had in the alley.

"Someone thinks a lot of himself." I gestured to the line forming behind him. "Also, that someone needs to order a drink because there are people waiting."

"What do you recommend?"

"Coffee."

"What kind of coffee?" He tapped his lips with his finger, considering. "Latte? Cappuccino? Macchiato? Filter? Espresso? I hope you use fair trade beans. I'm thinking espresso, but only if your machine is set and calibrated to pull a double."

What were the chances we had yet another thing in common? I'd applied to Buttercup my first year because I love everything about coffee, from the rich, complex taste to the heavenly scent and from the warmth to the caffeine buzz. It's one of my comfort foods, easing me back to life in the morning but keeping me relaxed at the same time.

"The split-style portafilter halves the shot for a single," I said. "So, do you want a double espresso?"

"Hit me. Or hit on me like you did the other night. I'm easy."

"I'm sure you are," I muttered under my breath as I wrote his name on the paper cup. Were his parents fans of the famous Italian writer of the *Divine Comedy*, or had they decided to set him up on a journey of redemption?

"Did you say something?" He put his hand to his ear. "I couldn't hear you."

"I asked if you would like something to eat with that," I said loudly. "I recommend the lemon squares. The shortbread crust is to die for, unless you don't have a sweet tooth, in which case I can't really talk to you anymore because I don't really understand savory people."

His lips quivered at the corners. "Savory people?"

"You know, the ones who order the cheese plate instead of dessert, or the chips instead of the chocolate bar." I leaned over the counter, dropping my voice. "Are you one of them? Because if you are . . ."

He studied me intently. "I'll take six lemon squares."

"The sensible thing to do would be to buy just one. What if you don't like them? You'll be stuck with six squares, and it will be my fault."

"'Sensible' isn't a word I would use to describe myself." His voice dropped to a low rumble that made me shiver. "Also, I like to share."

Beside me, Haley made a show of fanning herself with her hand.

At least we didn't have that in common. I'd always done the sensible thing. Basketball was the sensible thing. Havencrest was the sensible thing. Staying home to recover after the accident was the sensible thing. Getting a part-time job at the local library during my recovery to help my mom with the medical bills was the sensible thing. The only times I hadn't been sensible, Isla had been involved.

After writing out the order, I handed the cup over to Haley, who was making no effort to conceal her interest in both Dante and our conversation. I didn't blame her. He had a dark, dangerous vibe that was utterly electric.

Crap. I needed to get it together. I was at work. He was just some random dude who oozed sex. Besides, I wasn't looking for a man. If I made the roster, I'd be spending at least thirty hours a week practicing and training on top of classes and work. And then there were the nightmares and the scars. I wasn't ready to open myself up body and soul to another person, and when that day came—if it ever came—it would be with someone solid and stable. Not some sexy sexpot straight out of my bad boy musician fantasies who had a woman for every day of the week.

"Did you just call me a sexy sexpot?" Dante gave me a quizzical look.

Dear God. I'd said it out loud. "No." My cheeks burned, and I crumpled the cup in my hand. "You must have misheard."

"You didn't stay for the show on Friday night." He scanned his payment card, dropping his gaze for the first time since he'd come up to the counter. "I made my bass talk when we played 'Sweet Child O' Mine.'"

"I had a busy weekend planned. I needed my sleep." I liked that he'd noticed my absence . . . maybe a little too much. "I'm sorry I didn't get to hear you play. I love McKagan's slinky four-bar solo."

His face brightened. "Do you play bass?"

I shook my head. "I never had time to learn how to play an instrument, but if I had to choose, it would have been the guitar. I can't imagine there is anything more cathartic than sitting in your bedroom strumming 'Stay With Me,' 'when the party's over,' or even 'Wind of Change' while you cry and sing through your tears."

"What about 'Hurt'?" he asked, stepping to the side so I could help the next customer.

"Nine Inch Nails or Johnny Cash?" I waved my hand in the air. "Don't bother answering that. It has to be the Johnny Cash version. The Nails dragged it out too much. Six minutes is too long to cry." I took the next two orders and then turned my focus to helping Haley.

"Nine Inch Nails's version of 'Hurt' was six minutes of musical genius," Dante said, resting his elbows on the espresso machine.

"Only if you're wearing earplugs."

He gave me yet another knee-wobbling smile. "I think this requires further debate. When are you done?"

"Thirty minutes," I said. "But then I'm heading straight for my basketball tryout. I'm surprised you didn't remember since it was part of the conversation you were listening to that didn't include you."

He sipped his coffee, and I couldn't help but watch the way his lips moved, or how his corded throat tightened when he swallowed. "I remember everything about that night."

So do I.

I was grateful for the chance to cool my heated face in the chiller where we'd stored the extra lemon squares. I took a few deep breaths as I filled the box. My chest wasn't tight the way it had been all weekend, and the stress headache that had kept me up all night was gone. I felt light, curiously relaxed, and inexplicably . . . happy.

"Don't eat them all at once," I warned, handing him the box. "It's not good to have too much sugar."

"Too late, buttercup." He looked back over his shoulder as he walked away, and his wide smile made his eyes crinkle. "I think I've just overdosed."

CHAPTER FIVE

"Mr. Brightside" by the Killers

DANTE

I think I've just overdosed? Had those words seriously left my lips? What the hell was wrong with me? I didn't do pickup lines or cutesy phrases. I didn't hang around outside buildings hoping for the chance of another conversation. Hell, I was the man who didn't have to chase after women. They came to me. Case in point: Madison Taylor.

"I've been looking all over for you." Madison trailed her finger along the box of lemon squares, her blue eyes calculating. "You left me unread."

I'd met Madison during a summer law internship program sponsored by the State Bar. I'd applied for the program not just for the paid work experience, but because it was run by some of the top prosecutors from the Cook County State's Attorney office, and I wanted to make those connections early to pave my way into the DA's office after I finished law school. Two weeks before the end of the program, Madison found out about my band and showed up at our gig with only one thing on her mind. I'd been happy to oblige and had assumed she'd get the message when I didn't respond to her texts. Clearly, I was wrong.

I forced a smile and moved the box away from Madison's red lacquered nails. "I thought we both understood that it was just one night."

I had a one-night rule because I wasn't interested in relationships.

I'd lost everyone I loved, and it had almost broken me. I couldn't open myself to that kind of pain again.

"But it was such a good night." She twirled a long strand of her blonde hair around her finger. "I didn't get a chance to show you everything I could do."

"I'm sure there are other guys on campus who will appreciate your talents." I wasn't usually so abrupt, but I was waiting for Skye to get off her shift, and after Quinn had chased her away with his comments about my extracurricular activities, I didn't want her to see me with a woman who clearly had only one thing on her mind.

"You don't know what you're missing." Madison huffed and walked away with an exaggerated sway of her hips.

I knew exactly what I was missing, and it couldn't compare to the connection I felt with Skye. It had been a long time since I'd felt anything for a woman that wasn't purely physical, but Skye was the whole damn package.

I moved to a more secluded area and checked my station fan mail while I waited. Over the weekend, I'd received an unprecedented six requests to meet random girls for drinks—I usually averaged one or two fan requests a day—a few demo tracks from local indie bands, and a reminder from Noah that he was expecting me to do more volunteer work around the station.

Fuck.

I loved the station, and I didn't want to see it close, especially for Noah's sake, but I wasn't about to get sucked into the tight-knit group of volunteers who helped the paid staff. Unlike me, they didn't just show up for their programs and take off when they were done. They spent all their free time at the station, hanging out in the lounge, throwing impromptu parties, talking about their problems . . . They were a family, and I was never doing the family thing again.

Skye showed up around ten minutes later. She had a bag in one hand and a backpack that was so heavy she was hunched over, giving me a good view of the cleavage at the V of her shirt. Not that I was looking. But I was. She may have been an elite athlete but damn she had curves.

I moved into her path, but she was so focused on putting in her earphones and staring at her phone that she almost walked right into me.

"Sorry . . . I . . ." Her voice trailed off when she recognized me, and her forehead creased in a puzzled frown. "What are you still doing here?"

"Waiting for you." I gestured to the athletics building, the white dome rising beyond the trees in the distance. "I thought you might be stressed about the tryout and I'm very good at being distracting." I gestured to her backpack. "I'm also adept at carrying heavy things."

She shook her head. "I can carry my own stuff. Besides, your hands are full of lemon squares."

"I'll eat them." I took out a square and offered it to her. "These came highly recommended."

"If I eat too close to any kind of intense activity, I throw up. It's not a good look on me."

I couldn't imagine anything that wasn't a good look on Skye, but I wasn't about to let the lemon square go to waste. I took a bite, and tangy sweetness burst across my tongue, softened by the crumbly shortcake crust. I finished the first square in a few bites and reached into the box for another.

"Are you seriously using the threat of a sugar overdose to blackmail me into letting you carry my bag?" She gave me a sidelong glance as we walked along the path. "You're twisted."

"An accurate description."

"You can carry this." She handed me a lunch bag with a Superman decal on the front. "I'm only allowing it to save you from sugar poisoning."

My fingers brushed against hers when I took the bag. The skin-to-skin contact was staggeringly powerful, and a buzz of awareness sizzled through my veins. "It seems you are a superhero after all," I said, inspecting the worn image of Christopher Reeve mid-flight.

"You remember that, too?" she asked softly.

"That night is etched into my brain." Aside from the fact that I processed information so quickly I didn't need to take notes in class, I hadn't been able to stop thinking about Skye and our kiss and our curious connection.

"The lunch box is an inside joke," she explained. "My friend Isla found it at a thrift shop and gave it to me. I missed my sophomore year and the last few months of my freshman year after I was in a car accident. She said I was a superhero for making it back." She moved in the direction of the fitness center, and I fell into step beside her.

"She's a good friend," I said. "But I do hope it's a joke. There is no better Superman than Henry Cavill."

"Are you kidding me? Christopher Reeve was the best. He was kind, humble, compassionate and noble with pure farm boy wholesomeness and a subtle sense of humor. What else could you ask for in a superhero?"

"Grit," I said. "Steel. Passion. Determination. The ability to dole out hard justice when necessary. Raw physicality . . ."

Raw physicality. Right there beside me. It was hard to concentrate on the conversation when she was walking so close that I could feel the heat of her body and breathe in her scent—wildflowers and coffee and something sweet.

"Yawn to the cookie-cutter superhero ideal," she said. "I like a nuanced hero. A person who is strong, confident, and brave but isn't afraid to show their soft side. Although I will give you that Cavill looked better in his suit than Reeves."

Out of the corner of my eye, I could see her watching me. "The Man of Steel screamed and cried in anguish during intense action sequences and emotional scenes. What more do you want?"

"A fur bed in a palace of ice."

My laughter took me by surprise. Except when I was with

Noah, or trying to charm a woman into my bed, I rarely laughed, and I hadn't laughed so loudly since Sasha died.

I heard a shout, the *thunk* of a ball. In the distance I saw a group of guys running down the sidewalk tossing a football back and forth, heedless of the people who were dashing to the side to get out of their way. Instinctively, I slid my hand around Skye's waist and pulled her to the side. Fast. But not fast enough. The ball bounced off her shoulder and onto the grass.

"What the fuck!?" I yelled, more annoyed at my failure to protect Skye than anything else. I grabbed the ball and hurled it at the guy who had hit Skye, putting all my energy into the throw. "Get off the fucking path!"

"It's okay, Dante." Skye's quiet voice penetrated the churn of blood in my ears. "The ball barely touched me."

I took a deep shuddering breath and tried to find the self-control I had so quickly and inexplicably lost. I couldn't remember the last time I'd been so close to releasing the anger that I kept tightly leashed. "I just . . . you didn't need that right before your big tryout. What if you'd been injured?"

"Then I'd be on the phone right now booking a plane ticket back to Denver."

That stopped me in my tracks. "Are you saying that if you don't make the team, you're leaving Havencrest?"

Skye shrugged. "I came here on a full-ride basketball scholarship to get a journalism degree, but I lost the money when I had to withdraw after the accident. The team is giving me another chance to try out, but my leg was so badly damaged it basically had to be rebuilt. I don't think all the rehab and training in the world is going to get me back to the level I was at when they picked me, but I have to try."

"It takes a lot of courage to come back," I said. "Most people would just give up. You're very brave."

"I'm desperate," she said with a sigh. "If I make the team, I'll qualify for athletic scholarships, but without them, there's no way

I can stay. I've already talked to my financial aid advisor. She's looking at other options for me, but I missed the deadlines for most other scholarships."

"What about journalism internships? I just finished a summer law internship, and it paid—"

"You're in law?"

"Finance," I said. "But I plan to go to law school. The internship was at the State's Attorney's office, which is where I want to work."

Skye frowned. "I wouldn't have guessed law."

"Because I'm not wearing a suit?"

"Because it's pretty much the opposite of who you are."

I suppressed a flinch. Music. Banter. Light "getting to know you" talk. I could do it all. But getting personal, going deep, trying to make me question my goal . . . that was off-limits for me.

"You don't know who I am." I knew my words had come out too harsh when Skye grimaced.

"No," she said in a cool voice. "I don't. I'm sorry if I pressed a nerve." She turned and held out her hand.

It took me a few moments to realize we'd arrived at the athletic center and she wanted her lunch bag. I handed it over, mentally kicking myself for being such a dick. She didn't need me dumping my issues on her when she was going into one of the most important tryouts of her life.

"Go kick some basketball ass." Lost in a maelstrom of emotions, I didn't know what else to say.

"Thanks." Skye hesitated. "Do you—?"

"Dante!" Madison waved from a nearby picnic table on the grass and gestured to the curvy woman beside her. "Come on over. I've got someone for you to meet."

My body jerked, and I shook off the haze that had clouded my mind. What the hell was I doing? I didn't get involved. I didn't connect. I didn't waste time wondering how I could spend more time with someone I'd just met. I was a free agent, unencumbered by the burden of emotion-draining relationships. Skye deserved someone who could be there for her, someone who could protect her, and that sure as heck wasn't me. I didn't even have time for this kind of drama. Skye had her goal and I had mine.

"I'll be right there," I called out. I wasn't about to break my rule for Madison, but her friend was cute, and I was up for a little flirting to chase away all the unsettling feelings. "I'm bringing you a treat and it isn't me." I held up the box of lemon squares and blew the girls a kiss.

I felt a prickle on the back of my neck and turned to see Skye watching me, her face devoid of any expression. When she turned away, I felt sick inside.

"Good luck, buttercup."

I watched until she was through the doors. She didn't even wave.

CHAPTER SIX

"Bad Day" by Daniel Powter

SKYE

"Skye?" Isla banged her fist on my bedroom door. "Are you going to come out? Do you want something to eat?"

"Leave me alone." I pulled the pillow over my head to block out her voice. I wasn't ready to talk about the disaster that had been my tryout. Not even with Iz.

"You've been in there since Monday afternoon," she shouted. "Now, it's Tuesday night. You haven't even gone to pee. I learned in my biology class that not peeing for that long could kill you. The pee goes back into your blood stream, and you die of pee poisoning."

"That's bullshit."

"Do you really want to take the chance? Is that what you want on your tombstone? 'Here lies Skye Jordan. Sister, daughter, friend. Too bad she didn't pee.'"

"I went to the washroom when you were at school and when you were asleep."

"What about water? You can only survive three days without water. You can go three weeks without food, so I won't give you a hard time about that—"

"I have water, Iz. I'm not stupid." I threw back the covers. Isla wasn't going to leave me alone and neither was my bladder now that she was pouring water into some kind of container outside my door.

"I need to see you," she said. "I can't spend another night worrying. Come out and just let me make sure you're okay."

"Fine. I'll come out. I'll use the washroom and fill my water bottle and then you have to promise to leave me alone. Do not talk to me about the tryout. Do not try to console me or say anything nice. I just need to stay in bed until my mom books my flight home." I yanked open the door and stumbled past Isla. I was still wearing my gym clothes, and my face, when I glanced in the washroom mirror, was puffy and red.

"I know you don't want anything," Isla said when I was done, "But I got your favorite high-protein matcha blueberry energy shake and a box of granola bars just in case you change your mind." She followed me down the hallway, her voice tight with worry. "I left them in your room."

"I don't need to eat healthy anymore," I grumbled. "I didn't make the team, Iz. That's the end of my basketball career. I can spend the rest of my life stuffing myself with pizza and cake, getting drunk, and hooking up with guys every night."

Isla grimaced at my harsh tone. "To be fair, that doesn't sound all bad. Do you want pizza? Cake? A bottle of vodka?"

"I want to crawl under my covers and indulge myself in a weeklong self-pity sesh." I felt like an elephant was sitting on my chest, crushing the life and breath out of me. I'd known my chances of getting back on the team were slim, but I hadn't realized how much hope had sustained me.

Isla looked more lost and distressed than I'd ever seen her. "Should I call someone? Your mom? How about Dante? Haley said he came to the coffee shop just to see you. Are you two—?"

"No. Of course not. He's a player, like that guy in the alley said. As soon as he saw two girls he knew, he couldn't get rid of me fast enough." I still couldn't wrap my head around how badly I'd misjudged him. I'd been touched that he'd waited to walk me to the tryout, but it was clearly because he'd had nothing better to do with his time. Still, I hadn't been able to stop myself from listening to his show and imagining what could have been as I fell asleep to his impeccably crafted playlists and the soothing sound of his deep voice.

"What can I do?" She followed me into the bedroom and threw

herself on my bed. "I feel useless. You haven't even told me what happened so I can get working on helping you fix things."

She wasn't going to leave me alone, so I told her. "I wasn't ready. Two months of training camp just wasn't long enough to get to the level I was at when they recruited me. I was slow on the court. I missed my free throws. I wasn't responsive to the team. And when it came time for the jump shots, my leg didn't work the way it should. I couldn't push off properly and I landed badly. It was like my leg didn't even belong to me. I fell on the last jump shot and I knew right away that it was all over. The coach confirmed it on my way out. At least she didn't keep me waiting."

"I'm so sorry, babe." She wrapped me in a hug that was better than a pile of blankets.

"You'd better start looking for a new roommate," I mumbled into her shoulder.

"Don't give up just yet," Isla said. "We'll think of something."

It was almost midnight after Isla and I finished talking. I was too wound up to sleep, so I pulled out my homework and tried to focus on my paper for my *Fundamentals of Reporting* class. I'd become interested in journalism when my tenth-grade English teacher recruited my class to start a school paper. I tried everything from music, sports, and news reporting to general interest pieces, but I knew I'd found my niche in my junior year when, as co-editor of the school paper, I inadvertently broke a major news story. It started off as a straightforward profile of the school's new principal, but quickly turned into an in-depth investigation when I did a fact check and discovered that the university from which she claimed to have earned her master's and doctorate degrees didn't exist, nor did the high schools she had claimed to work at prior to joining us. We published the front-page story and one week later she resigned.

I knew then that I'd found what I wanted to do with my life if I couldn't make it to the WNBA, and Havencrest, with its prestigious journalism program, was the perfect place to pursue that dream.

Unable to focus, I put away my work and grabbed my headphones before tuning in to WJPK to listen to Dante's show. I was a big fan of indie radio and I'd listened to a wide variety of the programs during my first year, but my intense training schedule and early morning practices meant that I was always in bed way before midnight, so I'd never even looked at what they offered past 9 P.M.

"Good evening, Chicago." Three words in that deep, low vibrato, and I was hot all over. I could almost feel Dante's arm around my waist, his hard body pressed up against me, his lips taking mine in that hungry kiss in the alley. I still couldn't understand what had happened outside the athletic center before my tryout. He'd gone from thoughtful and kind to cold and distant in a heartbeat. And then he'd left me for two girls at a picnic table without looking back.

He set the mood with Autograf's "Nobody Knows (feat. WYNNE)." The downtempo electro beats and soulful vocals were perfect for late night listening, but it was the lyrics that really resonated with me, the yearning for something we're not sure even exists.

"Tonight, is request night," Dante said when the last notes of the song faded away. *"Hit me with the reason you're here with me tonight. Are you cramming for an exam? Just home from the bar and too wired to sleep? Or are you missing someone tonight? One word. One feeling. As always, your messages are anonymous. Your secrets are safe with me."*

I didn't care about the music he was going to play. I would have been happy to listen to him read his shopping list, sports scores, or even the bus schedule. There was something conspiratorial and intimate about listening to that honeyed voice alone in the darkness. Before I could stop myself, I typed the word "Fear" and hit SEND.

Fear had defined my life ever since I'd lost my parents when I was three years old. Fear of footsteps, creaking doors, and shadows in the darkness of the many foster homes I was shuffled through before I was adopted. Then it was the fear of disappointing my new parents and being sent back to foster care.

After the accident, I went through a new set of fears: never being able to walk again, play basketball, or make my father's dream come true. I'd been afraid to leave the safety of the hospital, and then afraid to leave home to return to school. But sleep was the worst fear of all. The accident still haunted me. I was afraid to sleep because of the nightmares, and afraid to be awake because some days the crushing guilt over my father's death made it difficult to go on. Now, I'd failed him, and I was afraid for my future.

From the first few notes of the mellow and pretty guitar line from Zach Williams's "Fear is a Liar," I knew he'd chosen my word. The song isn't exactly upbeat, but it reminds us that things are going to be okay.

"*Tonight is for everyone who's feeling afraid,*" Dante said over the music. "*Whether it's monsters in the dark, fear of failure, or fear of loss, I'm here for you tonight.*"

I felt those words in my chest, in my heart, like strong arms giving me a hug. I lay back and fell into the power of the music, drowning my heartache in song.

My phone dinged and I checked the screen. Dante had responded to my anonymous message.

"Are you safe? Should I call 911?"

My heart squeezed the tiniest bit. He hadn't lied when he said he was there for his listeners. I considered telling him it was me, but I didn't want him to think I was just another groupie who was so obsessed she'd tracked him down on the air, especially after the way we'd parted. Anonymity gave me the freedom to just be me.

"Im ok. Tx for asking."

Zach Williams faded into Julia Brennan's "Inner Demons," and I closed my eyes. For the first time in over a year, I didn't hear a shout of fear, the squeal of tires, or the shatter of glass. I didn't think about the past and I didn't worry about the future.

Instead, I sank into the voice that wrapped me in warmth and carried me away.

CHAPTER SEVEN

"Head & Heart" by Joel Corry and Mnek

Skye

Isla's "something" was to drag me out of bed at 7:00 A.M. every morning for the next three days to "get on with my life." I went to class, applied for jobs, filled in applications for the few scholarships still available, and met daily with a very sympathetic student financial advisor who was doing everything she could to help me stay in school. In my spare time, I worked extra shifts at Buttercup. Even though Dante had shown me that his reputation as a player was well-deserved, my heart skipped a beat every time I heard a deep voice, and a small part of me kept hoping he would stop by to say hello.

By Friday, I still hadn't found a new source of funding. I told Isla that if I hadn't figured anything about by the end of the following week, I'd have to return to Denver. Of course, she got in touch with Haley and the two of them decided to take me to a frat party to cheer me up. What better introduction, she said, to my new life of drinking, eating bad food, hooking up with strangers, and staying up late than a frat party where everything came free?

"Did you try the Purple Jesus?" Isla shouted over the music as we took a breather in the kitchen so I could help myself to another carb-and sugar-laden plate of potato chips and donuts. The DJ wasn't too bad. His playlist had bounced from "Closer" to Justin Bieber's "Sorry," with plenty of upbeat tracks like "Hey Ya!" and "Hips Don't Lie."

"Where is it?"

"In the bathroom."

"Why is it in the bathroom?"

"They made a bathtub full of it." She held up a paper cup. "Most people are just sticking their heads in and drinking straight from the tub, but I was smart. I asked for a cup."

Even after our pre-party tequila shot warm-up, I wasn't drunk enough to even contemplate drinking from a frat house bathtub, especially since the house smelled of stale beer and the sweat of dozens of unwashed bodies. I gently pried the cup out of Isla's hands and put it on the kitchen table, which held a buffet of potato chips, beef jerky, and something that looked like chicken fingers. "I think we should dance. They've found a DJ who can play some decent music."

Haley joined us in the living room, where the music was blaring and the room was filled with jocks, ballers, sorority girls and frat boys, a few artsy types, and some awkward freshmen. Other than the small table where the DJ had set up his equipment, there was a conspicuous absence of furniture, but it just meant more room to dance.

"Rugby player heading your way at six o'clock," Isla shouted in my ear as she thrashed her arms around to her own personal beat. "He's kinda cute."

The rugby player introduced himself as Aaron. His neck was so thick he could barely look over his shoulder. Someone had told him I was on the DII basketball team, and he wanted to talk athletics—best protein shake, earliest wake-up, number of times puking during a workout. He was a tight end who had won many trophies, and he was desperate for me to come to his room to see them. Aaron wasn't a dancer, so he stood beside me, keeping away the roving hands of his frat brothers while sending his pledges to bring me fresh drinks.

"I need to get away from Aaron," I said to Haley. "I'm not used to drinking and I've had so many shots, I almost forgot the moves to the Macarena. He keeps offering to take me upstairs and I'm worried I might say yes because I just want to rest my head. It wouldn't be a good situation."

"You don't want to hook up with him?" Haley asked. "He's a hottie."

"He's not really my type." There was only one guy I wanted to sleep with, but I was sure he'd found someone else to warm his bed on a Friday night. And even if he hadn't, I wasn't interested in being another notch in his belt.

We grabbed Isla and headed outside to sit on the grass so I could clear my head. The air was crisp and cool and a welcome relief from the sticky heat inside.

"I was playing shot pong with a guy who looks like Tom Holland." Isla took a sip from the bottle of vodka she'd taken from the makeshift bar. "If I'd kept winning, he would have gotten lucky tonight."

I took the bottle and put it to my lips, grimacing at the bitter taste as the vodka slid down my throat. "I think he was making his own luck, babe."

"Skye could have had the hottest rugby player on campus, but she's still pining for Dante," Haley blurted out.

"What are you talking about? I haven't mentioned him at all this week."

"You didn't have to." Haley grinned. "You've spent every shift at Buttercup staring out into the hallway with a dreamy expression on your face and jumping anytime you hear a deep voice."

"She listens to his show at night." Isla gave me a playful poke in the ribs. "Every morning she rants about the songs he played and didn't play, and why would he play this song after that one, and what about the ten songs that were better for this theme . . ."

I folded my arms and huffed. "I thought you guys were my friends."

"We are your friends," Haley said. "That's why I think we should make it happen. This might be your last chance . . ." She trailed off when Isla gave a warning shake of her head, but she was right. It was highly likely that by this time next week I would be back in Denver.

"Nothing is going to happen," I said, taking another sip. "He never even came by the coffee shop to find out how the tryout went. He's got women coming out his ears—usually two or three at once."

Haley took the bottle and added a splash of vodka to her drink. "He is sooo hot. I'd bang him if I had the chance."

"You can't bang Dante." Isla snorted a laugh. "Skye is going to bang him."

"I'm not banging him. I'm moving back to Denver. No time to bang."

We collapsed into a fit of giggles while Haley scrolled through her phone.

"His show is on right now." Haley turned up her speaker and I leaned in to listen. ZZ Top's rock classic "La Grange" had us immediately bouncing up and down.

"Let's make a booty call for Skye," Isla said, brightening.

"Don't you dare."

"He missed out big time with you." Isla swayed to the side. "Big. Time."

"Yeah, he did," Haley agreed, nodding. "You would have banged the beast . . . I mean best."

"She would have banged the beast best." Isla fell back, laughing. "Oh God. My stomach hurts. Do it, Haley. Call him at the station. Tell him he made the wrong choice."

I opened my mouth to protest, and then closed it again. It wasn't fair that I'd met someone I could connect with and now I had to leave. It wasn't fair that I'd been in a stupid accident that had ended my basketball career. It wasn't fair that the medical bills had sucked up the last of our family savings. I'd lost everything. Why not talk to him one last time? Why not tell him what he'd missed? I had nothing left to lose.

"I'll do it." I pulled out my phone and called the station. Too late, I realized he might recognize the number from the time I'd texted to give him the word "fear."

"WJPK. DJ Dante. Do you have a request?"

My heart pounded in my chest, the adrenaline rush cutting through the alcohol-induced haze that had made me think this was a good idea. "You missed out," I said. "Big time."

"Who is this?"

"You'll never get a chance to connect with someone who really gets what you're about." I grinned at my girls, who were nodding encouragingly. "Enjoy your life of pre-show groupies and seducing women with lemon squares when you could have had something great."

Before he could speak, I ended the call and dropped my phone on the grass. Bile rose in my throat and I slapped a hand over my mouth. "Oh, God. What did I just do? Why didn't you stop me?"

"It was fun," Isla said. "And now you've got him out of your system. Who should we drunk-dial next?"

Dante's show was still playing over Haley's tinny speaker. The last notes of "La Grange" transitioned into Pitbull's "I Know You Want Me."

"He knows it's me," I groaned. "I shouldn't have mentioned the lemon squares."

A few seconds later my phone vibrated in the grass. I stared at it in horror. I was such an idiot. Hand trembling, I pushed it toward Haley. "Take it. I shouldn't be trusted with a weapon of that magnitude ever again."

Haley lifted the phone to her ear. "What do you want me to say?"

"Don't answer it!" I shrieked. "Just . . . text in a request. 'Shame' by Elle King."

Haley lifted an eyebrow as she typed. "Is this you telling him you're embarrassed by your drunk dial?"

"No." My lips quivered with a smile. Excessive alcohol was making me brave. "It's an invitation to come and party with the bad kids."

Haley barked a laugh and sent the text. "Look at you embracing your wild side. I have to say I never imagined our straitlaced Skye getting totally shitfaced, drunk-dialing her crush, and inviting him to party with us tonight."

"Who Are You" faded into "Shame." My phone vibrated again.

"If he already knows it's you," Isla said, lying languid in the grass, "why don't you just talk to him?"

"We are talking. This is our language. I could send him tracks all night." I took another drink of vodka as I scrolled through my playlists looking for another song to request.

"You're hiding." Isla pushed to her elbows and took the bottle to finish it off.

"What am I going to say? He literally ran away from me at the athletic center to share the lemon squares I told him to buy with two other women. This kind of conversation is better."

"I thought you were all about taking risks and embracing life tonight," Haley pointed out. "If you do have to leave, this might be your last chance to talk to him in person."

"A good friend would tell me not to drunk-dial him again."

"I never said I was a good friend." She snatched my phone and pressed the screen. "I'll call him for you."

"No . . ." I grabbed the phone, but not fast enough. Before I could end the call, Dante answered.

"What's up, buttercup?"

"I didn't mean to call," I stammered. "It was a mistake. I thought you were someone else."

I shot a pleading look at Haley and Isla and mouthed "help," but they were too busy laughing to intervene.

"Who did you think I was?" Dante asked.

"Why does it matter?"

"I need to know how much competition I'm facing for the lemon squares at the coffee shop. Do I need to show up first thing in the morning to make sure I get one? Are there dudes wandering around with boxes of lemon squares seducing all the single ladies on campus? These are important things to know."

"Very funny. It was a mistake. Just pretend it never happened. Goodbye."

"Skye. Wait."

I heaved a sigh. "What do you want now?"

"Is this something you do all the time?" he asked, his voice amused. "Calling up dudes to let them know they missed out?"

I didn't know whether to laugh or throw up. "You're the first. I've never been this drunk before. I've never been to a frat party. I've never eaten so many carbs and so much sugar at once." I was leaving next week, so why not go out with a bang.

His tone changed from warm and teasing to something wary and sharp. "What frat party? Where are you?"

I told him the name and he sucked in a sharp breath. "They aren't good guys, Skye. Don't you know their reputation?"

"Haley was hot for a rugby player on the men's team, so she forced us to come."

"Don't tell him that," Haley called out. "I was hot for him but definitely not after he stuck his whole head in that bathtub of Purple Jesus."

Dante groaned. "Tell me you didn't drink from the bathtub."

"I didn't drink from the bathtub. I'd have to be unconscious to get over my disgust. We were drinking shots, but then Isla stole a bottle of vodka—"

"I didn't steal it," she mumbled. "It was just sitting there unattended."

The deep bass of AC/DC's "You Shook Me All Night Long" pounded through the speakers, making the entire house tremble. Until I'd mentioned it to Dante, I'd almost forgotten this might be my last night to party. "It's dance time," I told him. "I have to go."

"Be careful."

"I'm always careful," I said. "That's why I've never had any fun."

CHAPTER EIGHT

"Don't Stop the Music" by Rihanna

SKYE

Haley and Isla were more than happy to dance with me, and we rocked the dance floor for the next half an hour. Who could leave when the DJ was killing it with his sick beats? Aaron found me again and offered us shots of something sickly sweet, then did his best to dance by wrapping his arms around me and swaying to Shakira's "The One."

"Let me go." I tried to push him away, but he squeezed me tighter. My pulse kicked up a notch and I looked around for Isla or Haley. "Aaron. I can't br—"

"I'm cutting in," a familiar voice said from behind Aaron's massive bulk.

I peeked around Aaron's shoulder and my breath caught in my throat at the sight of Dante's glowering face. For a moment I couldn't speak. I was shocked, surprised, embarrassed, humiliated, mortified, and thrilled all at once. I closed my eyes and prayed that when I opened them, I wouldn't be in Kansas.

"The hell you are." Aaron had to physically turn us so he could look Dante in the eye because his neck didn't twist that far. I took the opportunity to pull away so I could see Dante in the flesh. Aaron slung a possessive arm over my shoulder, and my back bowed slightly from the extra weight.

"It's okay," I said. "I know him."

"You know me," Aaron said, tightening his grip. "We're spending the night together."

"Do you mean we're spending the night together partying or you think we're going to spend the night together in be—?"

"She's with me." Dante's voice was calm and controlled but his clenched jaw hinted at anger, barely restrained.

"What the fuck?" Aaron scowled and released me to get up into Dante's face. He was taller and wider than Dante, and thick with muscle, but Dante dominated the space with the force of his presence alone. A few of Aaron's rugby buddies looked over with interest, and my pulse kicked up a notch.

"We're together," I said quickly. "Dante and me. I'm sorry if you got the wrong impression."

"You? With him?" Aaron laughed. "You think I'd believe that? He's a NARP. We"—he gestured back and forth between us with a thick finger—"don't do NARPs."

NARP was short for Non-Athletic Regular Person, and Aaron was right. Elite college athletes usually dated each other because it was hard for NARPs to understand our strict diets, limited alcohol intake, early bedtimes, and pre-dawn morning practices. Not that they didn't sometimes cut loose like Aaron and his rugby buddies had done tonight, especially after a big game, but they would suffer for it at practice tomorrow.

"I'm a NARP, too," I said, swallowing past the lump in my throat. "I'm not on the basketball team anymore."

"It's okay. You're still hot as fuck." His arm slid down my back and he slapped my ass.

"Hey . . ." I turned to give him a piece of my mind, but Dante swooped in so fast I didn't see him move. He shoved Aaron in the chest with two hands, sending him stumbling back into two girls who were dancing behind him.

"Get your fucking hands off her."

Aaron's face darkened and tension crackled in the air. I'm not sure what would have happened if another rugby guy hadn't come up and clapped Aaron on the shoulder. "Dude. Not worth it. Beer funnel in the kitchen. Let's go."

I waited until Aaron had disappeared into the kitchen to do a little shouting of my own. "What the hell was that? Were you going to start a fight? Because he slapped my ass? I can bench press a hundred twenty pounds . . ."

Shut up, Skye.

". . . and in high school I held the team record in the squat, bench press, and power clean."

Oh God. Stop.

"I can look after myself." I flexed my biceps for him, the small ripple barely visible on my bare arm.

Shoot me now.

"Understood." Dante nodded. "I'll be sure not to get on your bad side."

"Why are you here?" I asked as I tried to wrap my head around the fact that he had actually come to the party.

"You invited me to party with the bad kids. How could I turn down that kind of invitation?"

My face flamed. "I was drunk. It was a drunk dial. You weren't supposed to take it seriously."

"How could I not take it seriously? Aside from the fact that you told me you were at a frat known for double-shotting to get women drunk, yours is the first booty call I've ever received."

I couldn't keep the sarcasm from my voice. "That's hard to believe. Haley told me your show gets more call-ins than any other at the station. I can't imagine you don't get the occasional booty call. In fact, I'd be shocked if you didn't because I've heard your show and your voice . . ." I trailed off when he smiled. "What?"

"You listened to my show."

Unable to meet his gaze, I stared down at the beer-and-mud-covered floor. "Maybe once or twice. Just to see if you played any decent music."

"Did you listen on Monday night?" He slid one hand around

my waist and every nerve in my body fired at once as the soft jazz notes of Peder's "The Sour" played over the speakers.

"Yes, and if you're going to play songs about getting over fear, then you have no business leaving out Rachel Platten's 'Fight Song' and Coldplay's 'Magic.'"

"Coldplay?" He snorted his derision. "They could have been the next Radiohead, but instead they cashed in on a mass-appeal pop styling and became U2 wannabes."

"I loved *Parachutes* and *Rush of Blood.*" I slid my hands over his broad shoulders and breathed in the scent of him, leather and citrus and masculine warmth.

"Hmm." He pulled me closer, his lips brushing over my hair. "There might possibly be one or two good tracks on those albums." Dante tightened his arm around me, and I softened against him. "Maybe three."

I pressed my cheek to his chest and caught a glimpse of us in the mirror over the makeshift bar. We looked good together, my body tucked perfectly against his, except for my ridiculous Cheshire cat smile.

Dante spun me around and my stomach heaved.

"I'm not feeling so good." I pulled away as bile rose in my throat. "I think I had too many shots. I need some air." Pushing my way through the crowd, I stumbled down the stairs and threw up in the bushes beside the house.

Dante held my hair until I was done and then left to let Isla and Haley know where I'd gone. He returned a few minutes later with a bottle of water and helped me over to the lawn, where we leaned against the trunk of a massive oak tree.

"I don't usually drink," I said, sipping the water.

He watched me, his eyes dark and warm, his smile cool and faintly amused. "I figured when you drunk-dialed me."

"It was my last hurrah," I continued. "I didn't make the team and I haven't been able to find any other funding options, so I'll be leaving next week. I'm hoping to get into one of the local colleges in Denver. It should be affordable if I live at home and work for the next year. There are some DIII teams at local colleges in Denver . . . I think one of them even has a journalism course. It doesn't have the prestige of Havencrest's journalism program . . ."

My throat tightened and I sighed. Some of the country's top journalists had graduated from Havencrest's journalism program—people I deeply admired. I'd never get the same opportunities anywhere else—or the connections. But I had to let it go. If I got onto a DIII team, I might still be able to make it to the WNBA. It was highly unlikely, but it was a chance I had to take.

"I'm sorry, Skye."

"It's better this way," I said, looking up at him. "I won't have to rely on money that comes with strings and obligations. People can take away things they've given you, but they can't take away something you've earned." I'd learned that lesson early in life after being shuttled from foster home to foster home, having to leave toys and clothes behind.

"So, this is your farewell to Havencrest." He rubbed his hand up and down my back in a soothing motion. "Drunk dials and partying with the worst frat on campus?"

"I haven't had much practice with self-pity. I thought alcohol would be a good way to fill the new void in my life."

"I can tell you from experience it's not a good idea," he said quietly.

I leaned back, resting against the tree beside him. "What was your poison?"

"Whiskey. It was the only alcohol in our house growing up. When that didn't do the trick, I moved on to harder stuff. Zero out of ten. Don't recommend. If I didn't have my music . . ."

"Wait! Aren't you supposed to be doing your show?"

"When you said you were here, I got the station manager to take over," he said. "I was worried about you, and he was happy to have a chance to showcase some of his favorite tracks. He used to be a DJ, too, and I think he misses that personal connection."

Another wave of nausea rolled through me, and I took a deep

breath, hoping I wouldn't embarrass myself yet again. "Why do you care?" I asked bluntly. "You didn't come by the coffee shop to ask about the tryout. For all you knew, I was already gone."

"I knew you were still around." He tipped his head back, looking up at the night sky through the branches and curling leaves. "I pass by the building every day on my way to class, and I could see you through the glass."

"Why didn't you come in and say hi?" I followed his gaze, but the sudden motion of my head made my vision swim and my stomach roil.

"I was kind of a dick before your tryout. I didn't think you'd want to talk to me."

Something bright bloomed in my chest. "You gave away my lemon squares."

His head dropped and he caught my gaze. "There was only one kind of sweet I wanted."

Wanted. I never got a chance to fully process his words.

One moment we were staring into each other's eyes. The next, I was puking on the grass.

CHAPTER NINE

"Dangerous" by David Guetta, Sam Martin

DANTE

Bob Gregory had been handling our family's legal matters since before I was born. His office was at the top of a steel-and-glass tower in The Loop, and it hadn't changed in the ten years since I'd last been to see him.

I helped myself to coffee and cookies in the meeting room after a suspicious receptionist called security to stand outside the door. Clearly, the city's top law firm didn't have many clients who showed up dressed in a leather jacket, heavy metal band shirt, and a variety of chains.

"Dante." Bob's worn, lined face showed no expression when he walked in to find me lounging back in the leather chair, my feet up on the shiny mahogany table. But then as a lawyer and fixer for businessmen in the upper echelons of power, including those like my father who were involved in organized crime, his poker face was part of the job. "Nice to see you again. I'm sorry we didn't get a chance to catch up last month at your grandmother's funeral."

"I can't say the same." I didn't get up to shake his hand. I had no respect for the man that helped my father get away with his crimes.

"Understood." Bob wasn't easily rattled. When I was only twelve years old, he'd watched calmly from behind his desk while my father beat me for daring to protest his decision to break the trust my mother had set up for my sister and me before she died.

"You said there was something we needed to discuss . . ." I wasn't interested in pleasantries. I wanted out of his shady law firm as fast as possible.

"Yes, it's about the money your grandmother left you in her will." He stroked the salt-and-pepper goatee that matched what was left of his thinning hair. "I am very sorry for your loss, by the way. I had season tickets to the Chicago Symphony. I never missed one of your grandmother's performances."

My throat closed at the thought of never hearing my grandmother play again. She was a gifted cellist and had encouraged my passion for music by introducing me to a wide variety of musical genres and teaching me how to play both the piano and her beloved cello. I had been devastated when she didn't step in to take custody of Sasha and me after our mother died, instead, leaving us to face my father's abuse alone. I'd dropped by a few times to see her after I left home, but my anger and resentment had made for some awkward conversations, and eventually I'd stopped making the effort.

"Her solicitors tried to contact me after the funeral, but I didn't return their calls or read the letters they sent," I said. "It was a difficult time. If you want to know anything about her estate, you should contact them."

Bob nodded in what was clearly feigned sympathy. "It's been difficult for your father, too. You may not be aware that your grandfather died intestate many years ago and your grandmother inherited his considerable estate. Of course, that money was meant to go to your father, but for tax reasons it made more sense for her to keep it, with the expectation it would then pass to your father upon her death. Unfortunately, we just discovered that your grandmother decided not to honor that agreement. Shortly after your sister's death, she put half the money in a living trust for you, which means that it did not become part of her estate when she passed."

"I didn't know about the trust." I had a vague memory of my

grandmother mentioning something about securing my inheritance after Sasha died, but at the time I was barely able to function.

"You probably also don't know then that her will divides the remainder of the money between you and your father, subject to payment of charitable bequests." Bob pushed a file folder across the table. "I've drafted the documents you need to sign to transfer the trust funds and your inheritance to your father—"

I stared at Bob, incredulous. "You want me to go against my grandmother's wishes and sign away the money she left me?"

"It was always meant to go back into the family business," Bob said, opening his hands in a placatory gesture. "This will ensure that things are as they should be."

The family business, Rossi Holdings, encompassed a little bit of everything from a real estate development company to casinos. My great-great-grandfather, a member of the Italian Mafia, had emigrated from Italy to Chicago to expand the enterprise. He brought with him extensive family connections, a head for business, and a nose for turning a profit. Over the years, the company had gone from success to success, the legitimate side supported by a variety of smaller businesses that were used to launder money from illegal activities such as drug trafficking, weapons dealing, smuggling, counterfeiting, and robbery. My father kept his hands clean with a team of clever mob-friendly lawyers and accountants to move his money around and a vast network of lower-level mobsters to do his dirty work.

"If things were as they should be," I said coldly, "my mother and sister would still be alive." I was tempted to go further, to tell him that I knew the truth—my father had murdered my mother and Bob had covered it up as a tragic accident, making use of both my father's organized crime and political connections to ensure the truth never came to light. But I had to play the long game. Sasha had taken her own life, unable to handle the burden of that secret on top of the constant abuse. Witnesses and evidence also had a way of disappearing in my father's world, and I intended to live to see justice done.

"I know you and your father haven't always been on good terms, but think of the future," Bob said, his voice dripping with honeyed insincerity. "Maybe one day you'll reconcile, and you and your father can run Rossi Holdings together."

"I'm not signing the papers." My father would never get his hands on my grandmother's money, but I also didn't want to keep it. Ultimately, it had come from a family business that was run by organized crime and I wanted no part of it. "I plan to donate it to charity."

Bob went utterly still. "We're talking seven figures. I was a student once and I know the financial struggles students face—"

"I'm not struggling." Between scholarships, band gigs, my summer internship, a side hustle providing essay-writing services on campus, and the money I'd saved while working at WJPK, I had more than enough to make ends meet.

Bob scratched his head, and I could almost see his brain do a mental shift. He wasn't just a lawyer. He was a fixer. His job was to make problems go away. "If you are set on donating it to charity, I can help you select some worthwhile organizations . . ."

Something niggled at the back of my mind. Noah needed money for the station. What could be more worthwhile than giving back for all the help he'd given me?

"I'm going to have my inheritance handled by another firm," I said, dropping my feet. "I'll send you the details—"

"Our firm is well-placed to help you with your charitable endeavors," Bob said in a pleading tone. "We've been serving your family for over two decades and would be happy to facilitate any donations."

No doubt my "donations" would be to charities connected to my father's businesses and wind up back in his pocket.

"Thanks, Bob, but I made some legal contacts this summer when I interned at the DA's office. I'm sure one of them can recommend someone to help me."

As expected, Bob paled at the mention of the district attorney. "Why don't you take some time to think about it? There's no rush."

"There is a rush." I grabbed the last cookie from the plate. "There are people who need that money more than me."

"Someone call an ambulance." Noah slapped his hand over his chest when I walked into his office later that afternoon. "I'm having a heart attack. Dante is here and it's still light outside."

"Hilarious." I lifted a box off one of the chairs and cleared away all the papers so I could take a seat.

"This feels serious," Noah said, his smile fading. He turned down his music—Leonard Cohen's "So Long, Marianne," one of his favorite songs of all time—and straightened in his chair. "Too serious for a Monday when I'm still recovering from the weekend."

"It is." I sprawled out in front of him, still buzzing with anticipation. I was about to solve all his problems with the click of a pen. "I just came from seeing my dad's lawyer. My grandmother left me over one million dollars. I want to give it to the station."

Silence.

Did he hear me?

"While I appreciate the gesture, your grandmother clearly meant for you to have that money," Noah said finally. "I'm sure she wanted you to use it so you could have a good life. Law school is likely going to cost you over two hundred thousand dollars if you go to a good school, and I'm sure you don't want to live above my garage forever. Have you seen the mortgage rates? And what about transportation? You may get the urge to buy a black 1967 Shelby Mustang GT500 that you'd let an aging station manager drive on sunny Sunday afternoons."

It took me a moment to process the fact that he was rejecting my offer. "Most of that money came from the family business," I protested. "I don't want anything to do with it, but I do want some good to come out of the bad."

Noah knew about my father's involvement with organized crime. He knew about everything, including Sasha's suicide note accusing my father of murder, and my plan to avenge both her and my mom. I'd never had any doubt that he would keep my secrets. I trusted him absolutely, and funding the station was the perfect way to pay him back for everything he'd done for me.

"That's very generous, but it won't solve our problems," Noah said. "Our total annual expenses are over three hundred thousand dollars per year, and that's with the rent subsidy we get from the university. If we want to stay on campus—and we do, because we are here to teach as much as anything else—we need to show the administration that the station is viable as an ongoing concern. I've spent years identifying grants specific to our needs. A lump sum will keep us afloat for a few years, but—"

"It could also mean you lose some of your long-term grants and that would hurt the station in the future."

Noah laughed. "Well, at least your education hasn't been a waste. It's important for students to understand what it means to be a nonprofit and how difficult it is to raise funding so they will be sympathetic to the struggles of nonprofits they encounter in the future."

"I feel like I missed out on an opportunity to learn about running a nonprofit radio station." During my first few years at the station, I was involved in everything from working the sound board to fixing the equipment and from managing volunteers and schedules to organizing the library. After I was accepted as a student, I dropped everything except my show.

"I'm always happy to teach," Noah said. "And with our finances tight this year, I'll be asking you to help out more than just doing your show. But I won't take your money, no matter how dire our circumstances. You have a life to live, Dante. I won't take that away from you."

"If I keep enough for law school, will you take the rest?" I persisted. "Or even just enough to fund something that isn't already covered by a grant—a new piece of equipment, a program, an event . . . ? I want to do this. For you and everything you've done for me, and for the station because this is where I got my fresh start."

Noah sighed and twisted his lips to the side, considering. "There is something. We were only able to hire one intern for this year through our joint program with the journalism department. Usually, we fund one position as a paid internship, and the journalism department takes care of the other. This year we had to divert the internship money to pay for operating costs. If you really want to help, you could—"

Skye.

"I'll fund the position," I said quickly. "And I know someone who would be interested. She's in journalism and—"

"I'll stop you right there," Noah said, holding up his hand. "First, the university has rules about scholarships and donations. Donors can set conditions but can't direct who receives the award. It would be considered a conflict of interest with some very serious and possibly criminal consequences. Your friend would have to apply like everyone else, and I can't guarantee I would choose her. I have to go with the best candidate." He waited for me to nod my understanding before continuing. "You would also need to give me your word that you'll keep back enough for law school, including all your living expenses. That's non-negotiable."

"You've got it." I could justify keeping the portion of the money that my grandmother had earned during her years playing for the symphony—it had come from her music and not from the family business.

"You also cannot be part of the selection process," Noah warned. "And you need to stay at arm's length so we can't be accused of bias. That means not being in a relationship with a particular candidate."

"I'm not. I promise. She—"

"Ah. Ah." Noah cut me off again. "I don't want to know anything about this person. I should really just offer the new position to one of the candidates I interviewed last term because the start date for the internship is next Monday. But to be fair to people who may have missed out last term, we can advertise it again with a deadline of this Wednesday. I can do the interviews Thursday and push the start date for the internship to give the university time to deal with the paperwork. If all goes well, the two interns could start together as early as next Friday."

I leaned back in the chair and groaned. Could he possibly make it any more difficult for me to help Skye? "That's not a lot of time."

Noah chuckled. "You should be thanking me for protecting your ass, not moaning like Ray Charles in 'What'd I Say.'"

"I groaned," I huffed. "I didn't moan. And it was in protest of all the roadblocks you're putting in the way of someone who really needs the job."

"The biggest roadblock will be the university administration." Noah toyed with the coffee cup in front of him. The pot was empty, and I made a mental note to fill it for him when we were done. "They are notoriously slow when it comes to setting up this kind of funding."

"I've just found a lawyer to help manage the legal aspects of the inheritance. I can ask him if there is someone in his firm who can help move things forward." I wanted Skye to have that chance, and if wasn't her, then at least someone else would benefit. "Any other hurdles? I honestly thought I was going to just waltz in here and write you a big fat check."

"No more hurdles," Noah said. "But I do have a question. In all the years I've known you, not once have you ever mentioned a woman in any other context than that of a one-night stand. I figured relationships were off the table for you, but I get the impression that this woman is different. Are you sure you want to do this?"

"She's just some girl I met," I assured him. "I hardly know her at all."

CHAPTER TEN

"There She Goes" by The La's

SKYE

"DO YOU NEVER LOOK AT YOUR PHONE?" Haley yelled at me when I arrived for my last shift at Buttercup on Tuesday morning.

"I was at the gym saying goodbye. Some of my friends on the team didn't know I'm flying home tomorrow and—"

"If you'd looked at your phone, you would have realized you didn't need to say goodbye. I've been trying to get in touch with you for the last hour." She thrust a piece of paper in my face. "I was at the station this morning to do my show and these flyers were everywhere."

"What is it?"

"An internship at the radio station for journalism students." She rattled the paper again, her voice trembling with excitement. "It's perfect for you."

I took the flyer and quickly skimmed over the details. An internship/scholarship in broadcast journalism at WJPK radio was being offered as a full-credit course for the school year. Not only would I be paid for my time, but the scholarship would cover my tuition fees and most of my living expenses. It was a dream come true.

I felt a flicker of elation but as quickly as it came, the tiny spark died under a deluge of fear and doubt. I couldn't apply because applying meant hoping and hoping meant facing the possibility of being crushed under the weight of another dream turned nightmare.

"I can't." Better to stay in the shadow of fear, where at least the familiar pain was a known entity, than to risk yet again being what my father had called me seconds before he died—a complete and utter failure.

"The deadline is Wednesday," Haley said, talking over me. "That's tomorrow so you need to get started . . ." She trailed off and frowned. "Wait. What? What do you mean you can't? Why are your eyes wet? Are you crying?"

"I think it's the cleaning fumes." I dabbed at my eyes with my sleeve. "I can't apply, Haley. I can't fail again. I've got nothing left. I wouldn't be able to bear it."

"Seriously?" Haley grabbed the break sign and slammed it down on the counter, calling out to the customers in line that we had to take a five-minute break to fix the espresso machine.

"You'll get fired," I protested as she pushed me into the small storage room where we took our breaks.

"I can get another job. You can't get another opportunity like this."

"It's broadcast journalism," I said, scrambling for an excuse. "I want to do print."

Haley snatched the paper from my hand. "Are you kidding me? This is perfect for you. Did you even read what's involved? Pitching story ideas, writing news stories, conducting interviews, booking guests, writing and structuring daily scripts, press release research, social media assistance, investigative reporting . . . all things they do in print journalism. All things you're good at and love to do."

"It also says radio reporting, conducting a radio show, and voice-over talent. The idea of going live makes me sick. What if I mess up? There could be hundreds of thousands of people listening."

"How is that different from playing a basketball game in front of an audience and missing a throw, or tripping and falling?" she demanded.

"Because you're part of a team. With this, the failure would be all mine."

"That's not how radio works," she said. "Newbies don't do their shows alone. They have someone in the next room handling the sound board and ready to step in and catch you if you fall. And so what if you fail? We all fail and get up, and we fail and we get up. That's what it means to be human. But each time we emerge a little bit stronger. I know you've been through hell and it must have been devastating to be cut from the team, but you can't let fear stop you from getting up again, especially when fate is giving you a helping hand."

"I've already got a plane ticket, Haley. I've packed my bags. Mentally, I've already gone. It's easier this way."

Haley pulled out her phone and waved it in front of me. "If you don't agree to fill in that application, I'm going to have to pull out the big guns."

"No. Don't tell Isla . . ." I stared at her in horror. There was no resisting Isla. She was a force of nature. The second she found out about the scholarship it would all be over. Knowing her, she'd run home, unpack my bags, fill in the application herself and cancel my flight. I had no doubt she'd even go so far as to show up at the interview and pretend to be me.

"It would be better if the decision came from you," Haley said in mock sympathy. "But I will not hesitate to resort to dirty warfare."

"Can I have a minute?"

"Take all the time you need. I'll cover for you." Haley left me alone and I pulled out my phone. She'd sent me six increasingly frantic messages about the scholarship as well as a link to the station website, and pictures from the station—a cozy lounge; Haley in front of a fluffy microphone with headphones over her ears in front of a wall painted to look like the cover of Pink Floyd's *The Wall*; a sound booth with a board full of switches; a library filled with old records, CDs, and 8-track tapes; and hallways covered in band posters. On their website, the schedule showed a wide variety of programming, but the predominant theme was . . . music.

I pulled up the playlist I'd saved from Dante's show about fear and listened to my favorite tracks—"The Arena" by Lindsey Stirling, "The Climb" by Miley Cyrus, "Roar" by Katy Perry, "Unstoppable" by Sia, and "Brave" by Sara Bareilles. I liked that he'd chosen songs by female singers, but even more I liked the way they made me feel. Unstoppable. Empowered. Brave. Strong.

I could do this.

I owed it to myself to try.

"Breathe." Isla made a sweeping gesture with her arms outside the door to the campus radio station, located in the basement of the student center. I'd managed to get my application in just before the deadline and my interview was in five minutes.

"Big breath in," Isla continued. "Hold it. Big breath out."

"I know how to breathe, Iz." My hands shook, my body vibrating with nervous energy. "I'm good. I've had interviews before."

"It was for me," she said. "I'm more nervous than you are. I have a vested interest in your success. I could easily find another roommate, but she's not going to send me fake emergency texts to help me escape bad Tinder or OkCupid dates, or calm me down when I'm wired, or knock on my bedroom door and shout 'fire' to get rid of a hookup who has overstayed his welcome."

Her comments reminded me of the frat party and I groaned. "What if Dante's there? That night at the frat party was utterly humiliating."

"It's been six days since the party and he hasn't been in touch, so I'm sure he's moved on," she assured me. "I thought it was actually very sweet how he insisted on coming with us in the Uber and carrying you to bed. It could have been much worse. You could have puked on him instead of all over the lawn."

I glared at her. "This isn't helping me relax before the interview."

"You brought him up." She snickered. "Or maybe not. You were kind of out of it when he brought you home, except for the sweet nothings you thought you were whispering to him, but in fact were saying out loud. Something about falling for him . . . and I think you wanted to lick . . . was it his tattoos or something else?"

"Isla!"

"Sorry. Forget about gorgeous, tattooed rock-star DJs who come for a booty call and have to leave with no booty because you're drunk as a skunk." She gave me a quick hug and then pushed me toward the door. "Go in there and kick some interview ass."

I took one last breath in the quiet hallway, then opened the door to utter chaos.

People were running, papers were flying, a small drone buzzed overhead. I heard shouts, laughter, and the odd scream. Guns N' Roses's "Welcome to the Jungle" blasted through the speakers, and an apple came rolling across the floor.

"Five points!" A guy in a checkered flannel shirt scooped up the apple and disappeared into a maze of wooden shelving.

"Excuse me," I called after him. "I'm here for—"

"Hi." A woman in a short green peasant dress, her auburn hair tied up in two ponytails, greeted me with a wave. "You look lost. I'm Siobhan, the assistant manager. Are you here to volunteer?"

"No, I'm looking for Noah Cornell, the station manager. I have a—"

"Noah." She shouted over the music. "Your lunch is here."

"I'm not . . ." I trailed off when she turned and ran down the hallway.

"I've got it! I've got it!" A short dude in a sweater vest burst out of the room beside me and hammered on a door with a flashing red light beside it. "Florida man tried to rob Target with a transparent bag on his head. I got an exclusive."

The door opened. A hand emerged, grabbed the papers he offered, and disappeared again. The dude heaved a sigh and leaned against the door.

"I'm looking for Noah," I said. "I have an interview."

"He's around here somewhere. Maybe try his office." He looked down at his watch. "Damn. I'm late for class."

"The office . . . ?"

A tall thin person dressed in black leather ran past us down the hallway. *Why was everyone running?*

"Derek," the dude called out. "Interviewee for Noah."

Derek halted mid-stride and returned to join us. "Follow me. I'll give you the grand tour along the way."

I hurried after him, breathing in the scents of brewing coffee, singed wires, stale pizza, and old books.

"That's the prep room," Derek said over his shoulder as we passed a room I recognized from Haley's pictures. It was painted bright green and filled with comfy couches, bean bag chairs, and small tables. "That's where we interview guests and hang out. There's a kitchen in the back."

We worked our way down narrow hallways filled with boxes of cords and electronic equipment with Derek naming the rooms we passed: Studio A, Studio B, classroom, production, newsroom, open office, music library . . . We passed a few closed doors, and then stopped in front of a crowd in the hallway.

"That's Noah." Derek nodded toward the tall man at the center of the chaos, then brushed past me and retreated down the hallway before I could thank him.

Noah had shaggy blond hair and a barely there goatee. I guessed his age at somewhere between fifty and fifty-five and his height at around six feet, not including the two-inch heels on his black cowboy boots. He wore a faded pink shirt with a black-and-silver bolo tie and skintight GWG jeans held up with a black studded leather belt. A silver hoop earring glinted in one ear as he turned his head from side to side answering questions at dizzying speed.

"Yes. No. Run it. Move the *Jazz Alive* show to nine P.M. *Rock Stellar* to Wednesday at six P.M. *Free Radical* should be primetime. Find me a jacket for the board meeting. Where's Chris? He's live in fifteen minutes." He looked between two people and frowned at me. "Are you from Skip?"

"I'm here for the internship interview."

"Not Skip." His face fell. "I guess I'll just die of starvation."

He gestured to the open doorway beside him. "If I collapse, tell Siobhan to find Chris. The show must go on even if the station manager is dead."

"Uh . . . Okay."

"Where's my lunch?" he called out. "Someone go see if the guy from Skip is wandering lost in the hallway. It's almost one P.M. I can't hear . . ." He looked at me and frowned. "Name again?"

"Skye—"

"I can't hear Skye over the rumbling of my stomach."

"I've got candy," I offered, digging into my purse. "I always carry it for emergencies."

"Hit me." He held out one hand to me and signed a document someone was holding with the other.

I handed him a small packet of gummy bears and he tore it open with his teeth.

"I read your application this morning," he said, popping a gummy bear into his mouth. "Sports person. Journalism major. Sophomore because you took a year off for medical reasons. You're planning to go into print."

"Yes, but—"

"Top three concerts of all time."

My gaze cut to the group in the hallway, all listening with avid interest. Was this going to be a group interview? I could feel my throat tighten until my gaze fell on the Rolling Stones poster on the wall. Music. It was my jam. "Classics or living legends?"

Siobhan high-fived the dude beside her. Behind them, I saw money changing hands.

"Good answer." Noah patted me on the back. "You passed stage one. Your prize is a visit to my office where we can have some peace and quiet."

Noah's office was no less chaotic than the hallway. Books, boxes, CDs, clothes, papers, and stacks of old magazines littered every surface. Not a single inch of his desk was visible, and the only two chairs were covered with concert posters from the '80s.

"I'll get those out of your way," Noah said, carefully lifting them from the chair. “We’ve got over one hundred shows on the air: news, social voices, critical analysis, cooking, comedy, environment, politics . . . but music is what we do best. Do you like music?”

“Yes, I—”

“Name a band you think I haven’t heard.”

“Angerfist.” It was still in my brain from the night I met Dante at the bar.

Noah stilled and studied me with interest. “Someone just mentioned that band to me the other day. How curious. Do you believe in coincidence?”

“No.”

“Me neither.” He waved me to the chair and raised his voice to a shout. “Everyone eavesdropping outside my office, disperse. When I’ve picked our intern, I’ll let you know.” He settled behind his desk and put up his feet. “We’re family here. Everyone wants a say when we bring in the new interns. Sometimes they even resort to bribery.” He gestured to an LP on his desk. “1977 The Beatles *With the Beatles* album. I got it a few years ago from one of my volunteers who wanted me to hire his younger sister. I told him I only take bribes if they are factory sealed, but they don’t influence my decision.”

I laughed, and my anxiety eased as we chatted. I told him about the accident and my failed basketball career, my interest in journalism and my love of music. Noah was chill and easy to talk to, especially when we got onto the subject of our favorite bands. He also had a wide range of knowledge—everything from politics to geology and from sports to international relations. I’d never met anyone who was so laid-back and yet so incredibly informed.

I was feeling hopeful when Siobhan walked in and slammed a handful of papers on Noah’s desk. “Chris is sick. He’s in the restroom puking out his guts. Bad sushi at lunch. That’s his show prep. We’re on in ten minutes and we need someone to take his place.”

“Hmmm.” Noah drummed his fingers on the desk, seemingly unconcerned about the crisis at hand. He looked through the open doorway at the gathering crowd and then his gaze returned to me. "You."

"Me?" I stiffened in my chair. "I don't have any live broadcast experience."

"Don't worry. Derek will be in the other studio handling the sound board, so all you have to do is talk. He's not bad. People thought it was funny when he made Siobhan sound like Mickey Mouse."

"I don't think . . ."

"Great." Siobhan handed me the papers from Noah's desk. "That's the show prep. Read it over and put the news stories in your own words. You just need to fill a three-minute news slot."

I looked at the papers as I stood and a wave of nausea gripped my stomach. After being shuffled through four foster homes as a child, I'd come to believe that there was something inherently wrong with me, that I was just never good enough. Even after I was adopted, I couldn't shake the fear that unless I was a perfect daughter, my parents would send me away. I carried that fear even after I left home. Failure carried with it the risk of being rejected and unwanted all over again.

"What if I freeze? What if I say something wrong or illegal or—"

"Anything you can think of has already happened on the air," Noah said. "We're still here disrupting the radio world, and most of the people who messed up are still alive." He gave a low chuckle. "Just go with it. Give it your own spin. Make it interesting. But don't be afraid to fail. We're a teaching station. No one expects you to get it right your first time out of the blocks."

"I don't want to get the station in trouble—"

"I'll take the board," said a familiar voice behind me.

I spun around so fast I stumbled and almost fell into Dante, who was leaning against the doorframe, arms folded, all cool and casual like he'd been there the entire time. Memories of my mortifying drunk-dial evening flashed through my mind: puking in the bushes, the booty call, and my nonsensical ramblings as he carried me to bed.

"Dante." Siobhan's eyes widened and then narrowed into a glare. "What are you doing here? I thought your kind went up in flames if you were exposed to sunlight."

"I'm also wondering why you're here," Noah said, tipping his head to the side in query. "My spidey senses are tingling."

"You said you wanted me to help out." Dante shrugged. "So here I am. I can handle all the on-air tests for all the interviewees."

"Hmm." Noah's gaze flicked from Dante to me and back to Dante. "What do you say, Skye? Are you in or are you out?"

I knew what he was asking. This wasn't just about the broadcast. It was about the job. Did I want it or not? I glanced around the office at the music posters on the wall, and then my gaze fell on Dante. "I'm in."

"You can't be worse than Siobhan," Noah said, smiling. "She sobbed on the air. It wasn't pretty.

"My cat had just died," she snapped.

"You don't have a cat. You're allergic."

"I'm allergic to you." She sniffed and marched away.

I followed Dante down the hallway to a spacious studio painted purple, with thick gray padding on the walls in an abstract pattern. Three swivel chairs had been pushed beneath a wide birch desk that held a laptop, screens, three huge microphones, and assorted equipment. Through the glass in the room, I could see a dude in a floral shirt pushing levers on a sound board as he talked into a huge mic.

"If you're on your own, you use Studio A," Dante said pointing through the glass. "Newbs use this studio with someone on the board on the other side." He gestured for me to take a seat. "We'll have three minutes after the previous show ends before we start. As a nonprofit, we don't run commercials, so we add a filler song to give our hosts a chance to change over. Any questions?"

"Has anyone ever passed out from fear before they got on the air?"

"You'll be fine," he said, laughing. "I'll be there to cover for you if anything goes wrong. We pull the same trick on everyone—someone is sick, we need an emergency fill-in, no one is available . . . Noah just wants to see if you're willing to step outside your comfort zone and be part of the team."

With only a few minutes to go, Dante quickly ran through the basics of using the equipment. He would handle all the sound adjustments from the board in the other room. All I had to do was put on the headphones, press the ON button, and read the news.

"Are you okay?" Dante asked.

My heart was pounding so hard I thought I'd break a rib. "Other than feeling like I'm going to be sick? I usually like to plan and prepare for things. Isla's the one who jumps on a plane and flies out to Denver, or sees a random guy at the bus stop and asks him for coffee, or—"

"Kisses a stranger in an alley? Drunk-dials him from a frat party?" He brushed my hair back, gently tucking it behind my ears before he reached for the headphones. I licked my dry lips, and my heart slowed its frantic beat.

"Yes." I realized what he was saying and quickly backtracked. "No. I mean, yes she would do something like that, but I wouldn't."

"But you did." He gently placed the headphones over my ears and his voice became muffled. "Maybe beneath the fear, there's a daring Skye wanting to be free."

While Dante adjusted the microphone, I quickly read through the show prep, trying to focus on the stories. Arson was suspected as the cause of a fire at a liquor store in Bridgeport. Walmart announced they were closing four stores in Chicago. Twenty sailboats in the south end of Monroe Harbor had been damaged in strong winds overnight, and a local developer had been arrested for drunk driving and got off with a slap on the wrist.

A green light flashed in the studio across from me and Dante left to trade places with the radio host. He gave me the signal and I heard the soothing baritone of his voice before I went live. "You've got this."

And I did.

Until I didn't.

CHAPTER ELEVEN

"Centerfield" by John Fogerty

DANTE

Noah didn't do meetings if he could avoid them. He especially didn't do meetings in his office involving more than one person because it meant he had to clean off his chairs. So, when he called me in to a meeting with Siobhan on Saturday morning, I was instantly on edge.

"What's this about?" I asked Siobhan while we waited for Noah.

"I have no idea. The internship is all but settled so maybe it has to do with getting you to do some actual work at the station like the rest of us." She lifted a box off one of the chairs while I cleared papers off the other.

I had a sinking feeling in my chest. Skye had been visibly upset after her newscast and had left the station before I could go after her. By the time the next show host arrived to take over, she was no longer in the building.

"Who did he pick?"

"Raj is the obvious choice." Siobhan sat in the chair closest to Noah's desk. "Six-time winner of the John Drury High School Radio Award, president of his high school radio club, and two years working at his local radio station before he came to Havencrest."

"Is that the dude who didn't know the difference between a bass and a six-string guitar?"

"At least he didn't go off on a rant about drunk drivers during the on-air test like Skye . . ." Siobhan snorted a laugh. "Talk about OTT."

"Skye gave an interesting commentary about that drunk-driving developer," I said, trying to keep my voice calm and even. "She did what journalists are supposed to do."

"Why are you defending her? Journalists are supposed to report facts, not opinions, and especially not opinions that are not backed up by facts, and double especially not in a voice dripping with emotion. Raj, on the other hand, was pure professionalism."

"I haven't made any final decisions," Noah said behind us. "Let's not jump the gun."

"I asked Raj his favorite band and he told me it was Limp Bizkit," I said, angling to get in at least one dig at the otherwise perfect candidate.

"Noooo." All three of us were momentarily united in our disdain for the whole "nu metal" genre which had dated very quickly.

"Despite his one flaw, he's the best candidate," Siobhan said. "Skye won't fit in. She's a sports person."

"So is the intern we hired at the end of last semester," Noah said. "Chad is on the soccer team. He read the news like a sportscaster. And you were happy with my choice even though his favorite band is Nickelback."

We all groaned again. Nickelback made almost every top ten list of Most Hated Bands.

"He's Canadian," Siobhan said. "It's in their DNA."

"I didn't fit in, and Noah gave me a chance." I was taking a risk backing Skye, but I had a strong feeling Noah already knew she was the person I'd been talking about when I first brought up the funding.

Siobhan laughed, but there was something brittle about the sound. "Are you kidding me? You are the living, breathing epitome of an indie radio DJ. You know everything about every indie band that ever existed. You can put playlists together in your sleep, go on air with no prep, and get ratings so high we need to request extra phone lines to deal with all your fans. You're in an indie band. You play, speak, and dress indie radio. Your problem, Dante, is that you do fit in, and you just can't accept it."

"I didn't ask for your opinion." Siobhan had a way of seeing right through me and it was annoying as hell.

"And I didn't ask for you to suddenly show up and get involved in staffing decisions when you haven't taken an interest in what goes on here in years," she snapped, finally revealing the reason for her rant.

"Let's put a pin in yet another heated debate," Noah said, holding up his hand in a placating gesture. "We have several good candidates: Julie, Pavel, Roman . . . I also liked Raj. He's got the most radio experience, but he doesn't know much about music. Skye has no broadcast experience, but we had a great conversation, and she knows her bands."

"We already have a Sporty Spice intern," Siobhan protested. "We need some variety."

"Skye doesn't do sports anymore." Noah's face softened. "She suffered serious injuries in a car accident that took the life of her father, and she lost her place on the basketball team."

"Oh God . . ." Siobhan groaned. "Your heart is bleeding again."

"I like to take the whole person into consideration when I'm choosing an intern," Noah said. "Not just the parts that meet the criteria for the job. Leave it with me. I'll pick the best candidate, as I always do."

"Why did you call us in?" I had a feeling Noah was going to go with Siobhan's choice, and I wanted to move on from the conversation in case I tipped my hand by pushing for Skye.

Noah sighed. "The university is moving ahead with its plans to repurpose our space, and I'm going to need all-hands-on-deck to save the station."

"Can they do that?" Siobhan's eyes widened in horror. "The station has been operating from the basement for over fifty years."

"It's their property. They are running out of space and it's easier to repurpose than put up new buildings." Noah slumped in his chair. He'd worked straight through the summer without a break, and it showed. Wrinkles had appeared at the corners of his eyes and mouth, making him look older than his fifty-five years.

"Aside from the fact that I'd be out of a job," he continued, "I don't want to see the university lose one of the best campus radio stations in the country. No one does the kind of programming we do. No one gives as much airtime to diverse voices, disruptors, and new bands. We need to make the university realize just what they would be losing."

"What's your plan?" Noah always had a plan. He came across as chill and relaxed, but that was only because he'd already looked ahead to what had to be done.

"I'm going to turn my focus to raising our profile. That means more time on the road and less time managing the station. We're going to be relying heavily on our volunteers and I need everyone to pitch in. We need to work as a team."

I sensed this was going somewhere I didn't want to go. "And you need us . . . ?"

"To lead by example." Noah fixed me with a firm stare. "Except for the paid employees, you, Nick, and Siobhan are the most senior volunteers at the station. Starting tomorrow, I am going to strictly enforce the ten-hour weekly volunteer requirement. I can't give you special treatment without starting down a slippery slope."

"I'm happy to help in any way I can," Siobhan said, shooting me a smug, sideways glance that told me her offer wasn't just coming from the goodness of her heart. Siobhan had managed to convince Noah to appoint her assistant manager even though the station had never had an assistant manager before. Sometimes I wondered if she wanted to take over. She loved the station and had always put in way more than her required volunteer hours, but Noah had been around for twenty-five years, and he'd told me once he intended to be around for twenty-five more.

"Ten hours of what?" My hands curled around the arms of the chair. "I'm not going to sell hot dogs in the quad or march in the homecoming parade waving a WJPK flag. This is my last year, Noah. I need to focus on my grades, or I won't get into law school."

"It's my last year, too," Siobhan pointed out. "But I'm willing to help out."

Noah lifted an eyebrow. He didn't appreciate ass-kissing, even from one of his favorite volunteers. "We need help with volunteers, managing the interns, organizing the library . . . whatever you want, but I'll tell you right now, you're either all in, or I give your show to someone who can make that commitment."

Every muscle in my body tightened. My show wasn't just a way to share my love of music and keep my listeners entertained. It was a way of connecting with people and giving them a catharsis for their pain. It was my way of vocalizing the emotions I couldn't otherwise share. It was my respite, my outlet, the one place I could be me. It was everything.

"You wouldn't."

"I absolutely would," Noah said. "I've let you do your own thing long enough. We are a family here at the station and being part of a family means pulling together in times of need."

"I'm not walking away from the show."

I won't abandon you.

Noah had saved me. He'd always been there for me, and never asked anything in return. The station was his life. How could I not return the favor?

"Then you know what you have to do." Noah smiled. "Welcome back to WJPK."

CHAPTER TWELVE

"Learning to Fly" by Tom Petty and the Heartbreakers

SKYE

"You're just giving up?" Isla's voice echoed through my now empty bedroom. "You're not even going to wait to see if Noah calls?"

I zipped up my last suitcase, trying to ignore Isla glaring from the doorway.

"I'm being practical," I said. "It's been six days, Iz. I know I messed up on air. I read the story about the drunk driver, and it took me back to my accident and I just lost it. You should have heard my rant."

"Why didn't you just explain? I'm sure they would have understood."

"I didn't want special treatment. I didn't accept it during tryouts—"

"Wait." Her eyes widened. "You were offered special treatment in tryouts?"

"I was offered accommodations because of the accident—they were willing to waive some of the drills because I hadn't had much time to train—but I turned them down. It wouldn't have been fair to the team. I wanted to earn my place fairly. I never wanted to worry that someone might take it away."

"You're a better person than me," she said. "When I see an opportunity, I just grab it and deal with the consequences later."

"I can figure things out when I get back to Denver." I shoved my team sweatshirt into my carry-on bag. "I'll work at the local library for a year, save money by living at home, and take the time to focus on training. Hopefully, I'll be able to get a place on one of the local university DIII teams next year."

"It won't be Havencrest," she said. "What about your dream of becoming a journalist? You could have played for a DI team, and you chose to come here instead."

My mind turned back to the conversation I'd had with my dad when it was time to choose a college. He'd wanted me to go to the University of Connecticut, which had produced the most players drafted in the WNBA and would give me the best chance of going pro. In an unprecedented act of defiance, I told him I wanted to go to Havencrest. Not only had they offered me a place in their prestigious journalism program, but they had also offered me a full ride. UConn had only offered me a one-year scholarship that I would have to reapply for each year and a place in their English program. Standing my ground had been the hardest thing I'd ever done, but I wasn't a naturally gifted athlete. I'd had to work damn hard to get to be selected, and chances were high that among the best of the best, I was going to fail. I needed a backup plan, and Havencrest was my best option.

"Skye?" Isla shook my shoulder, pulling me out of the memory. "I think you just need a good night's sleep and then you'll realize it's not over until it's over. Why don't I make you a nice warm cup of milk with a little diphenhydramine and doxylamine mixed in?"

"I wasn't really ready to come back," I told her. "I still can't sleep. I have nightmares. I can't walk properly. I need more time to process and heal."

My words didn't ring true, even to myself. I didn't want to leave. Over the last week, I'd had a tiny taste of an exciting new life that didn't revolve around the strict training and eating habits required of a top athlete and I wanted more. My days didn't start at 5:00 A.M. and my nights didn't end at 9:00 P.M. I didn't have to count calories or pounds, measure protein, or take fistfuls of supplements. I'd experienced a new side of life, and the longer I stayed, the harder it would be to go.

"I'll cover your rent." Isla's voice wavered. "Or I'll convert the dining room and take in another roommate. Or I can sleep on the couch, and we can bring in two people."

"Babe . . ." My voice broke. Leaving Isla was the hardest part of going home. "You can't cover everything, and I won't let you." I pulled my suitcase out into the hallway. I'd found a last-minute discounted ticket for later that evening and I wanted to be ready to go. "Where's my phone?"

"Oh. No." She slapped her forehead with her hand, overexaggerating each word as if she were in a middle school play. "Your phone is lost. You can't leave. I'll take your suitcase back to your room."

"Iz," I sighed. "Where did you hide it?"

"Microwave." She gestured to the kitchen. "I thought about cooking it but then the place would burn down, and I don't have insurance."

I grabbed my phone and checked my notifications. Three missed calls from the station and a message from Noah asking me to call him right away. My hand went to my mouth, and I tried to push down the hope that swelled in my chest.

"What is it?" Iz froze in the doorway. "What's wrong?"

"Noah called." I was shaking, trembling, trying to keep myself together as a tidal wave of emotion crashed over me. Hope got bigger and bigger and wouldn't go away. "Would he call three times to tell me I didn't get the position?"

Her hands found her hips. "Was he a dick?"

"No. He was a really nice guy."

"Then he's not calling with bad news. You need to call him back."

I swallowed past the lump in my throat. "I want it so bad, Iz, I don't think I can handle finding out for real that I didn't get it."

"I knew all that crap about wanting to go back to Denver was bullshit." She held out her hand for the phone. "If you don't call him, I will."

"I'm not ready." My finger hovered over Noah's number.

"You can never be ready for the big moments," Isla said. "That's why you just have to dive in."

"Welcome to WJPK!"

Siobhan stood on a chair and introduced herself to the new crop of volunteers and interns gathered in the station's lounge on Friday morning, only two days after I'd received the call from Noah. We'd been treated to muffins and coffee as we mingled with the more experienced volunteers and show hosts. I still hadn't been able to get my head around the fact that Noah had picked me. I was staying at Havencrest. I hadn't failed.

After running through the basic rules of the station, Siobhan introduced us to the paid employees, who, along with Noah, reported directly to an elected board of directors. "They run station, but you are its heart," she said. "You'll be involved in everything from promotions to sound engineering and from research to production under the supervision of the senior volunteers: me, Nick,"—she gestured to a tall, lanky dude with a thatch of dark hair—"and . . ." Siobhan trailed off when Dante walked in, sending a wave of whispers through the room. ". . . Dante. Fresh from his coffin. Thanks for joining us." Her voice dripped sarcasm. "I wasn't expecting you to show up until the sun set."

Dante didn't miss a beat. "I smelled fresh blood."

One of the female volunteers giggled and he rewarded her with a grin.

"Nick does all our jazz and blues shows," Siobhan continued. "I handle all our news programming, and Dante does our highest-rated show, *Dante's Darkness*. He's never been around the station during the day. I personally think he might be a vampire, but Nick spotted him once in an economics class in full daylight and he wasn't going up in smoke. I'm still not sure about the fangs, but I'm sure by the end of the year, at least four or five of you will be able to enlighten us."

Ouch. There was some bad blood between Siobhan and Dante, but if it affected him, he had the best damn poker face I'd ever seen.

"We have two new interns this year, Skye and Chad." She waved a vague hand in my direction and then pointed out a tall blond dude dressed in a rugby shirt and a pair of cargo shorts. "They'll be with us until the end of the year."

Siobhan's little speech reminded me that my internship was a reprieve and not a permanent solution. Between the scholarship and my job at Buttercup, I would have just enough money to make it to the end of the year, but I would need a kick-ass summer job and some serious financial assistance to fund my junior year. Rinse and repeat for senior year.

"Dante is our internship mentor this year." Her gaze cut to Dante, who was leaning against the wall, arms folded across his delectable chest. "If you are interested in our next round of internships, he's the man to ask."

"Internship mentor?" Dante's head jerked up. "I thought you handled the interns?"

"Oh, you didn't know?" Her tone was nothing short of vicious. "I thought Noah would have told you since you guys are so close. Jade just handed in her notice so I'm handling programming as well as the volunteers until he hires a new programming director. You're handling the interns, making sure they meet their internship criteria, finding things for them to do, liaising with the journalism department . . ."

"I'm going to talk to Noah." Dante brushed past me and stormed out of the room.

Nick stepped in to tell us stories about on-air disasters, production nightmares, and past volunteers. He was laid-back and easygoing with a wicked sense of humor and he quickly eased the tension in the room. I had a feeling we were going to get along well.

After Siobhan had given us a quick tour, I went to see Noah to sign the scholarship paperwork, but as I approached his office, I heard angry voices coming through the open door.

"I'm not a babysitter," Dante grumbled. "Find someone else to look after them."

"We talked about this. I don't have anyone else," Noah said, his voice strained. "You spent two years working full time with me before you decided to get your finance degree. You know how I like things done. Siobhan is already putting in way more than her ten hours a week. I can't ask her to take on more."

"What about Nick?"

Noah's voice dropped to a low murmur and Dante sighed. "I'll take the guy but not Skye."

"That makes no sense," Noah said. "They're both in the same program. They both must meet the same requirements. Their work will be different depending on their interests and abilities, but that's minor. What's going on? Is she—?"

"No. It's nothing like that."

I knew I should walk away. It wasn't nice to eavesdrop, especially on a conversation that involved me, but I was frozen in place. This was my childhood nightmare all over again.

I don't want her. We were supposed to get a boy.

Six weeks after I'd been adopted, on my way downstairs for a glass of water, I overheard Dad arguing with Mom in the kitchen. I was six years old and had already been through four foster homes. Traumatized by my last experience, I'd found an escape in the books my social worker had given me one Christmas.

We need to send her back.

She can't even throw a ball.

I want a kid who has a chance of making it to the NBA and living my dream.

I felt a gentle hand on my shoulder. Nick was behind me, an apologetic look on his face.

"Sorry you had to hear that," he said. "I'm not sure what's going on with Dante."

My face flamed at being caught out. "Noah asked me to come and sign some papers after the tour and I—"

"Skye?" Noah called out. "Come on in."

Nick followed me into the office, his comforting hand still on my shoulder. "If you need someone to train the interns," he said, letting them know we'd overheard the conversation, "I'm happy to help out."

Dante's gaze dropped to Nick's hand and his jaw tightened. "It's a timing issue. I'll work it out."

His explanation only partly made sense. He could have told Noah he could only manage one intern, but he'd specifically named me. I could only think of one reason—two, if I counted both the kiss and the drunk dial. Maybe he thought I had some kind of fangirl crush.

"If you can't work it out, then Nick can help." Noah met Dante's blank expression with a smile. "Problem solved."

"Dude." Nick raised his fist and Dante gave him a bump on the way out, but didn't even look in my direction.

Noah's phone rang and he gestured for us to give him a minute. Alone in the hallway, I went to find Dante.

"Dante. Wait." I caught up with him at the bottom of the stairs outside the station. "I overheard you with Noah. If this is about what happened at the frat house and I said something that made you uncomfortable . . . I'm really sorry. I've never had that much to drink, and I'm so embarrassed. I didn't mean whatever I said. I'm not interested in you that way. You're not my type. I want to keep this professional—"

He held up a hand, a pained expression on his face, and his words in the office became a mantra in my head that wouldn't let go.

Not Skye. Not Skye. Not Skye.

I stumbled back, reaching blindly behind me for the door handle, the urge to flee almost overwhelming. It was my father all over again.

I don't want her.

My hand found the handle and I yanked open the door. I looked back over my shoulder. Dante was gone.

CHAPTER THIRTEEN

"Desire" by U2

DANTE

"Hey, dude." Nick slid into the seat beside me at the back of Professor Davidson's microeconomics class on Tuesday afternoon. Nick and I had several classes together, and now that there was a possibility we'd be training interns together, he seemed to think we were best friends—saving me seats, waiting for me in the hallway, and even giving me the apple from his lunch.

I introduced him to Molly, who was sitting on my other side. We were in the same project group, and she'd been angling for a hookup since the first time we met.

"Did you get the written assignment done?" Nick pulled out his laptop. "I totally forgot about it until last night. I'm good with numbers but I can't put a sentence together to save my life. I got a crap mark on the last one and if I don't do well this time, I'm screwed."

"If you need help, I've got people who can write it for you." I handed him a business card for my side hustle—an essay-writing service that brought in more money than all my band gigs and scholarships put together. "It's all online. Totally anonymous. Every essay is unique and run through plagiarism checkers and AI detectors before it's released. I only hire people who get As, and my rates are the best on campus. You won't get this kind of quality anywhere else."

Nick took the card and frowned. "Seriously? You write essays for people? Is this even allowed?"

"I don't write them. I run a website that puts together people willing to write essays with people who need essays written. I manage the business and take a percentage of the fee."

Nick used my QR code to pull up the website and whistled. "It's not cheap. I'm desperate, but I still need to eat."

I saw an opportunity I couldn't pass up. "If you take on all my promotional hours at the station—handing out flyers, waving banners, selling hot dogs—I'll give you unlimited access to essays for the rest of the term."

Nick's eyes lit up and he patted me on the shoulder. "Now, that's what friends are for. You've got a deal."

We weren't friends. I didn't have friends. I didn't have time for friends. My focus was on doing everything I could to get into law school, and if that meant running a side gig that was slightly in the gray to help pay my tuition, then that's what I would do.

"I used it and got an A." Molly patted my thigh, letting me know she was still open to hooking up. I gently moved her hand away. Two weeks ago, I would have taken her up on the offer, but I hadn't been able to stop thinking about Skye.

It made no sense. Aside from the fact that I had to stay away from her—thanks for that, Noah—she'd made her feelings clear. *I'm not interested in you that way. You're not my type.* Very different from the sweet words she'd mumbled when I carried her to bed after the frat party. "*You get me. I've never met anyone like you.*"

Any girl at Havencrest would be falling over herself to be with me—hell, there was one right beside me—but not Skye. Nope. She wanted to "keep it professional." What did that mean? Friends? Colleagues? Teacher/student—*Fuck me.* How could I "keep it professional" when I'd wanted her ever since that mind-blowing kiss?

"Feet down, Mr. Romano."

With a sigh, I dropped my feet from the chair in front of

me. Most professors took one look at my clothes and ink and assumed that because I wasn't taking notes, I was just there to waste time. But nothing was farther from the truth. I was an auditory learner. I absorbed and processed material better when I could focus on listening. It was why I had such a strong internal sense for music, and why music was such an important part of my life.

"Don't forget we're meeting the interns this afternoon at the radio station," Nick whispered loudly. He'd insisted on attending the first few meetings so he could be up to speed in case he had to step in and give me a hand.

"Do you work at the radio station?" Molly's eyes widened. "My friend Rose and I have always wanted to check it out. She said I have the perfect radio voice."

Maybe that's what I needed. A distraction. With Molly and Rose at the station, I wouldn't be thinking about how right Skye had felt in my arms the night I had carried her to bed, or how her dark hair had fanned out over the pillow when I laid her down, or the way her long lashes brushed her cheeks when she smiled. I'd be able to "keep it professional," just like she said.

"I'll be there just before four," I said, "if you and your friend want a quick tour."

"I hope that means you're planning to share," Nick murmured, keeping his voice low. "Talk me up. Tell them about my show and stuff. That's what best friends do for each other."

I didn't know that much about Nick except that he did a few jazz and blues shows at the station, he was an economics major, we were in a few classes together, and he couldn't write for shit. I'd never made the effort to socialize with him or anyone else at the station. What the hell was I supposed to say?

"Is there a problem back there?" Professor Davidson stared straight at me, even though the only trouble I'd ever caused in class was putting up my feet.

"No, sir."

"Then keep it quiet."

I looked over and Nick and shrugged an apology, grateful that I didn't have to do the things that best friends apparently did.

I regretted my decision to bring Molly and Rose to the radio station the moment I walked in the door. What the fuck had I been thinking? "Keeping it professional" meant keeping it real, and the reality was that there was only one woman I wanted to see.

After giving them a quick tour, I brought them to the lounge and showed them some of the memorabilia Noah had collected over the years—framed pictures of now-famous musicians who had gotten their start at the station, vintage concert posters, and an ashtray rumored to have been used by Johnny Cash. Nick arrived with his guitar, and I had no choice but to make the introduction a "best friend" would make.

"I've got some interns coming in for training, but Nick can take you to see one of the studios," I told them. "He does a couple of jazz and blues shows here at the station." I struggled to think of things to say about Nick to hype him up. "He's an economics major and . . ." I gestured to his guitar for lack of anything more to add. "He plays guitar."

"I'm in a band." Nick gave me a quick nod of appreciation. "It's nothing like Dante's Inferno, but we do originals as well as covers. We haven't had any gigs yet because our bass player graduated last year, and we haven't found a replacement . . ." He gave me a hopeful look.

I felt a twinge of guilt that I didn't even know Nick was in a band, and even worse that despite the fact I'd never spent the time getting to know him, he wanted me to join them.

I was saved from making excuses when Chad and Skye walked into the room. Skye's gaze slid to Molly and Rose and her face went from smiling to expressionless in a heartbeat. I silently cursed myself for being such an idiot.

Nick offered to show Molly and Rose the studio while I ran

through the schedule with Chad and Skye and talked them through the internship requirements. If Chad hadn't asked questions, I wouldn't have looked in his direction. My eyes kept drifting to Skye, noticing details I had no business noticing: the blush on her cheeks, the wisps of hair that had escaped her ponytail, the glisten of her soft lips. The way her Weezer band T-shirt clung to the curves of her breasts did things to me that it shouldn't, especially because it was fucking Weezer. WTF?

"Did you see the game last night?" Chad asked, pulling my thoughts away from the danger zone. "I thought for sure the Grizzlies had it, but the Bulls managed to find the energy to battle back in the fourth quarter to turn a blowout into a tie."

"I haven't been following them." Skye's pained tone made the skin on the back of my neck prickle. Of course she wasn't following them after she'd lost her basketball dream. But Chad didn't pick up on her lack of enthusiasm. He just kept talking.

"What about you?" he asked me.

"I don't follow sports." I'd never been a big sports fan. Never enjoyed watching the Super Bowl or any other game that meant my dad would spend the afternoon getting drunk and the evening beating on my mom.

"I follow all the sports," he said. "My goal is to be a news anchor, but I plan to start out as a sportscaster to get my foot in the door. I'm going to be the next Dan Rather. I look great on camera. Any chance of getting my face on the screen during the internship?" He turned from side to side, with a self-mocking smile. "I don't have a bad side."

"This is a radio station," I pointed out.

"Yeah, but c'mon. What about TikTok, Insta, or YouTube? I could be the face of WJPK."

Skye shifted in her seat, and I shot her a sideways glance. Her hand was covering the lower part of her face, but I could see the corners of her eyes crinkle with laughter.

"We do have a public-facing opportunity coming up . . ." I pretended to give the idea some serious thought. "You'd get your picture in the campus paper. You might even make the local news if you play your cards right."

"That's what I'm talking about," Chad said, his face brightening. "Where do I sign up?"

"Go find Nick and tell him you want to help out next Friday. He'll sort you out."

"What did you send him to do?" Skye asked after Chad had gone.

"The station runs promotional events every week to raise our profile and entice volunteers. They're running a hot dog stand in the quad next Friday. Nick's in charge."

"I'll go and talk to Nick, too," Skye said, grabbing her backpack. "I'm happy to help. What about you?"

"I don't do hot dogs, buttercup." The name suited her. She made me think of sunshine and flowers. Beautiful and bright.

"I'm not a buttercup."

"If the apron fits . . ."

Her laughter warmed me like a familiar song, and after she'd gone, I picked up Nick's guitar and tried to capture the sound and the feeling of having messed up yet another thing in my life.

I ran through a few options in my mind and decided on Sam Smith's "Forgive Myself," a song about self-forgiveness and the struggle to come to terms with one's own mistakes and flaws. I played the opening chords and started to sing, losing myself in the music until I heard someone sigh.

"That was beautiful." Skye was standing in the doorway, eyes soft and distant.

"You shouldn't sneak up on people," I said lightly, dissembling. Although I was used to performing in public, I felt naked in that moment, stripped of the walls I'd built to keep feelings in and people out.

"No sneaking was involved." Her lips curved in a gentle smile. "I came back for my water bottle, and I didn't want to disturb you."

"OMG. Dante! Was that you?" Molly pushed past Skye and

walked into the lounge with Rose behind her. "I could hear you down the hallway."

"Molly and I are doing a group project together," I explained as Molly joined me on the couch. "She and Rose wanted to see the station."

"Dante's not a group project kind of guy." Molly patted my knee in a gesture that was more possessive than friendly. "He thought it would be more efficient if he just did it himself. But we're bringing him around."

"So, you're a control freak." Skye grabbed her water bottle and moved to the door. "Is that why you don't do hot dog stands? Too much socializing with people; not enough hands on the wieners?"

Laughter burst from my chest, so unexpected it startled me. There hadn't been much laughter in my life until I'd met Skye. "Did you really go there?"

"Yes." Her gaze dropped to Molly's hand on my leg and her smile faded. "You seem to bring out my bad side."

"I didn't know you had a bad side."

Skye turned in the doorway. "Neither did I."

CHAPTER FOURTEEN

"Wonder" by Shawn Mendes

SKYE

"*Avoidance . . .*" Haley read from her online psychology textbook, raising her voice above the clatter in the fast-food restaurant where we'd met for our weekly Thursday lunch. She'd managed to find a booth at the very back with windows overlooking the dumpster-filled alley. A perfect metaphor for my life.

". . . the practice of keeping away from a particular individual named Dante because of the anticipated negative consequence of such an encounter or having anxious feelings about talking to him because he's so hot."

I put down my soda and glared. "It does not say that."

"But it does sound like you," Isla said, laughing. "You haven't gone to the radio station since Tuesday when Dante serenaded you and turned you into a pile of mush."

Sometimes Isla's teasing cut too close. Noah was flexible about time so long as we put in the requisite hours, but I had been avoiding going to the station and I couldn't put it off any longer. The reality was that I was afraid to go back. Dante had made me feel things I wasn't ready to feel.

"You weren't even there. And he didn't turn me into mush. He played guitar and sang a moving song. I was moved. That's what happens when you hear a moving song."

"What part of that involves running away?" Isla tipped her

head to the side and lifted her eyebrows. Seriously. She was being so annoying.

"I didn't run away. I had a class." I raised my voice over the rumble of the garbage truck backing into the alley.

Isla lifted a knowing eyebrow. "You told me that morning the class had been canceled."

"I was worried I might have missed an email that it was on again." I shoved three french fries in my mouth at once so I didn't have to answer any more irritating questions. *Skye likes Dante. Skye likes Dante.* It was like being in middle school all over again.

"I think she's definitely showing avoidance," Haley said. "Dante makes her feel anxious feelings."

"Why don't we talk about Isla and her bartender. Yet another one-night stand."

"Deflection." Haley grinned as she scrolled through her screen. "'*To avoid uncomfortable feelings associated with a man who turned her into mush, the deflector will try to move the focus from herself to a friend named Isla.*' Guess who is rocking her psychology course? I might just declare that as my major."

"I'm not deflecting," I grumbled. "I'm just pointing out an interesting fact. And you should return that online textbook because it's full of lies."

"Do you know what's interesting?" Isla asked. "The part of the 'avoidance' definition about anticipating negative consequences. You're afraid of getting hurt if you let him get too close."

"Do you know what's not interesting? Being psychoanalyzed by my friends when I'm just trying to have a meal." I shoved the last few bites of my burger in my mouth. I'd avoided hamburgers when I was training. Red meat. Cheese. Carbs. All the bad things. I had missed out on so much.

I stared out the window watching a truck driver empty the dumpster as I scrambled to think of a new topic of conversation so they would stop talking about Dante. After a few minutes, the driver and his partner jumped out and proceeded to empty the blue plastic recycling containers into the truck as well.

"Look at that." I pointed out the window. "They're putting the recycling in with the garbage. If you want to talk about something worthwhile, talk about that. It's criminal behavior." My dad had been obsessive about separating recycling from garbage. One item in the wrong container and we lost our television privileges for the night.

Haley scrolled on her phone. "Let me read that 'deflection' paragraph again."

"Or better yet, tell Dr. Haley how your last two boyfriends were dicks and cheated on you." Isla stole a handful of my fries. "That would make anyone wary of getting involved in a relationship."

"I'm not interested in being in a relationship with anyone, and especially not Dante, who showed up at the station with two women and then tried to add me to his harem with his siren song," I snapped. "He knows my weakness is music. He knows he has a voice that makes people swoon. He played me."

"Or maybe it was heartfelt," Haley said. "One of the reasons his show is so successful is because he is genuine with his listeners. He asks them to share their pain and gives them the music to express those feelings."

Haley was right. I listened to Dante's show every night and it was authentic and real and deeply emotive. But it was easier to think that he was trying to manipulate me than to consider the alternative. I'd had two failed relationships. I'd spent my life trying to get into the WNBA and I hadn't even come close. I'd tried to make my father happy and instead he'd died angry and bitterly disappointed after I'd told him it was likely I was going to be cut from the college team. I couldn't take any more rejection and I couldn't make any more mistakes.

"I have to go. I don't want to be late for work at the station, which, by the way, I am not avoiding."

Haley walked with me around the building, and we cut through the back alley. One of the restaurant workers was outside talking to the truck driver. I thought I saw something change hands, but it happened so fast I figured it was just a handshake.

"If you need help overcoming your avoidance problem, I can

help." Haley grinned as we parted ways for opposite ends of the campus.

"I can't avoid Dante," I said. "He's effectively my boss."

Chad was standing in the hallway with a clipboard and a pen when I arrived at the station.

"Nick asked me to manage the hot dog stand," he said. "I've been able to get everyone to sign up for a shift except Dante." His mouth turned down and he gave me a sad puppy dog face. "He likes you. Maybe you could get him to sign up. Even just for an hour. I'd like to have a hundred percent success rate."

An image of Dante and Molly all cozy on the couch flashed in my mind. "He doesn't like me."

"Skyyye." He whined, but with a smile. Chad didn't seem to have an unkind bone in his body. He was a ray of sunshine in an otherwise dreary world. "I'm a guy. He's a guy. I know how guys act when—"

"Stop." I held up my hand. "Don't say it. I'll ask but I'm not making any promises."

Chad grinned. "I knew I could count on you."

"Hey, interns," Siobhan shouted down the corridor. "Stop gabbing in the hallway. The microphone in Studio A is broken. Dante's going to the storage room to get another one. You should go with him, so you know where it is."

"I've got a class," Chad called out. "Otherwise, I would have loved to be of service."

"Laying it on a bit thick there," I whispered.

His laughter made his eyes crinkle. "That's what the girls say."

"Ew. Chaaad." I mimicked his earlier whine. "Don't. Just . . . don't."

"Skye, you go with him," Siobhan called out from the doorway of the studio. "I'm pretty sure Dante keeps his coffin down there, and since he's been wandering around in the daylight, he probably needs to recharge. I hope you make it back alive."

My heart skipped a beat when Dante walked out of the studio. I hadn't seen him in two days, and it suddenly felt like forever. Had he been that gorgeous on Tuesday? Was that why I'd been frozen in place watching him play?

"Are you ready for an adventure, buttercup?" Dante seemed all cool and relaxed, like he hadn't poured his heart out in a song only to have me bolt from of the room like a startled deer when Molly sent a message anyone with half a brain could understand.

"Is there something about this storage room I need to know?" I looked back over my shoulder as I followed him away from the stairs and down a dimly lit hallway. "Do we need supplies? A head-lamp? Hardhat? Pickaxe? Should I leave a trail of breadcrumbs?"

"Officially, we're not supposed to be down here." Dante pushed open a metal door to reveal a dark, narrow hallway. "The building was built in 1906 and the foundations are crumbling, but we ran out of storage room and the university wouldn't give us any extra space. Noah only lets a few people down here and no one is allowed to go alone in case the walls cave in."

I lifted my gaze to the exposed beams and pipes in the ceiling, then to the cracked concrete walls and stained, uneven floor. My pulse kicked up a notch and it became difficult to breathe. "I wouldn't do well if there was a cave-in. I can't handle small spaces. Maybe you should take someone else . . ."

The overhead lights flickered on and off. Dante looked up at the ceiling, a frown creasing his brow. "Or, was his concern ghosts . . . ? I can't remember."

"Jerk." I punched him in the arm, and he gave a chuckle.

"I'm kidding. It's old, but it's still safe. I wouldn't bring you down here if it wasn't."

"Good to know you're not the type of guy to put innocent interns at risk."

"What is your type?" he asked over his shoulder. "You said it wasn't me, so . . ."

"Sports guys, I guess." I didn't have anything to lose by being honest. "My dad was very controlling when it came to my free time because my focus was supposed to be on basketball. He would only let me date other athletes because they understood the lifestyle—going to bed early, waking up at four or five in the morning to practice, watching what I ate, no drugs or alcohol . . ."

"Sounds dull."

"He didn't want me to date at all," I said. "He thought it would distract me, but my mom was worried that I'd miss out on high school experiences and wouldn't . . . know things when I left home."

A smile tugged at his lips. "So, your mom wanted to pimp you out?"

"That's not—"

"I'm just messing with you," he said. "So, sports people. What are they like? Never had one myself."

"Usually, the only thing we had in common was sports." I bit my lip considering whether to share. "I only had two serious boyfriends—one in high school and one my freshman year—and they both cheated on me, so I'm kinda done with the whole relationship thing."

"They were idiots."

My stomach tightened, expecting some kind of quip, but he wasn't laughing. "Yeah, they were."

"What about musicians," he said lightly. "Ever date one of those?"

I bit down on a smile, grateful he was walking ahead and couldn't see me. "I heard they have huge egos. I don't think we'd fit."

"Good thing I'm humble."

"This underground space is amazing," I said as we made our way through a maze of hallways. "From the outside you'd never realize there was so much down here."

"Most of the buildings on campus have hidden rooms and passages. When I first started at the station, Noah told me all about them. He found out about them from the previous station manager. The engineering science building has a hidden tower that can only be accessed through one of the libraries and the arts building has a theater under the existing theater that nobody uses. I've visited them all."

Before I could respond, he stopped in front of a red steel door. Someone had taped a handwritten sign on the chipped paint that read, *Abandon all hope. WJPK storage*, and beneath, in small letters, *Vampire lair.* He turned on the lights as we walked in, and the door closed with a bang behind us.

"Sorry," he said when I jumped. "The doorstop has been missing for years."

I breathed in the scent of stale air and moldy paper as I looked around. Boxes filled with electronics, torn posters, old cassette tapes, CDs and magazines littered the floor. Metal shelving units lined the walls, stacked with more outdated technology. As I moved farther in, I saw tables bowing under the weight of old computers and printer parts. No coffin in sight.

"Isn't it too damp down here for some of this?" I pulled out a 1980s edition of *Rolling Stone* magazine with a picture of Guns N' Roses on the front cover.

"We ran out of space in the music library." He searched through one of the boxes. "Noah prioritized keeping the vinyl upstairs. Even though everything is available digitally, he is reluctant to get rid of this stuff."

"That's such a shame." I rifled through the box of magazines and pulled out one with Nirvana on the cover and another featuring Pearl Jam. I held up one in each hand. "Best grunge band of all time?"

"Pearl Jam, of course."

"Seriously?" I put the magazines back in the box. "I can't believe someone who shares my love of music wouldn't appreciate the genius that is Nirvana."

"I can't believe the words that are coming out of your mouth," he retorted. "I think I might just have to leave you down here with nothing but a CD player and Pearl Jam's greatest hits until you come to your senses."

"You won't get a chance to leave me down here because I found the microphones we were sent to get," I said, spotting the box on the shelf overhead. I put my phone on the shelf and went up on my toes to reach it.

"Don't move."

I froze, precariously stretched with my fingertips on the box above me. "What's wrong? Is it a spider? I'm not afraid of spiders. Mom and I always used to carry them outside if we found them in the house."

His voice cracked, then roughened. "It's not a spider." He came up behind me and reached for the box. His chest pressed against my back, flooding my body with warmth.

"Did you think I couldn't get it myself?"

"I don't care if you can get it yourself. You look . . ." He trailed off, leaning closer, so close I could feel the heat of his body, the brush of his arm on my hair. Electricity crackled in the air between us, making my skin prickle.

"How do I look?" I glanced back over my shoulder. He hadn't moved, one hand planted on the box above my head, the other only inches away from my hip. His eyes burned into mine and I couldn't stop the stream of images in my mind: Dante pinning my hands to the shelf. His hand sliding across my stomach and down . . .

"Like something out of a dream." He brushed my hair over my shoulder, his lips gently skimming down my neck.

The lights flickered again. I heard a pop and crackle and then the room was plunged into darkness. My heart pounded and for a moment I was back in the crumpled car with my father unconscious beside me.

Shouting. Yelling. Blinding snow. Tires squealing. Bright lights. Big noise. Darkness. Pain.

"Skye?" Dante wrapped his arms around me and pulled me tight against his chest, bringing me back to the present. His voice was quiet, faint, as if he were far away and not right behind me. The thinly veiled panic in his voice overrode the fear that had frozen me in place.

"What happened?" I picked up my phone and turned on the flashlight.

"I think we blew a fuse."

"I guess we should go and report it."

"Yeah." His voice sounded so wrong, I turned in his arms so I could see his face, my hands moving to his chest to steady myself.

"Are you okay?" I looked up but could barely see the glimmer of his eyes.

"Not a fan of the dark."

I wrapped my arms around him and gave him a hug. "I totally get that. I associate bad things with the darkness, too. Some happened when I was young, and I blocked out the details. And there was the night of the car crash. I was trapped for hours while the emergency team tried to figure out how to free me. It took a year of therapy before I could handle dark enclosed spaces, and I still have nightmares."

"And yet here you are." He rested his forehead against mine. "All cool and calm and comforting me when I should be comforting you." He tightened his arms around me, and we held each other as my phone light flickered in the darkness.

"I've got you," I whispered.

"I've got you."

I pressed my cheek against his chest. "Your heart is still beating hard."

"That's because I want to kiss you right now," he said quietly. "In a terms of endearment kind of way."

A wave of heat crashed over my body, and I pulled back just enough so I could look up and meet his gaze. "What does that mean in the context of all the women who seem to be enamored of you?"

"This is totally different." He cupped my jaw, rubbing his finger gently over my cheek. "*You* are totally different."

Part of me thought—no, knew—this was a mistake for so many reasons. But I did want to kiss him. Because he was my bad boy musician fantasy come to life. Because I was lost in his eyes, drunk on the temptation of him. Because for the briefest moment, he'd dropped his walls and let me peek inside at a soul as bruised and battered as mine.

"No regrets. No expectations. No promises." I slid my arms around his neck and ragged breaths drew us together and apart.

I'm not sure who kissed who first. All I know is that his lips were softer than I remembered, velvet, his touch light, but there was a desperation behind his kiss, a need as urgent as my own. His mouth moved to my shoulder, my neck, the curve of my ear, his breath warm against my skin. I threaded my hands through his soft hair, and he found my lips again, taking the kiss deep, his tongue stroking mine, devouring the last of my resistance. A moan escaped my lips and I ran my hands down his back until I reached the edge of his T-shirt. His skin was hot, his muscles firm under my touch. I heard his breath hitch, felt his body stiffen.

"Skye . . ." My name came out in guttural groan as he wound my hair around his fist and took control, baring my throat to the heated slide of his lips, moving me where he wanted me to go. I fell into it, fell into him, his voice, his hold, triggering a darkness inside me, the same yearning I'd felt in the alley for something I wanted so much it scared me.

My body dissolved into his until we were one person, not two. I had never experienced feelings so intense, a want so fierce it was fire in my bones. Every part of me that had died in that car crash came alive, and my universe became Dante. His heat, his strength, his breath, his hands—holding me, moving me, driving me wild. I pressed my full body against him and felt the hard length of his erection against my hips.

His breath hitched, and he pulled back, his chest heaving in the same fractured rhythm as mine. "We need to stop. I want you, but not like this."

My body was humming, vibrating with the curious sensation of following my own desires. "Yes, like this," I whispered, taking a step so I could press my lips to his. "I want you." I'd never been so forward. I didn't make first moves. I'd been so focused on being the perfect daughter and making my dad's dreams come true that I hadn't had time for anything except basketball, my grades and writing for the school paper. My relationships had been entirely one-sided—more to assuage my mom's worry that I was missing out on life experiences than anything else. My desire had been buried under a mountain of guilt. But right then, all I wanted was to be the opposite of that girl. I wanted to be free.

He licked his lips, and his brown eyes met mine, making my stomach tighten. I don't know if he would have said yes, but before he could speak, I heard footsteps in the hallway.

"Dante?" A woman's voice called out. "Are you still down here?"

"Fuck." Dante ripped himself out of my arms and stumbled back, leaving me instantly bereft. "It's Siobhan. She can't see us like this." He grabbed his phone and shone the light around the room until he located a box overflowing with electronics. "Grab the mics and I'll find the rest of the equipment."

Still stunned by his suddenly cool demeanor, I took down the box while Dante frantically tossed cords and wires into a plastic container. He had just pulled the container off the shelf when the door banged open. Light sliced through the darkness, stripping away the veil of shadows and laying bare the stark reality of our surroundings. Our intimate enclave was nothing more than a crumbling graveyard for discarded memories and broken dreams.

"Noah wants all the mics," Siobhan said, walking into the room while Nick propped open the door. "We had to come all the way down here because you didn't answer our messages."

"Can't get a signal down here," Dante mumbled. "You wasted your time. I knew he'd need all the mics. Skye's got the box. We need to stop by maintenance on the way back. Fuse blew again." His cold, clipped tone was a shock after the warmth of our moment in the darkness.

Siobhan looked around the room, her gaze landing on me. "What's wrong with you?"

My stomach tightened at what she might have seen in my face, and I tried to cover it with humor. "I thought I saw a coffin."

Her frown gave way to a snort of laughter. "I'm just surprised he didn't bite you."

"You and me both."

Nick took another box from the shelf, and we made our way single file down the hallway with Dante behind me bringing up the rear. Just before we left the basement, he leaned forward to whisper in my ear, "Skye, I'm . . ."

"Don't say anything." I didn't want to hear that it was a mistake or that he had regrets. I wanted to keep it perfect and beautiful and soul-shattering so I could pull out the memory in the dark times and remember what it felt like to feel wanted.

CHAPTER FIFTEEN

"Come with Me Now" by Kongos

DANTE

When I first told Noah I wanted to become a lawyer, he pulled some strings and convinced one of the intellectual property law professors to take me on as a research assistant, a position usually reserved for law students. I didn't love the work. Law wasn't my passion, and it was a struggle to summarize the stacks of cases the professor asked me to read each week. But the money was good, and it gave me a chance to make connections in the law school and boost my resume with legal experience.

Although he wouldn't admit to it, I had a feeling Noah also had a hand in my admission to Havencrest, too. I'd dropped out of high school after Sasha died and lost myself to drugs and alcohol, spiraling out of control until he'd found me busking me on the street. Not only had he helped me clean up and given me a place to stay in the suite above his garage, he had also helped me get my high school diploma, and he'd encouraged me to apply to college. I think he'd hoped I would go into the music program, and maybe if vengeance hadn't become the driving force in my life, I would have.

I hated to disappoint Noah. I owed him everything. I had been brutally honest with him about my past and he had never judged me. In all the years I'd known him, I had only ever kept two secrets. The first was the essay writing service I started when I realized I needed an extra source of funding to pay my tuition. Noah already let me live rent free in exchange for help around his house, and he had been more than generous when he'd helped me get my life on track. I couldn't ask for more. The second secret I ever kept from him was Skye.

That kiss in the basement was a huge mistake. I had put her at risk. I'd put Noah and the station at risk. Hell, I'd put my whole law career at risk, although to be fair I'd already done that with the essay writing service. But I couldn't help myself. I'd never met anyone like her. Our chemistry was off the charts. Still, the guilt weighed on me. I hadn't contacted her since we'd parted ways the previous afternoon. I needed to back off. Keep my distance. Maybe Siobhan or Nick could take over the interns and I could take over the volunteers . . .

"Hey, bro." Nick punched me in the arm, pulling me out of thoughts. "Where have you been all class? You were staring into space. Are you on something? You got some for me?"

"I had an early meeting with the prof at the law school so I only got a few hours' sleep."

"I got an A on that paper your essay writers did for me," he held up his phone to show me the mark on his screen. "I've been telling everybody I know about it. You should consider doing more advertising . . ."

"It has to be word of mouth," I said. "It falls into a gray area when it comes to academic conduct."

"Why are you doing it then?" He grabbed his backpack and followed me out of the classroom. "Don't you need to be squeaky-clean to get into law school? Aren't you worried you'll get caught?"

I was worried, but I couldn't stop. Just like I hadn't been able to stop myself from kissing Skye in the basement. It didn't make sense. Money wasn't an issue anymore. I'd managed to get scholarships that, together with the research assistant money and the gig fees from the band, were more than enough to keep me afloat. I had always wondered if I had some kind of self-sabotage gene—the same thing that had made me defy my father over and over again even though I knew I would suffer the consequences.

"I don't know," I said honestly. "I started out doing it for the money, and then I told myself I was helping people . . . now . . ."

"I'd tell you to shut it down, but it's the only reason I'm getting through school." Nick grimaced. "Does that make me a bad person?"

"I don't think you could be a bad person if you tried."

"Tell that to the girls," Nick said. "It's just one strikeout after another for me. I'm hoping Chad comes through for me tomorrow at the basketball game in the park. He's going to introduce me to the girl who does the *Bollywood Mix* show. Are you coming?"

Fuck. I'd forgotten that Chad had set up a team-building basketball game for Saturday afternoon and Noah had thought it was such a great idea, he'd made it mandatory for all the volunteers. I didn't usually show up for team-building events, but I was feeling guilty about breaking my promise to Noah about Skye and . . . Skye would be there.

The sensible thing—the only response—was to say no. But when I opened my mouth the word that came out was "yes."

I wasn't sure if it was because the station volunteers had a secret love of basketball or because Noah had made the team-building exercise mandatory, but almost everyone showed up for the basketball game on Saturday afternoon—including Skye, who had brought Isla along for moral support.

Chad split the group over three courts. I joined Skye, Nick, Haley, Siobhan, and Chad on one court playing against the hip-hop, rap, and metal show hosts, who wore matching shirts and had already come up with a team song.

"Why don't we have a team song?" Chad complained, glaring at our team. "You're all music people. Couldn't you come up with something on the fly so we don't have to just sit here when they try to intimidate us with their metal screams?"

Isla looked over at Nick with interest. "You're a music person, too? DJ, musician, singer, or just obsessed?"

Nick brightened. He'd been down since striking out with the

Bollywood Mix DJ on their way to the park. "I play guitar and sing, although not as well as Haley. I could write a team song."

A smile spread across Isla's face. "Will it have a scream at the end?"

"If you want a scream, I'll give you a scream." He moved to sit beside her and they spent the next ten minutes with their heads bent over his phone.

Skye went to practice hoops at the other end of the court. She wore leggings and a crop top that showed off her toned body, and my mind went somewhere it shouldn't go when I was about to get involved in a contact sport. I grabbed a free ball to show off my signature move while everyone warmed up. It was a dribble drive with my right hand, followed by going behind my back and to my left. I finished with a reverse dunk and looked for Skye as I hung on the rim for an extra second, trying to appear as if I wasn't showing off, even though I was.

Skye had stopped shooting hoops to watch me, so I called Chad for a pass and shot a basket from fifteen feet out on the baseline coming off the screen. I wasn't a pro player like Skye, but I could hold my own on the court.

Her lips quivered with a smile, and she gave me the briefest of nods. Maybe she didn't hate me for the way I'd left things after all.

We organized our team and the game started on a high after we sang our new team song, ending with a scream. We were having fun, draining jumpers like there was no tomorrow, and scoring big points. But soon, the vibe shifted. The metal/rap crew decided they didn't like losing and started in with the trash talk and some excessive physical contact. We refused to call fouls, even when Chad took a slug to the face as he shot a jumper. Nick tripped the bastard as he ran back down the court. I stared the metal dude down when he opened his mouth to complain.

The metalheads had realized Skye was our ringer and focused their attention on her. Ben, the host of the metal show, started gratuitously touching her chest when she shot in front of him and applying hard pressure to throw her off-balance. My pulse kicked up a notch and I felt something dark stir inside me, something I'd buried when Sasha died. I moved to block him and got in his face. "Touch her like that again and I'll break your fucking nose."

Skye glared at me as she ran past. "I've dealt with worse," she said. "I can handle it."

Nick called the foul. We resumed the game, but the dude misinterpreted my threat as a challenge and became even more aggressive, holding, pushing, and throwing elbows. The trash talk became a mix of physical intimidation and personal comments, and then Ben deliberately body slammed Skye on her way down from shooting a jumper. She flew backward, hitting the ground with a loud thud. Her left foot twisted, and she grimaced in pain.

Red sheeted my vision and my pulse surged in my ears. When I saw Haley and Isla run over to help her, I crossed the court toward Ben.

"What the fuck?" I grabbed him by the shirt and slammed him up against the chain-link fence so hard it rattled. My body vibrated with tension, and the darkness I'd held back for so long came out with a roar.

For some reason, Ben didn't seem to sense the danger. "Hey, it's not my fault she can't keep up."

I shoved my forearm into Ben's throat. "Let's see how you keep up when I toss you around the court."

Ben struggled in my grip, his eyes widening with fear. "Chill, bro. It's just a game."

"Dante." Nick stepped in front of me and put a hand on my shoulder. "Let him go. Skye's okay. He took it too far, but it won't happen again. He's not worth it."

Nick tugged on my arm again and the darkness receded. With an irritated growl, I released Ben and made my way to Skye, who was on one foot, supported by Haley and Isla.

I was still so riled up, I could barely string two words together. "Sit."

Skye lifted an eyebrow. "Excuse me?"

I dropped to one knee in front of her. "Let me see."

She drew in a shuddering breath and lowered herself to the bench. Haley and Isla offered to get some ice, giving us a few moments alone.

"Are you okay?" I lifted her foot to my knee.

"Yes." She put a gentle hand on my jaw, tilting my head until our eyes met. "Are *you* okay?"

No, I wasn't okay. Now that my mind was clear, I kept having flashbacks to the night I'd found Sasha in the tub. I'd spent my life trying to protect her from our father, but I hadn't been able to protect her from herself.

"Dante?" Skye's voice was a light in the maelstrom of emotions that were swirling inside me. "What happened?"

I tried to shake it off, focus on the warmth of her touch. "He hurt you. I want to tear him apart."

"While I appreciate the sentiment, I don't need you to tear anyone apart on my behalf." She cupped my face with both hands and dropped her forehead to mine. "What I need is for you to channel that protective anger into kicking some metalhead ass."

Her gentle voice was doing strange things to my stomach and something in the air was making my damn eyes water. Maybe getting back on the court was a good idea.

Haley and Isla returned with ice and attended to Skye's ankle while I joined the rest of the team. Ben wisely sat out. The remaining players didn't know what hit them. Twenty minutes later it was high fives and victory hugs as the losers turned tail and walked away to the dulcet tones of Nick and Isla's new team song, to which they'd added extra screams.

"Yeah. Run to mama," Isla called out. "Go listen to your black death doom music on a cheap dollar-store speaker."

"This was supposed to be a team-building exercise," Chad muttered. "We were here to make friends with the other people at the station, not alienate them."

I returned to the bench where Skye was testing her foot. "I'll call an Uber," I offered when she winced.

"It's not that far. I can hop if I have a shoulder to lean on."

I crouched down in front of her, giving her my back. "I'll carry you."

It took a moment before she understood, and then she laughed. "Piggyback? I haven't done that since I was a kid. I'd be too heavy for you."

"Go on," Isla said with a grin. "It will take forever if you call an Uber and then you'll miss out on the food trucks."

With a sigh, Skye wrapped her arms over my shoulders. I lifted her and reached back to settle her against my hips. She fit perfectly against me, her body soft against my back. Safe. She was safe with me. Something inside me loosened and sighed.

"Why did you ghost me?" she asked quietly as we trailed behind the group.

I looked back, frowning. "What do you mean?"

"I mean we had a moment in the basement and then you ghosted me. You didn't respond to any of my messages. I just wanted to make sure we were on the same page about what happened since we have to work together."

"You said in the basement that you didn't want me to say anything." I'd been relieved I hadn't had to tell her it was mistake, but now it seemed I needed to be clear, even though I regretted every word. "What happened shouldn't have happened."

She let out a ragged breath and her grip loosened around my shoulders. "Okay. That's fine. I just don't want things to be awkward between us."

"It's not . . . what I want," I continued, hating myself for having to lie. "It's complicated."

"I get it. You don't need to explain. I'm sure you've got girlfriends lined up and—"

I stopped so suddenly, she almost lost her grip. "I haven't been with anyone since I met you." And it wasn't because the opportunities weren't there. Molly was still trying to get me to go out with her. Even Rose had dropped some hints. But there was only one woman I wanted—the woman I couldn't have.

Skye didn't respond, so I carried her the rest of the way in silence.

CHAPTER SIXTEEN

"Jealous (I Ain't with It)" by Chromeo

SKYE

Chad was in his element at the WJPK hot dog stand. He smiled, shook hands, handed out flyers, and kissed babies like he was on the campaign trail, leaving me, Haley, and Nick to do the grunt work. But I had to hand it to him, we'd had a steady stream of customers since we'd set up the tables and the barbeque in the middle of the quad.

"Who would have thought hot dogs would be such a huge hit?" Haley sliced open buns beside me. "We'll make a fortune."

"I hope so." I wiped my hands on the apron I'd thrown over my *Dante's Inferno* hoodie. I don't know why I'd put on the hoodie. Dante had made it clear our kiss had been a mistake, but it was soft and warm and part of me wasn't ready to let go of our connection. It was a sunny, crisp fall day with the barest hint of the cold that would be coming for us soon. "Isla helped me put up dozens of posters across campus and I stood at the door to the gym every morning this week to hand out flyers after training."

"Training?" Haley frowned. "I thought you were done with basketball. How long have you—"

"I'm not doing it as seriously as I did before." I turned away to flip over a row of hot dogs. I didn't know why I felt guilty, but I hadn't even told Isla my plan. "I'm eating badly. Drinking alcohol. Not getting enough sleep. But I am going to the gym every day to keep up my fitness and skills. I enjoy basketball and if things don't work out with journalism, I could try to get on a lower-level team, or even become a coach. It's a safety net."

"It's a net alright," Haley said. "But it's not keeping you safe; it's keeping you trapped. The university picked you for the journalism program because you are an amazing writer. You just need to believe in yourself."

"It's still hard to let go of the dream," I said. "It's all I've got left of my dad." Haley knew all about my family and the pressure I'd been under to make it to the WNBA. "I was a disappointment from day one, and it was the last thing he said to me before he died."

"It was your dad's dream," she pointed out. "Not yours. And he's the disappointment for never seeing you for who you really are. My parents are the same. They think singing is a phase for me, and after I get a nice shiny college degree, I'll forget all about it."

"Four bad boys. One plate," Nick called out from the grill. "This isn't the time for chitchat."

"One plate?" I grabbed a paper plate. "Who can eat four hot dogs at once?"

"That would be me."

I almost dropped the plate when Ethan Williams walked down to my end of the table. I'd had a serious crush on Ethan in my freshman year. He was the captain of the men's basketball team, a legacy from a wealthy family, and sheer perfection when it came to physical specimens of the male form. We'd never exchanged words and I'd thought he was oblivious to my existence, so it had been a total shock when he came up to me after my first game of the season and asked me out. Even more of a shock when he made it clear after he'd taken me out for dinner that he expected me to sleep with him in return.

From his sudden switch in temperament—he went from social to sulky in a heartbeat—I suspected my refusal was a shock for him, too. But he was so far out of my league I didn't feel comfortable around him. He'd been more interested in talking about himself than getting to know me, and I didn't like the way he pressured me for sex. He expected things simply because of who he was, and I couldn't relate. Nothing had ever been handed to me on a silver platter.

Of course, Ethan hadn't given up. He asked me out over and over again, and the day before Christmas break, he showed up drunk at our dorm begging me to let him in until he passed out on the front step. I had to call my coach, who called his coach to come and pick him up. Haley said people like Ethan didn't like to lose, as if I were some kind of conquest. But I wasn't so sure. He'd sent me a message after my accident telling me how sorry he was and that he hoped I got better soon. I appreciated the gesture. Broken and bruised inside and out, I was nobody's prize.

"I heard you were back." Ethan flashed a row of perfectly white teeth as his deep-blue eyes made a slow sweep of my body. "You look great . . . really great."

Ethan also looked great. At six foot five, with the body of a Greek god, curly blond hair, and jaw that looked like it had just been freshly chiseled, he stood out among the mere mortals around us.

My body grew warmer from the heat in his eyes, and I managed to stutter out something that I hoped sounded like "thanks."

"I saw you a couple of times at the gym, but it was always during practice, and I couldn't stop and say hello." He ran a hand raggedly through his hair. "I asked around about you and heard you were cut from the team. I'm really sorry. It must have been hard, especially after what you went through."

Ethan remembered me. He'd seen me. He thought I looked great. He'd asked about me at the gym. Up close, he was even better looking than I remembered.

"I'm Haley." Haley stuck out her hand. "Skye and I are friends. I've seen you play. Ball. At a game. Here. It was good. You were good."

Haley's unnaturally stilted voice made my lips quiver, and I had to look down at the grass and think about midterms and the music column I was writing for the school paper, and whether the paper plates and napkins people had dutifully been putting in the recycling bin would just wind up in the trash, just so I didn't laugh.

"Nice to meet you, Haley." Ethan's dazzling smile almost outshone the sun.

Haley shot me a sideways glance that screamed "I think I'm

gonna die" before leaving us to help plate the hot dogs. Ethan and I chatted briefly about his plans for the upcoming year. He was hopeful he would get drafted by his first-choice team, but he was struggling to keep up his GPA because he didn't have time to study.

"I never got a chance to apologize for being such a dick after we went out," he said, keeping his voice low. "I'd just had some bad news from home, and I didn't handle it well. I started drinking and doing crazy shit. I got myself in a bad place. It took almost losing my entire career to sober me up."

"Thanks," I said. "I appreciate the apology."

"Friends?"

I nodded. "Definitely. Friends."

"Hey, guys! We've got some hungry customers waiting," Nick called out. "I need a hand."

I gave Ethan an apologetic smile. "I'd better get back to work."

"My frat is having a big party tonight," he said. "You should come. Bring some friends."

I sensed someone watching me only seconds before Dante appeared out of nowhere and dropped his arm over my shoulders. "Sounds fun. What time should we be there?"

Ethan's smile faded. "I didn't know you were with someone . . ."

"I'm not." I pushed Dante's arm away. I still hadn't gotten over what happened in the storage room, and the feeling that the whole thing had just been a game to him. "We work together at the radio station. He does the late night show as DJ Dante." I introduced them and Ethan held out a hand that Dante shook after a moment of hesitation.

"Skye and I know each other from basketball." Ethan gave me a dazzling smile. "And we went out before her accident."

Dante sucked in a sharp breath. I could almost hear the tension sizzle in the air.

"If you're interested in checking out my show and you forget my name, it's written on the front and back of Skye's hoodie." Dante spun me around to show the band name embroidered on my back and then spun me back to face Ethan.

"It's the name of your band," I said gritting my teeth. "Don't you have somewhere to be? A show to prepare for? Homework to finish? A date to seduce in a dark basement?"

"Skye's a natural on radio." Dante flicked my ponytail back and forth. "You should have heard her do the news. She had a lot to say about the city's relaxed stance on drunk driving."

"I messed up," I said to Ethan. "He's just being nice."

"That's me." Dante leaned an arm on my shoulder. "Nice. I'm a nice guy. That's why I'm here. Selling hot dogs. Being part of the team."

"What's gotten into you?" I pushed his arm away. "If you're really here to help then go and give Nick a hand."

Dante reached behind me and pulled on the strap of my apron. "Your apron is untied. I'll fix that for you first."

"Four hot dogs." Haley gave Ethan his plate. "I saved the biggest ones for you."

Dante mumbled something behind me that sounded suspiciously like "cocktail size."

"I'll let you get back to work," Ethan said. "Will I see you tonight?"

I opened my mouth and Dante yanked on my apron strings, pulling me back toward him.

"What are you doing?" I snapped. "Any tighter and I won't be able to talk."

"Good."

"We'll be there." Haley shot me a worried look, waiting for my confirmation. I had a sudden flashback to the day Dante had brought two women to the station. Something wicked flared inside me and I gave Ethan a nod.

"Yes, definitely."

"Oh. My. God," Haley said as Dante muttered something unintelligible under his breath. "Why didn't you tell me about him? Did he just fly here from Olympus? Did you see that body? And that jaw? I just looked him up on my phone, and he's for sure going to the NBA . . ."

I tried to focus on what she was saying, but Dante was right behind me, his hands still holding my apron strings. I could feel the heat of his body and the delicious whisper of his breath against my neck.

"What's got into you?" I looked back over my shoulder at his scowling face. "Let me go."

He released me right away and I put my hands behind me to untie the straps. "What was that?" I demanded.

"What was what?" His scowl turned to a look of pure innocence. "Your apron needed to be tied."

"Not like this." I could feel multiple knots. "It's going to take forever to untie."

"You don't want your apron falling off when you're cooking hot dogs or making dates with Ethan." There was an edge to his voice I hadn't heard before. "It's not safe."

"I didn't make a date with Ethan," I said, acutely aware that Haley and Nick were listening to our conversation with interest. "I had one date with him a long time ago and things didn't work out. I was honestly surprised he remembered me."

"I'm honestly surprised he didn't order more hot dogs so he could spend even more time talking to you."

"I'm just happy he came out to support the station."

Dante's forehead creased in a frown. "I'll tell you what's coming out . . ."

"Dante," Nick called out. "I need a hand. I can't keep up."

"Well, that was the most interesting thing that has happened all week." Haley picked at the knots on my apron. "Which one of the two hottest guys on campus do you want? And I'm asking for the simple, selfish reason that I'll be happy to take your leftovers."

"I don't want either of them. I'm not looking to get involved with anyone right now," I said. "I've got training, the internship, work at the coffee shop, and my classes to juggle. I'm also writing for the school newspaper, the *Havencrest Express*. Dante and Ethan are just friends."

"Dante was right that Ethan bought the hot dogs just to talk to you. Look across the quad. He's giving them away."

I didn't want to look so I focused on opening another package of hot dog buns. When I first came to Havencrest, I would have literally died if Ethan had bought four hot dogs just to speak to me, but now, even after his apology and kind words, he didn't make my heart or my knees weak. Too bad the man who made me melt had no interest in anything more than kisses in the dark.

"And Dante . . ." Haley continued. "He wasn't giving off 'friend' vibes. Do you want my psychological analysis of the situation?"

"No."

"Too bad, because you're getting it. Dante has never come to a single fundraiser in all the time I've been at the station. Even after Noah said it was going to be all-hands-on-deck, he somehow got Nick to agree to take all his hot dog stand shifts. And yet, here he is doing something he hates to do. Why do you think that is?"

I looked over to see him watching me. He pointed to his chest and then his eyes and then at me—the mafia gesture for "I see you." I couldn't fight my laughter, and his face lit up with a smile.

"Maybe he's changed," I said. "Maybe he just wants to help save the station."

"Or . . ." Haley countered. "Maybe he's here for you."

The fundraiser was a huge success. We sold out of hot dogs just as the sun began to set. Although the local media didn't show up, I took a picture of Chad in his WJPK apron with a hot dog in one hand and a professor's baby under his other arm and promised him it would appear alongside the article I was writing for the *Havencrest Express,* about the importance of indie radio. After we had packed everything away, I messaged Isla and invited her to meet us at the station for celebratory drinks. She and Nick had been messaging each other since last Saturday's basketball game and I had a feeling she would want to see him.

"Anyone interested in a Friday-night game of pick-up?" Chad asked after Haley had passed out vodka shots in paper cups.

"I think we should plan for less-volatile team-building activities,"

Nick said, sliding a glance in Dante's direction. Dante had stayed for the rest of the event and helped us clean up when it was done. I'd been expecting him to leave, but he'd come with us and was now sitting in the corner, strumming on a guitar.

"If you want to get people here excited about an event," Haley said, "organize a Dungeons & Dragons campaign, trivia night, cosplay party, or take them on an adventure to see an undiscovered local indie band at a dive bar."

"Haley and I told Ethan we'd be going to his frat party," I offered. "He said we could bring friends."

Dante gave an annoyed grunt. "Maybe you should reconsider. You don't have a good track record at frat parties."

"Excuse me?" My voice rose in pitch. "I went to one frat party, and it was my first time drinking that much. I get a pass." What the hell was going on with Dante? He'd told me last Saturday that what had happened wasn't meant to happen. But then he'd told me he hadn't been with anyone since he met me, and I had no idea how to respond. And then he'd shown up and gotten into a pissing contest with Ethan that apparently wasn't over.

Dante angrily strummed the first few bars of The Jeff Healey Band's "Stuck In The Middle With You," and all my confusion coalesced into a ball of irritation.

"You're not stuck anywhere," I snapped. "No one is forcing you to come to the party."

"What about breaking into an empty building?" Isla suggested. "I'm taking an anthropology elective and my prof sent a couple of us over to the old social science building to look for a skull that had gone missing when they moved the department at the beginning of the term. It was cool being in there with no one around, and I thought it would be the perfect place to play hide-and-seek."

Isla's idea was met with enthusiasm from everyone but me. "How would we even get in?" I reached for another paper cup. This evening was going to require a lot of vodka, whether I went to the frat party or not.

"I can pick the lock," Dante said.

"Why do you know how to pick locks?"

"It's one of the many skills I developed as a child. I binged lock picking shows on YouTube and then asked my grandmother for a set of lock picking tools for Christmas to perfect my craft."

I opened my mouth to ask more about this juicy tidbit he had bestowed about his life, but something in his face made me think twice.

"What if the building has structural problems and the roof falls on us? What if they catch us. I don't want to get kicked out of school."

Dante started to play Kenny Rogers's "Coward of the County" and I shot to my feet. "Are you kidding me? I'm no coward. Someone take away his guitar before I smash it over his head. Are you guys listening to this?"

"Babe . . ." Isla shook her head. "We don't speak music the way you do, but whatever he's saying, I don't think you need to worry. I was in there and it all looked structurally fine. If someone sees us, at worst they'll tell us to get out. Lighten up."

"Every time you tell me to lighten up, bad things happen," I reminded her, thinking of our visit to the frat house.

"Every time you choose the straight path, you miss out on all the fun," she retorted. "Can't you feel your heart pumping already? We'll have an entire building to ourselves."

"I've been in there recently, too," Dante said. "The university is planning to renovate all the empty buildings as student residences and Noah got permission for me to check them out. He's planning to argue that they'll have more than enough additional space without including this building in the mix. I wouldn't let us all in if it was dangerous."

"Are you sure?" I looked over, only to find Dante's steady gaze on me.

"I would never let anything happen to you," he said. "Trust me."

CHAPTER SEVENTEEN

"Bad Girls" by M.I.A.

DANTE

Everything I did had a purpose. My degree, the summer internship, and my legal research job were stepping stones to becoming a lawyer. Music—both the band and the radio show—was my escape; it fed my soul. I had no room in my life for anything else—relationships, friendships, sports, or even recreation. So, what was I doing breaking into the social science building with the WJPK crew late at night? At first, I told myself it was for Noah and the station—I was being part of the team. And then it was to keep everyone safe.

I didn't expect to have fun.

Racing through the empty corridors of a three-story building at night with only the glow of streetlamps through the windows to light the hallways and my phone to illuminate darker corners was nothing short of exhilarating. I couldn't remember the last time I had done something for the sheer enjoyment of it, to feel my heart pound and my cheeks ache from smiling. I also couldn't remember the last time I'd seen Skye, but now that I knew Nick was the seeker, I was desperate to find her.

I heard shouts, a slam, the pounding of feet. I caught a glimpse of Nick heading in my direction through the glass door and ducked into a dark alcove under the stairs. A minute later, I heard footsteps, a gasp, and then Skye barreled into the alcove and slammed into me.

"Skye!" Nick bellowed. "I saw you."

It wouldn't take Nick long to find us under the stairs. I grabbed Skye's hand and we ran down the hallway, checking door handles along the way.

"Here," she called out. "This one is open."

We made it into the storage closet and closed the door only moments before Nick's heavy footsteps rang down the hallway. It was almost pitch-black inside, save for the faint light spilling under the door from the hallway. The air was stale and musty and heavy with the scent of cleaning supplies. Skye turned the lock and then pressed her ear to the door.

"He's not moving," she whispered. "I think he knows we're here."

I heard the rattle of a doorknob and then another and another. My pulse raced as if the danger were real. I couldn't remember the last time I'd felt such an adrenaline rush. Nick's shoes squeaked and suddenly the doorknob rattled. Skye jerked back and spun around into my arms.

We held each other, hearts pounding together, until his footsteps faded away in the distance. Skye let out a ragged breath. "I think he's gone."

That was my cue to release her, but I didn't want to let her go and she didn't seem to be in a hurry to leave. I could feel every inch of her soft body against mine. So close. Too close. There was zero chance she didn't know what she was doing to me.

"Dante." Her voice was soft and smooth like whiskey, with a ragged edge that I felt in my core.

Zero chance.

I couldn't kiss her—shouldn't kiss her—just like I shouldn't have kissed her in the basement. I needed to stop the freight train of desire that was taking away my power of rational thought. I'd made a promise to Noah. The risks were too high.

"So . . ." I swallowed hard. "You and Ethan." I'd wanted to punch Ethan when I saw the way he'd been looking at her, his gaze roving over her body, mentally stripping away her clothes. I knew that look. I knew the thoughts. I was that man when I met an attractive woman. But Skye wasn't any woman, and Ethan's blatant hot dog seduction had flipped some kind of switch in me that I didn't know I had, and all I could think was *mine.*

She let out a rough breath. "What?"

"Ethan said you guys went out." She was still locked tight in the circle of my arms and every time she shifted her weight, the brush of her hips against my cock was an exquisitely painful pleasure. "Are you going out again? Was tonight supposed to be the night you and Ethan—?"

"Shut up, Dante." She pressed her lips to mine and kissed me.

Every shred of conscience I possessed disappeared the moment I tasted those sweet lips. *Fuck Ethan.* Fuck not wanting to get between her and someone who wasn't bound by a promise to stay away. Fuck being a gentleman and not wanting to risk being caught.

She kissed me with an enthusiasm that wiped my mind clean of everything except her. The bittersweet taste of vodka on her tongue as it tangled with mine. The fresh scent of flowers as I brushed back her hair. The pillowy softness of her lips and the sound of her desire as she groaned into my mouth. *Damn.* The girl could kiss.

We were both desperately out of breath. She whispered my name again and this time I took control, threading my hand through her hair to hold her in place. Our mouths crashed together, lips hard and demanding. We kissed like we were desperate, ravenous, possessed. I backed her up against the wall, running my hands up her sides and under her shirt to touch her warm skin.

"Skye . . . is this . . . ?"

"Yes." Her hands tightened on my shirt, nails digging into my chest, a painful pleasure that went straight to my cock. "Unless you don't want to."

I ground myself against her heat. "Does this feel like I don't want to?" I wanted her. Needed her. Here. Now. If I was honest with myself, I'd wanted her since the moment we met.

"It feels perfect." She rocked her hips against the rigid fly of my jeans, and raw desire ripped through my body, fast and jagged as lightning.

"Do you know what you're asking for?" I gritted out. "I'm not a hugs and caresses kind of guy. I like to be in control. I'm not..."

Good.

"I know what you are. I listen to your show every night. You are in every song you choose to play. You break rules. You don't give a fuck about what others think. But you care about people—your listeners especially. And right now, you are what I want. I don't do things like this. I've only ever had sex in a bed. But you make me want to do things... bad things... things I've only seen in movies or read in books."

Fuck me.

I slid my hands under her thighs and lifted her to my hips, groaning as her legs wrapped around my waist. "I knew you were trouble."

"I've never been trouble. But I want to be trouble now." She nipped my bottom lip and I felt that bite in every inch of my cock.

Christ. I couldn't believe this was happening. She wanted me and not baller boy. Me and not someone else. My blood heated with possessiveness. *Mine.* I ground against her core, torturing myself by drawing a needy whimper from her lips. "Do you really want our first time to be in a storage closet?"

"Storage rooms seem to be our thing." She tugged up my shirt, slid those soft hands across my chest.

If I'd thought my heart was racing from an hour of running around the building, it was nothing compared to the way it was pounding now.

"Can you be quiet for me?" I licked the side of her neck, tasted the salt, breathed in the scent of her body, her honey-fragrant hair as I lowered her to the ground. "Or will you scream when I make you come?"

"Such a dirty mouth." She pushed my shirt up and over my head, then smoothed her hands over my chest, pulling a growl from my throat.

"You've got no idea." I pulled out my phone and turned on the flashlight. The narrow beam illuminated metal shelves filled with cleaning equipment, a few mops and buckets and . . . Skye. *So beautiful.* I placed the phone on the shelf before yanking her tank top and bra off in one swift motion. I took a long moment to drink in her perfection in the dim light. "You've got beautiful breasts, buttercup. I wondered what you were hiding under all those flowers."

A smile teased her lips. "Were you really?"

"Fuck, yes." I ran my hands up her rib cage to cup all that softness. "My imagination didn't do you justice." I bent down and swirled my tongue over her nipple before sucking it hard into my mouth. Skye cried out and then slapped a hand over her mouth.

"You can't do that again," she said breathlessly.

"Did you like it?"

"Yes, but . . ." She trailed off when I took her other nipple between my teeth, giving it the same attention. This time when I sucked, she buried her face in my neck and groaned.

"How long do you think we have?"

"Not long enough for me to taste you the way I imagined." I made quick work of her clothing, sliding her jeans and panties over her hips until she was gloriously bare. My fingers brushed over slippery skin. I recognized the feeling of scars, although I couldn't see them in the shadows. My heart ached for her. I knew how it felt to have your skin permanently marked, because I had scars, too.

So damn perfect. Her body was a delicious combination of lean muscle and soft curves in all the right places. I was so fucking hungry for her I could barely think straight.

"Your turn." She yanked on my belt and opened my fly. Soft hands wrapped around my cock. The sensation was so hot a tremor rippled through my body. She tightened her grip and my cock surged in her hand, taking me dangerously close to the edge. It was a painful effort to gently move her hand away.

"I want you soaking wet for me before I give you that." I drew her close, pressed my lips to her neck, breathing in her scent as I slid my hand down her body and parted her thighs. "Good girl."

She sucked in a sharp breath and shuddered against me. *Fuck.*

Could she be any more perfect? I got off on being in control, and knowing she got off on being praised did strange things to my stomach.

I cupped her breasts, gently squeezing the soft weight in my palms as I rubbed my thumbs over her nipples. She trembled and dragged her teeth over her bottom lip. With a groan, I trailed my fingers over her belly, through the soft down of her mound, and then along her hot, wet center.

She moaned and her head fell back against the wall. Taking my cue, I pushed a finger deep inside her slick heat.

Skye cried out and clamped around me. My blood rushed downward and I rocked the heel of my palm against her clit.

"I'm going to take good care of you." I brushed my mouth against her ear, nibbled the delicate shell.

"Yes." Her breath came out in a rasp. "Please."

I dropped to the floor in front of her and her eyes widened. "What are you . . . ?" Her words fell away when I brought my mouth to her pussy.

Skye gasped and her hand threaded through my hair. The scrape of her nails on my scalp sent a sizzle of heat to the tip of my cock. I wouldn't be able to do this for long without losing my fucking mind, but the feel of her hot, wet heat beneath my tongue, the salty-sweet taste of her arousal, and her soft moans were impossible to resist. I licked her clit in a slow, teasing motion, gauging her response. When her moans became more desperate and her hips rocked toward me, I eased two fingers inside her and pushed them deep.

"Are you going to come for me like a good girl?"

I was rewarded with a loud whimper and the clench of her pussy around my fingers.

Fucked. So fucked.

My fingers curled inside her as I drew her clit into my mouth. She came with a choked scream, muffling the sound with her arm as her inner walls clenched so tight, my cock throbbed in response.

"You good, buttercup?"

"So good," she whispered, pulling me to stand. "But I want more."

Don't tempt me.

"They'll be looking for us now. Nick is probably heading this way."

She grabbed the belt hanging from my open jeans and yanked me close. "Then you'd better be fast."

It was an invitation I couldn't refuse.

I shoved my clothing down and sheathed myself with a condom from my pocket. "Look at me."

Her gaze snapped to mine, her beautiful eyes clouded with lust as I lifted her against me, supporting her back against the wall. "You are so fucking sexy. I could spend hours eating your pretty pussy. Next time I won't just take a taste."

Skye's face flamed and she dropped her gaze, thick lashes brushing over soft cheeks. I put a finger under her chin, lifting her face back to mine. "Kiss me."

I didn't usually kiss much during sex. I enjoyed women. I loved giving them pleasure. But I didn't need the intimacy that came with a kiss. Skye was different. I didn't want this to just be another encounter where we'd both get off and never see each other again. Not just because we had to work together, but because I felt something for her—a connection I still didn't understand.

My tongue tangled with hers as I slid my cock into her hot, wet heat. She moaned into my mouth and the sound vibrated through me, taking me to the edge before I'd even started to move.

"Fuck." She was so hot, so wet, so damn tight, I groaned at the sensation. It took every ounce of effort not to come right then. I curled my hands under her ass and pushed deeper, stopping to let her adjust. "Are we still good?"

Skye nodded. "You can be . . . rougher."

Holy fuck.

I braced myself against the wall with one hand and slammed into her until I was buried to the hilt. Her breaths quickened and I picked up the rhythm, my abs flexing with the power of my thrusts. Skye wrapped her arms around my shoulders and moved with me, her breasts bouncing, hard nipples brushing against my chest.

"Ask me to make you feel good." I searched her eyes, making sure she was still with me. "Tell me you want it."

"Yes. I need it," she gasped. "I want it. I want you."

Her words scrambled my brain. I skimmed one hand over her hip and across her smooth belly until I found her clit. Soft, swollen. I rubbed it with my finger, tracing gentle circles while we moved hard and fast together. Her soft groan finally broke the last threads of my control and we came together, riding out the waves of our orgasms until we collapsed against each other in the flickering darkness.

For a long moment we stayed like that, a crush of limbs and sweat and clothes. I was afraid to move. Afraid to see her face in case I'd gone too far. Afraid of what would happen tomorrow when I thought about implications of what we'd done.

I pulled her up and studied her flushed face. She looked like she'd just rolled out of bed, with her hair partly out of its tidy ponytail and her cheeks so pink and pretty. I kissed her softly, holding her weight as she collapsed against my chest.

"Are you . . . is everything okay?"

"Yes." She pulled back, a smile playing at the corners of her lips. "You may have ruined me for other men."

Other men?

"That was the plan." I tried to lighten my tone as I stood, but I couldn't get her words out of my head. *Other men*. What other men? Was this just a one-off for her? A box to tick in her quest to experience everything she'd missed in her years of training? If so, I should have felt happy. I didn't do relationships. I was a one-off kind of guy and I'd made that promise to Noah.

So why did the idea of Skye with *other men* make my stomach tighten?

"We should go," she said as I gently lowered her to the floor. "We've been away a long time." She gathered up her clothes and we quickly dressed. She was cool and calm. Detached. I could feel the distance growing between us even before she stepped out of the closet and into the light. It unsettled me. For the first time in my life, I wasn't the first one to walk away.

"Skye . . ." I reached for her hand to pull her back. I needed something. A touch. A kiss. Some form of connection that would ease the strange, pent-up emotion that had knotted my stomach. My hand waved through the empty air. Skye was gone.

CHAPTER EIGHTEEN

"Riptide" by Vance Joy

SKYE

Isla was hunched over the kitchen table with her laptop and an energy drink on Saturday evening when I came back from the library. I hadn't seen her since Friday night after our game of hide-and-seek when she and Haley had left with Nick and Chad for a few drinks at the campus bar, and Dante had gone to the station to do his show. I'd begged off, telling them I needed to get up early to go to the gym and put a dent in all my assignments, but the truth was I needed space. Isla messaged later that night to check up on me and let me know she was spending the night at Haley's place, and I'd switched to video and told her what had happened, right down to how I'd run away.

I'd had a terrible night's sleep afterward, tossing and turning and wondering if I'd made a terrible mistake. I knew Dante's reputation. He'd already ghosted me once after our encounter in the basement. I had hoped my morning workout would help me sort out my feelings, but it was the walk past the social science building to the library later that afternoon that had finally sent my thoughts down another path. Of course, that ended the minute I walked into the kitchen.

"How was the library?"

"Fine." I dropped my backpack and grabbed a protein shake from the fridge. Old habits die hard.

"Did you stop at any storage closets along the way?" Isla asked.

I groaned and sat at the table across from her. “Don’t make me regret telling you.”

“Did you message him?” She tapped on her keyboard. Isla was a multitasker. She usually had a show streaming on her iPad, two or three conversations going on her phone, and at least six tabs open when she was working on one of her labs. “Or, more importantly, did he message you?”

“No and yes.” I pulled out my phone and opened one of the tabs I’d saved over the course of the afternoon. I’d been looking up information on universities turning to private sector and public-private partnerships to address student housing needs. Dante’s comments about the university’s plans for the empty buildings on campus had given me an idea for an article that would do double duty for both the university paper and my investigative journalism class. Was there really a need for that much student housing? Some of Isla’s science labs had been scheduled for as late as 9:00 p.m. because there weren’t enough classrooms. Why, then, close the social science building? Was it possible that once private money became involved, profit would take the driving seat instead of student need?

“Yes?” She looked up at me over the rim of her cup and lifted an eyebrow.

“Yes, but I left him unread. I didn’t want to know what he said.”

“So you’re going to ghost him?”

“I ran away afterward,” I pointed out. “It’s not like he didn’t have a clue that something was wrong. He told me after we kissed in the basement that what happened shouldn’t have happened, so how is this going to be any different? I don’t even know if Noah has rules about stuff like that.” My pulse kicked up a notch. “What if I lose my internship?”

“What if you don’t announce it to Noah?” she suggested. “No one knows except you, me, and Dante. And was it really a bad decision? It sounds like you both had a good time.”

“It was the best sex I’ve ever had,” I admitted. I’d never felt comfortable enough with anyone I’d been with to be as assertive as I’d been with Dante. He’d made me feel safe. He’d been caring, but also controlling in a way that had made me feel free to let go. It would have been perfect except for my concerning reaction when he called me a "good girl." His praise had sent little sparks through my body, lighting me up inside, making me want to give more, do better. What did it say about me that it turned me on?

"Maybe you should just talk to him," she said. "Maybe it was the best sex he ever had."

"I can't. I still need to process." I shook the bottle in my hand. "And what if he wanted to tell me he thought it was a mistake? I don't want him throwing it in my face like he did last time. It's better if I just assume it was a one-off and act like it never happened. It's safer that way."

I had no intention of falling for a brooding musician who ran hot and cold, but life wasn't sticking to the plan. Although I wanted to blame it on my sudden freedom from the rigors of training, there was no denying our chemistry. Every time we were together, sparks flew and I became incapable of rational thought. I needed to slow things down. Guard my heart. I knew all too well the emotional price for failure.

"How was your night out?" I asked, trying to steer her off a subject I'd been trying not to think about all day.

"Nick asked me out for coffee. Just us. I said no."

She immediately had my attention. Isla didn't talk much about her hookups and I'd never heard her talk about a guy in the context of anything other than friendship. "I thought you liked him."

"I do. He's a nice guy." She stared at her screen, but her fingers didn't move. "Drop-dead gorgeous, super smart, plays in a band, writes songs, makes me laugh, kicks ass on the basketball court. What's not to like? I invited him to spend the night with me at Haley's place last night and he said no. He said he didn't want to ruin things between us. He wants to get to know me first."

"Add 'gentleman' to his list of qualities." I had to hand it to Nick. If he'd spent the night with Isla, he would never have had the chance at anything more. She would have kicked his ass out in the morning and never looked back.

"I don't want him to get to know me, so I said no to coffee." Her hand fisted on the keyboard, so I sat down beside her.

"I know you, and I think you're pretty great," I said. "Why don't you give him a chance?"

"Because . . ." Her voice quivered. "If he wants to be anything more than a hookup or a friend, then at some point, I'd have to tell him what happened to me and then he wouldn't want me anymore. He'd look at me with disgust or pity, and I couldn't take it."

I covered her hand with mine. "For the record, I don't think a guy who would give up an invitation to spend the night with you just to get to know you better would ever look at you in disgust or pity, but I totally understand. You need to play it safe; just like me. And when the time is right for you, if it ever feels right, I have a feeling he'll be right there waiting because, Iz, you're worth waiting for."

On Monday morning I got approval from both my university professor and the managing editor of the *Havencrest Express* to go ahead with the story about the empty buildings. I spent the next two days immersed in my investigation and discovered that six buildings slated for redevelopment had been sitting empty for four years, and nothing had been done since the contracts were signed. After hitting roadblocks obtaining documents from the university administration, I decided to do a shorter piece bringing attention to the fact that the university had partnered with private developers to repurpose the old buildings, which would give outside interests control over most of the student residences on campus.

I wrote all day Wednesday and managed to get the piece in hours before the evening deadline. Isla called Haley over to celebrate, and we partied so hard I had to drag myself out of bed the next morning and was almost late for my shift at the station.

"You look rough," Chad said on Thursday morning when he walked into the lounge to find me collapsed on the couch, waiting for the painkillers to take effect so my brain would start working properly.

"I sent in my first investigative piece to the *Havencrest Express* yesterday and it's coming out this morning." I groaned and flipped to my side to get away from the glare of my lights. "I might have celebrated too much. I can barely remember what we did all evening."

I had a vague memory of asking Isla and Haley why they thought Dante hadn't contacted me since our storage closet sexy times and them daring me to use Isla's phone to anonymously message his show to prove I wasn't afraid to tell him how I felt. I'd never been able to resist a dare so I'd sent a message asking him to play Jake Scott's "Like This." It's a song about giving up and then finding someone who sparks a fire inside you, and wanting to stay in that moment, wondering if something might happen between you.

"Next time, call me over." Chad filled a coffee cup from the pot in the corner and brought it over to me. "I have a special hangover cocktail that works in under fifteen minutes. Can you stomach raw eggs?"

"God. No." I groaned and sat up so I could drink the coffee. "Don't talk about food."

"How are my interns doing today?" Dante walked into the lounge wearing a black Jake Scott *Goldenboy* hoodie. I spat my coffee out on the tile floor.

"You okay, buttercup?" He came over and thumped me gently on the back. "Did it go down the wrong way?"

I nodded, making an indecipherable noise while my brain spun out of control. First, he was acting . . . normal. Like we hadn't had sex in a closet and then ghosted each other all week. And then there was the hoodie. Was it a coincidence? Did he know I was behind the call, or had he decided to pull out that particular hoodie because of the request? And how did he just happen to have Jake Scott merch? I had a bad feeling that he knew it was me, and I'd revealed too much about myself with the song.

"I'll go see if Noah is ready for us." Chad made a hasty and awkward exit that heightened my state of unease. Was it that obvious something had happened between Dante and me?

I looked up from my half-empty cup, trying to think of something to say. "Are you a Jake Scott fan?"

"I played for one of his opening bands at the House of Blues." He grabbed some paper towels and wiped up the mess at my feet. "Noah got me some last-minute session work filling in for a bass player who got sick. He hadn't really been on my radar, but I like his stuff. He's got great energy on stage."

My mouth dropped open, and nothing came out. I wasn't sure if I was more surprised that he liked a pop singer who sang love songs mostly for a younger crowd, or that he'd played with the opening band.

"Surprise is a good look on you," he said, his voice amused. "I'll make a note to surprise you more often."

"Have you had any other gigs like that?"

"A few." He sat on the couch beside me, placing his hand on the cushion beside mine, close enough to touch. "Noah knows everybody in the music industry in Chicago. He's been trying to get me to quit my band and do some session work. If I wasn't planning to go to law school, I'd try and make a living playing bass. My dream would be to go on tour but that was never going to happen with Inferno."

"Did you quit the band?"

Dante shrugged. "They weren't serious about playing."

"I'm sorry. I know what it's like to have a dream taken away from you."

"Thanks, buttercup." His eyes drifted from my face down to the cup clutched in my left hand. "Rough night?"

"I submitted an investigative story about the empty buildings on campus to the university paper and I might have celebrated a little too hard."

"You should have sent me a message. I would have celebrated with you." He moved his finger the tiniest bit and stroked my pinky. A bolt of white lightning shot through my body and went straight to my core.

"Hey, guys." Chad appeared in the doorway, and we jerked our hands apart like guilty teenagers. "Noah's waiting in his office for us."

We made our way down the hallway. Noah was at his desk looking paler and more tired than I'd ever seen him. His hair was out of its usual ponytail and hung limp around his face, and he had dark circles under his eyes.

"You look like shit." Dante cleared off a chair for me. "Is everything okay?"

Noah waved a dismissive hand. "Too many late nights trying to figure out how to convince you to give up saving the world to become the next great bass player."

"You didn't have your morning coffee." Dante gestured to the empty pot. "I'll fill it up so you don't keel over from caffeine withdrawal."

"Law isn't such a bad profession," I said after Dante had gone. "He can help a lot of people."

Noah shook his head and sighed. "The world will lose a great musical talent. I want my legacy to include a picture of him on the wall when he becomes the next John Entwistle and people will know he got his start here."

"He's more of a Jaco Pastorius." I lowered my voice and tried to mock his famous line about being the greatest bass player in the world.

"My voice is a bit lower." Dante was standing in the doorway, a smile spread across his face.

Noah laughed. "She's got the ego right."

Chad and Dante cleared off two more chairs and we went over the work Chad and I had done the past week. The strong aroma of freshly brewed coffee filled the air, reminding me that I'd spat out my caffeine fix on the floor.

"I've been trying to expand our programming because we have

too many empty slots during the day." Noah poured his coffee and leaned back in his chair. "Chad has agreed to do two sports-related shows, but I also want to add some more spoken-word news programming . . ."

I didn't know if it was the gleam in Noah's eyes or Dante's awkward shift in his seat that made my skin prickle. "What did you have in mind?"

"I read your article this morning in the *Havencrest Express*. Excellent work, and very relevant for us at the station. I'd like you to do an investigative journalism show and break a story that will put us on the map."

"Uh . . . do you not remember my last on-air experience?" I swallowed hard. "I was so sure you weren't going to hire me that I was standing at my door with a packed suitcase when you called with the offer."

"Hear me out," Noah said, raising his hand. "It would be a great experience for you and a profile-booster for the station. I've already called your investigative journalism prof and he said he'll consider giving you course credit for the show. Think about it. Did a professor receive an undisclosed grant from a pharmaceutical company to fudge his results? Did the head of a faculty get paid off to let a politician's son into a particular program? Find me a story so high profile, the university won't be able to take our space without a major outcry."

I felt an unfamiliar rush of pride at Noah's praise and his confidence in my ability. My dad had rarely had a good word to say no matter how great my achievements. I was never good enough—never fast enough, never scored enough, just never enough. But this wasn't basketball. I didn't have any experience. I knew I could do the research and writing, but talking live on the air . . .

"I'll handle the sound board for you," Dante said, as if he knew what I was thinking. "All you have to do is talk."

Noah had faith in me. Dante would be on the other side of the glass. They believed in me. It was time I believed in myself.

"Okay." I twisted my hands in my lap. "I'll do it."

CHAPTER NINETEEN

"You Sexy Thing" by Hot Chocolate

SKYE

Chad wanted to celebrate our new show assignments with a visit to the campus sports bar on Friday night. He made an announcement over the station intercom, and by the time Isla, Haley, and I arrived the bar, the WJPK team was out in force.

"Cheers to Skye's new show." Isla held up her drink and we all clinked glasses.

"All I can think about are all the things that could go wrong," I said. "I'm not telling my mom about it or any of my friends back home. And you guys are not allowed to listen."

"As if." Isla snorted a laugh. "Haley already said I can come to the station when you're on-air. You're getting all the support in the world. Not just from Dante."

I glanced over at the bar where Dante was sitting with two women and one of the metal DJs from the basketball game. As if he knew we were talking about him, Dante looked up from his conversation. His gaze dropped and then he made a slow, leisurely perusal of my body that left me feeling like I'd been stroked with soft velvet. I'd worn a pair of tight dark jeans, sparkly flats, and a silk top with spaghetti straps that was open down the back. Isla had refused to let me put my hair up in its usual ponytail and had smoothed and teased it into gentle waves that fell across my shoulders.

"Jesus," Haley whispered. "I would die if a man looked at me like that. Why are you so afraid to talk to him about what happened in the closet?"

"What am I going to say? It was amazing, but it was just a one-time thing. A heat-of-passion moment. I don't need to hear him say it. And this morning was perfect. He acted like it hadn't happened and everything was the way it was before." Except that he'd touched my pinky and set my body on fire.

"My inner psychologist is thinking a lot of thoughts," Haley said. "Also, I'm not sure he thinks it's a one-time thing. He's looking at you like he wants to lick you all over."

"He's probably got those two women all lined up for an evening of fun."

"Skye. Hey." Ethan tapped me on the arm. He was tall and as gorgeous as ever in a blue polo shirt and jeans, his blond curls tamed into submission. "I saw you come in. Can I buy you and your friends a drink?"

I glanced over at Dante, who was still chatting with the DJ and the two women, one of whom now had a hand on his arm. "Yes, but no tequila. I had a bad experience at a frat party and that part of my life is now over."

"Frat parties or tequila?"

"Both. That's why we didn't join you at the party the other week."

"I was disappointed you weren't there." He casually brushed my hair back over my shoulder. Haley choked on her drink. Isla frowned. She knew all about Ethan's apology but refused to accept he had changed.

"I'm going to play pool with Nick," Isla said abruptly. She gave Ethan a curt nod and headed across the bar.

"We're celebrating Skye's new investigative reporting show," Haley said into the awkward silence. "Do you know any juicy scandals involving the sports teams? Who's hooking up with who? Who's heading for the pros? Who got shitfaced at a party and went for a naked swim? She's looking for a good story."

"I'm the wrong guy to ask about gossip," Ethan said. "But I'm sure one of the guys can spill some tea." He gestured to the cluster of ballers at the back of the bar. "Why don't you join us?"

My gaze slid back to Dante and his duo. "Sure," I said to Ethan. "Let's go."

Haley and I were more than ready to dance when the band finally took to the stage later that night. We'd had a few drinks and a fun conversation with Ethan and his friends, one of whom had seemed enthused by the idea of digging up dirt on other sports teams. Isla was still over at the pool table with Nick, pretending she didn't know how to play so she could hustle a few extra dollars from the overly cocky sports types. Dante and the two women had disappeared.

The band's opening song, "Welcome to the Jungle," hit like a ton of bricks and instantly whipped the crowd up into a frenzy. Musically and lyrically, it was the perfect song to set the mood.

"You're being watched," Haley shouted in my ear when the song transitioned into "Won't Get Fooled Again." I followed her gaze expecting to see Ethan, but instead I saw Dante, sprawled in a chair facing the dance floor, legs parted wide, his gaze fixed on me—carnal, intent. I hadn't seen this side of him before, but it set my blood on fire.

When the band launched into "Let Me Entertain You," Dante crooked his finger and beckoned me over. I'd never thought of myself as a sexual person, never flirted or played games, and although I liked the way I looked, I'd never considered myself pretty. But the way Dante's eyes roved over me, as if there were no one else in the bar, made me feel like I was the sexiest woman in the whole damn world.

In that moment, I didn't care about Ethan or the two women who had been flirting with Dante. I didn't care if he'd slept with every woman on campus, or even if he was about to tell me our closet encounter was just a one-night stand. Dante made me feel things I'd never felt before. He made me want to take risks. He made me feel seen in the depths of my soul.

Taking a deep breath, I flipped my hair back and walked toward him, slow and sexy with a little sway of my hips. By the time I reached his chair, his hand was fisted on his thigh, and his lips were pressed tight together. He was wearing a bronze medallion around his neck and his jaw was rough with a five o'clock shadow. He gave off serious dark-and-dangerous vibes, and I could almost see the energy pulsing beneath his skin.

"Looking good, buttercup."

"Feeling good." I tried to force my lips into a sultry pout, but they decided to spread into a grin instead. "Are you going to dance?"

He lifted his chin in the direction of the ballers' table. "Not wanting to start a fight."

I looked back over my shoulder, following his gaze. "Ethan? That's not going to happen."

Dante gave a rumble of approval and drew me between his spread legs, his gentle touch on my hips sending lightning bolts of pleasure through my veins.

"You've been avoiding me," he said, not unkindly.

It had been one week since our encounter and although we'd both been so busy our paths had only crossed that one time in the station, there was no point denying it.

"I was working on my story and I just . . . I didn't know how things stood between us. The last time, you said it was a mistake, and I know you have some kind of one-night rule and I'm fine with that, but—"

"I do have a rule," Dante said. "But that was definitely not a mistake. At least, not to me."

"But you avoided me, too," I pointed out.

"I was giving you space," Dante said. "I was worried I'd pushed you too far, but when you reached out with that song . . ."

My cheeks flamed, and I groaned. "You knew it was me? I used Isla's phone."

"I know your music." Dante chuckled. "It was like you'd picked up the phone and called me."

"You're different tonight," I said, trying to distract myself from the throb of arousal between my thighs. "You seem . . ." I trailed off when I heard Isla shout, her voice barely audible over the music, but the tone made my heart skip a beat. "I have to go. Something's wrong."

I pushed my way through the crowd toward the sound of her voice, pulling up short when I saw her and Nick facing off with some rough-looking dudes near the pool table. They were heavily muscled, hair buzzed short, arms fully inked. One of them had spacers in his ears and tattoos on both cheeks.

"I've seen them here before," Dante murmured in my ear. "They're always causing trouble."

"We won fair and square." Nick pushed Isla behind him and held up a hand in a warding gesture.

"She's a fucking ringer," one of the guys shouted. "She said she didn't know how to play."

"I said it had been a long time." Isla's voice wavered the tiniest bit. "You're just pissed because you thought you'd take advantage of me and now the tables have turned."

"Isla's been playing pool since she was three years old," I told Dante. "She's a bit of a hustler, although like she said, it's not her problem if people make assumptions."

"Look, we don't want a fight." Nick backed up a step, forcing Isla to retreat with him. "We're leaving. The table is yours. Just chill out and have a good time."

"This is not going to end well," Dante muttered under his breath as they made their way to the door. "We'd better go with them. I'll round everyone up and meet you outside."

I followed Nick and Isla out into the cool night. Dante joined us a few minutes later with Chad, Haley, and Derek.

"We need to get out of here," Dante said. "They're not going to let this go."

Too late. Before we even had a chance to process what was happening the three guys from the bar were blocking our path.

"Hey, man." Nick held up his hands in a placatory gesture. "We don't want any trouble."

"I want my fucking money." The tall guy grabbed Nick's shirt. Nick responded with a punch that sent the guy reeling. Two of the dude's friends grabbed Nick and held him while the tall guy positioned himself to return the blow.

Before he could swing, Dante moved to stand between them, all cool and casual like there wasn't a storm brewing. "I don't want to fight you," he said.

"I got no beef with you," the tall guy snarled.

"They're my friends and that means their issues are my issues," Dante said calmly. "And I repeat, I do not want to fight you. Just go back inside, have a drink, and—"

"Fuck you." The dude threw a punch, clipping Dante's jaw. Dante recovered quickly and slammed his fist into the guy's stomach, sending him staggering backward. His friend with the spacers released Nick and joined in the fight. Dante dodged his punch effortlessly and countered with a swift right hook, knocking him to the ground. The impact reverberated through the air, drawing the third guy into the fight. He landed a solid punch that made Dante grunt, but Dante countered quickly, sweeping his assailant's feet out from under him and jabbing an elbow into his back as he went down.

The first assailant came at him again with a left hook. Dante ducked the swing and drove his fist into the guy's face. The sound of bones cracking echoed through the air as the dude crumpled to the ground, blood gushing from his nose.

"Behind you," Nick yelled.

Without even a moment of hesitation, Dante whipped around and delivered a vicious back kick to the guy with the spacers, sending him flying into the street. Cradling one arm, the dude pushed to sit and spat out a mouthful of blood along with a string of curses.

Still wired with adrenaline, Dante spun a full circle, hands up and ready to fight as he glared at the three men sprawled on the ground around him. His eyes were pure black, his face taut, lips pulled back in a grimace. He looked feral, vicious, almost out of control. "Who's next?" he shouted. "Who's fucking next?"

"Dante." I put a hand on his shoulder and spoke quietly in his ear. "They're not getting up. No one wants to fight you."

"Yeah, bro." Nick gently tugged his arm. "Let's go."

"Skye," Ethan shouted from the doorway. "Come back inside. You and your friends can join us. We'll keep you safe."

Dante and Nick had already gone ahead and were cresting the grassy hill that led back to campus. I hesitated for only the briefest second before I shook my head. "Thanks," I called out. "We're all good. Everything is under control."

CHAPTER TWENTY

"The Sound of Silence" by Disturbed

DANTE

I didn't know why the whole stupid gang decided to follow me to the station, but there they fucking were. Five little shadows and Skye. They didn't seem to realize the danger. I'd tried my whole life not to be like my dad. I thought I had a handle on my anger. I couldn't have been more wrong.

"Thanks, man," Nick said. "I mean, really, thanks. No one has ever stood up for me like that before. You're the best friend I've ever had. You killed it out there with that spinning back kick. You could go pro." He jogged beside me yammering like a puppy, replaying the fight scene by scene until I was tempted to hit him, too, just to shut him up. *You meant business. Three guys down. That punch. That kick. So much blood.*

"It was my fault." Isla came up behind us. "Nick was in trouble because of me. You saved us both."

I didn't want their gratitude. I didn't want to talk. I didn't want to listen. I felt like I was crawling out of my skin. I couldn't breathe. No matter how fast I walked, they wouldn't go away. I just wanted silence. I wanted to crawl back into the darkness and pretend the fight had never happened.

"I think he needs space," Skye said quietly behind me. "Just give him time to chill."

"Back off, everyone." Nick dropped back a few steps. "Skye's right. This is what happens in a big fight. You're pumped up on adrenaline and it's hard to come down. I'm looking after him."

I would have laughed if I hadn't wanted to throw something. I knew exactly what happened in a fight. People got hurt. Over and over and over again.

"You've still got a couple of hours before your show," Nick said when we reached the road that led to the student center. "Do you want to grab a beer? Or just come to my place and chill?"

"I need to prep." It was an effort to form the words, harder still not to just yell at everyone to go away.

"I'll make sure everyone gets home," Nick said, pumping my hand so hard I thought he was trying to rip it off. "I've got your back. You don't have to worry."

I wasn't worried. I wasn't responsible for these people. I didn't give a damn whether they got home or not. But something in his face stopped me from sharing those thoughts. No one had looked at me like that since Sasha died. Like I mattered. Like I'd done something good. Like I was a goddamned hero.

If only he knew.

I moved to leave, and Skye put a gentle hand on my arm. "Are you okay?"

Unable to bear her touch, I jerked away. I couldn't look at her, couldn't bear to witness the fear and horror in her eyes. She'd seen me now—the worst of me. A monster. Not a man.

"Skye, please just go. I need to be alone." I walked quickly, wanting to put as much distance between us as possible, until finally my chest loosened and I could breathe again. It had been too damn easy to step into that fight, too easy to loose my fists, too easy to break that guy's nose. The second he punched me, I was right back in the family kitchen taking a beating from my dad so I could keep Sasha safe. But this time I wasn't a helpless child. I was a man, and I could make sure that no one hurt the people I cared about ever again.

I was grateful Noah wasn't at his desk when I finally arrived at the station. One look at me and he would have demanded a recounting and then I would have had to deal with his disappointment. It would have been too much to bear. Hell, I was still such mess, there was no way I could do a live. I didn't want to listen to other people's problems while I was struggling with my own. I'd taken jiu-jitsu to learn how to defend myself and control my anger, but ten years of study and a black belt had all been in vain. Instead of deescalating the situation, I'd resorted to violence. No one was safe around me.

After checking the equipment in the studio and cueing up a recorded show, I made my way to the music library and lay on the couch in the darkness, staring at Noah's vast collection of vinyl. Somewhere on those shelves, there was music that would take away my pain, but for the first time in my life, I couldn't think of a single song.

I don't know how long I lay there before I heard the thud of the front door, the ring of footsteps. I tensed, expecting Noah to walk in, but Skye appeared in the doorway instead, her face creased with concern.

"I know you said you wanted to be alone, but—"

"How did you get in here?" Gritting my teeth, I stared at the ceiling and waited for the axe to fall. I'd scared her and she didn't want to see me again.

"I was worried, so I called Noah. I told him you'd been in a fight and I needed the door codes so I could check on you. He said he can be here in half an hour—"

"Tell him not to come."

"I don't think you should be alone." She hadn't moved from the doorway. She was probably terrified to be near me.

"Noah is the last person I want to see." I grabbed my phone and sent Noah a message telling him I was fine.

Lies.

"You're hurt," Skye said. "I'll get the first aid kit."

I didn't deserve to be cared for. I didn't deserve her sympathy. "I should have just walked away," I said bitterly.

"He took a swing at you. What were you supposed to do? He didn't give you a choice."

"There's always a choice." I pushed up and crossed the room to the bins where Noah kept his boxes of 8-track tapes. I wanted to listen to something raw—pure, real music from a time when people played with nothing more than an instrument and an amp.

"If you hadn't stepped in, he would have hit Nick. Maybe Isla. Chad would have gotten involved because he's an act-first-think-later kind of guy, and maybe the rest of us would have joined in and we don't know how to fight. You saved a lot of people a lot of pain."

"I broke someone's nose," I shouted at her, throwing one of the empty boxes on the floor. "Do you know what that means?"

"No. I don't." Despite my outburst, her voice was calm and even. "You don't share very much about yourself. I don't know anything about your family or your friends. I don't know about your childhood. I don't know why this has affected you so badly. I don't know what classes you're taking or even where you live . . ."

Share? I'd shared everything about myself outside the bar. I'd just shown her the man I really was—violent, unpredictable, uncontrolled. I was my father's son. Dangerous. Deadly. She should have been running away. I needed her to run away.

"I don't know what it means," she continued. "Tell me. Help me to understand."

"It means I'm just like my dad," I gritted out. "It means that during the day I'll put on my suit, shake hands with bankers and politicians, run a multimillion-dollar business, give to charity and get write-ups in the local papers, but at night . . ." I drew in a ragged breath. "At night, I'll come home, and I'll drink and beat my wife for no reason other than I can. And when my son tries to protect her, I'll beat him, too. Or sometimes I'll beat on him just because he looked at me the wrong way. And when the doctors and teachers report the bruises and broken bones and the police and social workers come calling, I'll use all my power and influence to make them go away."

"No one came to save you," Skye said quietly, her eyes wet and glittering.

I willed myself to stop. I had only shared this story with Noah and I'd made him promise not to go to the police. But I couldn't stop. The words kept coming in a torrent of pain, and there was no way I could slow them down.

"No one." My hands shook so violently I couldn't pick up anything else to throw. "And then one day, I'll start looking at my daughter in a way no father should look at his child. But every time I do, my son will get in my way and I'll punish him for interfering. My wife will know that she has to leave. By then, she'll have secretly gathered enough evidence of my criminal activities that she thinks she'll be safe if she takes the children and goes to the police. But I'll discover her plan. I'll confront her, and in a fit of rage, I'll push her down the stairs and she'll break her neck."

"Oh my God." Skye gasped and covered her mouth with her hand. Tears welled up in her eyes. Now, I was hurting her, too.

Stop. Stop. Stop. But I couldn't. Skye needed to know the truth. She needed to know what kind of man I was and why she'd been right to be hesitant. She should know why this couldn't work and why she should run away while she still had the chance.

"Of course, I'll pay people off and it will get recorded as a tragic accident," I spat out. "I won't know that my daughter knows the truth, that she saw everything, and because there was no justice, she'll lose hope in the world. I won't know that her brother can't save her, and when she takes her own life, she'll leave a letter begging him to make me pay for my crimes."

Skye had a big heart, a soft heart. I could see the sympathy in her face. I could see her pain. She took a step toward me, and I held up a warning hand. I didn't deserve what she was offering. I didn't want her words or her touch or even the sound of her voice. I wanted to retreat to the shadows and get swallowed by the darkness.

"What was her name?" she asked softly.

"Sasha." It fucking broke me, that question. It destroyed me, that question. It told me I'd finally been seen. So why wasn't she running away?

"Why are you still here?" I shouted. "Why didn't you go with everyone else? Why don't you go back to the bar . . . to Ethan? Or are you so desperate that you came here because you thought I was a sure thing?" I regretted the words the moment they dropped from my lips, even more when pain flickered across her face.

"I came here because I could see you were hurting. I was trying to be your friend."

"I don't need friends," I spat out. "I don't need you. Just . . . leave."

Skye turned and stumbled into the hallway. I heard the hitch of her breath, the fading sound of her footsteps, the rattle of the handle as she unlocked the front door.

My hands curled into fists as tight as the band that seemed to be squeezing my heart. Could I be more of an idiot? She'd come to support me and I'd hurt her. She was the best thing that had ever walked into my life, and I'd pushed her away.

"Skye. Wait." I ran down the hallway, catching her just as she pulled open the door. "Don't go." I came up behind her, wrapped one arm around her chest and pushed the door closed with the other. "Please."

She shuddered in my arms, and I pressed my forehead against the back of her neck. "I'm sorry. That wasn't about you."

For the longest moment she didn't speak. I could feel her chest heave with every breath as she stayed motionless by the door.

I kissed her hair, brushed my lips along the slim column of her neck. "I need you," I whispered, gently turning her. "I want you. Please stay."

CHAPTER TWENTY-ONE

"I Wanna Be Yours" by Arctic Monkeys

Skye

I want you.

I wanted a boy.

I need you.

Can we send her back?

Dante's words sparked something inside me. I spun around to face him, my back up against the door.

"Skye . . ." His face was creased in pain, cheek bruised, temple bloodied.

"I can't believe you would say what you said." I slapped him, hard, across the face before he grabbed my hand and slammed it up against the door. Far from being alarmed, a thrill of excitement shot through my veins as his steel gaze held me in place. I wasn't afraid of him, this broken, hurting man who had a protective streak a mile wide, because I was broken, too.

When his mouth slammed down on mine, all those feelings coalesced into liquid desire. Too much. Too intense. Light and dark. Hard and soft. Everything inside me embraced it, reckless and wild.

Dante grabbed my free hand and pinned it with the other over my head. My back arched to accommodate the stretch, my breasts pressing against his chest, sending a wave of heat through my body.

I heard a creak, the sound of footsteps, a howl, and then the first beats of Michael Jackson's "Thriller" filled the station.

"No one else is here. I have pre-recorded shows for emergencies," Dante said in answer to my unspoken question.

"Is this an emergency?"

Dante parted my legs with his hard thigh and ground his hips against me, letting me feel the steel of his cock beneath his fly. "It is most definitely an emergency." His mouth came down on mine again and I couldn't think, couldn't move, couldn't do anything but feel.

He was ruthless, relentless; hands, mouth, fingers everywhere. I sucked in a desperate breath, drawing in the scent of him. Sweat. Whiskey. Autumn leaves. It hit me in the belly, stirring something deep and dark that uncurled without warning.

I moaned my desire, and he spun me around, pushing me up against the cold, hard door. "This shirt . . ." His fingers trailed down my spine beneath the strings that kept it together. "Has been driving me crazy. Do you know what it does to a man to get a glimpse of something he shouldn't see?" He unhooked my bra and slid his hand under my shirt to cup my right breast in his warm palm.

"So soft." His rough fingers pinched my nipple, sending a shower of sparks through my veins.

Need sliced through me, hot knives of lust that threatened to consume everything that I was. Could I do this? Could I strip off everything and show him my scars in the light?

Dante squeezed and toyed with one breast and then the other until my nipples were hard, and I was aching with need. Using his weight to hold me in place against the door, he yanked open my jeans and slid his hand into my panties. His fingers grazed over my sensitive clit and then down to my center.

"You're soaked."

I shuddered when he slid a finger inside me. If I hadn't had his weight, his heat and strength behind me, I might have collapsed from the sheer intensity of the sensation.

"Such a good girl." His lips nudged my ear, his breath hot on my skin as he replaced one finger with two, moving them rhythmically until I was rocking against his palm for the friction I needed for release.

The whisper of cool air on my skin as he eased my jeans over my hips with his free hand yanked me back to my senses and the imminent exposure of my scars. What would it feel like to show him everything? To be enough just by being me? To be free of the fear and shame?

"I need to touch you, Dante."

He released me and I spun to face him, wild hands tearing off his shirt, roaming over skin slicked from heat. I pressed my lips to the inked designs on his pecs and felt the steady rhythm of his heart beating in his chest.

"I want you." I shifted my weight, unable to ease the ache between my thighs.

"I want you, too, but I want to do it right this time. You deserve more than basement rooms and closets and hallways."

It was my out. I could end this now and he'd never see my scars. I wouldn't have to deal with his revulsion or horror or sympathy or whatever was going to show on his face when I stripped myself bare. There would be no awkward silences. No pain in my heart. No regrets.

No Dante.

"This is right." I kissed him hard, grinding my hips against his hard length. "I like you like this. I like the sense of danger. I like breaking the rules. I want to feel you lose control."

I craved him—his smell, his taste, the power that rippled beneath his skin—with a primal hunger that wouldn't be sated by soft blankets and clean sheets. I wanted to be taken, possessed. I didn't want to be enough. I wanted to be everything.

"I can't lose control." His voice cracked, broke. "I don't want to hurt you. Look what happened tonight."

"You won't hurt me." I was so wet I wanted to sob. Empty and aching, my self-control hanging by a thread. "I won't let you."

His hands slid under my ass, and he lifted me to his hips, easily carrying me to the lounge with my legs wrapped around him. He shut the door and flicked on the light before pinning me against the wall.

"You want it like this?" He fisted my hair and tugged my head back.

My breath left me in a rush. "Yes."

He yanked off my bra and shirt, powerful hands squeezing my breasts until everything inside me started to melt. I fell back against the wall when I felt the sharp edge of his teeth on my nipples and begged for more.

Dante lowered my feet to the floor and tugged my jeans over my hips. I grabbed his hand before he went too far.

"There's something you need to know." I swallowed hard, my body tensing. "My legs were crushed in the accident. The left one was injured so badly they basically had to rebuild it. I have . . . a lot of scars. Not just on my leg but all over my body. You wouldn't have seen them in the dark."

For a moment, there was only silence between us, and then he took my hand and pressed it over the ink on his shoulder. "I have scars, too." He squeezed my hand, then pointed to various other places on his shoulders and arms that were covered by intricate designs. "I had them inked so I didn't have to look at the constant reminder about how my dad preferred me to an ashtray."

My heart squeezed in my chest as I traced over the circular designs that marked the places he'd touched. "You've turned them into something beautiful."

He kneeled before me, trailing soft kisses over my belly and then down as he lowered my clothing over my hips. For a long moment—too long—he just looked at the V between my legs, his gaze burning into me until my clit throbbed, desperate for the attention of his talented mouth.

But his lips didn't go where I wanted them to go. Instead, he worked his way down my damaged leg, kissing each and every scar. His tongue traced one mark, then the other, until my skin began to anticipate every gentle touch. He teased me with a rush of heat when his lips touched unbroken skin, and moments of longing when he kissed the long silvery lines and patches that had no nerves left to feel. So soft. So tender. So unlike the man who had pinned me to the door only moments ago.

A whirlwind of sensations exploded inside me. Except for my mom and the healthcare workers, no one had ever seen my scars. Not even me, because I'd stopped looking when the bandages came off. In my world of pretend, I was still whole.

My hands fisted against the wall, every muscle tensing as he trailed gentle kisses along my calf to the sensitive skin behind my knee. A sound escaped my lips. I didn't know if it was arousal or fear.

Dante looked up, his eyes darkening with pleasure. "Do you know what I see?"

I shook my head, my heart pounding so hard I could barely hear for the rush of blood in my ears.

"I see a survivor." He kissed the delicate skin of my inner thigh, "I see courage. I see someone much stronger than me, someone who doesn't hide."

His words caught me off guard, and I felt a warmth spread through me that had nothing to do with the physical heat of the room or what he was doing to my body.

"Open for me." He nudged my legs apart, guiding me to lift my damaged leg to his shoulder before he spread me wide. His eyes heated as he studied me, his pleasure evident from his husky voice. "Good girl."

A shockwave of arousal punched me in the gut, stealing my breath away. His praise washed over my body, the knowledge I'd pleased him sending a flush of heat through my veins. I tucked the curious reaction away to worry about later because the friction from the stubble on my inner thigh as he kissed his way to my center was about to unravel me on the spot.

His dark head moved closer until I could feel the heat of his breath on my clit. My hips tilted upward, my body seeking relief.

"Look at me, buttercup."

He held my gaze as he licked over my clit, easing the sensation before opening his mouth around me. After only a few strokes of his tongue, my back arched and heat blossomed in my core. My knees buckled, but his hand shot out, pinning my thigh against his shoulder as he stroked me, his tongue doing wicked things that ripped a choked whimper from my throat.

He'd rocked my world in the storage room, but I'd never experienced anything as wild and intense as the way he took me in that moment. His heated gaze locked on mine as he spread me wider, filling me with two fingers and then three, building a fire inside me. In the background, over the speakers, his whiskey-smooth voice echoed around me while his real-life groans rumbled from his chest.

"Please." I tugged on his hair, pulling him closer, letting him know with the rocking of my hips how close I was to release, how desperate I was to feel him where I ached the most. Finally, he closed his lips around my clit and sucked as he pulsed his fingers in a merciless rhythm.

My vision went white as every single nerve ending in my whole body fired at once. A massive tidal wave of pleasure crashed over me, battering my senses until the world dissolved around me.

After a second, I opened my eyes. Dante was on his feet, holding his fingers over my lips. "I want to watch you taste yourself."

I managed a nod and he thrust his fingers into my mouth, humming in approval as I licked off my own salty-sweet desire. I'd never done anything that felt so decadent, dangerous, and filthy all at the same time.

"Fuck, you're hot." Dante leaned forward to kiss me, sweetly and slowly, his tongue exploring every inch of my mouth until he had banked the fire inside me again.

"I need you inside me," I murmured as I traced the curves and spirals of the ink on his shoulders. "If you don't fuck me, I might have to slap you for real, and this time I won't miss."

He smiled down at me and ran a finger along my jawline. "Are you threatening me?"

The hint of warning in his eyes and the controlled power in his voice turned my body into liquid heat and a tremor of need shook my body.

"No. Yes. I just . . ." Words failed me as he shrugged off the rest of his clothes, his muscles rippling with power barely restrained.

I let my gaze roam boldly over his magnificent body as he retrieved a condom from his jeans and slid it over his thick, hard erection. He was perfectly built, all hard planes and angles, his skin slick with sweat and beautifully inked. I imagined licking my way down his body, over the rippling six-pack and along the V-shaped lines of his pelvis to the intimidating length below.

"Walk over to the bulletin board and turn to face it," he said, his voice low and full of gravel.

Heart pounding with excitement, I did as he asked, resting my cheek against the cool cork surface. Dante came up behind me and drew my hands above my head.

"I want you like this," he murmured in my ear. "I want to fuck you in exactly the same position you were in when we were down in the basement and you were reaching for the box. You looked so damn sexy. Your shirt had ridden up. I could see your back, the curve of your waist, and this beautiful ass, just begging to be touched." He squeezed my rear, ripping a soft moan from my lips. "I wanted you so fucking bad . . ." He kicked my legs roughly apart. "I've fantasized about fucking you like this every night, buttercup. Every. Fucking. Night."

He brushed my hair aside and kissed my nape, sending a delicious shiver down my spine. He followed that shiver with his lips, feathering kisses down my back until he reached the cleft of my ass. I tensed in wary anticipation of him going somewhere I wasn't ready for him to go.

"Maybe another time." He pressed a kiss to each cheek. "There's too much I want to do with you tonight."

He stroked between my legs with one hand while he pinched my nipples with the other, stoking my need again until I was writhing against him. His erection rubbed against my cleft and a frantic ache pulsed between my legs. Once wasn't enough.

"*Dante . . .*"

"I got you." He thrust into me in one hard, singular motion, digging his fingers into my hip with one hand, while he held me secure with the other.

I didn't know what turned me on the most—the fact that he wanted me in that moment, or that he'd fantasized about me at night when I'd been fantasizing about him.

"Don't stop . . ." I rocked against him, driving up on my toes and back again. I was desperate, aching to have him completely, hard and raw and wild.

With a shuddered breath, he pulled back and pushed fully inside. He was everywhere. His voice from the speakers surrounding me. His groans vibrating against my back. His hands on my skin, his breath hot on my neck, his cock filling me with every hard thrust.

He took me roughly, slamming into me, pushing me toward orgasm in a way I'd never felt before. My hands fisted against the corkboard as the pressure inside me grew and my lower half started to tighten. When I cried out, he pushed deeper, hitting the sensitive spot inside me while his fingers brushed over my clit in a move perfectly timed to send me straight over the edge.

"Yes. Yes. Yes." I let out a guttural groan as everything spun out of control. Pleasure exploded inside me, a firestorm of sheer sensation that streamed through my body electrifying every nerve ending until I came apart at the seams.

"Skye. Fuck." Dante pounded into me deep and hard, until finally his body went rigid and he came in a rush of white-hot heat.

I fell forward, resting my forehead on the corkboard while my body shook with the aftershocks of Dante's raw and wild fantasy sex. Bracing himself with one hand on the wall, Dante sagged against me, heaving his breaths.

"Are you okay?" He eased out of me and turned me around for a gentle kiss.

"More than okay. That was the hottest sex I've ever had."

"Me, too." He quickly disposed of the condom, wrapping it in paper towels before tossing it in the trash. When he returned, he swept me up in his arms and carried me to the couch.

"Shouldn't we get dressed in case someone comes? Noah . . ."

"Isn't coming." He threw a blanket over the cool leather and stretched out, patting the space beside him. "Cuddle time."

"I heard a rumor that you didn't do cuddles." I grabbed another blanket and spread it over us as I lay down beside him. "I heard you were a wham-bam-thank-you-ma'am kind of guy."

"I never met anyone I wanted to cuddle with." He kissed the pads of my fingers one by one and then found my mouth, drawing out my desire with long, deep strokes of his tongue. "I also never told anyone about my scars except for Noah. He's the one who suggested the tattoos. He said it could be a fresh start. I believed him until I realized the old me was still there, lurking in the shadows."

"They're beautiful." I traced the intricate designs with my fingers, treble and bass clefs and staffs with musical notes. "Do those notes represent anything?"

"Songs my mother used to sing." He covered my hand with his. "I was twelve years old when she died. The birds are for my sister, Sasha. She loved to listen to them sing outside her bedroom window. I lost her four years after my mom. Now she's free to fly with them."

"Dante . . ." Emotion welled up in my throat. "I'm so sorry. It was hard losing my dad, but I can't imagine how it must have been for you to lose both of them, and you were so young . . ."

He stiffened and his jaw went taut. "I don't want to talk about it."

"I understand. But if you ever do, I would love to hear about them." I put my arm around him and we held each other in the quiet of the night.

"My mother would be horrified if I came home with my leg all inked up," I said lightly, hoping to pull Dante back from the shadows that clouded his face. "She would think I'd turned to the dark side."

"You have turned to the dark side." He ran his fingers through my hair, smoothing it out over my shoulders. "You've seduced a poor radio station DJ during his show. Tomorrow, you'll probably pretend it never even happened."

"I thought that was *your* modus operandi."

"I can't pretend this didn't happen," Dante said, tracing patterns on my shoulder. "I don't want to pretend it didn't happen. I'm not good at letting people in, but you snuck through my defenses when I wasn't looking."

"Sneak attack," I said, trying again to lighten the mood. "Kinda what you did to me. I never would have imagined letting someone see my leg, much less touch my scars. But then I would never have imagined having sex with a tattooed bad boy in a radio station to Michael Jackson's 'Thriller.' You've definitely ruined me for other men."

"And I've shared one of my deep dark secrets. That means there can be no other men." He tucked me against his body, my head resting on his chest where I could hear the steady beat of his heart.

"Do you see me complaining?" I slid my hand over his abdomen and down under the blanket. He was hard again, and his cock swelled in my grasp. The idea that I could arouse him sent a shimmer of triumph through my body.

"I see you want to be fucked again." His hand slid down my back, fingers digging into my ass. "If I time it right, you'll be screaming to 'Bohemian Rhapsody,' one of my top-ten songs of all time."

"Let me up." I tried to pull away but only succeeded in sliding against his erection. "I can't have sex with you now. That's like saying *The Avengers* is one of the best movies in the world. I can't . . ." I gave a dramatic wave. "I just can't."

"You should have thought of that before you decide to tempt me again." He twisted his hips, dropping me to the couch so I was lying beneath him. "Now, I have to do something about it. But this time, I'm going to go slow. I'm going to kiss every inch of your body and every single scar. I'm going to make you so hot and so wet you'll agree that 'Bohemian Rhapsody' is the greatest rock song of all time." He leaned down to take my nipple in his mouth, licking and stroking until I was writhing beneath him.

"Will I also be so hot and so wet that you'll make me come many times and fuck me into oblivion?"

Dante released my nipple and slid his hand down to cup me between the legs. "Are you going to be a good girl?"

His words should have sounded patronizing but instead a wave of heat flushed through my body. This time instead of worrying about why it turned me on, or what it said about me, I focused on how it made me feel. Hot. Wet. Sexy. Safe. Accepted. Complete.

Something that made me feel this good couldn't be bad. And besides, we had passed the point of no return. I wanted to drown in the blissful feeling of his praise. I needed to hear it with a soul-deep longing that went into my bones.

"Yes," I said, rocking against the heel of his palm as the first words of Dante's favorite song played over the speakers. "I'll be the best girl ever."

CHAPTER TWENTY-TWO

"Howlin' for You" by the Black Keys

DANTE

Noah wasn't the kind of man to care about the state of his house, so I did a double take when I walked into his kitchen the next morning and saw the floor.

"What happened here? I didn't even know you had tiles." The three-bedroom red brick vintage home in Forest Glen was too big for just one person, but Noah had bought it from the previous station manager for a bargain basement price. He'd converted the top of the garage into a suite, and the big backyard was perfect for his rescue dogs to play.

"Bella is in town." He looked up from his tablet. His senior cat, Calico, was asleep in his lap. "I thought I should make an effort, so I hired someone to come in and tidy the place up."

"Since when do you hire people when you've got me?" Part of my deal with Noah included helping with the household chores and looking after his pets in exchange for free rent.

"It's your final year. You've got a lot going on. I didn't want you to have pick up all my shit just because Bella decided to visit."

"Your sister's cool. I don't think she'd care." I'd met Noah's younger sister several times over the years. She was the only member of his family to stay in contact after he'd been disowned for following his dream of becoming a professional musician instead of working in the family business. "But she'll probably tell you that you look like you need a meal and two weeks' worth of sleep.

Seriously, Noah. She's going to be all over your ass when she sees you." Noah's iconic Misfits tee was so loose around his chest, the skull's eyes were almost crossed.

"Saving the station has become a full-time job. I've never filled in so many applications or attended so many meetings in my life. I think I've worn out my bolo tie." He rubbed Calico's furry head. "Did you just come here to piss on me or was there a purpose for your visit?"

There were a lot of purposes for my visit, none of which I was able to articulate. There was the fight and the whole scholarship fiasco that meant I was lying to two people I cared about and putting Skye at risk; and then there was Skye making me feel things I wasn't ready to feel.

I had been comfortable with my hookups and one-night stands. No expectations. No commitments. No heartfelt discussions revealing uncomfortable truths in the middle of the night. Skye had taken my comfortable life and turned it upside down. She didn't hide her scars behind secrets and ink. She pushed through every barrier that stood in her way. To be worthy of her, I needed to do the same.

"It's about the fight," I pulled up a chair at the table, dropping my head to my hands. Might as well start with the easy one and work up to the part where I'd sabotaged the best thing in my life before it even began.

"Did the other guy start it?"

"Some dude at the bar went after one of Skye's friends who was hustling him at pool. We decided to leave, but he came outside with two friends. Nick and Chad were gearing up to get involved so I took the bastards down so no one got hurt."

Far from judging me or even being annoyed, Noah smiled. "You defended your friends."

"You're missing the point," I snapped. "I broke somebody's nose. It was the wrong thing to do. Violence wasn't the answer."

"Sounds like self-defense to me," Noah said, gently moving

Calico to the floor. "All that time and effort you put into jiu-jitsu was worth it."

"Jesus Christ, Noah. I hurt someone. What if I'm like my dad after all?" Then it didn't matter how I felt about Skye. It didn't matter about the scholarship. I couldn't get close because there was no way I could risk doing to anyone what he'd done to me.

"Did you keep hitting them when they were down? Did anyone need an ambulance?"

I stared at him aghast. "Of course not."

"I didn't think so." Noah put a hand on my shoulder. "That's because you're not your father. You have the strength and the compassion to know when to stop."

I let out a shuddering breath. Noah tightened his hand on my shoulder, letting me know he was there but not invading my space while I processed what he'd said.

"You're a good man, Dante. You're not your father. You'll never be him. You've changed your name. You've cut him out. Now you need to let him go and start living your own life."

It was the same old discussion we'd always had. I'd been open and honest with Noah when I decided to leave my full-time job at the station and go to college with the goal of becoming a lawyer. But I couldn't move on. Sasha's final words were burnt into my soul, and I owed it to her to see my father brought to justice. "I'm living my life. It's just not the life you want me to have."

"It's not the life you deserve." Noah refilled his cup from the pot in the corner. "That guilt you are carrying is a heavy burden to bear. There is a world of happiness out there if you can just walk away."

I wanted to believe him. Over the last six weeks I'd had a taste of a life that wasn't driven by guilt or vengeance. I wasn't utterly consumed by the black hole at the center of my chest. I'd seen light at the end of the tunnel. I'd felt pure emotion stir my heart, and I wanted more.

My fingers uncurled from the edge of the table, the tension

easing in my chest. I was going to tell him about Skye and the scholarship. Maybe he could help me untangle the mess.

"There's something else . . ."

"Can it wait?" Noah asked. "I need to take a shower before Bella arrives. We've got some meetings over the next few days, and she wants me to be presentable."

"No problem." I bit back my disappointment. "I'd better go. I don't want Bella screaming at me because you're not ready on time."

"Dante," Noah called out as I pushed open the back door.

"Yeah?"

"I'm glad to hear you're finally making friends," he said with a grin. "But no more fighting in the playground."

"Fuck off, Noah."

He laughed and I realized I hadn't heard him laugh like that in a very long time.

Midterms kept Skye and me apart for the next four days. We messaged constantly and shared our study playlists. I preferred chill or instrumental beats. Skye listened to Spanish flamenco guitar. I don't know why it surprised me. She was a woman of hidden depths. Of course, it didn't stop me from dragging her about it. Seriously? Spanish guitar?

She showed up at the station on Wednesday in a pair of tight black leggings and a form-fitting running jacket for a quick lesson on how to use the sound board. Chad was already in front of the mic with the headphones on, listening to himself croon "Blue Suede Shoes."

"I'm planning to go for a run when we're done and I didn't want to waste time going home to change," she said when I couldn't tear my gaze away.

"Very commendable." I tried to think about baseball and grades and things that didn't involve Skye in tight clothes. "We like healthy interns at the station."

"And interns like healthy bosses." She licked her lips, and I felt every stroke of her tongue as a bolt of heat in my groin. "Maybe you should take up swimming. I noticed they had Speedos for sale in the athletic center."

"Naughty," I muttered under my breath. "This is a workplace. No suggestive licking of lips or inappropriate imagery allowed."

"I thought you liked naughty," she whispered when Chad was looking the other way. "Or is that not what you want?"

What I wanted was to get Skye alone again. What I wanted was my hands on her body and her lips pressed against mine. What I wanted was to take her home so I could spend another night with her, but this time in my bed. Instead, I had to deal with switches and microphones, sensors and headsets.

After I explained all the equipment and showed them how to cue up their music, Skye practiced with a pre-taped podcast and Chad did a fake live staring at his reflection in the glass as he reported about a bar fight that ended in a local man sprawled on the ground with a broken nose, all because he'd been hustled at pool.

"How did you learn to fight like that?" Chad asked, taking off his headphones. "You had that guy down in three seconds flat and you didn't even break a sweat. You should join the wrestling team."

"Jiu-jitsu. I've also done some karate and boxing. I've never been into team sports." Team sports required parental involvement. They meant using team locker rooms where you couldn't hide your bruises. They meant leaving your little sister alone for hours at a time.

"I can see that," Skye said. "You're more of a lone wolf type."

"It sounds like you've given that considerable thought." I liked the idea that she'd been thinking of me even though we hadn't seen each other for almost a week.

"Are you fishing for compliments?"

"I don't have to. The compliments write themselves."

Skye lifted an eyebrow. "And there's that ego we've heard so much about."

And there was the woman who kept slipping past my walls. I pulled up Duran Duran's "Hungry Like the Wolf" from the music database on the screen. Moments later the room was filled with the polished keyboards and powerful guitar riffs of the 1980s pop sensation. Over the years, people had debated the meaning of the song, but at its essence it was about a guy who wanted to get it on with a girl. Skye looked over at me and laughed.

"Why don't you do a few more mock broadcasts," I said to Chad. "I need to get Skye's opinion on something."

"What is it?" Skye asked, half jogging to keep up with my strides as I slammed open the station door and led her partway down the storage room hallway.

"This." I took her hands and pressed her palms to my face. I needed her touch, her lips, her eyes on me like I needed to breathe. I wanted to feel her, connect. I needed to know that the other night had been real.

"My opinion is ten out of ten. Highly recommend." She pressed her lips to my neck, and then we were clutching at each other, arms and hands and mouths and tongues until we were so close, we were like one person, not two.

"I missed you." I rested my forehead against hers, our lips close enough to touch.

"We message or video every day."

"It's not the same." I breathed in the scent of her hair, pressed my cheek against her temple. I didn't understand this, the naked need, the all-consuming want. I felt raw, exposed, adrift for the first time since Noah saved me. I usually pushed people away. I didn't know how to keep them.

Her mouth softened in a smile, and she rubbed her nose against mine, her lips one breath away. I could smell her; feel her pressed against me. "I'm not going anywhere."

Relief crashed over me like a tidal wave of emotion so fierce I thought I would crack in half.

"God, Skye—" I cupped her face in my hands and kissed her. Touching. Tasting. Harder. Deeper. With a fervent, urgent need I'd never known before. I broke for air and buried my lips in her neck, feathering kisses over her collarbone, her chin, and cheeks.

She tasted like rain and sunshine. My heart was pounding against my chest. I thought I might explode.

Skye pulled back with a low groan. "Chad will be waiting for us."

"Fuck Chad."

"I was hoping you'd fuck me instead."

I pulled her close. Kissed the top of her head.

"Let's get rid of him and we'll have the station to ourselves for at least ten minutes."

Skye laughed. It was the world's most beautiful sound.

We didn't have to get rid of Chad. He had a hot date with a shot-putter who was apparently an expert with balls. After he'd gone, Skye and I headed upstairs. Our ten minutes alone had become ten seconds when the next show host arrived early.

"All that kissing made me hungry," she said. "Do you want to grab some pizza?"

"I thought you had to run."

"I already worked out today. I just needed extra stress release, but you took care of that."

My chest puffed with satisfaction. I'd done that. I'd helped her relax. I could get her food and help with that, too.

"I'm in. I've been eating leftover lasagna three nights in a row."

"Was it frozen lasagna or did you make it yourself?" Her hand brushed against mine as we walked toward the pizza restaurant, sending a bolt of electricity straight to my groin.

"I learned how to cook after my mother died. My dad wasn't into the whole parenting thing. My sister and I ate Fruit Loops and ham sandwiches every day for a month until I figured I'd better learn how to make something else, or we'd die of malnutrition." Except for Noah, I'd never talked to anyone about my family. It was both freeing and disconcerting. I wanted to let her in, but I couldn't let her get too close.

"You were a good big brother," she said. "She was lucky to have you."

We reached the counter, and I pulled out my credit card. "I have a responsibility to ensure our interns don't die of starvation so I'm buying, unless you order something boring like pepperoni and then you're on your own."

"Ham and pineapple."

I tipped my head back with a groan. "That's the musical equivalent of Apocalyptica. Mixing contrasting styles like classical music and heavy metal just isn't right. Next you'll be telling me you listen to Mumford & Sons or the Avett Brothers."

"I think they're innovative and refreshing, just like pineapple on pizza." She tipped her head to the side. "What are you going to have?"

"The Wild Man. It's got everything on it except pineapple because that would just be wrong."

"So, your musical equivalent is Mr. Bungle, or maybe Naked City." She gave me a sideways glance. "I'm learning so much about you today. You don't talk much about yourself so I have to collect what little tidbits I can."

"Can I show you something?" The words came out before I could stop them, but I was already keeping one secret from her. I didn't want to keep any more.

She tipped her head to the side. "Is it something that shouldn't be seen in public and could get you arrested?"

"No. Jesus. What kind of guy do you think I am?"

"I don't know. You are as mysterious as you are multifaceted. We've had sex twice and I still feel like I don't understand you."

"Come on an adventure with me and I'll show you who I am."

She rested her chin in her hand, her eyes sparkling. "I might have seen enough the other night . . ."

"I'll try your pizza," I offered.

Her eyes lit up. "You have to swallow it. No gagging. No spitting it out . . ."

"Did you really just say that?"

I could see the moment understanding dawned on her face. Her laughter, bold and beautiful, rang out around us. "I did just say that. You're a bad influence. But you have a deal. I'm up for an adventure. You take a bite and I'll come with you."

I would do anything for Skye, so after we got our food I took a bite of her pizza, holding her gaze as a disgusting combination of tangy sweetness and salty cheese assailed my taste buds.

"What do you think?" she asked.

"Do you have a bucket?"

CHAPTER TWENTY-THREE

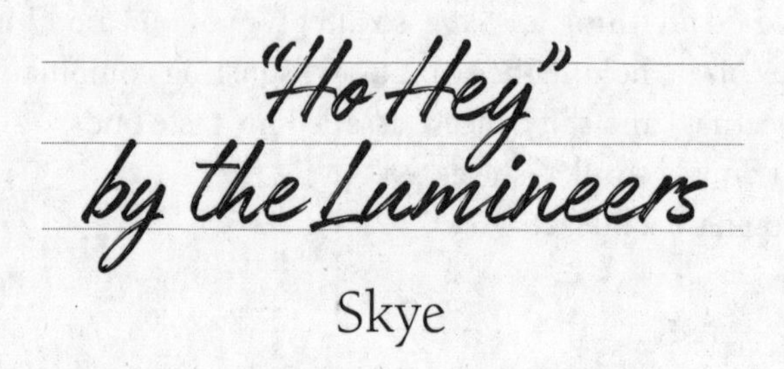

Skye

Of all the places I had expected Dante to take me to reveal his hidden secrets, the university's engineering science building wasn't even on the list.

"It's after hours," I pointed out as he took me around to the side entrance. "The doors will be locked."

"That didn't stop me when we played hide-and-seek." He pulled a thin wire from his wallet and jimmied open the door.

"I see the whole 'bad boy' persona you've got going on isn't for show." I took a quick look around before walking inside. "You are, in fact, truly a bad boy."

"When we get to where we're going, I'll show you just how bad I can be." He pulled me into his arms as soon as the door slammed closed behind us, kissing me with a desperate hunger that left us both breathless and panting.

"Is this just a sex thing?" I wrapped my arms around his neck, every shred of my previous resolve gone the moment his lips touched mine. "I thought you were going to show me secrets I hadn't seen before."

"I am," he said. "I just needed to get that out of my system." He took my hand, and we walked through the quiet, empty corridors, occasionally stopping to look through the windows of the science labs.

"I was never good at science." I peered into a lab filled with black tables and stools and shelves piled high with beakers and boxes and rubber tubing. "My brain doesn't work that way. Too many protocols and methodologies to follow. Too many tests and theories and failed experiments. I wanted the whole story, something I could follow from beginning to end."

"You're a big-picture kind of person," Dante offered.

"I don't mind asking the hard questions, but when I ask them, I want definitive answers. You can't tell a story when the facts are changing, or when a tiny mistake can have huge consequences. My tenth-grade chemistry teacher cut a stick of phosphorus on his desk instead of in water and set the entire lab on fire."

"My eleventh-grade chem teacher blew off one of his fingers," Dante said. "He liked to show us his half finger before every experiment as a warning to be careful."

"Is that why you chose to major in finance?"

"Finance wasn't a choice. It's a means to an end."

We left the labs and walked up the stairs, our footsteps echoing in the stairwell. Except for our hide-and-seek adventure, I'd never been in an empty building at night, but there was an intimacy in the darkness. No one could see us. No one could hear us. I could share my secrets, and no one would ever know.

"Basketball wasn't a choice for me either," I admitted. "My father made it to the NBA but he kept getting injured and he had to drop out after only one season. He wanted a son to live that dream for him and when my parents were told they couldn't have children, they applied to adopt. He was bitterly disappointed I wasn't a boy and wanted to send me back. I'd already been through several foster homes and was terrified of being rejected again. I played basketball to make him happy so he wouldn't send me away. I thought if I made his dream come true maybe he would love me."

"Jesus, Skye." Dante wrapped his arm around my shoulder and gave me a hug. "I can't even imagine how hard that must have been."

"I wasn't naturally athletic, so I had to work twice as hard to be half as good as everyone else," I continued. "My dad was all in as a coach, but he was very tough to the point of being abusive." I told

Dante about Jonah and how devastated my father had become when he found out Jonah would never be able to do competitive sports. "My dad became unbearable. It was all about him. My failures were his failures. I was never good enough."

"I know that feeling," he said quietly.

"It's not like I hated playing ball. I liked being part of a team and I enjoyed the competitions and pushing myself to be the best I could be. It really helped me grow as a person. It gave me strength. It's just . . . I would have liked to feel I had a choice, that I wasn't on the court simply because I was afraid of being sent away."

We reached the end of the stairwell and Dante led me into a small engineering library. He jumped over the turnstile and held out a hand to help me.

Laughing, I hopped over the turnstile, unassisted. "I may not have wanted to be a baller, but I can still jump."

We walked past the tall metal shelves, breathing in the slightly musty air as we headed into the reading room.

"Get ready to be amazed." Dante pushed on a built-in bookcase on the back wall, and it swung open to reveal a hallway framed in dark wood. "This is one of the secret passages I was telling you about."

"Oh my God. This is the coolest thing ever." I turned on my phone light as Dante pulled the door closed.

"The latch to open it is here," he said, pointing to a small handle. "I've explored all the secret passages from the previous station manager's map, but this one is my favorite. It's where I come when I need to get away."

He led me up a worn wooden staircase to an outdoor balcony sheltered by a small roof. Beneath us the campus, and beyond, the city, spread out in a twinkle of lights.

"It's magical."

Dante grabbed a blanket from behind the door and spread it on the ground. We snuggled up against the wall and enjoyed the view in comfortable silence.

"Another ten out of ten," I said, looking up at the night sky. "Highly recommend."

Dante pulled me into a straddle over his lap. "What else is a ten out of ten?"

"Hmmm." I kissed him softly on the lips. "Radio station sex is up there."

"What about hidden passageway secret balcony sex?" His hand slid under my shirt, gently cupping my breast.

"Can anyone see us up here?"

"I doubt it," he said. "This is the tallest building on campus. But even if they could, no one would be able to identify us . . . Would it matter?"

I felt a small thrill at the thought of being caught. Dante must have been able to read my mind because his voice dropped to a low growl. "She likes that idea."

"She does indeed." I flicked open the button at the top of his jeans and slid my hand beneath his fly. He sucked in a sharp breath, his erection growing impossibly hard beneath my palm.

"Fuck." His head fell back, chest rising as I wrapped my hand around his cock and gave it a tight squeeze.

I'd never felt confident enough to lead before. I'd never felt secure enough to take what I wanted, but Dante was different. I could be myself with him. He listened. He heard. We connected.

"I owe you from the other night." I lowered his zipper and eased him out. He was thick and hard, the skin of his shaft smooth and hot to the touch. Dropping down, I gave the head a little lick.

"Christ." His hand fisted my hair, and he pulled me up. "If you're going to put me in your mouth, you'd better kiss me first."

As soon as our lips connected, his tongue dove deep, stroking over mine relentlessly until my hips were rocking against his shaft, my thighs trembling, my body taut with need.

"Take off your shirt." His voice was rough and thick with desire.

I yanked my shirt and sports bra over my head. The cool air made me shudder and my nipples tightened.

Dante's forehead creased in consternation. "Too cold?"

"Not if you heat me up."

"With pleasure." He yanked my hips forward, making my back arch and my breasts rise. His lips molded around my left nipple, and he drew it between his teeth while he fondled my breast. Hunger pulsed through my veins, and my clit throbbed as if begging for a touch.

"If you keep that up," I panted, "I won't be able to do what I wanted to do."

He drew my other nipple into his mouth, sucking harder. I had planned to take control, but the edgy pain on the sensitive peak was so intense, his hand in my hair holding me so firm, his fingers so tight on my hip, I could barely think.

"What do you want to do to me?" he murmured against my mouth. "Tell me. Give me dirty. I want to hear you say the words."

I pulled my bottom lip between my teeth. I'd never done dirty. There were words I thought, but never said. Books I read that made me blush. The idea of saying those words out loud was, at the same time, terrifying and powerfully erotic.

Loosening his grip on my hair, I slid down between his legs and wrapped my hand around his shaft. He was fully erect, hot and heavy in my hand. "I want to lick the head of your cock." I flicked my tongue over the smooth tip and his body went rock hard beneath me. "I want to squeeze your dick so hard you can't stay still." I pumped my hand, feeling the heat of him against my skin as I dragged my fingers up and down until a drop of moisture beaded at the top. "I want to suck you dry." I looked up. Dante was staring down at me, his jaw tense, eyes glazed. Arousal thickened the air. Skin and sweat and something darker.

I drew him into my mouth, taking him deep, struggling to encompass the sheer size of him. He groaned, fisted his hands in my hair, and held me tight. Making my tongue flat and stiff, I licked up and down, dragging my tongue along the seam of his head before diving deep again. He pulsed against my tongue, his body vibrating around me.

"Fuck me with that dirty mouth," he moaned, urging me faster.

I released him, then doubled down, working him with my hand while I swirled and stroked with my tongue, tasting salt and sweat and the essence of him. He rocked his hips in time to my rhythm, his muscles taut and hard.

I'd never had a man at my mercy before, never imagined I'd get off on watching him fall apart. My breasts ached, and heat flushed my skin. I ground myself against his thigh as I brought him to the edge.

"Christ. No." He released me abruptly, his hands dropping to my shoulders to push me away. His cock slid between my lips, and I sat up, confused.

"Did I do something wrong?"

"I can't get off when you're needing to get off." In one swift motion he had me on my back. Moments later he'd stripped away the rest of my clothes. "You grinding against me is the fucking hottest thing I've ever seen."

"You can take care of me after I take care of you." My words seemed pointless now that he had me pinned to the ground.

"That's not how it is with me." He wasn't even looking at my leg, my scars, the worst of me. His entire focus was down below, where I was wet and aching for his touch.

"Spread your legs for me, buttercup. Show me how wet you are, how much you need me." His gaze lifted to my face as I slowly spread my legs apart. I licked my lips in anticipation of the words I needed to hear.

"Good girl."

Heat washed over me, setting me on fire. This time I pushed away all the questions and misgivings and accepted it for what it was. It didn't matter why. His praise gave me a deep erotic pleasure that made me feel hot and achy inside. It turned me on like nothing else, and damned if I wasn't going to embrace it.

I let out a shuddering breath when Dante pumped two fingers inside me. I didn't care if the whole university could see us now. I didn't want him to stop.

"You aren't fighting it this time." He added a third finger and pressed them gently against the sensitive spot deep inside me, sending tingles down my spine.

"I like how it feels when you tell me I'm a good girl." I rocked my hips against his fingers, unable to stay still. "I'll deal with the why some other time."

"Just like that," he murmured. "Move like that."

"I need . . . More."

"Not yet." He pulsed his fingers with enough pressure to take my breath away while slicking my wetness around my clit with his thumb. "Take it for me. I know you can."

I felt a rush of heat between my thighs. My fingers tangled in his dark hair and I groaned my frustration as heat rose inside me. "No more teasing. Do me now."

"I get off on giving what I know you can take," he said lightly. "I had no control as a kid, and now I need it." He leaned over to press a kiss to my lips, all while his fingers pulsed inside me, his thumb circling closer and closer to my clit. "I'm not going to deny myself the pleasure of tormenting you because of what happened in the past, and I'm not going to waste time trying to figure out the psychological complexities of why I get off on keeping you on the edge for as long as I can. I'm just going to enjoy it."

"How about you enjoy it a little faster and a lot harder." I grabbed his hand and pulled it closer.

"That's not how this works." His eyes twinkled in the darkness. "You need to be a good girl and take what I give you."

My breath quickened, my pulse thudding in my ears. I reached out to grip his biceps, needing something to hold on to, spreading my legs wider as he continued the slow rhythmic pulsing that was driving me wild.

"Please . . ." I was so wound up, so tense that I thought my body was going to split apart.

Finally, he pressed his thumb over my clit and every nerve cell inside me fired at once. It was an effort to stifle my scream as my orgasm flamed through my body, then faded to a flicker, leaving me languid and spent.

Dante sheathed himself with a condom from his back pocket. Then he slid an arm around me and flipped me. "Over you go."

"Is this another fantasy of yours," I said over my shoulder as he positioned me on my hands and knees.

"Studio A." He leaned over, his weight against my back, his hand gently squeezing one breast and then the other. "You were on all fours, plugging in a cable that had come out of its socket."

"And you thought . . ."

He gave a deep rumble. "I thought you had one hell of a sexy ass."

"It's very hot that you wanted to do me on the filthy floor of the studio," I said, amused.

"I would do you anywhere." He grabbed my hair with one hand and pulled my head back, forcing my back to arch. "Very nice," he murmured before he shoved his knees between my thighs, pushing my legs apart.

"I can't move." I tried to push back and take what I wanted but was held firm by the weight of his body as he leaned over me to run a finger through my wet folds.

"That's the idea." He positioned his cock at my entrance as his fingers moved over my clit, touching me in the way he knew would drive me crazy.

Just when I thought I couldn't take any more, his grip on my hair tightened and he plunged into me as deep as he could go.

My breath caught in my throat and I let him take control, driving into me over and over. Everything inside me started to tighten. I braced myself, fingers curled into the blanket, hungering for the dark, dangerous thrill of him. Power rushed through me, electric and wild. We climbed together, naked but cloaked in darkness, exposed in body and soul.

"Fuck. Skye." With one last savage thrust, he reached his peak, and I reached mine. We came apart together sheltered by a blanket of stars.

Dante's heavy body collapsed over me. His fingers twined with my mine still clutching the blanket. He pressed soft kisses to my shoulder, his lips sliding to my nape, the light pressure making my nerve endings stir and tingle.

"You're cold. Let's get you dressed." Dante rearranged the blankets while I pulled on my clothes. After we were dressed, I settled between his spread legs. His chest was warm against my back, thick arms keeping away the chill. For a long time, we just sat together, enjoying the silence, enjoying each other.

"I feel like I can see all of Chicago from here," I said, staring out into the twinkle of lights. "Where does your family live?"

"I grew up in a house in River Forest. After my mother died, my dad bought a condo in The Loop and stayed there most of the week. Sasha and I had to fend for ourselves, although my grandmother would stop by occasionally to check on us or bring us a meal. I haven't been back there since Sasha died. I don't even know if he still has the house. He's not a sentimental kind of guy." His body tensed and his arms tightened around me. I could feel the rapid beat of his heart against my back, hear his breaths turn raw and ragged. I sensed the shift in the air around us even before a cool breeze sent goosebumps rippling across my skin.

"We'd better get going." He released me and eased me forward to stand up. "My show starts soon and I need to get to the station."

I felt that gentle push as a sting of rejection. What had I been thinking? I knew he was sensitive about his family, but the closer we got, the more I wanted to know about him. So much about Dante was still a mystery to me.

"I have to get going, too." I jumped to my feet. "I . . . uh . . . I promised Isla I'd help her with an experiment." Even though I knew it was irrational, I felt sick inside. Maybe this was why Dante didn't get close to people. Maybe this was where he drew the line, and this night would be our last. Before I knew it, I was caught in a spiral of anxiety that tightened my lungs and stole my breath away.

Can we send her back?

Dante looked over at me, frowning. "You're not going to come?"

"I didn't think you'd want me there," I admitted. "I know I shouldn't have asked about your family."

"I want you there," he said softly.

I swallowed past the lump in my throat. "Then I'll be there."

"Skye?" He walked over to me and cupped my face in his hands, drawing me close.

"Yes?"

"I'm not them."

"Who?"

"All the people who didn't want you. Your dad and anyone else who didn't love you for who you are."

Emotion welled up in my throat and my eyes watered. I had that love from my mom and from my brother Jonah, but there was still a part of me that was broken from three years of foster fails and a childhood knowing my father never really wanted me and desperately trying to make him love me anyway.

"I think I'm allergic to something up here." I dabbed at my eyes with my sleeve.

"I hope you're not allergic to me because I'm not going anywhere." He pressed a soft kiss to my forehead.

He wanted me. Not the idea of me—my baller boyfriends just wanted to flex about dating an NBA player's daughter and my dad wanted a sports star—but the real me. Skye who loved music. Skye who felt happiest when she was chasing down stories. Skye who would have sex on a secret balcony under the stars.

"I am kinda hot for you," I whispered, hoping he'd get the reference to the iconic Van Halen song. Technically, he wasn't really my teacher—more a mentor or even a boss—but the song fit.

A smile spread across his face and he played on the words of the song. "Do you have it bad?" He kissed each of my cheeks and the tip of my nose, making my heart flutter.

"So bad," I whispered. "So very, very bad."

CHAPTER TWENTY-FOUR

"Chasing Cars" by Snow Patrol

DANTE

The morning after I took Skye through the secret passageway, I went home.

I hadn't been to the house in River Forest since the day I'd found Sasha in the bathroom in a tub full of blood. She'd left a note taped to the mirror, handwritten on the puppy dog stationary I'd bought for her twelfth birthday. Sasha had always wanted a dog, but my father refused. Looking back, I had a feeling he knew a dog would try to defend Sasha from his abuse, and he had enough trouble dealing with me.

I had never forgiven Sasha for taking her life the way she did. She knew I would be the one to find her. She knew I would to try to save her. She knew I would haul her out of the bath slippery and wet and naked, while I begged the 911 operator to tell me what to do. She knew I'd be alone. Not just then, but forever after.

She knew and she did it anyway.

I'd blocked the house from my mind the way I'd blocked everything else about my family. I didn't talk about it. I didn't think about it. As far as I was concerned, my life started the day hers ended and my memories of the past were gone.

But then I met Skye and my walls started to crumble. First my loss, then my pain, then stories about Fruit Loops and ham sandwiches. When I told her about my house, something broke inside me and the memories came flooding back.

Once upon a time, I had a home.

I borrowed Noah's car and drove to River Forest. I didn't know what possessed me, only that I had to go. Maybe some small part of me actually thought my father would have kept the house out of sentiment, or even as real estate investment. I imagined I would walk inside and see my mother's paintings on the wall—vibrant colors and abstract designs that had made her the darling of modern art collectors. I would see the couch where she would curl up with Sasha and me to watch movies on the big-screen TV, run my hand over her treasured collection of vinyl records, and brush the dust off the turntable where she played her old-time rock 'n' roll whenever my father was out of town. My feet would sink into the thick carpet where we'd danced and belted out the lyrics to her favorite songs. I would see her everywhere in all the things she'd left behind.

And I would see Sasha, hiding in her pretty pink bedroom from the shadows in the night.

I parked a few blocks away and walked down the quiet tree-lined street until I reached the Victorian heritage home that I'd lived in until I was sixteen. For a split second, I thought it was still our house, but with a fresh coat of paint, and new front door. But I didn't recognize the cars in the driveway, or the tire swing hanging from the oak tree in the front yard. The bicycles on the lawn were pink and pretty and someone had set up a teddy bear tea party on the front walk.

It took me a long time to process that my home was gone, along with all the memories inside it. He hadn't even given me a chance to save a few mementos. No record collection or turntable. No paintings. No birthday cards or even one of the stuffed animals that Sasha had slept with every night.

I couldn't move, couldn't breathe. I felt as if my heart had been ripped out of my chest all over again. Somewhere in the darkness I'd nurtured a flicker of hope and now it was gone.

Just like they were gone.

Just like the pain had been gone until I tried to let light into my life.

I didn't know how I made it back to the station for our weekly intern meeting with Noah. I didn't remember walking back to the car, or driving through the city. I didn't remember going to class or how I wound up in a chair in front of Noah's desk.

"You're early," Noah said. "And you look like shit."

"So do you." His face was gray and the circles under his eyes were so dark it looked like he was wearing makeup.

"I have a reason. This station is my life and I'm not going to let it fail."

"I have a reason, too." My voice caught, broke. "My mother had a vinyl collection that included original pressings of *The Black Album*, *Led Zeppelin*, and *Electric Ladyland* and now it's gone. Everything is gone." It was a strange thing to blurt out with no context, but music filled the space when I didn't have words.

Noah's face creased in sympathy, and I knew he understood. He was the most intuitive person I'd ever met. "Rare vinyls, but not that hard to replace if you had, say, an inheritance in your pocket. If she'd had a copy of Wu-Tang Clan's *Once Upon a Time in Shaolin,* that would have been something. Or even *The White Album,* not for the overrated musical genius but because it's worth almost $1 million. Now, if you told me she'd had a copy of Tommy Johnson's 'Alcohol and Jake Blues,' that would be a tragedy because the master tapes were destroyed."

And just like that he pulled me back from the brink. "I can't stand his yodel."

Noah pointed a finger at me across this desk. "Then you, sir, cannot call yourself a musician. Get your ass in here tonight before your show and I'll give you a Tommy Johnson education. I might even let you listen to this." He held up a twelve-inch vinyl of Miles Davis's *Kind of Blue.* "I picked it up for two grand from an old lady who only listened to it on Sundays."

"Thanks, Noah."

He gave me the briefest of nods. "Don't thank me. Thank Miles and the father of the Mississippi Blues."

I managed to get it together before Skye arrived with Siobhan and Chad. They brought their own chairs and squeezed between the boxes and piles of papers scattered across the room. I couldn't look at Skye. She hadn't done anything wrong, but I couldn't handle what she'd triggered inside me. I'd put walls up around my past for a reason and I had to stop them from crumbling, or I'd crumble, too.

"I've read your updates about the volunteers and interns," Noah said. "Everything looks on track except the broadcast portion of the internship. Where are we with that?"

"Chad has done a few sports shows," Siobhan said. "Still waiting for Skye."

"I've been doing more digging into my story about the empty buildings," Skye said. "My journalism professor helped me file some formal information requests because the administration won't give me access to their files. What I've got isn't broadcast-ready yet. I've also been looking into an issue with the garbage and recycling on campus and Professor Stanton just agreed to let me conduct an investigation as my year-end project."

"Garbage?" Noah didn't seem very enthused about Skye's project, but her eyes lit up at the question.

"The university is mixing the garbage and recycling. I've been watching the pickups around campus. Two weeks ago I thought I saw something suspicious going on between the truck driver and one of the building maintenance crew, but I wasn't close enough to see what went down. My gut tells me there's something there, but I don't know what it is . . . yet."

Noah folded his hands behind his head. Nothing about his

expression had changed, and yet I sensed his disappointment. "Anything else in the pipeline?"

"I met some ballers in the bar the other week," she said quickly. "I told them I was interested in any gossip about the sports teams. One of them came up to me in the gym the other day and said he might have something for me. I'm meeting him for coffee next week."

My breath caught and I bolted up in my seat. "Who? Ethan?"

"No, it wasn't Ethan." Her forehead creased in a frown. "You don't know him."

"Why does this dude need coffee to spill the tea?" I folded my arms across my chest. "Why not just tell you in the gym where there are lots of people around?"

Skye gave an irritated sniff and folded her arms, too. "Maybe since he's spilling tea about the team, he doesn't want to do it where the team is practicing."

Noah's gaze slid from me to Skye and back to me. "I have faith in Skye. I'm sure she'll find us a big story." He coughed and then coughed again. I picked up his Bob Ross coffee cup so he could take a drink and realized it was empty. Only then did I realize his coffee pot was empty, too.

"I'll get you some water," I said, standing. "And I'll fill the pot."

Noah cleared his throat and waved me away. "Water is for wimps. And the machine is busted. I was going to buy a new one but they have too many fancy gadgets. I like things simple. I don't need milk steamers, silver pods, or adjustable trays. I'll go upstairs after we're done and pick up a cup of the swill they're trying to pass off as java."

Noah without coffee was like my house without my mom. "I'll run up and get it now."

"We're in the middle of a meeting." Siobhan glared at me. "I don't have time to sit here waiting for you to run errands."

"Seriously, Shiv?" My voice rose as all the emotion I'd managed to push back down threatened to explode. "Everything you have here—your show, your friends, your job—it's because of Noah.

You can't wait five minutes? Noah needs coffee like you need fucking air to breathe."

"Dante? Are you okay?" Skye reached for me, and I bolted out of my seat.

"Don't." I didn't need her sympathy. I didn't need her soft voice and her worried frown. I needed her to be angry. I needed her to hate me as much as I hated myself. I needed her to leave me alone so I could go back to my world of ice where I didn't to think or feel or remember.

"It's cool." Noah shrugged. "I'm not going to die because I missed my afternoon coffee."

My ears were ringing, and I could barely see his face. Even if he didn't need the coffee, I couldn't stay here. Not with Skye in the room. Not with Noah looking so tired with a broken coffee pot and an empty cup on his desk. Everything just felt wrong.

"Haley is just getting off her shift," Skye said, gently. "Why don't I ask her to stop by with some coffee?" She smiled at Noah, clearly trying to lighten the mood. "I assume one tray will be enough?"

He gave her an appreciative nod. "Colombian. Black. And tell her to make sure it's fresh or I'll cancel her show."

"Noah. Emergency." Derek popped his head in the door. "Khavy isn't going to make it for his show today and neither is Ryan. There's some bug going around, and they both have it."

Noah didn't drop a beat. "Make a quick Kidcore playlist for the first half hour until Siobhan and I can find someone to sub in—Black Eyed Peas, Nickelback, Coldplay—anything safe sounding and radio friendly. Nothing with an edge or sense of danger. Lots of Imagine Dragons."

"I thought you were trying to save the station, not tank it," I said, channeling my pain in the language I knew best. "Imagine Dragons are tied with Florence and the Machine when it comes to churning out overly dramatic wannabe-epic tunes."

"What are you talking about?" Skye looked up at me aghast. "Florence is one of the greatest voices of all time. Have you heard

'South London'? Her songs make me cry because of the way she captures ordinary moments of life."

"Fake arena-style pop tunes," I muttered.

"What's fake about it?"

"Everything. The structure, the sound, the drums. She can sing well, but I don't feel the emotion. I thought you understood music."

Skye winced at the blow but wouldn't back down. "I thought *you* understood music, but clearly you're just a hack."

"Stop." Noah dropped his feet and pointed from me to Skye. "That. Right there. We need that on the air."

Skye shot him a puzzled glance. "Two people arguing about music?"

"Yes." He jumped up. "Two people who know music, who understand it, having a lively discussion. It's interesting. It's engaging. Dante is obviously wrong because have you heard *Ceremonials*? Great album."

"See?" Skye smirked at me for all of two seconds before her face fell. "Wait. What? You want me to do a live? Have you forgotten my interview?"

"I don't forget anything," Noah said. "And the point of interning at a teaching station is to learn new skills. Dante will handle the board and run the show. You'll just be there as a special argumentative guest who is going to get some on-air experience with a safety net."

"I'm not argumentative," Skye snapped. "I'm right."

"We'll argue about it later." Noah fixed his gaze on me. "It's time you let someone into your studio. It will be a learning opportunity for both of you."

"And if I refuse?"

"I'll cancel your show." Noah nodded at Derek, who'd been following the conversation with interest. "Why are you standing here gawking? Get that Kidcore on while I stop these two from melting down. Siobhan, find someone to take the second slot. If you can't, then Chad can talk sports."

"Yesss." Chad pumped his fist. "I brought in a mirror after my last show so I could watch myself the next time I was on-air. It's practice for when I'm on TV."

"I haven't prepped," Skye pointed out after Siobhan and Chad had gone.

"Just don't mention Imagine Dragons and you'll be fine." I couldn't keep the sarcasm from my voice.

"What's with you today?" Skye turned on me. "Imagine Dragons might not put their best foot forward with their singles but the deep cuts are where it gets real. You clearly haven't listened to 'Uptight,' or 'Hopeless Opus.'"

"You're prepped," Noah said to her. "You can thank Dante later."

Skye marched ahead of me to the studio, her back stiff, hands clenched by her sides. I could almost hear her thoughts. *What if I mess up? What if I'm not good enough? What if . . .*

Her anxiety was enough to pull me out of my own emotional crisis. "He won't fire you," I said. "He won't take your scholarship away. You're safe, Skye. And I'm right here. Nothing is going to go wrong. Trust me."

She looked over her shoulder but her eyes were as cold as ice. "I trusted you until you started acting like a dick."

I felt her anger like a knife through my heart, but it's what I needed, what I wanted, what had to happen to drive her away.

"We need a name for our show," I said after we'd taken our seats. "We can't just go on and start talking."

She sucked in a sharp breath and her eyes widened. "I thought this was a one-off to help Noah out and when everyone is back, he won't need us again."

"Then you still don't understand how Noah works. He has no scruples when it comes to the station. He will ask, beg, and demand to get what he wants. If you open the door a crack, he'll push right in. He needs more programming to fill the dead air and now he's found it."

"I can't believe I walked right into his trap." She twisted her hands in her lap. "I'm going to fall apart from the stress. Say something encouraging."

"No one knows music like you do." I forced a smile. "Except, of course, me."

"That didn't do it."

I couldn't do it. I couldn't push her away when she looked like she wanted the floor to swallow her up. I couldn't stomach her pain even though five minutes ago that was exactly what I'd resolved to do.

"I've got you." I checked over my shoulder to make sure the hallway was clear and then I pulled her in for a kiss.

My heart slowed. Heat rushed through my veins. She filled the emptiness with light and soothed my aching soul.

"Better now," she whispered against my mouth. "Maybe you're not such a dick after all."

I forced myself to pull away and check the clock. "We have ninety seconds. What about that name?"

Skye twisted her lips to the side. "What about Sound Off? The Musical Divide? The Clash of the Chords? Or Rhythm and Discord?"

I looked at her with newfound appreciation. "You came up with all those ideas in ten seconds?"

"I like words." She shrugged. "It's who I am."

"I like the Musical Divide."

Skye laughed. "Of course you do."

"What do you mean?" I put on her headphones before grabbing my own.

"You fail to appreciate the genius that is Imagine Dragons," she said with a grin. "There will be no closing that divide."

I put on my headphones and reached for the mic. "Buttercup, prepare to be schooled."

CHAPTER TWENTY-FIVE

"Blame It on Me" by George Ezra

SKYE

On the surface, everything seemed fine between me and Dante after our unsettling encounter in Noah's office. Although we couldn't be seen in public together—Noah had spies, Dante said—we spent the next two weeks stealing kisses in hallways, sneaking into buildings for secret sexy times in hidden rooms and passageways, and making forays into the basement storage room for "spare parts" that involved quickies on a table that he'd cleared off for the sole purpose of keeping my feet off the floor. We messaged on the days we didn't see each other and had a blast on Thursday afternoons doing our show. But still, I couldn't shake a sense of unease.

When we were alone together, we talked about music, school, work, and my journalism investigations. We discussed weather and world events, Isla and Nick's obvious attraction and Chad's determination to find a girlfriend before the end of term. I told him stories about my life growing up, the articles I'd written for my high school newspaper, and the guilt I'd felt when I got more satisfaction from breaking a story than winning a basketball game.

We talked about me, but we never talked about him. It was liked he'd locked a mental door the day after he'd told me after his sister and his family home, and no matter how gently I pushed, he wasn't going to let me through.

"Earth to Skye." Haley waved a hand in front of my face, blocking my view of the espresso machine while I was trying to pour an Americano. "Hot dude. Twelve o'clock. He's staring at you. I think he might be a stalker or else he's trying to mentally project his coffee order into your brain."

I looked up and laughed when I recognized the man walking toward us. "It's just Blake. He's on the men's basketball team. I got to know him at the bar the other night when Ethan introduced us. We're meeting after I'm done with my shift." I waved as the tall, blond, lanky wing shuffled up to the counter with a smile so wide I could count all his pearly white teeth. I introduced Haley because I knew she wasn't going to leave my side until I did. Blake gave her a polite smile, but the spark wasn't there.

"I'm off in ten minutes," I said to Blake. "Do you want to grab a table and I'll meet you in the student lounge?"

"I'll see if I can find a booth in the corner." He glanced from side to side. "I don't want anyone to see us talking."

"What's that all about?" Haley asked after he'd gone. "It's Friday night and you'd better not be planning to ditch Isla and me for hot stuff over there because you promised you'd come to hear me at the open mic tonight."

"He's helping me with an assignment." I desperately wanted to tell her I had found my first-ever informant—he had sent me a cryptic message about some tea he wanted to spill—but disclosing his identity was a surefire way to ensure I'd never win the trust of an informant ever again.

"Is he helping you with an assignment?" she asked, keeping her voice even. "Or . . ." She rocked her hips. "Helping you with an assignment."

"Haley!" I had to turn my face away so she couldn't see me laugh. "I'm shocked."

"Someone who gets all the hot guys can't be that shocked."

"What guys? I have no guys." I pulled a row of cups from the box on the floor and stacked them on the counter.

"Seriously? You have Dante, and don't pretend nothing is going on. The minute he walks into a room, your face lights up. Sparks fly. Then you're scurrying off somewhere together on the pretense of getting things no one needs. Nick figures there's nothing left in the basement storage room. Why don't you guys just come out and say you're together? Or, were you together and now you're not together and you're moving on with Beautiful Blake?"

"Blake is just a friend," I said. "And, I don't know what Dante and I have together." I bristled at having my biggest worry dragged into the light. "We haven't DTRed and I kind of want to keep it that way."

"Sounds like a situationship to me," Haley said, refilling the tea bags. "Do you do things outside of the bedroom?"

I glanced over to make sure there were no customers waiting who might overhear our conversation. "We've never been in a bedroom together."

"I did not want to know that," she said. "Where's the bleach? I need to erase that image from my brain."

"He told me he lives in the suite above Noah's garage, but he's never invited me to visit." I grabbed cloth and scrubbed at the already clean counter. "For all I know he doesn't even have a bed."

"Okay. That's not normal. So far so bad." Haley raised an eyebrow. "Have you met his friends?"

"I've met everyone at the station . . ."

"We weren't friends with him before you and Chad showed up," Haley said. "So, the answer is no. When someone starts making you a priority in their life, they'll start to introduce you to people that are close to them."

Dante had lost the people closest to him. He'd quit his band. He had Noah, Nick, and the people at the station, but as far as I knew he didn't have any other friends. "How many psych classes have you taken?"

"When something interests me, I go all in," she said. "The problem is I don't stay interested for long." She pulled out her phone and scrolled through the screen. "One last question. Do you have a deep emotional connection or are you just a hookup or a booty call?"

I didn't need to think about that one. Dante and I connected on so many levels. Music. Ambition. Losing a parent. Past pain. "Connection."

Haley twisted her lips to side. "I was going to diagnose you with a bad case of situationship, but the connection thing kinda throws that off. You should talk it through."

"That's what Isla said."

"Isla thinks he's seeing someone else." Haley left me hanging as she took the next order.

"What do you mean Isla thinks he's seeing someone else?" I demanded the moment the customer moved aside.

Haley shrugged. "She says you've never invited him over for the night, and the closest she's ever seen him get to a PDA was when he gave you a piggyback ride at the park and then at the bar when you were talking to him and he touched your hip."

"He said Noah wouldn't approve given our roles at the station, so we have to keep things hush-hush."

"Noah doesn't give a damn about people getting together," Haley said. "People are always hooking up at the station because we're all the same kind of people. Siobhan dated last year's intern, and someone caught them going at in the lounge."

Her words shook me to the core. "Noah didn't care?"

"He was happy about it, actually. He said Siobhan needed a little love in her life."

My breath caught as I grabbed my purse from beneath the counter. I tried to rally even though I felt like I was dying inside. "I need a little love in my life, too, so do I care what this is? No. All I care about is that I'm having fun right now with someone who makes me happy. Even if it has to be a secret." My voice rose in pitch, wavered. "Why can't I have that? Why is everyone trying to take it away?"

Haley stared at me with a horrified expression. "I'm not trying to take it away. Of course I want you to be happy. Just ignore me. Sometimes I read things in my textbooks and I get excited about applying them and I forget real people with real feelings are involved. You do you and fuck anyone who isn't with you on the journey."

"I have to go and meet Blake." And then because I knew she

was still upset after my outburst, I said, "I'll tell him you're single and fabulous."

Haley brightened. "Tell him I like blond blue-eyed dudes who are tall and into sports. You can tell him to listen to my show, or better yet tell him to come to the open mic at *The Gilded Lily* tonight, but don't tell him about my donut addiction."

Blake had managed to find a quiet alcove in the student lounge, a large, open space lined with mismatched couches and chairs, some with cushions torn and stuffing spilling out. Groups of students huddled together under brightly colored posters and flyers from various events, their faces lit up by the glow of their laptops and phones.

"So, what's the scoop?" I asked, handing him a free apple to keep him sweet.

He looked around and then leaned forward, lowering his voice. "I heard something I thought you might be interested in, but I'm not sure because it's a bit heavy, and you were asking about people getting shitfaced or DUIs or hooking up with profs and stuff."

"I'm interested in everything," I assured him. "Heavy, light, and in between."

"I was wondering . . . I mean . . . um . . . Would you . . ." He stuttered and stammered for a few more words until I realized he wanted something in exchange for his information.

In that moment I felt like a seasoned reporter. How should I play this? Favors? Bribes? Arm-twisting? "What do you want?"

His cheeks reddened. "Maybe we could go for a drink some time."

"I . . . uh . . ." I'd just told Haley I didn't want to put a label on what Dante and I had, and whatever it was had to be secret. So, what did I say?

"You're seeing Ethan," he said quickly. "I get it."

"Ethan? No, I'm not with Ethan." I'd seen Ethan at the gym a few times over the last few weeks, and we'd chatted briefly, but other than that, the spark between us seemed to have died after I'd blown him off outside the bar.

"He told us—the team—you were off-limits," Blake said. "I figured that's because you were together. Are you with someone else?"

Why was this coming up again after I'd spent weeks keeping the issue of our relationship conveniently buried away? Things were good with Dante. I didn't want to ruin them with awkward questions about the status of our relationship and whether we were exclusive. The little girl in me who had been so desperately terrified of being sent away had decided that willful blindness was the way to go if it meant I could have a little happiness after eighteen months of utter despair.

"Maybe?" I shrugged. "Sort of. It's a casual thing." The strange feeling in my stomach belied my words. Why had Dante lied about Noah? Was this all just a game to him? Was he seeing other people?

Blake's face fell. "Sure. I get it."

I mentally chastised myself for being such an idiot, and gave up trying to sort out all my conflicting emotions in favor of doing what it took to get the scoop because I was a journalist, and I wasn't about to lose a source because I couldn't get out of my own damn way. "I'd love to have a drink sometime."

"Cool." He smiled briefly and then leaned closer. "I'm not the kind of guy who would rat on my team, but I heard something that really got under my skin, and I need to know if it's true. I remembered you telling us at the bar how you didn't miss basketball that much because you loved everything about journalism, and you wanted to dedicate your life to finding the truth. I thought this might be right up your alley."

I was almost vibrating with excitement. I had a gut feeling that whatever he was about to tell me was something good.

"You can share it with me, and I won't tell anyone it came from you," I said. "I totally understand how you feel about the team. They're family."

"I knew you'd get it." He swallowed hard and lowered his voice to almost a whisper. "I was in the locker room late one night because I'd stayed to practice my throws, and I overheard two seniors from the football team talking. One of them, I'll call him Dave but that's not his real name, had hooked up with a girl who used to be a personal assistant to one of the basketball coaches. She told him that there had been a big cover-up involving a member of the basketball team. Apparently, the dude had done something so awful that the university was going to kick him out, but the head coach convinced the higher ups to let him stay because he was pretty much guaranteed a spot in the NBA and—"

"That's everything for the university rankings."

Blake nodded. "I know Dave. He's spotted me in the gym a few times. He's a good guy—very religious. I don't think he'd lie about something like that."

I didn't realize I'd been holding my breath until it came out in a rush. "Did Dave say what the dude did, or who was involved or even when it happened?"

Blake hesitated and then shook his head. "They left the locker room, and I didn't hear the rest."

"This is huge." It was an effort to keep my voice down. "I just wish I knew how bad is bad. Did he kill someone? Or hurt someone in a fight? Or was it a sexual assault? Did he have a drug problem?" My mind was whirling with possibilities.

"I need to know, too," Blake said. "I don't think my chances of going pro are very good and I've been thinking about transferring schools. If there is some kind of scandal involving the team, I don't want to be here. I thought if you could find the truth, then I could make an informed decision."

"Could you ask Dave if he would be interested in talking to me? Or if he would be willing to put me in touch with the personal assistant?" My hand was literally shaking. This was potentially huge. Bigger than my building story. More exciting than garbage. "It would be totally confidential."

Blake shook his head. "I wasn't even supposed to hear that conversation. It was hard just coming to you."

"I get it. I'll see what I can do." I had no idea how I was going to squeeze information from an unknown source, but I was in the gym every day. I still had my connections with the athletic community, and if all else failed, there was Ethan, who knew everybody.

Blake's eyes darted over my shoulder and then widened. I huffed an irritated breath. I didn't need to look over my shoulder to know Dante had found me.

"Hey there," I said when he joined us in the alcove. I looked to Blake and then away, silently trying to remind Dante that I had mentioned meeting someone from the team when we were in Noah's office, and I needed him to back off.

Dante stared at Blake like he'd done something to offend him. "Who's this?"

Message not received.

"Blake. He's on the men's basketball team. We're catching up on old times." I introduced Dante as a friend from the radio station. The men nodded at each other but didn't shake hands.

"What happened in these old times?" Dante sat beside me on the worn red couch and threw his arm across my shoulders.

"It's none of your business." I pushed his arm away. "I'll meet you over at the coffee shop in about ten minutes. We're almost done."

"Actually, I should get going. I have a class." Red-faced, Blake picked up his bag. "Let me know if you find anything out."

"Thank you," I said. "For everything. I won't let you down."

I waited until Blake was out of earshot before I rounded on Dante, who had his feet up on the coffee table and a scowl on his face.

"You just cost me what might have been the biggest scoop of the year. You were totally out of line."

"Was I?" A tiny muscle pulsed at the base of his jaw. "The minute my back is turned, you're off having a secret rendezvous with Blake the baller. What were you going to do next? Shoot some hoops together? Drink protein shakes in the moonlight? Go for a run in your tights?"

For a moment, his anger made me forget about my own. "Are you . . . jealous?" Jealous would mean there was something between us that wasn't the situationship Haley had thought it might be.

"Why would I be jealous?" Dante folded his hands behind his head. "It makes sense that you'd go for someone like him. He's your type. You told me in the storage room that you preferred to date athletes."

"I told you I dated athletes because I wasn't allowed to date anyone else in high school," I spat out. "Or don't you remember that conversation?"

"And yet you picked him," he said bitterly. "An athlete."

"I didn't pick him." I turned on the couch to face him. "If you take even thirty seconds to think back to our meeting with Noah, you would know who he is. And even if I did pick him . . ." I knew I should stop myself, but Haley had wound me up and Blake hadn't helped. I couldn't keep my head buried in the sand anymore. "What does it matter? You've made it clear you want this thing between us to be casual at best."

With the floodgates open, the words just came pouring out. I didn't care that people were listening to us. Everything I'd been holding in, all my questions, worries, and fears needed to be heard.

"You won't let me touch you in public," I continued. "We've never gone out together, not even for a drink. I haven't met your friends or seen where you live. We haven't officially told the people close to us what this is, if it is anything. And you lied to me about Noah. Haley said he wouldn't care that we're together. Is it because you're seeing someone else?"

Silence. Dante stared at me, his face an expressionless mask. Finally, he took my hand and pressed my fingertips to his lips. "No. There's no one else."

I let out a shuddering breath, trying to separate his words from my fears. "I know we never agreed to be serious or exclusive but don't come down on me because you set the rules and I'm playing your game."

"You don't think I'm serious?" Dante moved closer on the

couch and placed my hand on his chest right above his beating heart. "I haven't been with anyone else since the day I met you."

"I didn't ask for that," I said, my stomach queasy.

"I want you and only you." Dante's voice dropped to a husky rumble. "I wanted you from the moment we met. And every time I see you, I want you more." He threaded his hand through my hair, and rubbed his thumb gently over my cheek, the emotion on his face so real and raw it made my heart ache. "When I saw you with Blake . . ." His Adam's apple bobbed when he swallowed. "I was jealous, Skye. So, fucking jealous. I can't lose you, so if this is what you need, let's make it official."

"I don't *need* to make it official." I pulled away. "I just want to understand what we have." Official meant commitment. It meant opening myself up to disappointing someone all over again. It meant taking the risk that I wasn't good enough all over again. My blood chilled at the growing realization that the reason I hadn't wanted to open this door was not because I needed a commitment, but because I knew I couldn't give it.

A pained expression crossed his face. "Isn't that why you brought this up? Because you wanted this out in the open? I'm touching you now."

"In an alcove where it's unlikely anyone could see us and in a lounge with only five people, three of whom are asleep," I retorted.

"What do you want?" His voice was laced with the thinnest thread of desperation. "Do you want to fuck right here, Skye? Or should we go where there are more people? Do you need an audience? What do I have to do?"

"Dante . . ." I stared at him aghast.

"I'm giving everything I can give you." His voice cracked with emotion. "What else do you need?"

"I don't know." My hands fisted on the couch. "I was happy just doing what we were doing. But then Isla thinks . . . and Haley said . . . and Blake thought I was with Ethan, and when I told him that wasn't true, he asked me out. I didn't know what we were or why it has to be a secret or whether I wasn't good en—"

"He asked you out?" Dante froze and his eyes hardened. "What did you say?"

"I said . . ." God, how did this become such a tangle? "I'd go for a drink with him sometime."

"Of course you did." His voice turned to ice, cold and unforgiving. "You've had your walk on the wild side and now it's back to polo-shirt-wearing clean-cut athletes named Blake. Was it fun, Skye? Did you enjoy getting your hands dirty?"

Gritting my teeth, I hugged my bag to my chest. "That's not fair. It's not like I led him on. And I agreed to go for a drink because he's helping me with an assignment. I'm not interested in Blake that way, and he didn't come here to ask me out. He said Ethan had told the team I was off-limits."

"Off-limits?" Dante barked a harsh laugh. "Now you're planning to date Ethan, too? Well enjoy. I'm sure he's everything you want."

"You don't understand—"

But it was too late. He was already winding his way through the tables toward the exit.

I wanted to follow him, but I simply couldn't move.

What just happened? My head was still spinning. He wanted me. There was no one else. He would make it official. He was jealous. But then the thought of me with someone else had sent him away. Was it me or was it him? I didn't know what was driving Dante, but I knew what drove me. He'd opened up, and I'd closed the door. I was still afraid—afraid of taking a risk, of making a mistake, of being rejected. And this time, instead of just hurting myself, I'd hurt someone else. Someone I cared about.

Someone who cared about me.

CHAPTER TWENTY-SIX

"Way down We Go" by Kaleo

DANTE

When Noah called me in to his office on the Wednesday after my blowup with Skye, I was expecting him to tell me that he wanted Skye and me to host *Musical Divide* on a permanent basis. Our ratings had been through the roof and the show was bringing some much needed attention to the station. I'd never hosted a show with anyone else, but it was easy with Skye. I'd become so involved in our spirited debate that I'd almost forgotten we were on the air. But after our conversation in the student lounge, I had no idea whether our show the next day would go on.

"Close the door."

The skin on the back of my neck prickled in warning. When had Noah ever asked me to close the door? Noah believed that people should learn how the station was run from every level and that included management decisions. He only ever closed the door for personal matters.

"What's going on?"

"What the hell is this?" Noah held up a flyer advertising my essay-writing service—a flyer I had never authorized. "I saw Nick pinning it to the corkboard. At first, I thought it was his business and I told him that if he wanted to continue being part of this station, he would have to take down the website right then and there. He said he couldn't do it. Damn idiot was prepared to take the fall rather than give you up. But I knew he was holding something back. I asked around and he'd recommended your business to a few other volunteers. They knew you were behind it."

I shrugged, at a loss to understand his fury. "I wanted to help people who weren't good at writing."

"Bullshit," he yelled, slapping his palm on the desk. "Do you think you helped Nick?" His face was red, the vein throbbing at the base of his neck. "What happens when he gets into the real world and he can't write for shit? You took something away from him—an opportunity to learn to do it for himself. After everything you've done to get as far as you have, how could you be so stupid?"

It took a long time before my brain could catch up. First, Noah never yelled. In all the years I'd known him, he'd never once raised his voice no matter how big the screw up. Second, Noah never swore or called people names, not even in jest. Third, he knew about the essay-writing service, but it seemed he didn't know about Skye.

"I told you I had a side hustle," I protested. "And it's not illegal. It's on the line. I don't write the essays. I don't submit the essays. I'm just a middleman bringing people together."

"It's academic dishonesty and you know it," he shouted. "You're putting your degree . . . hell, you're putting your whole future at risk."

"It hasn't been a problem so far."

"Is it the money? You promised me you'd keep enough of your inheritance to get you through law school." He ran his hand through his silvery hair and a clump came off in his palm. He absently tossed it in the garbage can beside him as if it happened every day. I felt the hair lifting on the back of my neck and my mouth went dry.

"It started off being about the money." I couldn't stop staring at Noah's hair. Why hadn't I noticed before that it was getting thinner? Was this just an old person thing and he was going bald like his dad—I'd seen the pictures in his house—or was it the stress of trying to save the station? "I didn't have enough to make it through my first year, and you'd already given me so much, I couldn't ask for more—"

"I have connections everywhere." Noah cut me off with an irritated wave. "I could have gotten you session work. I could have sent producers and music execs to hear your band play. I could have taken your solo demos to big names in the industry . . ." He heaved a sigh. "But no. Instead of coming to me . . . instead of following your real passion and using your gift to get you out of a jam, you chose to fuck up your whole damn life . . ."

Again. He didn't say it, but the word hung heavy between us.

"Are you going to report me?" I would never have thought to ask that question before, but I didn't know this Noah who yelled and thumped his desk. I didn't know this Noah who I suddenly realized was too thin and too pale, and who didn't even have a paper cup of coffee to replace what he'd usually have from his broken pot.

"No, you idiot, but I am trying to save you. I'm sick and tired of watching you sabotage yourself over and over and over again. Every time something starts going right, you do something to make it go wrong. You're doing well at school and then you pull something like this. Instead of session work, you hook up with a band full of drug addicts. It's like you don't think you deserve a good life."

"What do you want me to say?" A sliver of anger curled inside me. Who was he to tell me how to live my life? "I'm sorry?"

Noah drew in a shuddering breath. "Maybe I'm taking something away from you by not turning you in. Maybe this is a lesson you need to learn. I could just pick up the phone and that would be the end of your time here at Havencrest. No degree. No more working at the station. No show."

My blood chilled in my veins at his thinly veiled threat. "You wouldn't do that."

"I would if I thought it would help you get your head out of your ass." His voice rose in exasperation. "What the fuck is going on? You're a smart guy, Dante, but do you really see yourself putting on a suit and sitting in an office cubicle day after day? Music is in your blood. The only time I ever see you smile is when you're doing your show or playing your bass. Your music touches people's lives. It speaks to them. And now you've put me in a position where I have to take it away."

The weight of Noah's words pressed down on me, suffocating me with the truth. Music had always been my solace, my refuge from the chaos of the world. Even though my focus had shifted to vengeance, the show gave me an emotional outlet. What would I do without it? My breath caught in my throat, and I felt like I was falling, as if I were in an elevator plummeting to the ground, every floor a person I had loved and lost and would never see again.

"It hurts me to watch you sabotage yourself," Noah said, his voice breaking, pulling me out of the abyss. "Music. School. Life. Love . . ." He held up a hand to stop me from speaking when I opened my mouth. "I know about you and Skye. Anyone with half a brain can see it. You were supposed to stay away, keep yourself safe, but you fucked that up, too. I'm only surprised it lasted this long because you seem determined to destroy anything good in your life."

Of course, he was right. I'd messed it up that very afternoon, and I didn't even know why.

"You always said you didn't want anything to do with your dad," he continued on his unprecedented rant. "But your whole damn life is about him. You can't keep punishing yourself because of what he did. You can't blame yourself for other people's choices or for things you couldn't control. You've given up everything on your quest to destroy him, but from where I'm sitting the only person suffering is you."

His words sliced straight through to my heart. He wasn't wrong, but I couldn't see another path. "What do you want, Noah?"

"I want you to believe you're worthy of a good life," he said. "You don't need meaningless hookups, shady side hustles, or a drug-addicted band. You don't need a degree you hate or a career whose sole purpose is revenge. You don't need to worry that the people you care about will abandon you because they will always be with you—if not in person, then in spirit." He touched his chest above his heart. "I want you to be the best man you can be. I want you to know you deserve the love of a good woman. I want you to have a career you love and music that feeds your soul. I'm canceling your show with Skye tomorrow to give you time to think seriously about your life. I want changes from you, Dante. Big changes. Or I will make that call."

I asked Nick to come with me the next morning to clean out my rehearsal space.

Noah was right. I needed to make changes and one of them was to cut ties with the band. Two months ago, I wouldn't have even considered asking for help. But Noah hadn't just made me rethink my life, he'd made me realize that I wasn't alone. I'd made friends since he forced me to put my hours in at the station, and it was time to open myself to a friendship that had been offered time and again.

Quinn and the other members of the band had come and gone by the time Nick and I arrived with Noah's SUV. Jules was waiting for us inside, smoking a cigarette while tapping out a one-handed beat on her drum kit.

"I didn't think you would ever walk away," she said after I introduced her to Nick.

"Quinn made it easy. After I sent him the text telling him I was canceling the lease, he responded with 'mushrooms chips pork rinds pizza coke.'"

Jules snorted a laugh. "What is that? His shopping list?"

"I think he was cataloguing everything he had in front of him. I'm guessing the mushrooms weren't the fungi kind and the coke didn't come in a can." I coiled up the cords to one of my amps.

"I don't blame you for leaving," she said. "But your timing sucks. I had just got us a gig at the Ironhorse for Sunday night, and I was planning to text you to see if you'd do a one-off for old times' sake. They were going to pay double the going rate because they had a last-minute cancellation. Quinn promised he'd stay clean all week, but if he was sending you text messages like that, it was doomed anyway."

I picked up my spare bass and played the bass line for B.B. King's "The Thrill is Gone." Jules joined in on the beat. Nick picked up my guitar and began to play. His sound was cool and clean and so damn good I almost dropped a note.

"Well, damn," Jules said to Nick when we were done. "I'd invite you to jam with us anytime, but as of today, Dante's Inferno doesn't have a name or a rehearsal space."

"I couldn't sit out from a girl trouble song. Nothing else soothes the pain." He shot a knowing glance at me. "You get it."

It took me a moment to realize not only that he knew about me and Skye, but also that he had girl troubles of his own, and I regretted not being a better friend. My shock must have shown on my face because Nick laughed. "Isla isn't very good at keeping secrets but I would have guessed about you and Skye after your first show together. Your chemistry is off the charts."

"So . . . you and Isla?"

Nick shook his head. "Not yet. But I'm in it for the long haul. She needs time and I'm more than happy to give it to her. She's worth waiting for."

I'd never shared anything personal with friends, not even Jules. I had managed to compartmentalize my life so successfully that nothing crossed through. Nick had given me an opening and damned if I wasn't going to take it. "I think I messed up. I saw her with another guy and—"

"No way." Jules stared at me, open-mouthed. "You? Serious enough about a girl to actually get jealous? She must really be something."

"She is."

Nick strummed the first few bars of Bruce Springsteen's "Secret Garden" and Jules picked up the beat. I joined in and we sang the vocals together. It felt good. Like coming home.

"Guys . . ." Jules grinned. "We're damn good together. How about we pick up that gig at the Ironhorse tomorrow night? I could try to sober up our keyboardist . . ."

"I've got a band," Nick said. "Well, part of a band. It's me and my friend Derek. He plays keyboard. We just lost our drummer to another band, and we've been looking for a bass player."

"Dante?" Jules lifted an eyebrow. "What do you think, and whatever you're thinking better come out as a 'yes.'"

I was still tripping on our last song, so the answer was easy. "Yes, but I think we need someone to do vocals."

"How about Haley?" Nick suggested. "She's an incredible singer, and she's always looking for opportunities to get on stage."

Nick gave me Haley's number and I sent her a message. Seconds later my phone rang. My phone never rang. I almost didn't recognize the sound.

"Are you serious?" Haley shrieked into the phone. "You want me to sing with your band?"

"I'm very serious. We need you to—"

"Yes!" Haley screamed so loud I had to hold my phone away from my ear.

I looked over at Jules and smiled. "We've got a band."

CHAPTER TWENTY-SEVEN

"This Is Me" by Keala Settle, the Greatest Showman Ensemble

SKYE

Despite Dante's reaction to my meeting with Blake, I was stoked about the basketball cover-up story, and spent the following week chasing down leads and dropping hints to the athletic center staff that I was interested in any tea they wanted to spill. For a few boxes of lemon squares and a tray of coffee, I got some juicy—albeit anonymous—stories about athletes involved in drunk driving accidents, academic dishonesty, affairs, secret babies and equipment sabotage, but nothing serious enough to warrant a major cover-up.

When my efforts with the staff didn't turn up any leads, I met up with my old teammates for dinner on the pretense of catching up, but really to find out if they'd heard any rumors. I spent Saturday doing a deep digital dive of both the university and local news for any mention of Havencrest basketball players involved in incidents or crimes, and when that didn't pan out, I dragged poor Isla to the athletic center on Sunday to drink protein shakes with me in the corner so we could eavesdrop on conversations.

"I've never seen this side of you," she said, watching me slide down my seat when a few ballers arrived for their protein shake fix. "Do you really think there's something to this rumor?"

"I feel it the way I felt the story about the high school principal with the fake résumé." I thumped my stomach. "It's here in the gut with two strawberry matcha açai protein shakes and a health bar that tasted like cardboard."

"Leave room in that gut for a few G and Ts," she said, laughing. "Apparently Nick, Derek, Haley, and Dante have put together a band and they're playing at the Ironhorse tonight. Everyone from the station is going to be there."

"Not me. Dante doesn't want to see me. He just walked away, Iz. He didn't want to talk, and when I messaged him, he left me unread."

"He hurt you by not wanting to go public with your relationship. You hurt him by making a date with some random baller who is clearly holding back the information you need for your story so he can get into your pants. You're afraid of being rejected, and Dante didn't help the situation by doing exactly that." She looked over and grinned. "How am I doing?"

"You've been talking to Haley about me."

"I'm insulted," Isla said. "Chemistry is just as important as psychology when it comes to relationships, although to be fair, Haley did say you have trust and commitment issues, and you're not going to make things right by hiding."

"I'm not hiding."

Isla pointed to the potted palm half covering our table. "You literally are hiding, and if you don't agree to come to the bar, I'm going to out you as spy to the entire men's basketball team and you'll never get your story."

"You are a cruel woman, Iz."

Isla grinned. "That's why you love me."

A few hours later, we were back in our apartment, warming up with a few margaritas while we got dressed.

"I've decided I'm not going to hide how I feel anymore," I called out to Isla, who was changing in her room. "I was trying to pretend that everything was okay with Dante when it wasn't. I didn't like having to keep what we had secret. It made me feel like he was ashamed of me, or maybe he had someone else. I'm on to a big story here, Iz. I'm kicking ass at school and at the station. I shouldn't have to hide. I'm going to tell him how I feel, even if it means finding out that he doesn't want me."

"If he didn't want you, he wouldn't have been jealous of Blake and he wouldn't have said 'Skye, I want you.' The question is, do you want him?" She walked into my room looking stunning in her favorite red strapless dress. "How do I look?"

"Fabulous. Are you finally going to tell Nick how you feel?"

"Of course not," she huffed. "Then he might want to go out and have dinner or drinks and then he might walk me home and then he might kiss me and that might lead to . . ."

"Sex." I opened my closet and flicked idly through my clothes. I still had the dresses I'd bought when I started college. Some of them had never been worn.

"Sex I can do," she said. "I've had a lot of sex since . . ." She waved a vague hand in the air. "I've erased all the badness with multiple sexual encounters. But Nick is different. He isn't therapy peen."

"Therapy peen? Is that really a thing?"

"My therapist said it's a way for me to take control. So yes. It's a thing."

"Sounds like it's an intimacy issue."

"Strangers know the deal," she said. "There are no expectations."

"Maybe it's time to stop trying to prove to yourself that you're okay with nameless strangers and start being okay by letting Nick in," I suggested. "If I can do it, you can do it."

"They're not always nameless," she said, with a grin. "I like to have a name to shout out when I'm pretending to come. 'Oh, Todd. You're so huge. Tyler, will it fit? Do me, Ryan. Faster, Scott . . .'"

Laughter bubbled up in my chest. "You're hopeless."

"So are you if you don't take your own advice." She reached into my closet and handed me a tight green sheath dress I'd bought for the year-end baller bash that I'd never had a chance to attend. "Go big or go home, babe."

I looked down at my scarred leg. If I could do this, I could do anything, including taking a risk on a man who made my heart sing.

"I'll need shoes."

Isla raced across the hallway and returned a few minutes later with a stack of shoeboxes. "Don't worry, babe. I've got you covered."

We drank. We danced. We sang. We danced some more. Music thrummed through me, making my heart pound. It was the perfect distraction from the air whispering over my scarred leg and the truth flowing from my battered heart. I was all in and tonight I wanted to let Dante know.

Dante played his bass as if it were an extension of his fingers, steadily, deftly weaving the band's rhythm and melody into an impenetrable musical cloak that I wanted to wrap around my naked self. There was something highly erotic about watching him play—an intimacy I wanted to share as his fingers moved over the strings, pulling me closer with every note. He was a different person on stage, so obviously born to make music. He was a performer. A rock star. And every time I looked at the stage, his gaze was fixed on me.

Near the end of the night, as the band moved into a slower set, Dante took the mic. "I don't sing very often," he said, his deep voice resonating through the speakers. "But this is a special song for a special girl, so be gentle with me." His hands moved over the strings and into the intro baseline to "Stand By Me." He controlled the bass in a way that was both powerful and graceful, commanding and elegant at once. Then he started to sing, and his eyes found me and never let go.

He was in my head, my heart, my very bones.

He saw me, and I saw him. He forgave me and I forgave him.

As the last notes drifted away, Dante put down his bass and jumped off the stage. The crowd parted as he made his way over to me.

Before I could say anything, he wrapped one arm around my waist, and pulled me against his body before covering my lips with his. He kissed me deeply, possessively, ravaging my mouth, leaving no doubt that I was his and he was mine and we were together in every sense of the word. My defenses gave way before the force of his desire, my back arching as he owned me with his passion.

I was undone.

It was too much, his kiss. Too good. It was like the perfect sunset when the sky is streaked with crimson and gold and every inch of your body is bathed in beauty. It opened me, his kiss, knocked down the walls and let the light rush in, sweeping away the pain and unveiling emotions so deep and true they bared my very soul. And there I was. The girl who had been hiding. The woman who had been afraid to follow her heart.

I wanted him. His lips. His hands. His breath. His body.

His kiss.

Our chemistry. Sparking, igniting, and melding us together.

A sound escaped my lips, a cross between a whimper and a moan. I could feel his heart beating in his chest. He kissed away my fear, my pain, my hurt, my insecurities and doubts. He was everywhere, everything, his lips on my neck, my collarbone, jaw, chin, and cheeks, destroying me with adoration and filling me up with fire.

"We've got one more song," he whispered in my ear. "Then I want to take you home."

CHAPTER TWENTY-EIGHT

"All of Me" by John Legend

SKYE

From the outside, Dante's apartment looked like an ordinary garage suite. The roof tiles and worn siding on the rectangular building were a match for Noah's two-story house and it had the same peaked roof and narrow windows. Inside the garage, a wooden staircase led up to a metal door, but there the similarities ended. As I crossed the threshold, I felt like I'd stepped into a music museum. Framed vintage band posters and signed photographs of musicians covered the walls, along with neon beer signs and wooden shelves bursting with music paraphernalia.

"Noah decorated this place before I moved in." Dante closed the door behind me. "He thrifted the furniture from various stores and flea markets. He was going for an eclectic look. He said I could change things around, but I didn't want to mess with his stuff. I kinda like it."

"It's very Noah." The mishmash of colors, textures, and patterns somehow worked together to create a space that was warm and inviting, a reflection of Noah's artistic personality.

"Where are you in here?" I studied the vintage guitars displayed in glass cases, some of which had been signed by musical greats.

"Right here." Dante gestured to the big wooden desk in the corner. "Textbooks, coursework, pens, calculator, mail, bills, LSAT study guide—I'm taking the test this Friday."

"Can I see your bass?" After watching him play all night, I was desperate to see it up close.

I could tell from Dante's smile he was pleased I'd asked. He unzipped the case and offered it to me. Understanding the importance of the moment, I took the instrument carefully with both hands.

"It's beautiful." I ran my fingers over the shiny blue metal-flake surface. Despite the warmth in the room, it was still cool from our trip home.

"It was my first bass," he said proudly. "It's a Fender with a custom maple neck and jumbo frets. I used to play it out of a small GK amp that fell off the back of a truck."

"You do like to play it close to the line," I said, teasing. "Where did you get it?"

Dante's smile faded. "The bass was a gift from my middle school music teacher. My dad wouldn't agree to pay for lessons, so my teacher taught me after school and on weekends in exchange for yard work. He let me bring Sasha and she would help in the garden and play in his backyard. It was a sanctuary for us. I was devastated when he moved away. I didn't realize at the time, but he was a pro session player and he'd toured with some big-name bands back in the day."

Everyone had left him. How did someone deal with that much pain?

"I would show you a few chords, but's hard to focus when I'm wondering what's under your dress." He returned the bass to its case, and then pulled me into his arms, his eyes hooded, primal, hungry.

"Why don't you take it off and find out?"

"I would be delighted to strip you naked, but first . . ." He swept me up in his arms and carried me into his bedroom. "I had fantasies of doing things to you in my bed and I'm going to make every single one of them come true."

"I'm happy to oblige."

Dante released me, standing, at the foot of his bed. His room was decorated much like the rest of the suite, but with far fewer adornments. A king-size bed with a plain-blue cover took up most of the space with a vintage dresser squeezed into one corner.

"I want you naked." He yanked off his T-shirt and I pressed a kiss to the bluebird inked on his bare chest.

"What a coincidence," I murmured against his skin. "I want you naked, too." I unzipped my dress and shimmied my hips until it fell in a puddle on the floor. I was wearing my only matching underwear, a white lace bra and panty set that I'd bought my freshman year when I'd had the world in my palm and thought that was the year I'd meet "the one."

"I like this." Dante slid one finger over the strap of my bra, then flicked it over my shoulder. "But I like you more without it." He unhooked it with one hand and tossed it on the bed, his gaze sweeping over my breasts as he rumbled with approval.

"Your turn." I trailed my fingers down his chest and over the trail of soft hair before I ripped open his fly and wrapped my hand around his arousal, hard and thick beneath my palm.

His breath hitched, firm hand clasping my wrist and drawing it away. "I want this to last. I want to take my time with you." He kicked off his jeans but left his boxers on, and there we were, bare save for the thin material between us.

Dante leaned down and kissed me, gently, softly, slowly melting me until I had to wrap my arms around his neck to stay upright. We kissed and we kissed, and we kissed until I was wet and aching and imagining that talented tongue thrusting somewhere else.

"I need to taste you." He eased me back onto the bed and lifted my heels to his shoulders, licking his lips as if I were a delicious treat. "Don't move." His voice was a low, teasing whisper in my ear as the rough pads of his fingertips glided through the wetness of my arousal.

Moaning, I jerked my hips up, chasing his touch. "More."

"You'll get more when I'm ready to give you more." He circled my clit with his tongue, making me shudder. His fingers were on the insides of my thighs, curling around from behind to spread me open, treating both legs the same. Scars or no scars, he was pulling me apart.

"Please." My cheeks burned but I was beyond caring. I fisted the covers, digging my heels into his shoulders.

"There's my good girl." He rewarded me with the thrust of a thick finger as he lowered his mouth back to my clit. So slow. So gentle. Not nearly enough.

"Are you trying to drive me crazy?"

He looked up, a wicked smile spreading across his lips. "I like you crazy. I like you begging. I like you totally out of control." He pulled out and pressed two fingers deep inside, sweeping his tongue through my folds in a rough, sensual stroke.

An inferno built inside me, my moans turned into whimpers and then sounds—pleasure, need, frustration, desire.

Dante added a third finger, stretching me deliciously wide as he continued to torment me with his tongue. He took me to the brink and let me hover until the pressure of anticipation verged on pain.

"Tell me what you want me to do," Dante said, his lips wet with my arousal.

"I want you to make me come. Please." I groaned, rocking my hips against the thrust of his fingers.

"Say my name."

"Dante. Make me come, Dante."

"Good girl." He closed his mouth over my clit and applied a slow, relentless gentle pressure that built and built, swelling up through my body, winding me tighter and tighter until finally I crashed over the edge, pleasure breaking over me like a cresting wave.

Dante's fingers never stopped, moving in a gentle rhythm inside me, stroking that sensitive spot that kept my pleasure at an erotic peak.

I sobbed a moan. "I can't . . . Too much."

"You can." He pushed up and stripped off his boxers, then

rolled on a condom from his nightstand. "But this time with me inside you."

"Like this?" I drank in the sight of him standing in front of me, his chest and pecs covered in tattoos, the ink swirling down his arms, his cock hard and thick with promise. He had a magnificent body. I could have stared at him all day.

"Are you done looking at me like you want to eat me?"

"I could . . ."

"Later." He grabbed me around the waist and flipped me over, positioning me on my hands and knees on the bed. "Right now, I want to fuck you looking at that sexy ass you teased me with all night. I want to fuck you knowing that all the other men in the bar wanted you but it's only me who gets to be inside you." He grabbed my hair with one hand, pulling my head back as he ran a rough hand along my spine from my nape to the cleft of my ass. "I'm going to be the one to make you scream."

"I like that you were thinking about me that way."

"You're gonna like me fucking you that way even more." He shoved my knees apart with his thick thigh then plunged inside me, releasing my hair to grip my hips instead. I sucked in an unsteady breath and pushed back, taking as much as he was giving me, showing him I wasn't fragile in any way.

"Skye. God, you're so fucking tight." His voice was thick, hoarse. I liked that I could do that to him. That I could affect him that way.

"You can be rough."

"I don't want to hurt you." He kissed the scars on my back, the sensitive spot at the base of my spine. My hips arched in his hands, taking him deeper, showing him how far he could go.

"Do you like it hard, buttercup?" He pulled out and thrust faster, harder, rough in the most delicious way.

"Yes. Make me feel good," I murmured. "Make me feel bad. Make me just feel."

"I'll make you feel fucking everything." He sped his thrusts, his hips slapping my ass. "You're gonna be a good girl and take it all."

My fingers curled into the bedding, gripping hard to brace myself as my body rocked with his thrusts. Holding me firm with one hand, he yanked my hair back and slammed me into orgasm with his hard, pounding rhythm. Moments later, he followed me over the edge, his guttural groan melding with mine.

His arm wrapped around my waist, and he rolled us until he was on his back and I was lying on his chest, tucked under his arm. He stroked his fingers in and out of the dip of my waist while we came down from the high. I liked the small intimacy of his touch, the way he connected with me as we shuddered together.

"We forgot the music," he said, reaching for his phone. "I made a playlist for the night I could bring you here."

"What did you call it? I hope it's not something lame like *Sexing Skye* or *Dante's Dick Dance* or *Banging the Broadcaster.*"

"How do you come up with these things so fast?" he asked. "You make my head spin."

"You're changing the subject." I leaned over, trying to peek at his playlist.

"I called it *The Sound of Us.*" He held it up for me to see and I quickly scanned the first few tracks. "It's our story."

"I can hardly wait to hear it."

As the first notes of John Legend's "All of Me" filled the room, Dante moved down my body. His first kiss was on the worst of my scars, and then he followed the mottled rainbow of white and red and silver that streaked me from hip to ankle, his lips pressing softly on every inch of my skin. He lifted each of my feet and kissed my toes, my calves, the sensitive creases behind my knees. His rough stubble against the soft skin of my inner thighs made me gasp and beg for his mouth where I was wet and aching for him all over again, but he only teased me with hot breaths and whispered promises for later in the night. He knelt between my legs and feathered kisses over my mound, my hips, my belly, and curve of my waist. He spent a long time on my nipples, sucking and licking each one into a hard peak before he trailed butterfly kisses along the undersides of my breasts, the valley between and the soft crescents above. Finally, he moved to the hollow at the base of my throat, my jaw, my chin, my cheeks, my forehead, a nip on my earlobes, and then, yes, finally, he came back to my mouth.

"Look at me, Skye."

I hadn't even realized I had closed my eyes, but there he was, his pupils dark but full of light, looking at me as if I were the most beautiful thing he'd ever seen.

"That's . . . it's perfect." His playlist was everything—deeply emotional, thoughtfully curated, exquisitely crafted, perfect in every way. It was about hope and longing and loss and love. It thrilled me and scared me at the same time. "I'll have to make you a playlist now," I said kissing his lips, so he didn't speak the words he'd shared in his songs.

"Do you know what I want to hear?" He rubbed his nose against my cheek, a sweet, intimate gesture that I felt deep in my heart. "The soundtrack of your life."

I had always imagined meeting someone who wanted to hear the soundtrack of my life—the roadmap of the major milestones that got me to where I was at that moment in time—because it meant they truly wanted to know me. There was no point denying it existed, and I was sure he had one, too.

"I'll tell you mine if you tell me yours."

"Deal." He rolled to his side, propping his head on his elbow. "First song."

"The Dora the Explorer theme song. I was three or four years old, and I remember standing outside my foster parents' bedroom door in the middle of the night belting out 'Doo doo doo doo doo DORA!' I think that's why they sent me away."

"You're too adorable to send away," he said, feathering a kiss over my nose.

"You just want more sex," I huffed. "Your turn."

"'Yellow Submarine.' My mom had a yellow car, and we sang that song every time we went for a long drive. We thought they were fun road trips, but she was keeping us from my dad when he came home drunk."

I squeezed his hand. "She sounds like a brave and loving mom giving you joy in the worst of times."

His faced smoothed, eyes shuttering for the briefest of moments. Then he said, "You're stalling. Next song."

"ABBA's greatest hits."

"Seriously," he said. "How old are you really?"

"I loved ABBA because my mom loved ABBA and I loved Coleman Hawkins and Frank Sinatra because of my dad."

"My mom loved musicals," Dante said. "We listened to the soundtracks to *Moulin Rouge*, *The Sound of Music*, and *West Side Story* on the way to school. My favorite was *Les Misérables*. I used to imagine singing 'Do You Hear the People Sing?' in front of my dad as a kind of defiant family uprising."

"Dante . . ." I cupped his jaw, rubbed my thumb over his bristles as if I could take away his pain.

"Sorry, buttercup." He turned into my hand and kissed my palm. "This is supposed to fun."

"It's supposed to be real," I said quietly. "Thank you for sharing it with me."

"What's next on your playlist?" he asked, turning back to look at me. "It's tween time."

"Katy Perry's 'Roar.' I felt like I'd been given the words to express all my complicated tween feelings."

"You as a tween . . ." Dante shook his head. "I can't imagine."

"I was a good tween. Five years after the adoption, I was still afraid my parents would send me away."

"I was a mess." He toyed with a strand of my hair, twisting it around his finger. "My mom had just died. I missed her so much. I spent the first few months playing David Guetta's 'Without You' on repeat."

Emotion welled up in my throat. It was a song about loss, about not being able to go on without the person you love. I moved closer and wrapped my arms around Dante, pulling him into a hug. "I'm so, so sorry."

"It got better when my middle school teacher offered to teach me bass," he said, burying his face in my hair. "Green Day's 'Welcome to Paradise' always reminds me of those days."

"I'm glad you had some happy times."

"Teen Skye," he said, perking up. "What was she listening to?"

"Omi's 'Cheerleader.' It was all about friends. They were my cheer squad."

"I tried to be Sasha's cheer squad," he said quietly. "I used to play Avicii's 'Hey Brother' at full volume to let her know I would be there for her no matter what, but it wasn't enough. She saw what my father did and couldn't live with it. She took her life when she was fourteen and I was the one who found her. My soundtrack ends with Chord Overstreet's 'Hold On.' Sasha died and a part of me died, too."

"You had to be so strong and so brave for so long." I brushed his hair back. "How did it not break you?"

"It did," he said. "I left home the day after her funeral. It was a dark time. Drugs, alcohol, anything to numb the pain. I wound up busking on the street and Noah found me. He let me stay here, helped me clean up, and gave me a job at the station. I broke ties with my dad and changed my last name so the family line would end with him. Revenge gave me a reason to go on. I'm going to destroy his empire and make sure he goes to jail."

My heart ached for him. He was living his life for someone else instead of living it for himself. But wasn't I doing the same?

"My last song is 'Tears in Heaven.'" It was a beautiful song about guilt and loss and regret that encapsulated the most devastating moment of my life. "I was arguing with my dad in the car right before the accident. He was so angry because I told him I was probably going to be cut from the team. He accused me of not working hard enough, of not trying hard enough, of not wanting it enough. He said I was the greatest disappointment of his life. And maybe . . ." I drew in a deep breath. "Maybe he shouldn't have adopted me."

"Jesus, Skye." His arms tightened around me.

"The thing is . . ." I struggled to put all the tangled emotions into words as eloquent as Eric Clapton's lyrics. "If I had tried harder, or if I'd been the player he wanted me to be, we wouldn't have been arguing in the car that night, and he might have seen the drunk driver cross the center line in time to avoid the collision."

"Don't do that to yourself," he said firmly. "His death is on the idiot who got into a car drunk. It's not on you. It will never be on you." He kissed my forehead. "You need a new last song."

"So do you."

"We should write our own song," he said. "Something upbeat."

"I think it should be a song that shows we learned from our experiences and can move forward unburdened by the past."

Dante gave an exasperated sigh. "I'll write the song. You can dance naked when I play it for you."

"I could dance naked for you now," I offered. "Put on some Joe Cocker." I'd never done any kind of sexy dancing for anyone, but I felt lighter after sharing my burden and I knew in my heart there was nothing I could do to screw this up. Dante accepted me with all my flaws.

Dante scrambled up the bed while I pulled on my clothes. He leaned against the headboard, gloriously naked, and folded his hands behind his head. "Dance," he demanded.

I lifted an admonishing brow. "Bossy boyfriends don't get treats."

"I'm your boyfriend." He gave a satisfied grunt.

"Yes, you are." I had to fight back a smile.

Dante licked his lips. "I'm going to get a treat."

I struck a pose, waiting for the first notes of "You Can Leave Your Hat On." "Only if you ask nicely."

His gaze darkened. "I'm your boyfriend. Boyfriends get treats."

"Yes, but you don't always get to be in control."

"Please." The word rumbled from his throat, carrying with it the promise that I wouldn't be in charge for long.

I unzipped my dress and rocked my hips in time to the music. "Good boy."

CHAPTER TWENTY-NINE

"Set Fire to the Rain" by Adele

SKYE

I was awoken the next morning by the scream of a siren and flashing red lights.

Bolting out of Dante's bed, I ran to the window. He'd left two hours earlier for his morning class, insisting I stay and sleep after our wild night together, so I knew the emergency vehicle wasn't for him. Still, my heart pounded as I pulled on my clothes and ran outside.

"Do you know this guy?" A paramedic waved me over to the back lane, where Noah was lying on a stretcher beside two turned-over recycling bins. His eyes were closed, and for a moment I thought he wasn't breathing.

"Noah Cornell. He's the station manager at WJPK radio. What happened? Is he okay?"

"He needs to take a trip to the hospital. Are you family . . . ?"

"He's my boss. I was just visiting his tenant who lives in the apartment above the garage. I'll give him a call."

"No." Noah's voice was barely a whisper. "Don't call Dante."

"He'll be worried," I said. "He would want to know."

"No." Noah shook his head again, so I let it go.

"Is there anything you need me to do before they take you to the hospital?" I asked as the paramedic hooked him up to an IV. "Do you need your phone or your wallet? Should I lock up your house?"

"Pets. Wallet. Keys."

"I'll be right back." I went in the back door and was instantly greeted by three wet noses and wagging tails. Growing up, I'd had a Border Collie named Maya who had been my constant companion until she passed away when I was thirteen, and I was able to give them the assurance they needed given all the commotion outside. I checked their food and water and grabbed Noah's belongings from the kitchen table along with the six bottles of pills on the counter in case he needed them.

By the time I was back outside, the paramedics were loading Noah into the ambulance. His eyes were half-closed, and he had a nasty gash on his forehead.

"Do you want me to come with you to the hospital?" I asked. "I can help with the insurance, call someone . . ."

Noah nodded. "Call my sister, Bella. And the pet sitter, Lisa. Where's my phone?"

"I've got it." The paramedic handed it to me as I climbed into the ambulance. "Good thing you had it on you and could call for help."

Noah gave me the code and I called his sister and pet sitter as the ambulance raced through the streets.

"My idiot brother is supposed to be resting, not taking out the trash or going to work," Bella grumbled over the phone after I told her the situation. "I told him this would happen if he pushed himself. I told him to take the treatment. But no. Stubborn ass wouldn't do it. Tell him I'll be there in a few hours."

I relayed her message and gave Noah's hand a squeeze. "What happened? Did you fall, or . . ."

"Pancreatic cancer." He swallowed hard. "It's terminal. It's getting more challenging to manage."

My breath left me in a rush. "Noah, I'm so sorry. Why didn't you say anything? We could have done more to help you. All the meetings and the running around you've had to do . . ." And then it hit me—the reason he didn't want me to call Dante.

"Dante doesn't know, does he?"

"No, and you can't tell him. He's already lost too many people."

I felt dizzy, my knees going weak, and I was glad for the bench they'd cleared for me to sit. "You can't keep this from him, Noah. He's going to wonder where you are."

"Meetings." He forced out the words as his eyes closed and his face twisted in a grimace. "Tell him I'm on a road trip."

I stared at him aghast. "I can't lie to him. Not about something like this."

"I'm going to give you something for the pain," the paramedic said to Noah. "It will knock you out for a bit. Is there anything else you need to tell her? Anyone else she needs to call?"

"Not Dante." His words faded. "Not yet."

With Noah's wallet in hand, I was able to handle the insurance and paperwork. It was clear he'd been at the hospital many times and had made an impression on the staff because so many of them came to see him while I waited for his sister to arrive.

By midafternoon, Noah had adjusted to the pain medication and was able to sit up in bed. His first words after he woke were about Dante.

"Tell me you didn't call."

"I didn't, but it's not fair to keep this from him." I had been tempted to call Dante anyway. I couldn't imagine how he would feel if he found out Noah had been there for hours and no one had called to let him know.

"He's not ready."

"No one can be ready to hear something like this, especially if it's someone they love." I had no doubt about the depth of Dante's feelings for Noah. It was clear from the way Dante talked about Noah that he was the father Dante never had.

"You don't understand," Noah said. "When I found him, he was living on the street with nothing but a piece of cardboard to sit on and his bass. I'd never met anyone so completely broken, and so alone. He was estranged from his father and grandmother, and he blamed himself for his sister's death. He was just sitting there waiting to die."

"He told me everything," I said, in case he felt he couldn't share. "Even about what his dad had done."

"Bastard didn't give a damn." Noah's face curdled. "He saw Dante fall apart and told him he was weak. It was only after Dante got his life back together and started university that his dad became interested in him again, and then only because he wanted Dante to take over the family business."

"I've never met him, and I hate him already." My hand curled into a fist. "I also hate the system that let him walk free. I'm glad you found Dante. You saved him."

"Music saved him," Noah said. "I would never have walked around that street corner but he was playing his bass and I could hear his pain—'Candle in the Wind,' 'See You Again,' 'Fire and Rain,' 'Fast Car,' 'Dog Years'—but I also heard genius. It didn't matter that it was coming from someone sitting in a filthy alley whose eyes said he was dead inside, because the music told me that there was still a tiny part of him that was fighting to survive."

That was me. After the accident. When I blamed myself for my father's death. When his last words were the embodiment of my biggest fear. When I was broken physically and emotionally and the doctors thought I would never walk, much less play ball again. But I had my mom and Jonah and Isla to pull me out of the darkness. Dante had been alone.

"I knew I had to help him," Noah continued. "Not just because his musical talent needed to be shared with the world, but because someone did the same for me." He reached for his phone and showed me a picture of an elderly man standing on a boat in the sunshine. "Dave Duncan." Noah smiled at the picture. "He was the station manager at WJPK before me."

"I saw his picture in your office."

"I put it up there after he left so I would never forget what he did for me." He tucked the phone away. "I found love when I was a young man traveling across the country with my guitar. Caroline was the most beautiful woman I'd ever seen with the most beautiful voice I'd ever heard. It was love at first sight and we went on the road together until she got pregnant. We settled down with our little boy, Knox. We had six glorious months and then . . ." He let out a ragged breath. "We lost him."

"I'm so sorry, Noah."

"She never recovered," he said. "One day I came home, and she was gone. She left a note telling me not to follow her. Every time she looked at me, she saw his face. She couldn't take the pain." A tear trickled down his cheek. "I tried to find her. Eventually, I gave up—not just the search, but everything. I was busking on a street corner when Dave found me and helped me get my life back on track, but I promised myself that one day I'd find her again. I told Dante that if he ever walked into the station and I was gone, that's where I would be—back on the road, looking for Caroline."

"That's a hard way to leave someone." I had been angry with my father, feared him, even resented him, but the shock of having him there one moment and gone the next was something I still hadn't fully come to terms with.

"Better to leave him with the knowledge that I was following my heart rather than chasing shadows to my grave."

"That's very death metal of you," I said.

Noah gave a weak laugh. "You remind me of Caroline. She loved music and people. She was curious and brave. But she couldn't find her way out of those dark places. I worry that Dante won't find his way out either. It's why I'm still here. I couldn't leave until I knew he had people to support him. But he's got friends now. And he has you."

I didn't see any point in hiding the truth since he seemed to know already. "Yes, he has me. I'm sorry if we broke any of your rules. Dante said we had to fly under the radar because you wouldn't approve, although I heard otherwise."

"I don't have rules about love," Noah said, shaking his head. "The heart wants what the heart wants. But I know why he said that, and it was for a good reason, so don't give him a hard time if it ever comes up."

"If you know he's got support, why not tell him the truth? We'll be here for him. I'll be here."

"You don't understand." He curled his fist around the bed rail. "He's got his LSAT this Friday. If he finds out I'm here, he'll come to the hospital and he'll sit on that chair and he won't get up, not even to write that test. He's been working toward that goal for three and a half years. I can't be the reason he loses his dream. I don't want him to resent me when I'm gone. I want him to have good memories to hold on to in the bad times, and there will be bad times because he wants to be a lawyer for the wrong reason. Revenge is nothing but a road to pain."

Noah's words resonated with me. I'd been on the wrong path, too. Basketball had been my father's dream, not mine. But it wasn't that easy to let go. I still kept up my training because I was afraid that if I stopped, I would have to admit I had failed my dad. Maybe it was the same for Dante. Maybe he couldn't let his law dream go because then he would have to accept his dad would go unpunished.

"I'm pretty sure he would resent you more for not letting him be here for you than he would if he missed the chance to pursue a dream that you are so sure won't make him happy."

"I know it won't make him happy." Noah drew in a shuddering breath. "He's not a lawyer, Skye. He doesn't spend his free time at legal clinics or pouring over law cases. He spends it in the studio, or with his band. Music is in his blood. It fills his soul."

"You fill his soul, too," I said. "He loves you like a father. He needs to know you're ill."

Noah tugged on the wires attached to his chest. "A better solution is to get the hell out of here and then it won't be an issue."

"Noah. You complete idiot." A short woman with flaming red hair and a bright-green coat walked into the room. "Get your hand off that wire. You're not going anywhere. I go home for a few weeks, and this is what happens. I'm not letting you out of my sight again . . ." She trailed off when she saw me and her green eyes widened. "Who's this? Your girlfriend?"

Noah threw back his head and laughed. "Christ, Bella. I know I'm hot but she's thirty years younger than me. This is Skye. She works at the station. Skye, my sister, Bella."

"You're working?" Bella's voice rose even higher. "For the love of God . . ."

"I have homework, so I'd better get going," I said, not wanting to get in the middle of their family drama. "I need to stop by Dante's place to get my stuff. I can also check on the dogs and take them for a quick walk if your pet sitter isn't still around."

"You're a saint." Noah tipped his head to the side "Please don't tell Dante about this."

I felt sick at the idea of keeping a secret from him, especially one of such magnitude. "I won't lie to him, Noah. I can try and avoid him to buy you some time, but—"

"Give me one week," Noah said. "There's stuff I need to do first, and it won't happen while I'm in a hospital bed."

"One week. And then if you don't tell him, I will."

After taking care of Noah's pets, I returned to Dante's place to get my bag. I made the bed and took a few minutes to wander around, checking out the concert posters on the wall and Noah's collection of vintage guitars. Music was everywhere, but I couldn't see even a flicker of Dante's personality reflected in the vast collection of memorabilia. Dante was a collector of experiences, not things. He felt music. He didn't need replica hells bells or shrunken Iron Maiden heads to bring it to life.

After I tidied up the bedroom, I went to his desk to find a piece of paper to write a sexy note. I was flipping through the mess when I saw my name.

For the briefest second, I hesitated. I had no desire to look at his personal papers, but I couldn't think of any reason why he would have a letter on Havencrest University letterhead with my name on it.

It only took me a few seconds to skim through the contents.

Havencrest's president had written to Dante to thank him for funding the WJPK journalism internship, and to let him know that the first recipient of his generous scholarship was me.

My breath left me in a rush, and I collapsed into the chair. I must have read it wrong. People who set up scholarships were rich. They didn't live above a rundown garage in an apartment filled with someone else's stuff. They didn't wear worn jeans and frayed T-shirts and eat pizza off paper plates.

Hands shaking, I read the letter again and again in the hopes that it wasn't really my name on the page. But no matter how many times I stared at it, my name stared right back. Bile rose in my throat and my vision blurred. My instinct had been right the day I'd packed up my bags to go home.

How could he do this to me?

Why did he lie?

My heart pounded so hard I could barely hear for the rush of blood in my ears. Noah had to be in on it, too. He'd just told me Dante had a reason for saying he wanted to keep our relationship under the radar—and that reason had to be the risk of someone finding out that the scholarship hadn't gone to the best candidate. Dante had probably agreed to fund the internship to save the station on the condition Noah hire me. Quid pro quo. But why? For an easy hookup? A challenge? Was it all just a game?

I felt utterly ridiculous, remembering my total shock when Noah had called to offer me the job after my terrible broadcast; the day I'd overheard Dante tell him he didn't want to supervise me; Dante's hot and cold, and his insistence we keep our relationship secret. Sweat beaded on my forehead and I dropped my head to my hands. Who else knew? Were the friends I'd made at the station really my friends?

Stupid. Stupid. Stupid.

My ears rang with memories of my father's words, his admonishments, his anger and disappointment. *How could you miss that shot? Why weren't you there to catch that throw? You are the greatest disappointment of my life.*

I couldn't breathe. There wasn't enough oxygen in the room. I pushed the chair back, grabbed my bag, and ran out of the apartment.

I had always felt like I didn't deserve Dante's praise—great job on the copy, excellent piece, good girl . . .

Pulse racing, caught in a spiral of panic and humiliation, I retched into the garden, bringing everything up.

I'd fallen for him, utterly and completely. I'd bought the whole damn story, but everything was a lie.

My heart splintered into a thousand pieces.

In the end, my father was right. I was never going to be good enough.

CHAPTER THIRTY

"Everybody Hurts" by R.E.M.

DANTE

I hadn't seen Skye for four days when she showed up at the station for our show. She'd called in sick for work, both at the station and at the coffee shop, and wouldn't respond to any of my messages. I'd tracked down both Haley and Isla, neither of whom had anything to say.

The sinking feeling I'd had all week got even worse when she arrived in the studio only minutes before I was about to send Nick out to find her.

"You've got three minutes," Nick said, shutting down the screens he'd used for his show. "I've put on 'City of Stars' to keep things mellow before you guys get into it. What's the topic for the day? Something juicy I hope. I was disappointed that Noah canceled your show last week."

"We're going to talk about the commercialization and authenticity of music." Skye took her seat beside me. "We can debate whether popular bands and artists have sold out their artistic integrity for the sake of commercial success."

Puzzled, I frowned. "I thought we were going to talk about punk rock."

"I thought this would be more appropriate since you are clearly the kind of person who believes in success at all costs, regardless of whether you undermine a person's competence or vision, whereas I believe in authenticity." She pulled on her headphones before I could respond, and I did the same, trying to focus through the maelstrom of emotions swirling in my brain. Skye wasn't just angry; she was furious, and I had a sneaking suspicion I knew why. Part of me had hoped she'd be happy, even grateful that I'd funded the internship, but another part of me had always known how she would feel about it, which was why I had never come clean.

After the filler song ended, I introduced the topic and turned the microphone over to Skye, who launched into the discussion without preamble.

"When a band achieves commercial success, they often have to make compromises, sacrificing their authenticity to please record labels and mainstream audiences. Some bands, however, would rather stay true to themselves and their vision. They don't believe in success at all costs."

"We can't fault musicians for wanting to reach more people," I countered, scrambling to find a way to justify my actions. "Taylor Swift reinvented her sound and became a world-famous artist. Success doesn't always equate to selling out."

"It's a betrayal." Skye slammed her fist on the desk. "True success in the music world has to be earned. It has to be authentic or you're just pretending to be someone else." For the first time since she'd entered the room, she looked directly at me. There was no warmth in her eyes. No smile on her lips. I'd betrayed her trust and had unwittingly cut deep to the heart of what she struggled with most.

"Maybe we should focus on giving people the benefit of the doubt," I offered, my voice tight. "There could be other reasons for their choices. We shouldn't assume that commercial success equates to a betrayal of their original vision."

We segued into a discussion of specific bands and the conversation became less heated and more like the usual banter that made Skye so much fun to work with. The time passed quickly and Nick opened the studio door as soon as we were off the air. "Noah wants to see you right away."

"Noah?" Skye jumped up from her seat. "What's he doing here?"

Noah waved us into his office and directed Skye to close the door. I hadn't seen him in almost a week, and I was unprepared for the drastic change in his appearance. Hollow-eyed, gaunt, pale, his cheeks sunken, Noah looked like he'd aged ten years and lost twenty pounds. The collar of his pink shirt gaped at his neck and his bolo tie hung askew. A feeling of dread crept over me and I gripped the nearest chair to steady myself.

"What the fuck happened to you?"

"Don't bother to sit down," he said, gesturing to my hand. "You're not here to chill out and relax. What the hell is going on?"

"Why are you here?" Skye demanded. "You're supposed to be—"

"Away." Noah cut her off with a glare. "Those plans changed, and thank God because I tune in to the station only to hear two people bickering under the thinly veiled cover of the most boring of musical debates."

"There was no debate," Skye said. "I found out that Dante funded the internship. I saw a letter from the university on his desk naming me as the recipient. You must have been in on it, too. I wondered why you picked me after my terrible broadcast, but now I know I got the position because Dante must have felt sorry for me. He never thought I'd make it on my own, so he likely made you hire me in exchange for donating money to the station. You didn't really me want me."

I was floored by how close she'd come to the truth, but it just proved she had the makings of a great journalist, and it was a small comfort that I had helped her on that journey.

"I recommended you to our board of directors because you were the right candidate," Noah said. "I did not know beforehand that there was anything going on between you and Dante. The board had the ultimate say and they could have refused my recommendation, but they agreed with my choice."

"He's not lying," I told her. "My grandmother left her estate to me. I wanted to help the station, so I offered to fund the internship. I did want it to go to you because I didn't want you to lose your place in the journalism program, but Noah wouldn't even let me give him your name. He said it had to be fair."

"Fair?" She gave a bitter laugh. "I would be shocked if Noah didn't figure out right away that I was the person you wanted him to hire, especially after you showed up at the station for the interviews. He would do anything for you. He loves you like a son. There is no arm he wouldn't twist. No hill he wouldn't climb. There is no fair when it comes to you."

"Skye . . ." Noah coughed, choked. He sipped some water, coughed again. Then he doubled over, coughing violently. He grabbed a tissue to cover his mouth and it came away full of blood. I couldn't move, couldn't breathe. A cold sensation skittered across my skin and my eyes fixed on the dry coffee pot beside his desk. When was the last time I'd actually seen Noah drink a cup of coffee? This wasn't a new illness. He'd been sick for a very long time.

"Should I call Bella?" Skye crouched down beside him. "Do you need to go back to the hospital?"

I had a sudden feeling that the floor wasn't stable anymore. "*Back* to the hospital?"

"He's been there all week," Skye said, handing Noah a glass of water. "Bella came to look after him."

I couldn't process what I was hearing. "How do you know?"

"I went with him in the ambulance on Monday morning."

"You took him there?" Fear found an outlet in anger and my body started to shake. "Why didn't you tell me?"

"He didn't want you to know because you have your LSAT tomorrow. He didn't want you to worry. I'm pretty sure that's why he's here and not in the hospital. He was afraid you'd wonder where he was."

I couldn't process what I was hearing. "What's wrong with you, Noah?"

"Pancreatic cancer," Noah sighed. "It's terminal. It spread everywhere. I didn't think you were ready to hear it."

Terminal.

I'm sorry, your mother didn't make it.

I'm sorry, your sister's gone.

I'm sorry, your grandmother passed away.

No. No. No. No. This wasn't happening. Not again. It was just a bad dream.

"But I could have helped you," I protested. "You didn't have to go through it alone. I could have found doctors, medicine . . ." My stomach twisted in a knot. "My inheritance. You would have had the best care. You can have the best care. I haven't finalized the other donations."

"I'm dying, Dante. Even the best care can't save me," Noah said. "There is nothing you can do, and I didn't want you to bear the burden of trying to stop the unstoppable."

The room seemed to spin, and the sound of my heartbeat thudded in my ears, loud and fast like a drum as the weight of his words sank in. Noah had been the one constant in my life, the person who believed in me when no one else did. He was my mentor, my friend, the father I'd never had. And now I was going to lose him. Just like I'd lost everyone else.

"How could you keep this from me?" I turned on Skye, finding in her worried face an outlet for my pain. "How could you sit there and talk about trust and authenticity while you were hiding a secret so huge it makes a mockery of everything you said? You know how I feel about Noah. You know I would want to help. You know about my family and how I couldn't—"

"Dante." Noah waved away the cup of water Skye was holding to his lips. "It's not her fault."

"It was her choice."

"It wasn't my choice," Skye said. "I wanted to tell you. I wanted Noah to tell you. But he wanted me to wait one week until you'd written your test and he'd handled his affairs. I had to respect his wishes. That's why I stayed away. I couldn't lie to you so I just . . . tried not to be around."

"Fuck the test," I shouted as I stumbled toward the door. "What about me? How about respecting my wishes? I thought we had something together. I thought you knew me, but you don't know me at all."

I heard a grunt, a soft thud. Behind me Skye screamed. "Call an ambulance!"

CHAPTER THIRTY-ONE

"Why Does My Heart Feel So Bad?" by Moby

SKYE

With Noah heavily sedated in the hospital, the station in chaos, and my heart in tatters, I fell back into the comfort of my old training pattern—spending at least an hour and a half every day in the gym working out, practicing on the court, and doing drills.

Pushing myself to train at the highest intensity possible meant I didn't have to think about Noah's brush with death, my fight with Dante, or even the scholarship that should have gone to someone else. I canceled the *Musical Divide* and spent only enough time at the station to meet the internship requirements. I hadn't made any headway with any of my investigations, and I began to wonder if I should turn my focus back to basketball and try out again for the DII team.

Isla tried to cheer me up with romcom nights, pints of ice cream, crazy dances, and long discussions about why she and Nick would never work, even though he'd told her he was willing to take things as slow as she needed to be comfortable. I took an extra shift at the coffee shop and gossiped with Haley about our customers, but too often I found myself looking for a glimpse of a leather jacket, or the swing of a bass.

How could I miss Dante but hate him at the same time? Some days I felt angry at him and other days I was heartbroken and missed him so badly my chest ached. I'd never cared for any of my previous boyfriends the way I cared about Dante. I'd never experienced the depth of feeling that had inspired so many breakup songs.

"Not another heartbreak playlist," Isla groaned two weeks after our on-air fight. Dante and I had never talked about a breakup, just as we'd never talked about being official, but I didn't want to see him, and it was clear he didn't want to see me.

I turned down the volume on my speaker. "This one is *Heartbreak Jazz*. It's different."

"It's depressing." She closed her textbook and tossed it to the far end of the couch. "I can't take it anymore. *Heartbreak Soul*, *Heartbreak Country*, *Heartbreak Rock*, *Heartbreak Beats*, *Heartbreak Metal*. When I asked you to move in, I thought it would be cool to have someone who knew everything about music because you would be able to pull up playlists for any vibe—studying, cooking, parties. It didn't occur to me that you would also know every breakup song ever written and play them twenty-four-seven while you pine for your lost love."

"I am not pining," I huffed. "I'm angry. I told Dante at the frat house that I didn't like things I didn't earn myself and then he went behind my back and set up the scholarship and then made sure I'd get it by showing up at the interview to help me and somehow roping in Noah. He didn't have any faith in me, and worse, he kept the secret even after we caught feelings."

"You told me you were getting good performance reviews at the radio station," she countered. "Noah gave you not one, but two different radio shows. He loved your piece on the empty buildings so much he wanted you to put it on the air. That doesn't sound like he made a mistake."

"I already told Siobhan that I'm not doing the investigative journalism show," I told her. "I don't feel like I deserve to be there, and that slot should go to someone who does. I've run out of leads on all my stories, and I'm beginning to question whether journalism really is the right path for me."

Isla let out an exasperated sigh. "What happened to the Skye who was finally embracing her passion? I think you're just afraid to face the truth."

"What truth?"

"The truth that it is easier to fall back on something that is comfortable and familiar than taking that leap into the unknown. Maybe Noah did choose you because of Dante, but it doesn't mean you won't be a good journalist. You've already proven yourself at the station with the story about the empty buildings. You're on to something with the basketball team. Your professor was encouraging about your garbage story. I've never seen you more excited about anything than when you're dragging me into back alleys to look into dumpsters or making me drink disgustingly healthy protein shakes so we can spy on hot basketball players. I don't know why you stopped believing in yourself, but are you really going to throw away your dream because you may have gotten a helping hand? Or are you that afraid of failing? Because this time, the only person who you would disappoint is you."

Isla had been harsh with me when I had sunk into a depression while healing from my injuries, but never as harsh as she was at that moment.

"You're afraid, too," I countered, bristling with indignation. "You're afraid to be with Nick."

"You're afraid because of you," she said. "I'm afraid because someone made me afraid." Her voice wavered. "And it wasn't even me he wanted. After it happened, he touched my hair and jerked back like he was in shock. He shone his phone light in my face and then he swore and said, 'You're not her.' Then he apologized over and over and said he thought I was someone else and he wanted to show her what she was missing."

My heart leaped into my throat. "Oh God, Iz. Why didn't you tell the police?"

"I did, but it didn't make a difference so I didn't tell anyone else. I was so ashamed that I couldn't fight him off, and even more ashamed I hadn't locked the door. I know it sounds crazy . . ." Her voice caught, broke. I pushed away all her books and papers and reached over to give her a hug.

"I had blocked it out," she mumbled into my shoulder. "But then I saw you being so brave after you lost your place on the team. You didn't give up. You found a new dream and threw yourself into it with all your heart. It made me think maybe I could move forward, too, but this was in the way. Now, you're afraid again and it makes me so angry because I need you to be strong. I need to see that you can come back from something bad so I know I can do it, too."

Emotion welled up in my throat and it was a long moment before I could speak again. "You're the strong one. You're the one who shook some sense into me and pulled me out of the darkness. I'm here because of you, Iz. And if I could come back, you can, too."

Later that night, I put on my headphones and tuned in to Dante's show. I knew right away it was recorded, but I didn't care. I needed to hear the strong, deep, resonant timbre of his voice like I needed to breathe. I needed his music like the blood in my veins. I needed to remember how it felt to hold him in my arms.

You are listening to DJ Dante on WJPK, the independent voice of Chicago radio. Next up is a song sure to make you forget all about winter for a while—"Born to be Wild."

I snuggled up in bed remembering the last time we were together. I closed my eyes and felt the soft press of his lips, the slow sensual knowing of my body, and the feeling of his arms around me when I shared the soundtrack of my life. I sank into memories of our secret forays, Dante holding me against his hips as we had sex against walls and doors, on dusty tables and rusty chairs. My fingertips trailed over my belly until they brushed the waistband of my pants.

We're going to spend the next hour diving deep into some metal rock mix that's perfect for late nights and broken hearts, taped Dante crooned over the radio before the first notes of Danzig's

"She Rides" filled my headphones. Slow and sexy, it is a song about a dangerous, powerful woman who embraces her wild side and is ready to take on anything despite the burden she carries.

Perfect for a little self-love. Not so perfect when I needed to get Dante off my mind. I still couldn't forgive him—not just for the betrayal or the secrets, but for not having faith in me, for making me feel that I wasn't good enough all over again.

I closed my eyes and imagined he was with me.

"Touch yourself."

My heart fluttered and I did as my imaginary Dante asked, brushing my finger over the sensitive bundle of nerves. Nice. But not as nice as his fingers, or even better, his tongue.

"Now your fingers."

DJ Dante was tormenting me now with Nine Inch Nails's "Closer," telling me through the lyrics how he wanted to feel me and drink me down. I felt like I was inside his head. I was him and I was me and we were pain and anger and longing and love.

I pushed two fingers inside me and brushed my thumb over my clit.

"Fuck yourself," imaginary Dante ordered me, his voice vibrating deep in my chest.

I teased myself the way he teased me through "I Hate Everything About You" and finally reached my peak when he played "Stairway to Heaven." And he was there with me, whispering, *"Good girl,"* as I went over.

CHAPTER THIRTY-TWO

"The Chain" by Fleetwood Mac

Dante

I hadn't been at the station for over two weeks when Siobhan finally tracked me down outside one of the lecture halls. I'd cut everything out of my life except class and visits to the hospital. Somehow, over the last few months, I'd lost sight of my goal and the lessons I'd learned over the years—that the people you love will abandon you, and if you let them in, they will hurt you in ways you could never imagine.

I couldn't get over how Skye and Noah had both betrayed me by keeping secrets. I couldn't stay angry with a dying man, but Skye had broken me. How could she be angry with me for not having faith in her when she'd done the exact same thing to me?

And yet I missed her. Her scent lingered on my pillow. Her laughter echoed in my ears. My arms ached with emptiness. I felt like someone had ripped my heart out of my body and replaced it with lead.

"Where have you been?" Siobhan accosted me in the hallway as Nick and I walked out of class. She'd clearly been waiting for me, and one glance at Nick's guilty face told me how she'd found me. Nick shot me an apologetic look and made a quick escape. "You've left me unread for two weeks."

"I'm done with the station. I need to focus on my grades."

"I'm running the station by *myself*," she spat out. "I got the board to agree to make you and me joint interim managers until Noah is back, and you haven't even bothered to show up."

"I've got a meeting with my father's lawyer in an hour, Shiv. I can't do this right now." Bob had left me a message about some paperwork that needed to be signed to close out my grandmother's estate and had insisted it couldn't be handled by the lawyer I'd hired to manage the scholarship.

I brushed past her and made my way toward the exit, but she quickly caught up to me and continued her tirade. "We all have stuff to do. This is my last year, too, and on top of keeping up with my coursework, I'm trying to run an entire radio station so they don't shut us down."

I couldn't understand why she was so upset. Siobhan had always wanted to be in charge. She wasn't a music person like Noah, but she loved the station. I loved it, too, but there was no way I could even walk through the door knowing Noah wasn't at his desk. "This is your dream come true," I said. "You've always wanted to run things. You're more than capable—"

"Shut it," she said, cutting me off. "I get that you're upset about Noah. We're all upset about Noah. But you don't get to hide away and pretend the station can run itself in his absence. Things are falling apart. There are thousands of emails in his inbox. I'm in engineering, not finance. I can fix a sound board but I can't tell the difference between a financial statement and a balance sheet."

I pushed open the door, hoping she'd take the hint, but she followed me outside into the cold. "Our ratings are falling," she continued. "Your show was our biggest draw, and now we're sinking in the charts. People are complaining about a lack of programming, the sound boards need to be replaced in both studios, and as far as I can tell there isn't enough money. It's a shitshow, Dante. I need you. The station needs you."

"I've never been a team player. You know that. If you need help, ask someone else."

Siobhan zipped up her jacket and pulled on her gloves. It was gray and bitterly cold outside, the ground covered in snow and ice, a cold wind blowing in from the lake making the minus-fifteen-degree temperature feel like minus-twenty-five.

"I thought you'd put your lonely vampire ways behind you after you started hanging out with everyone," she said. "You were helping with the interns. You took on a new show and even started a new band. I even saw you smile a few times. It scared me."

"It was all a big mistake. I lost focus, but it won't happen again." The icy wind blew through my shirt, making the hair on my arms stand up on end, but I didn't bother with my jacket. After feeling numb for the last few weeks, I welcomed the pain.

"You've got friends at the station who care, Dante. Even me." Siobhan's voice softened. "If you want a shoulder to cry on or you want to go for a drink and talk about how Noah is stuck in the eighties and how he needs to realize no one wants to see a fifty-five-year-old man in skintight black jeans, I'll be there, albeit with a string of garlic around my neck. You don't have to deal with this alone."

I couldn't imagine wanting to open up and spill out my secrets to Siobhan, but I appreciated the offer, and I gave her a nod. "Thanks, Shiv, but I don't need anyone."

"But we need you," she continued, raising her voice over the crunch of our boots on the half-shoveled pavement. "You've been at the station longer than anyone else. You understand Noah's crazy library system and why his programming choices include medieval tavern music and folktronica. WJPK is his life, Dante." Tears welled up in her eyes. "And now he's dying. Are you really going to let his dream die, too?"

Of all the people I expected to see at Bob's office when I walked into the boardroom later that afternoon, my father wasn't one of them.

"I wasn't expecting an ambush." I paused on the threshold, torn between walking away and finally putting the whole estate business to bed.

"Your father was here on another matter and when I mentioned you were coming in, he asked to see you." Bob made his way to the door. "I'll get the documents and give you two some privacy."

I hadn't seen my father since Sasha's funeral six years ago. He even hadn't bothered to pay his respects to my grandmother—his own mother. If Noah hadn't insisted I go to her funeral, she would have had no family to say goodbye.

Age hadn't been kind to my father. His thick, dark hair was almost gone, save for a smattering of gray around his temples. He'd gained weight, too, his once athletic build now overtaken by a bloated stomach. We shared no common traits except for the streak of anger that underpinned his violence and that I had channeled into revenge.

"What do you want?" I said into silence.

"We have things to discuss."

"If you're after Grandma's inheritance, I gave it all away." It felt good to stick it to the old man, to finally have hurt him in a way that I knew would matter.

"You gave some of it away for that stupid scholarship," he said. "Your lawyer hasn't had a chance yet to arrange the charitable donations you asked him to make. I asked him to hold back until after we'd had a chance to talk. He was very helpful after I paid him a visit. I made him an offer he couldn't refuse." He smiled, like it was a good thing that his success had come from threatening people and making them fear for their lives.

Damn. I should have known transferring the money out of Bob's firm wouldn't be enough. My father could get to anyone.

"Of course you did, because that's all you know. Fear and pain. If it wasn't for Mom, who taught me about love and sacrifice, trust and loyalty, I might have turned out like you."

"Jesus Christ," he spluttered. "You think you had it so bad? My father broke my arm, my nose, even my fucking leg. He beat me with a cane, strangled me unconscious, and held my head underwater until I almost drowned. But he made me a man—a man strong enough to run a multimillion-dollar business in a sea full of sharks."

"He never hit his wife." I desperately wanted to let him know

I knew what he'd done to my mother, but I wasn't an idiot. She'd found out about his criminal operation and planned to leave him and go to the police, and he'd killed her for it. I had no doubt he would do the same to me if I wasn't careful. "He didn't abandon his children. He didn't drive his daughter to suicide. He may have been abusive to you, but he was a better man because in his own twisted way, he had honor. You have nothing."

"You're a whiny bastard." He raised his hand for the dispassionate slap he'd often meted out to anyone who displeased him.

Adrenaline surged through my veins—not the fear I'd felt as a child, but the anger of a man who was more than capable of taking him down. I caught his wrist and held his hand aloft. "Don't even try it."

He wrenched his hand away, his lips twisting in a snarl. "You talk about honor, but I've had my people do some digging. I know you set up that scholarship for your girlfriend. I know the station manager was involved. I can make their lives very difficult—admissions, career, job, freedom, and finances all at risk. I don't have to tell you about the legal ramifications of what they've helped you do. I'm sure you know from your stint last summer in the DA's office." He snorted a laugh. "One word from me and your whole house of cards comes tumbling down. Your woman, that long-haired hippie you live with . . . I'll make sure they pay the price."

I was about to tell him that I'd lost Skye, I was about to lose Noah, and I didn't give a damn about what happened to me when something niggled at the back of my brain. He had threatened Noah and Skye, but he hadn't threatened me, and if anyone was going down, I was the obvious choice.

Why?

"What do you want?" My father always wanted something, and I had a feeling what he wanted was me.

"I want to know when you're going to get your damn act together and come and help me run the family business," he growled. "It's been handed down from father to son for generations. There is more money in it than you could ever spend in a lifetime. You did something right getting a finance degree, but after you graduate, you need to come the fuck home."

I almost laughed at the irony. He needed me. Despite four marriages and countless mistresses, he had no other children. I was his only heir. And damned if I wasn't going to use it against him. "I'm going to law school. I've never been interested in real estate, and it sounds like your business isn't doing so well if you're trying to get money from me."

A wary tension thickened the air as his posture shifted, turning defensive, but his shoulders retained their hostile slant. "We've expanded from real estate into the waste management business," he said. "We've won bids for commercial and residential recycling and refuse collection and processing contracts across the city. We've secured four of six residential zones, as well as the universities and colleges, and now we're looking at O'Hare Airport. Most of the contracts are only three years, so money must constantly change hands to keep us in the game, and it has to be clean."

"You need Grandma's money for bribes." A statement. Not a question. I was more surprised that he was being honest about it than that he was doing it at all.

"That's how the world works," he said. "There are a lot of palms to grease: the city's chief procurement officer, cops, on-site security, state and local officials, and now the Alpha Institute that is preparing a report on long-term city waste and recycling policy. Our competitors are complaining that we've almost got a monopoly on waste hauling in the city. We need a clean source of funding that can't be traced back to me."

"So, really, this isn't about reconciling and bringing me into the family business. You just want my money." My hand curled into a fist at my side, and I cursed in silent self-reproach. Despite everything he had done, despite my hatred of him and my determination to see him punished for his crimes, some small part of me had nurtured a tiny hope that he still wanted to be my dad.

"I need my fucking son by my side while I take the business to the next level," he shouted, spittle bubbling at the corners of his mouth. "You belong with me, not in some rundown radio station playing stupid songs. I'm done talking. You *will* come back and work in the business. You *will* transfer that money to me. If you don't, I *will* fucking destroy you and everything you love." He spoke with cold indifference, as if it didn't matter to him one way or another whether he ended the family bloodline in a sheer act of revenge.

I didn't even take a beat before I pulled open the door.

"Not if I destroy you first."

CHAPTER THIRTY-THREE

"Girl on Fire" by Alicia Keys

Skye

Exams were over. Christmas had come and gone. I'd gone back to Denver, hugged Jonah, cried in my mother's arms, and now I was back in the dreariest month of the dreariest year in the dreariest city of all. Noah was back home but not back at work. He'd finally agreed to treatment, and he'd had some good days and some bad, but overall, he seemed to be getting stronger. Bella had moved in to care for him and coordinated visits so Dante and I weren't there at the same time. I hadn't heard from Dante since the day Noah collapsed in his office. I didn't know if I ever would.

"I think Blake wants to talk to you," Haley said as she pulled down the coffee shop Christmas decorations. "He keeps walking past the shop, staring at you, and then he scurries away."

"If he wanted to talk to me, he would have done it already. I see him at the gym every day and we always say hello. I figured he had nothing else to tell me, so I moved on with the investigation. I've been reviewing all the university's audited financial statements and finance reports to see if I could find something that indicates a payout, and I've started poking around for information again to hopefully fire up the rumor mill. Ballers just love to gossip."

"Look at my girl back to doing what she does best." Haley grinned. "I like to see you back in form."

"Isla gave me a good talking-to before I went home for Christmas," I said. "It was the verbal equivalent of a slap in the face. And then I went home, and my mom and brother wanted to hear all about my investigations, and it got me excited about being a journalist all over again."

"Blake is still there," Haley said, looking out into the hallway. "He's acting like informants do in the movies. I'm just surprised he hasn't slipped you a note asking you to meet him at midnight in an underground parking garage where you'll be ambushed by two men in dark trench coats driving a black SUV who will shoot him before he can tell you what he has to say. You should probably wear a bulletproof vest in case they shoot you, too. That way, when I come looking for you and start crying because I think you're dead, you can sit up and say, 'Ow that hurt,' and I'll be so relieved I cry happy tears and then I'll hug you and we'll go home and have pizza."

Haley could always make me smile. "That was frighteningly specific."

"It was drama time at home over Christmas," she said. "Too many relatives. Too little space. I hid in the basement and binge-watched crime shows, so I know how these things go. If I don't make it as a singer, I'm going to apply to the FBI to be a criminal profiler."

"You almost passed out when I cut my finger the other day," I pointed out. "They see a lot worse than little boo-boos."

She gave a shrug. "I don't have to be in the field. I could sit at the computer, and someone could call me baby girl and make me blush."

Laughing, I looked up and caught Blake watching me. He jerked his head toward the door, indicating he wanted to meet me outside. What if Haley was right and Blake did have more information about the cover-up? Maybe he'd come here because he didn't want anyone at the gym to see us together.

"I suppose I should find out what he wants," I said, taking off my apron. "Cover for me. I want to catch him before he runs away."

I pulled on my jacket and hat and went out into the bitter cold. Blake was skulking behind some bushes near the front door—as much as a six foot six basketball player could skulk with his head poking up over the hedge.

"Oh hi," I said, pretending I hadn't seen him peering over the hedge. "I just came out for a breath of air to freeze my lungs."

Blake didn't even smile at my joke. Instead, he looked around and then pulled me into the bushes.

"What the . . . ?"

"I think you stirred something up by asking so many questions around the athletic center," he said. "Yesterday, the coaches pulled us into a meeting and told us they'd heard that people were spreading rumors about a cover-up involving a member of the team and there was nothing to them. They told us to ignore what we'd heard and focus on playing ball. But every time I turned around, they were whispering or having closed-door meetings. We didn't even have a coach at our last practice. They're running scared."

"Scared of what?"

"Of people finding out that the dude who did whatever they covered up is still around." Blake tucked his hands in his pockets. "I didn't tell you last time because I didn't want to believe it. I told myself it was probably a DUI, or a bar fight or something minor like that. There are only fifteen guys on the team, and we're close, you know. Like brothers." He drew in a ragged breath. "But then you started poking around and people started talking and the coaches started acting weird . . . I couldn't take it anymore. I had to know, so I went to talk to Dave." He hesitated. "That's not his real name."

"I remember," I assured him. "He's the football guy who hooked up with the former personal assistant to one of the basketball coaches. What did he say?"

Blake looked around and lowered his voice. "I told him I'd overheard him talking in the locker room about a cover-up on the basketball team, and I was trying to decide whether to transfer schools and I just . . . needed to know the truth. He was cool about it. Like I said before, he's a good guy and the idea that the university covered up a sexual assault—"

"Sexual assault?" My stomach tightened. I would definitely have to stop talking about the case in front of Isla. "How could they let a known rapist stay on campus? He's dangerous."

"Exactly." Blake's face tightened. "When he told me, it made my transfer decision easy. I can't play on a team knowing one of them hurt a woman and got away with it, and I can't respect an institution that would cover it up to protect their reputation. I have a little sister . . ."

"I totally understand." I was still reeling from the revelation. "Did he know the name of the baller they're protecting?"

"No. The personal assistant had signed an NDA and since she works on campus she had to be careful. She only told him what she did because she'd been seeing pictures of the bastard splashed all over the news and it pissed her off that he was about to become rich and famous when he should be in jail." Blake shuddered. "My sister wanted to come to Havencrest. I called her up right after I talked to Dave and I told her no way, but what about other people's sisters? There's a fucking rapist loose on campus—a dude I practice with every day."

"Do you have an idea who it might be?" With only fifteen players on the team, it wouldn't be hard for Blake to figure out who the university was protecting.

Blake's jaw clenched and he shook his head. "I can't go there, Skye, because if I knew for sure, I'd do something that would mean the end of my basketball career. That's why I'm coming to you."

I wanted to promise him that I'd blow this out of the water, that I'd expose the cover-up and bring the bastard down. But I couldn't do much with what he'd given me. I needed facts, evidence. I needed to get to the source. "I'm going to do everything I can to get to the truth."

"You're pretty good at this journalism thing." Blake hesitated. "We never got to have that drink . . ."

I liked Blake but there was only one guy I wanted to be with. "I'm still sort of with the guy you met in the lounge. It's . . . complicated."

"If it ever gets uncomplicated . . ."

I leaned up to kiss his cheek. "I'll let you know."

Blake may not have wanted to reveal any names, but now that I knew the personal assistant still worked on campus, it didn't take me long to search through past administrative directories for the athletic center and cross-reference them with current university admin listings. I came up with a list of five names, and all it took was another tray of coffee and a box of lemon squares to get my new friends in the athletic center admin office to confirm that Marisa Staples, now executive assistant to the chair of the Department of Rehabilitation Medicine, was the key to my investigation.

Of course, Marisa wasn't interested in talking about her time working with basketball team. She'd responded to my email inquiry with a big fat "no comment" and brushed me off when I approached her in the hallway. I'd even sent her a coupon for a free coffee and lemon square, but she never showed up.

"Why don't you wait outside her office and spill coffee on her?" Isla said, flipping over the next card for our game of Texas hold 'em. Chad, Haley, and Nick had joined us for lunch and I'd given them a brief outline of what I knew so far. I hadn't mentioned the sexual assault because I was worried about triggering Isla. The last thing she needed was to hear that there was another rapist loose on campus.

"Because that's too obvious. She'll probably get angry and then she'll never tell me what I want to know. That will be the end of my story."

"Is this for our year-end project?" Chad asked. "I've been struggling to find anything worth investigating."

"I have something else I'm working on for the year-end project," I said. "But if this turns out to be something big, I might just use it instead."

Chad rubbed his hands through his hair. "It's not fair. You get something so juicy you might have to throw coffee on someone, and I can't even find out if the gluten-free flour they use in the gluten-free pizza is safe for celiacs."

"One of my psych profs said that when you want someone to open the door, you don't break it down; you make them want to open it for you," Haley said. "Maybe there is a reason she doesn't work for the basketball coach anymore. She might want to talk but since she still works for the university, she's afraid of losing her job."

"Is that how you took all my money?" Chad asked Isla, who had cleaned him out in the first two hands. "You made me want to give it to you?"

"Chad, Chad, Chad." Isla shook her head as she threw five dollars on the table. "Don't try to blame me for your ego getting the better of you. Were you not at the bar when I hustled those guys at pool? Did you think my skills were limited to sticks and balls?"

Nick snorted a laugh as he folded. "I'm not even going to touch that one."

"Who thinks Isla's bluffing?" I studied the cards on the table. I still had some skin in the game, but Isla was a master.

"Look at this cute face." Nick rubbed his knuckles gently over Isla's cheek. "Do you really think she could hide anything from you?"

"Don't be fooled. She's trying to get us to fold." Haley folded, but I threw in my five dollars. I might have played it safe at the beginning of the year, but now I wasn't afraid to take a risk. "I'll see you . . ." I trailed off as an idea took root in my mind. "What if I bluffed and told people I had enough evidence to run my story?"

"I thought you didn't have any evidence," Isla said, fanning out her hand of nothingness for everyone to see.

I'd never beat Isla before, so I made a big show of scooping up the money. "And you didn't have anything in your hand, but I paid to see you anyway."

"Won't you get in trouble if you go around saying stuff that isn't true?" Nick asked. "How bad is the thing the baller did? Is it a crime?"

"Yes."

"Then shouldn't you just go to the police?"

"I have no proof," I said. "I have a guy who said he talked to another guy who said he talked to a girl who said she knew something. Not much to go on. And the university has already covered it up. That means they've buried the evidence."

"I'm beginning to think my gluten flour story isn't so bad," Chad mused. "It's low risk, easy to investigate, and yet it could save lives."

"Maybe I tell Blake I'm planning to run the story and he 'misunderstands.'" I punctuated the last word with finger quotes as I put the pieces together. "He tells someone I've got the evidence and that person tells someone else, and soon the people who are the most worried will crawl out of the woodwork and expose themselves to try and stop me from going public. I don't have to spill coffee on anyone or hunt them down. They'll come to me."

"Sounds dangerous," Isla said. "What if they threaten you? Or worse?"

"They can't risk doing anything until they know what evidence I have and who I've told."

"I don't like it." Nick folded his arms. "What if they break into your apartment looking for evidence like they do in crime shows? You and Isla aren't safe. I've got a friend in engineering who used to be a locksmith. I'm going to bring him by your place to check your doors and windows." He pulled out his phone and stepped away to make the call.

"What the hell was that?" I asked Isla.

"I told Nick everything," she whispered. "I wanted him to know why I couldn't get into a relationship with him, even though we really click."

"That was very brave." I squeezed her hand. "How did he take it?"

Isla's eyes watered even as her lips quivered with a smile. "He was furious. I'd never seen that side of him. We were in the food court, and he threw his tray on the ground. He couldn't believe the police hadn't caught the guy. He wanted to go down to the police station right then and demand they reopen the investigation."

"He's protective of you," I said. "Not that I'm condoning violence toward plastic trays, but it was kind of sweet."

"Now, he waits for me after my night class to walk me home, and when I'm studying late at the library, he shows up with a pizza picnic. Next week, after I get back from visiting my parents, he's taking me to learn Krav Maga. He said he's in no rush and he's happy to be friends for as long as it takes. He said I'm worth waiting for."

"Oh, Iz." I was happy for her. She deserved someone as kind and thoughtful as Nick. She deserved to be someone's everything. I just wished I could be someone's everything, too.

CHAPTER THIRTY-FOUR

"I Melt with You" by Modern English

Dante

James Dunn from the university's legal department didn't look much older than me, despite the sweater vest he wore over his rumpled blue shirt, and the thick black glasses he put on to read the list of famous WJPK alumni posted beside the station's front door.

"Thanks for meeting with me," he said, shaking my hand. "I know this must be a difficult time for you and everyone at the station with Noah ill and—"

"I didn't have a choice." After the guilt trip Siobhan had laid on me before Christmas, and with Noah home and feeling well enough to guilt me into helping Siobhan run the station, I had reluctantly agreed to meet with James after he'd sent a message about an urgent legal matter.

"Should we go to your office?" He gestured awkwardly down the hallway.

I took a step forward and my body seized. It had taken all my willpower to walk through the door, but I couldn't go any farther. There was no way I could sit in Noah's office if he wasn't there. I'd lost too many people I cared about. I couldn't handle the stark reminder that I might just lose another.

"Let's grab a coffee upstairs." I led James up to the food court and we ordered our drinks.

"I actually just came for quick chat," James said after we'd found a quiet table in the corner. "The university wanted me to pass on the message that they don't want you to run the story."

"What story? We have an extensive programming schedule. You'll need to be more specific." I silently cursed Siobhan for not giving me a heads-up about what was going on.

"The story about the men's basketball team."

"I don't know anything about it. If you'll excuse me for a moment, I'll touch base with Siobhan." I stepped away and sent a quick message. Siobhan replied right away saying that Chad had mentioned that Skye was investigating a possible cover-up involving someone on the team.

It didn't take me long to put the pieces together. Skye was clearly on to something, and the legal team was worried enough to send James to pre-empt a possible broadcast. Damn, she was good.

"I'm up to speed," I said, taking my seat. "What exactly is your concern?"

James sighed. "Are we really going to play this game?"

"Why don't you call it what it really is? A fishing expedition." I sipped my bland coffee, wishing I'd suggested Buttercup instead. It had been too long since I'd seen Skye and she could have shed some light on the story. "You want to know what we know."

His jaw tightened. "It doesn't matter what you know. What matters is that WJPK leases space on university property and is an integral part of the university community. That means we all need to be on the same page when it comes to anything that may impact the university's reputation."

I leaned back in my chair and imagined myself ten years from now in James's place. Is that what lay in store for me after I'd put my father away? Sweater vests and rumpled shirts and veiled threats to college radio station volunteers?

"Are you trying to curtail the freedom of the press?" I asked. "It's in the community's interest to know when someone is doing something that is illegal, unethical, or questionable when it comes to societal values. That's why we're here. That is the beauty of independent radio. We are not beholden to advertisers, which puts us in the unique position of being able to ensure those truths come to light."

James lifted an admonishing brow. "Are you seriously going to put the station at risk for something that happened over two years ago? Maybe you should talk to Noah." His voice took on a condescending tone. "I know you're just a student and you're filling this role on an interim basis, but this is a very serious matter—"

"Oh, I understand it's serious." I leaned forward, giving him my full attention. "Honestly, I wasn't sure the story had teeth. But now I know it's worth pursuing."

"I haven't said anything," James said, scrambling. "I just came here to raise a concern."

"And I heard you." I held out my hand for a goodbye shake. "I'll pass the message on to Noah, but you should know that he feels the same way I do about the purpose of independent radio and freedom of press. If he were here, you wouldn't have even had the courtesy of a handshake."

I texted Skye as soon as he was gone. *I need to see you.*

"What are you doing at a rival coffee shop?" Skye's voice pulled me out of the coursework I'd tried to lose myself in while waiting for her to show up. It seemed like forever since I'd seen her, and I took a moment to drink her in. Her hair was loose, falling in dark waves across her shoulders, and her red sweater clung to her curves. She was beautiful. Seriously beautiful. Inside and out.

"I couldn't be in the station."

Her dark eyes softened with understanding and she took the seat across from me. "You said you needed to see me."

I needed to see her like I needed to breathe. The story was just an excuse. But I didn't know how we stood, and part of me was still hurt from her betrayal. "What the hell is going on with this basketball story?"

She startled and I realized my words had come out harsher than I'd intended. "I'm sorry." And once I'd said the words, the rest was easy. "I'm sorry about not telling you about the scholarship. I didn't mean to make you feel less capable. I didn't want the money and Noah wouldn't take it, and I knew you needed it. I also knew you wouldn't take it as a gift so I set up the scholarship hoping I could help you and other people like you in the future. I'll admit there may have been some self-interest on my part, but as Noah said, he insisted that the selection had to be fair. Maybe he figured it out, but he would never have compromised the integrity of the station by hiring someone he didn't think was capable of the job. You are an amazing woman and you've been an incredible asset to the station. No one would refute that."

There was a maelstrom of emotion behind her dark, quiet eyes, and for a heartbeat I thought my apology might not be enough.

"You grovel pretty well." Her lips quivered with a smile. "I like the 'amazing woman' part. Next time you should lead with that."

I reached over and cupped her cheek, the simple touch melting something inside me. "Will there be a next time?"

"If you accept my apology, too." She turned her face to kiss my palm. "I'm sorry I didn't tell you about Noah. He put me in a terrible position when he asked me not to tell you. He was worried you wouldn't write your LSAT and he didn't want you to resent him if it meant you couldn't follow your dream. I did it under protest."

I moved my chair beside her and kissed her long, slow, and deep, feeling that connection between us snap into place.

"I missed you," she murmured against my lips.

"I missed you, too. I'd suggest we take this down to our favorite basement storage room, but I didn't just ask you to see me to apologize. I had a visit from the legal department about your story."

"No way." Skye pulled back, her eyes sparkling. "It worked!"

"What worked?"

Skye told me about her meeting with Blake and her plan to bluff the administration into showing their hand. "I figured if there really was something to the story, they would be afraid of it getting out, and come to me."

"They came to me instead," I said. "They think we're planning to break it on the air."

"I wish we could." Skye sighed. "I still can't substantiate anything, and even if I could, I would send it to the *Havencrest Express* first because it would have the most impact."

"I'll pretend that didn't hurt on behalf of all our news broadcasters."

Skye laughed. "Did you get any information from the legal guy?"

"Nothing except he said it happened two years ago, and it was serious enough that he was there to make veiled threats. I didn't give in."

"Very impressive." She leaned up to brush her lips over mine. "Maybe you should give up law and become a journalist."

"That would make Noah happy—the giving up the law part. Although he has supported me every step of the way, he's never held back his views on my decision not to pursue my music."

"He just wants you to be happy."

I wrapped my arms around her and pulled her close. "I'm happy now."

CHAPTER THIRTY-FIVE

"Pompeii" by Bastille

SKYE

I went straight to the gym after my shift at the radio station the next day with my heart lighter after reconnecting with Dante. I was still buzzing with the thrill of knowing there was something big behind the story Blake had shared with me. Isla had left that morning on a field trip to see a chemical spill in New York, but I'd sent her multiple messages and received a wide variety of emojis in response.

"Hey, Skye." Ethan folded his lanky frame onto a nearby weight bench as I did my hammer curls. He was wearing a Havencrest Warriors T-shirt that hugged his muscular body like a glove. "I see you training here every day now. I hope that means you're planning to give up journalism and come back to playing ball. You were a great player. I think the team made a mistake not giving you another chance."

"Uh . . . thanks, Ethan." I wasn't sure what that was all about. I hadn't seen him since I'd blown him off at the bar when Dante had made mincemeat of three guys without breaking a sweat.

"I could put a good word in for you for next season," he said. "And I'm always here to help out if you need a practice buddy."

I put my weights back on the rack. "Thanks."

"Anything for a friend." He flashed his panty-melting smile. "I just want you to know I'm not the same guy from when we first knew each other."

"I believe you." He seemed almost desperate for assurance, and

I hadn't seen anything that would make me think otherwise. "You seemed different when we met at the hot dog stand, and I appreciated you coming out to help that night at the bar."

He let out a breath that almost seemed like relief. "That's what I'm talking about. I'm a good guy. I was going through some stuff that year, but I got myself sorted out."

"I'm glad to hear it, Ethan." I picked up another set of weights, hoping that he'd take the hint that I wanted to focus on my workout.

"Maybe we could go out for a drink sometime," he said. "You'll see I really have changed."

"I'm seeing someone." My heart gave a happy little jump. "But there are two soccer players on the mats who I'm pretty sure would be interested in a drink with the great Ethan Williams."

His gaze flicked to the stretching area and he smiled. "Thanks, Skye. And thanks for understanding. Friends?" He held out his fist and I bumped him.

"Of course. Friends."

Ethan made his way over to chat up his admirers. I finished my workout and quickly changed. Dante was meeting me after his class, and we were going to pick up some burgers and head back to his place to join Noah and Bella for dinner.

I had just left the locker room when Michael Sunderland, the men's head basketball coach, flagged me down. He'd been head coach of Havenhurst's men's basketball team for fifteen years and had five national titles under his belt. "Skye. I was waiting for you. Do you have a few minutes to chat in private?"

I'd never had a conversation with Michael. He was college basketball royalty. I couldn't imagine what he wanted to chat about unless my plan to flush out the cover-up story had worked too well.

"Um . . . sure." I sent a quick message to Dante to let him know I might be late, and then followed Michael down the hallway.

"We can talk in here." Michael opened the door to one of the sports meeting rooms, where five men in dark suits sat around a large table.

"Am I in some kind of trouble?" I gave a wary laugh, standing half in and half out of the open door.

"No. Not at all." Michael gestured to an empty seat. "We just want to talk about an amazing opportunity for you."

I was getting a bad vibe about the meeting, mainly because of the number of people in suits and that fact that no one was smiling about the "amazing opportunity."

"Is this going to take long?" I asked. "I was supposed to meet a friend after my workout and if I'm going to be late, I need to let him know."

Michael shrugged. "We need about half an hour of your time."

I sent a quick text to Dante to update him, and then turned on the app I used to record my lectures. Although it was illegal to record a conversation in Illinois without the consent of both parties, my gut was telling me to do it, even if the only person who heard it was me. By the time I was seated at the table, another suit had joined the meeting.

Michael introduced the people in the room: two lawyers plus representatives from the university president's office, public relations team, and conduct board.

Smiles. Waves. "Nice to meet yous,"s and a casual, "Dev from legal has an NDA we need you to sign."

Uh-uh. Nope. I'd learned in my journalism classes that we should be wary of signing NDAs. "I can give you a pinky promise," I said, crossing my fingers behind my back, "but I'm not signing any legal documents without a lawyer." I was pretty sure it wasn't easy to juggle schedules to get so many suits around a table at once, so I moved to stand, calling their bluff.

The lawyers huddled. Nodded. Dev took back his NDA. I called it a win for Journalism Law 201.

"So, what is the amazing opportunity?" I decided to take charge since I was already tired of being in the dark.

"We'd like to offer you a guaranteed place on the women's basketball team for next season," Michael said. "We'll send you to a training camp over the summer to get your skills back up to where they were when you first joined the Warriors, private coaching during the season, guaranteed playtime during games, and you'll have our focused efforts to get you picked in the draft. This isn't an offer without teeth."

Whoa. I felt like the floor had dropped out from under me. Everything I had ever wanted handed to me on a silver platter. It was almost too good to be true.

"We have a contract prepared." Dev slid another document across the table, along with a pen. "You can sign it now, but I do have to recommend you get independent legal advice."

One of the suits glared at Dev and then shifted his gaze to Michael, making some kind of silent entreaty.

"We've never made this kind of offer before," Michael said quickly. "But we've seen you training here every day and we don't want to lose someone with your skills and that kind of dedication. I had to do a lot of convincing to get everyone to sign off. If I were you, I'd lock that down before someone changes their mind."

There was a curious, almost desperate, vibe in the room that made my skin tingle. I studied all the people at the table, trying to figure out what was really going on. First the lawyer talking to Dante, then Ethan acting odd, and now Michael and his amazing opportunity . . .

Blake tells someone I've got the evidence to run a story and that person tells someone else and soon the people who are the most worried will crawl out of the woodwork . . .

It had gone exactly as I'd planned.

"What's this really about?" I leaned back and folded my arms the way Isla did when she was bluffing. "There is no way you're that desperate to have me back, considering I failed the tryout, I've got a wonky leg, and you've got hundreds of young aspiring basketball players out there just waiting for their shot."

A few sideways glances. Shifting in seats. Someone drummed a thumb on the table.

"We understand you've been looking into rumors that may involve one of the players on the men's basketball team," Michael said. "We're concerned that you may have been misled or that you may release unsubstantiated information that could damage his reputation or indeed the reputation of the team or even the university. We just want to make sure we're all on the same page."

My offer wasn't an offer. It was a bribe. They didn't need my skills. They needed my silence. If I signed the contract, I would be part of the team again and with that came an NDA that would prevent me from speaking up. The lawyers had just taken a gamble that I'd sign on the dotted line and the NDA Dev had given me earlier wouldn't be necessary. They'd also taken a gamble by throwing an "amazing opportunity" at me to stop me from releasing "unsubstantiated information," which suggested that the information they believed I had was most likely true. Otherwise, why we were all here? And who was this about? They assumed I already knew.

And I did. I could feel it in my gut.

No wonder Ethan was so desperate to be friends.

"If I accept your offer, what happens to Ethan?" I asked, taking a calculated risk. "Does he just get away with it? No repercussions?" I'd played a lot of poker with Mom and Jonah during my recovery, but no one had taught me more about bluffing than Isla.

"Who said anything about Ethan?" Dev asked.

"I was just talking to him in the gym. He wanted my assurance that we would still be friends." It was a less-than-subtle attempt to suggest Ethan had tipped his hand, but Michael took the bait.

"Ethan's a good guy who got in a bad situation and just made some poor choices," Michael said. "He's got a bright future ahead of him. He doesn't deserve to lose a chance at a successful NBA career because of a fifteen-minute mistake two years ago."

"Michael." Dev shook his head, attempting to cut Michael off, but it was too late. I had my confirmation.

Fifteen minutes. Two years ago. Something was niggling at the back of my mind and it was becoming difficult to breathe.

"Ethan did the right thing and reported it to us right away," Michael continued, seemingly oblivious to the consternation of Dev and his legal buddy whose sole function seemed to be writing everything down on his legal pad. "We had a long talk and he understood that kind of thing could never happen again. He made some promises, and he's kept them—no drinking, no drugs, no dating, low profile—so I think on that front nothing else needs to be done."

My brain was putting the pieces together and the picture that was forming was making my heart hurt. I tried to take a deep breath, but my lungs were seizing up and my vision was blurring and my ears were filled with white noise.

"Skye?" Michael's voice seemed far away. "Are you okay?"

I dug my nails into my leg and the jolt of pain pulled me back into the room. "He raped someone," I said bluntly. "How could you possibly think nothing else needs to be done?"

"No one said anything about rape," Dev interjected, trying to shut down the runaway train. "There have been no allegations, no accusations, no charges, no witnesses, no proof . . ."

Marisa Staples likely had proof. She'd been working for Michael when this whole thing went down. I would have to find a way to convince her to talk.

"That's right," Michael said. "It was just a fumble in the da—" He cut himself off at the warning hiss from Dev.

"Well, I guess that's it." Michael pushed the document across the table as if I were all ready to jump on the "amazing opportunity" to play basketball for a university that had covered up a sexual assault. "Once you sign, we'll need one more thing from you to make this official. You've stirred up some bad rumors with all your questions and we need Ethan going into the draft with a squeaky-clean image, and that includes him being in a stable, happy relationship. We thought you, being the daughter of an NBA player, would be excellent PR."

"You want me to go out with Ethan?" I asked, incredulous. "The rapist?"

"Maybe let's not use that word," Michael said. "It's got some bad connotations—"

"You don't say."

"It would just be for show," the PR dude said, piping up for the first time. "We'd plant a few stories, spread some rumors, get a few pictures of the two of you together . . . that kind of thing. After the draft, you can go your separate ways. We're just asking you to play your part."

"If it's a safety issue, let me assure you there is nothing for you to worry about," Michael said. "He was young and he'd been drinking, and he thought he was with his girlfriend—"

"Michael." Dev shook his head in warning, but Michael waved a dismissive hand. "I'm an up-front guy and it's better if she knows the truth than the false information she was going to spread." Turning back to me, he said, "It was a case of mistaken identity, and he's had to live with the guilt for the last two years. He's worked hard to get to where he is. We don't want a little thing like this to derail what promises to be a very successful career."

Dev's legal buddy leaned over and whispered something in his ear but I wasn't listening. I wasn't breathing. I wasn't moving. *A case of mistaken identity.* The final piece of the puzzle slipped into place.

"You're not her."

My ears rang. The room dimmed. Bile rose in my throat. I doubled over in my chair and tried not to throw up all over the floor.

"You're not her."

No. Isla wasn't me. But we'd shared a room two years ago in the freshman dorm. I'd gone away for the weekend a few days after I'd turned Ethan down for the third time that month. He'd been angry. No one had ever turned him down before. I never imagined he'd break into our dorm room intending to sexually assault me and assault my beautiful Isla instead.

"I need to leave." My eyes watered and I grabbed my phone and the contract off the table. "It's a lot to think about and I need to get some legal advice."

I needed more than legal advice. I needed all the advices. What was I going to say to Isla? How was I going to tell her without breaking her all over again? Did I go to the police? Did I tell my friends? Should I call my mom? Where should I go?

I ran out of the building, tears streaming down my face, until I hit something solid and warm. Strong arms wrapped around me, and I breathed in Dante's familiar scent.

"I'm here, Skye." He hugged me tight. "I came as fast as I could. Who do I need to kill?"

CHAPTER THIRTY-SIX

"Perfect" by Ed Sheeran

DANTE

I knew this feeling. It was part of me, written into the fabric of my being with the blood of the people I'd loved and lost. It was in the round scars that marked my skin and the cracked bones that had never healed quite right. It was in the tears that had coursed down my cheeks as I sat beside Noah's bed and in the ache that had seized my heart in the time Skye and I had been apart.

Helpless.

All I could do was hold her. I couldn't make her pain go away.

"I'll kill him," I said again, tucking her against my side. We'd dropped off dinner for Noah and Bella and then come straight to my place, where I'd been holding Skye on the couch for the better part of an hour. "Or I can arrange for it to happen. I'm pretty sure my father knows a guy."

"I don't care about Ethan." Skye looked up, her lashes still wet with tears. "I care about Isla. I don't want her to have re-live the nightmare all over again."

"You can't take that choice from her."

"What if I sent an anonymous tip to the police? They'd have to investigate him. They should still have the DNA samples . . ." She swallowed hard. "He thought it was me, Dante. He wanted to 'show me what I was missing.' He must have told Michael he was drunk and played it down, but he had to get through the main door and then find our room, which suggests he knew what he was doing."

I hugged her tight and tried to process what she was saying. How did a person deal with that kind of revelation? It was big—much bigger than classes or grades or even our fight.

"Why waste money hiring a guy when I can do it myself?" I mused. "I'll pick a fight with him. Pretend it was an accident. Claim self-defense . . . At worst, I'll go down for manslaughter and I'll be out in five years, maybe less if I get time off for good behavior."

Skye punched me lightly in the arm, but at least I got the glimmer of a smile. "You're not going to jail for me."

"I can't think of a better cause."

"There is more at stake here than just one man. The university is willing to cover up a serious sexual assault on campus to save their reputation. They've put women at risk. They've denied Isla the justice she deserves. They must be called to account."

"If you turn down the offer and expose them, it will be the true end of your basketball career," I pointed out. "The end of your dream. You'll never play here or anywhere else. You might not even be able to stay at Havencrest."

"It was my father's dream." She met my gaze, her eyes still swollen with tears. "And I lived it for him because I was afraid he wouldn't love me and that he'd send me away. But I have a new dream now, and no one can take it from me. I have never felt more alive than when I was investigating this story. I can make a difference in the world as a journalist. I can give Isla the justice she never had and hopefully others, too."

"Are you going to call her tonight?"

"She's back in two days. I think it's something I need to do in person."

"I love you." I said it not just because I wanted her to hear it, but because it needed to be said. "You are the strongest person I've ever met. You are brave, smart, fierce, and loyal, and the only person who has ever truly seen me. You are the person I would always choose to have my back. You are best song in the playlist of my life."

Silence. For a heartbeat I thought I'd said too much, but then her eyes softened, and she kissed me gently on the lips. "I love you, too. You are the most amazing man I've ever met."

I chuckled and pulled her into my arms. "You don't know how long I've been waiting to hear that, but you might not think I'm so amazing when I tell you that I've put you at risk. My father found out about the scholarship and threatened to expose us if I don't give him my inheritance and join his company. He's moved into waste management and needs money for bribes."

"Don't give in to his threats because of me," she said. "I can take care of myself, and this time you'd better believe it."

"I'd give it all to keep you safe." I pulled her into a straddle across my lap and nuzzled her neck, breathing in her scent of lavender and vanilla and crisp winter air. "Are you still angry with me?"

"After those beautiful words? No. Are you angry with me?" She peppered little kisses along my jaw.

"I was never angry with you. I was angry with myself for not putting all the pieces together and realizing Noah was ill." I pulled her closer. I was so hard, and it had been so long . . .

"Is this the part where we get to have make-up sex to the apology playlist you told me about when we first met?" She rubbed her palm over my cock, making me groan.

"This the part where we have make-up sex to all my apology playlists," I said. "I hope you don't have any plans tonight."

Skye's phone woke us the next morning after a wild and crazy night.

"Who is calling you this early?" I pulled her into my arms, ready to resume where we'd left off only a few hours ago. "Haven't they heard of messaging?"

"It's ten A.M.," she said, reaching for her phone. "And some people still prefer to talk."

"Tell whoever it is that you're busy being pleasured by a sex god." I cupped her lush breasts and squeezed them in my palms.

"Down, boy." She slapped at my hands. "I need to take this call."

With a grumble, I released her and then pressed kisses to her nape while she talked on the phone.

"It was Michael, the men's basketball coach," she said, after she was done. "I don't know how he got my number, but he wanted to know if I'd gotten my legal advice yet. It hasn't even been twenty-four hours. If I wasn't waiting to talk to Isla first, I would have been even more determined to write my story because he's clearly worried. I just don't want to put her through any more trauma."

I leaned over and kissed her. "What could we do to distract you until Isla gets back?"

"Hmmm." Her lips quivered with a smile. "I can't think of anything."

I slid a finger through her slick folds. "You're very wet. It feels like you're already thinking of something."

"You say the nicest things."

"You're supposed to say them back," I murmured. "You're supposed to tell me I was amazing in bed, the best you ever had, the sex was mind-blowing. That kind of thing. Nice words mean free legal advice."

"Everything you just said is true." Her back arched with pleasure as I pushed two fingers deep inside her hot, wet heat. "You've ruined me for other men."

"Fuck, that's hot." I gently withdrew my fingers. "Stay right there. I need you on top of me."

"As if I could move." She lay languid on the bed, watching as I grabbed a condom and rolled it on. Moments later I was back on the bed and pulling her into a straddle on top of me. I'd fantasized about having Skye like this so many times, it was yet another dream come true.

"Ride me, baby. I want to watch you come all over my cock."

"We need music." She reached for her phone. "I think this position calls for a little 'Mustang Sally.'"

"A little energetic for ten A.M., don't you think?"

"If you can't keep up . . ." She leaned over, crushing her breasts against my chest. So hot. So sexy. So utterly addictive. I kissed her lips, the dimple in her cheek, the hollow at the base of her throat. She groaned and dug her fingers into my pecs, a delicious pleasure pain that almost sent me over the edge.

"Where's the riding, Sally?" I gripped her hips and lifted her over my cock.

"Are you trying to turn me on with this primitive display of strength?" She slammed down so hard, I let out a guttural groan of pure pleasure.

"I'll do anything for you."

A sly smile spread across her face. "Make me come."

Holding her hips, I pushed into her, fast and deep. Skye responded by grinding against me. God, she felt good. I could feel her flexing around me, the downward tilt of her hips a perfect match for my upward thrusts. We fell into a steady rhythm that had the headboard thumping against the wall.

"That's it, baby." I teased her, spreading her moisture around her clit but not touching, sliding my fingers down and then up again until her body was shaking, and she was panting for release. When I couldn't take it any longer, I pulled out and slammed into her, over and over, my fingers digging into her hip to hold her in place. I felt her legs quiver as she approached the edge and slid my fingers over her clit. She climaxed with a sharp intake of breath, her inner walls clamping down on me so hard, I came in a rush.

Skye collapsed on top of me, and I wrapped my arms around her, holding her tight against my chest. "I still can't get used to having sex in a bed," she murmured into my neck. "It's all very tame."

"You just rode the Mustang," I grumbled. "What's tame about that?"

"Do you know what I need?" She wiggled on top of me as she reached for her phone.

My eyes watered at the painful pleasure. "Give me a few minutes. Your Mustang needs a rest."

"I should have known that's what would happen if I went for an old edition."

I heard the first few notes of ZZ Top's "Bad Girl" and a smile spread across my face. "Are you a bad girl, Skye?"

"Very bad." Skye laughed and eased herself down between my legs. "I hope you can keep up."

CHAPTER THIRTY-SEVEN

"Believer" by Imagine Dragons

SKYE

Isla took the news better than I expected. She was more angry than shocked, and sickened that I had been Ethan's real target.

"I am so sorry, Iz," I said after I'd told her about Ethan and the meeting and the team's ridiculous attempt to buy me off. "I never imagined he would do something like this. I wish—"

"Don't even go there," she said, holding up a hand. "It's not your fault. Ethan is responsible. The university covered it up. All I want from you is a promise that they'll pay for what they did."

"It's possible your name might come out even if it's kept confidential," I warned.

"If that's what it takes to put him behind bars, then I don't care who knows," she said. "I'm tired of hiding in the shadows. I'm tired of being afraid. And I'm sick that the university let him walk around campus, putting other women at risk. Write the story, Skye. Give me justice. Do what you do best."

I wrote the story.

Isla and Dante checked it over for me before I submitted it to Professor Stanton, who was also the editor in chief of the *Havencrest Express*. Two days later, he called me into his office.

"You did excellent work," Professor Stanton said after I'd settled in the chair across from his desk. "This is an incredible article with far-reaching repercussions for the university. I think you've got a real talent for investigative journalism." He hesitated, sighed. "I just wish we could publish it."

My breath left me in a rush. "I don't understand. You just said it was good."

"It is good. This is the level of reporting I would expect to see from a journalist out in the field. But the university administration wants it buried."

"But you're a journalist," I protested. "You can't be complicit in the cover-up. This goes against everything you teach."

"I *was* a journalist." His shoulders sagged. "Now I'm a professor whose tenure is contingent on towing the party line. The administration suspected you were going to write the story and came to me in advance with a warning. They made it clear that if I sign off or help you get it published, my tenure will be at risk. I have a mortgage and children who are going to college. I can't throw my career away, no matter how good the cause."

I couldn't move, couldn't breathe. This wasn't just about the cover-up. It was about Isla and how she'd suffered. It was about justice for survivors. It was about all the women who'd been afraid to speak their truth. It was about me.

"A rapist is loose on campus," I said. "Other women are at risk."

"I am assured that the basketball player in question understands that one more slip and his career in basketball is over."

Never in my life had I felt such rage. "It was a rape. Not a slip. Not an incident. Not a mistake. I used pseudonyms in my story to protect my sources, but I will tell you that I know the survivor. She's my friend, and I have witnessed firsthand the devastating effect of his actions. You can't do this."

He opened his hands in a helpless gesture. "They have me over a barrel, Skye. I don't have a choice. These are the kind of real-life issues you're going to face if you pursue this career. Sometimes the best stories never see the light of day. Sometimes justice is never served."

"Do the other members of the journalism department know what a hypocrite you are?" I couldn't believe the words coming out of my own mouth. I was the girl who had spent her life hiding her passion to make her father happy. I was the girl who was afraid to step out of line in case I was sent away. I was the girl who didn't make waves.

But I wasn't that girl anymore. I'd survived a car crash. I'd lost my dream and reinvented myself. I'd done things in the last few months I'd never have imagined doing—breaking into buildings, talking live on-air, holding my own in meeting full of suits, having sex in public spaces, falling in love. I was stronger, braver, bolder than I had ever been before.

Professor Stanton bristled. "They know how the world works. They know that idealism often buckles under the weight of survival. The men's basketball team brings a huge amount of money to the university. Not only that, but the boy's father is also a major donor and has considerable political influence in the city. Even if your friend goes to the police, I would be surprised if he got anything more than a slap on the wrist."

"I believed in you." I grabbed my bag and made my way to the door. "I thought you stood for something greater."

"I believe in passing the torch," Professor Stanton said. "I was on the board that had final approval of your internship. Noah gave us three names, but you were his top choice and after reading your application, and his notes from the interview, I fully agreed with his recommendation. You are a survivor, Skye. You've been through more in your short years on this earth than many people endure in a lifetime, and it has only made you stronger. There is more than one way of getting a story out, and if anyone can bring this injustice to light, it's you."

I called an impromptu meeting of my WJPK friends in the student lounge later that afternoon. Nick and Isla were on one of the worn red couches. Chad and Haley had pulled up two wooden chairs. Siobhan was sitting beside Derek on a bench. Dante was leaning against the wall, looking very Kurt Cobain in his ripped jeans, graphic tee, and black-and-white Chuck Taylors.

After Isla shared her story and everyone had time to process and hug her, and stop Nick from destroying the furniture, I told them about the investigation and the meeting at the athletic center. I also told them about the university's interference and Professor Stanton's remarks. And then I told them my plan.

"I want to record the story and break it on the air," I said. "I thought about going to the press, but Dante pointed out that I would lose control of the narrative. They would focus on the NBA angle, which would sell more online subscriptions. But my concern is the university cover-up, which has wider implications for the student body. We're telling you about it because it could have serious repercussions for the station, and we wanted to get your views."

"Did you talk to Noah?" Siobhan asked. "This would be the station's biggest story, at least since I've been around."

"Dante talked to him earlier this afternoon and he said this was exactly what indie radio is all about." Dante had been uncharacteristically quiet since he'd gone to talk to Noah about my plan and I'd had a niggle of worry that Noah wasn't doing as well as we'd hoped.

"How do you feel about it?" Haley asked Isla. "The most important thing is that you get justice."

"I'll go to the police tomorrow after the story goes live," Isla said. "I didn't go earlier this week because I didn't want to take the risk that they would make Skye shut down her investigation. Once the story is out there, it will be more difficult to cover anything up. Best-case scenario, Ethan will face criminal charges and the university will be exposed, which will hopefully force them to change their policy with respect to sexual assaults on campus."

"That's the bravest thing I've ever heard," Chad said. "I'm all in. Whatever you need. If you need a face for the station when the television crews roll in, I'm your man." He smiled wide, showing his pearly-white teeth. "New veneers."

"I'm in, too," Haley said. "For Isla and for making the campus a safer place."

We didn't have to ask about Nick. He hadn't left Isla's side since she'd told him about Ethan. He'd slept on our couch, walked her to and from class, and made sure she was never alone.

"I'm in," Siobhan said. "Especially if it's got Noah's stamp of approval. Why don't you come in first thing tomorrow and I can set you up to tape it?"

"Why not do it live tonight?" Derek said. "I've got a show in an hour. You can come with me and take my slot. It's in the prime-time window so you'll have good numbers. The university already knows about your story. They'll be covering their tracks. The sooner you get it out there, the better."

"Because my first live experience wasn't a good one," I pointed out. "It's one thing doing the show with Dante when all I have to do is talk about music, and he handles everything else. It's another to fly solo with something that is too important to mess up. I don't want a single word lost to stutters or microphone squeaks or a finger on a wrong button that means I cut out. I don't want to lose the audience by going off on a rant again."

"You won't have to fly solo," Derek assured me. "I'll be there. I can handle the board, deal with any sound or mechanical issues and fill in the time if there is any dead air. And once you're done, I can go back to my regular programming."

I liked the idea of getting the story out there right away. The university had already shut down Professor Stanton. What else were they prepared to do? "I thought you made someone sound like Mickey Mouse," I said, considering.

"It was just a few squeaks," he protested.

"We'll all come," Haley offered. "You might need more bodies around if they try to stop you."

"Whoa." Chad held up his hands. "I'm not in if this is going to get violent. I can't risk any damage to this face. It's the key to my future."

"I was thinking witnesses, not a throw-down." Haley couldn't hide the sarcasm in her tone as we packed up to leave. "But don't worry. If it comes to that, you can just run away."

"Is something wrong?" I asked Dante as we walked across the campus, our boots squeaking in the snow. The wind had picked up and even with my thick jacket, hat, scarf, and mittens, I could still feel the chill.

"I expected the old Noah when I went to tell him what had happened," he said quietly. "I thought he'd jump out of his chair and drive himself to the station because he was so incensed he just had to be in the thick of the action. And he was incensed. He said this is exactly why we need independent radio, but then he said it was up to me to carry his torch. I don't think he plans to come back."

"His cancer is terminal," I said gently. "Maybe he doesn't want to spend his last days fixing broken microphones and juggling programming schedules. Maybe he could put that burden aside because he knows that the station is in good hands with someone who loves it as much as he does."

"I can't run the station. I'm going into law," Dante protested. "I owe it to my family. They need justice."

"What do you need?" I stepped back as Dante pulled open the door to the student center. "Or maybe the better question is, what do you really want? It took me a long time to answer that question for myself, and it was only when I really got my teeth into a story that I realized journalism was what I really wanted to do."

We trooped down the stairs, but our conversation faded into silence when we saw chains on the station door and a huge yellow sign that read "Closed."

"How can they do this?" Haley tugged on the door handle, ratting the chains. "Doesn't it violate some kind of law?"

Nick shook his head. "It's their building. Their property."

"Did they find out Skye was going to broadcast the story instead of going to print?" she persisted. "Did someone rat us out?"

"Professor Stanton hinted to me that there was another way

of going public, but he wouldn't have done that and then turned around and betrayed us. I got the feeling he really wanted this story to get out. Other than him, no one knew the plan except us."

"What are the permanent employees going to do?" Siobhan asked. "They have families and mortgages. They can't just be terminated with no notice or severance. And you have course credits riding on your internships. I think we need to get a lawyer involved."

"And in the meantime, they find a way to bury the story." I looked over at Dante. "Can you pick the lock?"

"You could be charged with trespassing," he warned. "And I could be charged with breaking and entering."

"Not if I tell them I was in the station when they locked the door." My mind raced as I considered all the possibilities. "Open the door and let me in, then lock it behind me. I'll say I was asleep in the lounge and woke up only to discover I couldn't get out."

A maelstrom of emotions flickered across Dante's face. "What happened to good Skye who didn't like to break the rules?"

"She's learned to let her bad girl free. I'm about to expose the university for covering up a sexual assault involving one of their star basketball players. I'm not worried about a little trespassing."

Dante frowned. "What about Derek?"

"I don't want anyone else involved if I'm breaking the rules," I said. "I know what to do. I just need to believe in myself. This is my story and I want to stand behind it."

"They'll probably send campus security to the station once someone hears the broadcast," Siobhan warned us. "They might try to shut Skye down before she can finish."

"They'll have to get through me," Dante said, as he worked the lock with the same small tool he'd used when we played hide-and-seek. "I might not be able to help inside, but I can do a hell of a lot out here."

"We could all help," Haley offered. "It will be like another game of hide-and-seek, except we'll make ourselves visible to the security guards and then hide to keep them distracted."

"If they do make it to the station, they'll have to deal with me," Dante said, as the lock fell open.

"Since when is the Lord of Darkness a team player?" Siobhan asked, one eyebrow raised in query.

Dante shrugged. "Since I realized I was part of a team."

"You know what this means?" Nick had an arm around Isla. "We need to sing our team song."

"Yes, we do." I pulled open the door. "But first, let's show this city what indie radio is all about."

My first solo show wasn't perfect. I stumbled over words, mumbled through a few sentences, and talked too quickly. But from the number of messages that popped up on the screen, and the stream of notifications on WJPK's social media, I got the message through.

Even if the university kicked me out, I was proud of what I had accomplished, and for the first time I wasn't afraid of the consequences. I knew what I wanted to do with my life, and if it wasn't at Havencrest, it would be somewhere else. No one was going to stop me.

I had just turned off all the equipment when I heard a rattle at the front door. Moments later it opened and Dante rushed in, followed by a security guard and a custodian.

"Are you okay?" He feigned concern, holding my shoulders and then pulling me close. "I got your message about being locked in."

"Thanks for rescuing me." I twisted my face into a combination of terror and utter relief. "Someone must have locked the door when I was taking a nap in the lounge before my show. I didn't know what was going on."

"I walked through the station before we locked it up." The security guard glared at me. "I didn't see you."

"I was under a blanket." I gave him my sweetest, most innocent smile as he led us back out into the hallway.

"Why was the station closed?" I asked the custodian as he relocked the door.

"The university partnered with a real estate developer to turn the building into student residences," he said. "I heard a condition of the offer was that the radio station had to be shut down immediately."

"Did anything else in the building have to shut down?" Dante asked. "Any of the businesses in the food court? Copy shop? Spirit store? Bookshop?"

"Nope." He followed us up the stairs while the security guard reported to someone on his walkie-talkie. "It's a shame. The station has been around as long as I have."

"Noah saw it coming," I said on our way to the campus bar where our friends were already celebrating. The air outside was crisp and icy and stung my cheeks. "I wish I'd put more time into that story. Maybe I could have done something to save the station."

Dante shook his head, his face creased in a puzzled frown. "It doesn't make sense. Why shut down the station and nothing else?"

"What are you thinking?"

"My dad said he would destroy everything I cared about if I didn't come to work for him and return the inheritance money. I didn't take him seriously because he's basically left me alone for the last seven years, but he's a real estate developer. It's not beyond the realm of possibility that he partnered with the university so he could shut the station down out of spite."

I slid my mittened hand into his. "Does he have the money to buy an entire building?"

"He owns Rossi Holdings," Dante said. "They are one of the biggest real estate developers in the state. He could buy multiple buildings, and now that he's moved into waste management and tied up some of the biggest contracts in the city, he could buy the whole campus if he wanted."

"Rossi? Was that your last name?"

"It was before I changed it."

"It sounds familiar. I feel like I've seen it on something." I pulled out my phone and flipped through my pictures. "Is this his company?" I showed him the logo on the side of the truck I'd spotted mixing garbage and recycling outside the athletic center.

Dante stared at the circular logo with the words *Rossi Waste*

Management Services written below. "I would assume so. It's not a common name."

It only took a quick internet search to confirm that Rossi Waste Management was indeed Dante's father's company.

"Should we sneak back inside?" I asked. "I've got enough evidence to run a story about how his company has been mixing waste and recycling and bribing people to look the other way. I've even got pictures."

"Babe . . ." Dante gave me a hug. "Enjoy your win before you start digging into another story."

I laughed. "That's what journalists do."

"My journalist," he said, brushing his lips over my hair.

"Yours," I agreed. "Now . . . How do you want to expose him? University press? Social media? *Chicago Tribune*? I'm not even going to try and submit my recycling story to Professor Stanton because I have a feeling the university will shut this one down, too."

"I've got a better idea," Dante said.

"Does it involve a trip to a hidden balcony at the top of the world?"

"It involves taking the pictures to my dad and making him reopen the station."

"Oh." I gave a heavy sigh. "Blackmail. I guess that could be kind of fun. But honestly, I was hoping to celebrate my incredible victory with some sex in an abandoned building and a new playlist."

"We're supposed to meet everyone at the bar to celebrate," he said. "They played hide-and-seek in the hallways to distract the security guard and forgot to tell him he was the seeker."

"That's a shame," I said. "All the excitement made me want to be a very bad good girl. It could be we were delayed coming to the bar because the custodian brought the wrong key."

Dante sucked in a sharp breath and his eyes narrowed. "Did I ever tell you about the tunnel under the math building?"

"No."

He tugged my hand, walking so quickly I had to jog to keep up. "It's soundproofed," he said. "No one will be able to hear you scream."

CHAPTER THIRTY-EIGHT

"The End" by the Doors

DANTE

I got the call the day after Skye's story blew up in the media. I had planned to visit my dad for a fun round of blackmail, but everything was put on hold when Bella told me Noah was missing.

"One day," she shouted over the phone. "I was away for one day to visit a friend, and I came to discover his car is gone, and his pets are with the pet sitter, ready to go to the new forever homes he arranged *last month*." Her voice rose on the last two words. "His phone and house keys are on the dining room table. I called the hospital and they said he'd canceled the rest of his treatments. We need to find him."

We spent the day driving around the city looking for Noah's distinctive red-and-white 1969 Dodge Charger RT. We visited his favorite bars and restaurants, shops, and parks. We called every contact in his address book and drove all the way along Lake Shore Drive in case he'd decided to freeze himself to death while taking in the view. It was like a farewell tour, and by the time the sun set, we'd resigned ourselves to the fact that Noah was missing because he wanted to be missing, and there was nothing we could do to bring him back.

We returned to the house and Bella ordered some food while I walked around taking stock of what Noah had left behind. Unlike my family home, his memories were still there—his collection of vinyl, the basketball hoop he'd put up to get me outside during my darkest days, pictures of his family and his pets, his favorite fringed leather jacket and worn cowboy boots, the green armchair where he sat every night to listen to his favorite songs, the table where he'd helped me fill in my university applications, a collection of bolo ties, and enough musical paraphernalia to open a museum. "He took his guitar," I said after I'd finished my walk down memory lane.

Bella looked up from the row of family pictures. "He's gone to find Caroline."

"I saw him yesterday." My hand tightened on the chew toy I'd found in the hallway. "I wish I'd known that was the last time I'd get to talk to him." I could barely keep it together. I felt untethered. I needed Skye, but she was caught in a whirlwind of interviews and radio and television appearances and I wasn't about to pull her away from her moment in the sun.

"Fuck." I threw the toy across the room. "I can't do this without him."

"Do what?" Bella turned to me, her eyes wet with tears.

"Life." I scrubbed my hands over my face. "I've lost everyone I ever loved. I can't lose him, too."

"You've been doing life on your own for a long time," Bella said. "And you're not alone. You've got me. You've got Skye. Noah said you've even managed to make friends. You've got your future all mapped out. If Noah thought you needed him, he'd still be here."

"I do need him." My voice cracked, broke. "I don't know what to do, Bella. I've known what I wanted to do for the last four years, but now I think I might be on the wrong path. I need to talk to him. If he'd just waited . . ."

"Then he wouldn't have gone. You were like a son to him, Dante. The thing that distressed him most was the idea of leaving you. He's been living with this illness for a lot longer than you know, but he hung on until he knew you'd be okay."

"Don't say anything else." I didn't think I could keep it together if she kept talking.

"He loved you, Dante," she continued, despite my warning.

"You gave him purpose—more than the station ever did—but he had one regret, and he was running out of time to make peace with that part of his life."

Before I could respond, she left the room and returned with Noah's Santa Cruz 1934 OM Brazilian guitar. Noah always said it was the greatest musical instrument he had ever had the privilege to play. The guitar had an unrivaled vintage tone that only got better with age. He'd paid over twenty thousand dollars for it and had only played it a handful of times, preferring the guitar that he'd owned since his youth.

"Noah told me many years ago that he'd been keeping this guitar for you, and I would know when it was time to hand it over." She placed the guitar in my hands. "I think he knew what you were struggling with, and this is his answer."

Emotion welled up in my chest, closing my throat. The Santa Cruz was everything that made a stringed instrument beautiful. It was pure music, and only a true musician could make it sing.

A few days after Noah left, I went to see my dad.

"The prodigal son returns." My father looked up from his desk, the faintest of smirks tugging at the corner of his lips. His office in The Loop was a vast expanse of glass, hardwood, and shining steel. A thunderstorm had rolled in and the gray clouds outside the floor-to-ceiling windows drained both light and life from the cold, hard space.

"This isn't a social visit." My feet sank into the plush carpet as I walked toward him, the acrid scent of cleaning products bringing back a host of bad memories. I handed him the envelope containing Skye's photos of Rossi Waste Management truck drivers paying off the university maintenance workers, as well as her short summary of the story she planned to run if my dad didn't agree to my terms. I had no qualms about blackmailing him. It was a language he understood. He was a master of dirty business tactics, and he'd taught me everything I knew.

"What's this?"

"Read it."

With an exasperated sniff, he opened the envelope. His jaw clenched as he flipped through the documents. Finally, he looked up at me with narrowed eyes. "What's this all about?"

"You tell me. One truck instead of two. One driver instead of two. Twice the pay for twice the load. And of course, garbage pays more than recycling. How do you think the good citizens of Chicago would feel if they found out all their hard work at protecting the environment, separating their recyclables from their normal trash, was for nothing? That the waste management company that had won contracts worth over eighty million dollars was actually working against them? They are paying a fee for a service that's not getting done."

"It's one guy." He tossed the papers on his desk. "A rogue operator. He'll be fired and that will be the end of it."

"There are multiple drivers doing this; not one guy," I said. "We have video evidence. Not only that, but we also have a team leader confirming on video that his instructions came from the top." I waved my hand vaguely around his office. "I can't imagine it's going to look good when you make your bid for the airport contract, or when your three-year contracts are up for renewal. I also wonder if the citizens who paid for the services they didn't receive will ask for a refund."

He understood the game right away. "What do you want?"

I took a deep breath and steadied myself, trying to keep my own emotions in check. "I want you to withdraw your offer for the building that houses the radio station and I want the station reopened effective immediately. I want your word that you won't file any reports about the scholarship and if you already have, then you'll withdraw them. Finally, I'll be keeping my inheritance money. I've hired a new lawyer to manage Grandma's estate and you will not threaten or blackmail her."

"That's it?" He snorted a laugh. "You are not cut out for business if that's the best you can do with the hand you've got. I'm embarrassed to call you my son."

It was everything I could do to maintain my poker face. This was only my opening gambit. I hadn't shown him all my cards.

"I've wasted too much time chasing after revenge," I said. "There is nothing you can do that will ever make up for what you did to me or Mom or Sasha. I know you pushed Mom down the stairs because she was planning to leave you and go to the police with evidence of your crimes. I know you used your criminal connections to cover it up. Sasha saw it all, and the burden of that, of seeing you walk free on top of all the abuse she had to endure, was too much for her to bear. She killed herself because of you. But I'm tired of being angry, tired of living a life where all I think about is how to destroy you. I have that power now, but what I really want is for you to be out of my life forever."

His eyes widened in disbelief, then anger flashed across his face. "You ungrateful little shit," he spat out. "I gave you everything. You wouldn't be where you are today without me. You wouldn't have had a life if I'd let your mother go to the police. Do you even understand that? We would all have gone down. We would have lost the business, the house . . . everything. You should be thanking me for breaking her fucking neck. It was a mercy compared to what would have happened to her if our family in the old country found out what she was planning to do."

For a moment, I couldn't talk. Even though I'd known he'd committed the crime, hearing him admit it, and without a hint of remorse or regret, was more painful than I could ever have imagined.

"You gave me nothing but fear and pain and loss." I kept my voice calm and even, acutely aware that the police and the FBI were listening and recording the conversation through the wire taped to my chest. This would be our last conversation and I wanted to make sure I said everything I'd always wanted to say. "You showed me how to be a bitter, angry, ruthless, soulless human being. But you're right about one thing. If I didn't hate you so much, I would never have enrolled in college. I would never have focused all my energy on getting a degree that would give me the skills to take you down. I would never have met the man who was more of a father to me than you will ever be. I would never have found my true passion. And I would never have found love."

Skye and I had finished the investigation together, hiding in alleyways, following garbage trucks in Ubers, and taking surreptitious videos from behind mailboxes and lampposts on the street. It had been a blast. She had written up the story and it was ready to go live on her new investigative reporting show at the station—the show Noah had wanted her to host.

I didn't expect an apology and I didn't get one. Nor did I see even a flicker of shame, guilt, or regret on his hard face.

"So, what now?" he spat out. "I agree to your demands, and this goes away?"

"Yes."

"Even after you become a lawyer?"

"I'm not going to become a lawyer," I said. "I was doing it for all the wrong reasons. Life is short and I don't want to come to the end and realize that I missed my chance to follow my dreams."

"You'll be cut out of my will if you do this," he said. "The business, the legacy, all the money . . . it will go to your cousin Silvio."

I'd met Silvio a few times as a teenager. He was a miniature version of my dad but without the good sense to stay out of jail. "He's welcome to it. I'm planning to make my name as a bass player and launch my music career."

"Jesus Christ." He snorted a laugh. "A bass player? You'll be back on the streets in less than a year."

"Not this time," I said. "I've faced my biggest fear, and it didn't destroy me. I'm going to be okay."

He tucked the photos and papers back into the envelope. "How do I know you'll keep your word?"

"Because I'm not you."

"Fine. I'll make the calls."

"Do it now while I'm here." It had to be now before the FBI and police waiting downstairs came up to ask him some questions. I'd finally decided that this had to end, and I'd gone to see the lawyers I'd worked with at the DA's office who'd brought in the FBI. I just had to hope that my father couldn't get to them the way he'd gotten to everyone else. Revenge had given me purpose, but it no longer defined my life.

I felt a weight lift from shoulders as he made the calls. It was finally over. No more dwelling on the past. I could finally look forward to the future—a future in which a police officer with a warrant would know to look for the brown envelope that would help take down my father's company.

"It's done." He slammed the receiver down. "We're done."

I took one last look at the face that was an older version of my own before I turned to leave and felt nothing. No longing. No regret. No love. "Goodbye, Dad."

"Dante."

I stopped in the doorway, and looked back over my shoulder, raising my eyebrow in query.

"You're just like your mother," he snarled.

"Thank you," I said. "That's probably the nicest thing you've ever said to me."

CHAPTER THIRTY-NINE

"Dangerous Woman" by Ariana Grande

SKYE

"Welcome to Dante's Darkness, the show where anything goes and you set the theme. I'm here with you when the rest of the world is sleeping."

I quietly opened the door to the radio station and slipped inside, listening to Dante's deep voice through my headphones. He'd texted me before his show to let me know his first blackmail attempt had been a huge success. His dad had withdrawn his offer for the building, which meant the station had reopened just in time for him to do his show. The only downside was that I couldn't run my recycling story. I told him not to worry. The world was full of stories, and that one was garbage anyway.

He started off with an apology to his listeners for the brief hiatus and explained there were some changes happening at the station. I knew they would forgive him. His show was a balm to every soul that wandered the night, including mine.

"Hope is our theme tonight," Dante crooned through the headphones. "Let's kick it off with Surfaces's 'Take it Easy.' You might recognize this band from their TikTok hit 'Sunday Best.' This track is a mood-booster that's going to send your mind on an island vacation. We'll follow it up with 'Good Day' by Mackenzie Bourg because that's gonna be your tomorrow."

Dante was alone in Studio A. I walked into Studio B across from him wearing nothing but my long winter coat, belted around my waist.

Five months ago, I could never have imagined stripping in front of anyone and letting them see my scars, but I was a different person now. I knew who I was and what I wanted. I was comfortable with my body. And I'd found someone I trusted with my heart.

Dante looked through the window and sent me a text.

What's up, buttercup?

I came to keep you company.

Is it raining?

No, but it's hot in here.

I leaned against the back wall of the studio and unbuttoned the first button on my coat as I fanned myself with my free hand. Dante was talking into the mic, his headphones on, but his eyes were fixed on me, a tiny furrow growing in the crease between his eyebrows.

I unbuttoned the second button and pushed the flap aside to show him what I wasn't wearing underneath. The furrow in his brow deepened. I cupped my breast and leaned back, closing my eyes.

My phone buzzed. It was hard not to smile.

What are you doing?

You are generating so much heat in there, I need to cool off.

Sit down and behave. I'm almost done.

I pulled out the chair and sat down, letting the coat fall open to give him a teasing look at my lack of underwear.

My phone buzzed again. Dante didn't look very pleased.

Stop

I slowly unbuttoned the rest of the coat and slid my hand between my legs.

Buzz.

Buzz.

I closed my eyes and touched myself to the angry buzz of my notifications. I briefly wondered what Dante was saying to his listeners, but I was close, too close to care.

My orgasm hit me hard and fast, making me arch up out of the chair, my coat falling completely open as Dante's eyes blazed in the studio across from me. I dropped my feet, accidentally kicking my phone off the table. Oops. I'd have to pick it up. I turned my back to him and bent over, flipping up the convenient back flap of the coat for maximum viewing pleasure. Then I gave a little wiggle. I wasn't a good girl tonight. Not good at all.

The door crashed open.

I jerked up and pulled the coat tight around me, eyes wide, innocence personified. Dante stalked toward me, his face taut.

"My office. Right now." He grabbed my collar and yanked the coat off, dropping it to the floor. "I've put on thirty minutes of prerecorded music. That should be enough to show you what happens to bad girls."

"I didn't know you had an office." I shivered under the heat of his gaze.

"The board held an emergency meeting today. I formally accepted their offer to take over as co-station manager with Siobhan until the end of term. They've also offered to extend the position after we graduate. Siobhan is planning to stay at Havencrest for grad school, and it would mean I'd be able to pay my bills and do session work until I've made my name as a bass player or joined a band."

My lips tugged at the corners. "So . . . You're the boss."

"That's right." He folded his arms across his chest. "And your boss wants you in his office, bent over his desk so you can be punished for your bad behavior."

"I thought it was good behavior." I brushed up against him as I walked out the door. "You were looking a little tired. I thought I'd do something to wake you up."

Dante grabbed my hand and pressed it against the bulge beneath his fly. “You succeeded.”

“Exactly how ‘up’ are you?” I could feel the heat of his gaze on my naked body as I walked down the hallway.

“So ‘up’ you’re gonna feel me tomorrow.” His voice was rough, low and husky with promise.

“Are you going to be okay in here?” I asked, pausing on the threshold of Noah’s office. Nothing had been touched since he left. The desk was still covered in papers. Boxes full of magazines littered the floors. Posters and band merch filled every chair.

Dante stood in the doorway for a long moment, and then he stepped inside.

“Yes,” he said, pulling me into his arms. “I’m going to be okay.”

CHAPTER FORTY

"Everlong" by Foo Fighters

SKYE

It was the end of the school year and Steamworks was packed. I hadn't been to the bar since the night I met Dante, and nothing had changed, from the teeming mass of bodies on the dance floor to the scents of stale beer and deep-fried chicken wings.

This time, however, Isla and I weren't there to find her fangirl crush or to take my mind off a basketball tryout. We were there for something much more important.

"Excuse me." Isla marched up to the six foot five bouncer guarding the back hallway. He wore a nametag that read *Brad* and he filled the entire doorway with his massive presence alone. "We're with the band."

Brad snorted in derision. "That's what all the girls say."

"Skye has Dante's name tattooed on her ass." Isla pushed me forward. "Show him your tramp stamp."

"It's not on my ass; it's on my hip," I snapped. "And it's not his name. It's a symbol for truth. It covers one of my scars. Why don't you show him your ass since you're wanting to let it all hang out?"

"Nick would kill him," she said with a shrug. "You saw him outside the bar the night I was hustling at pool. If Dante hadn't been there, he would have taken them all down."

I kept my thoughts on Nick's fighting skills to myself. Isla had finally found closure after Ethan was arrested. She had been able to move on and let Nick into her life, and he could do no wrong in her eyes.

"Maybe we should text the boys and let them know Brad won't let us through." I pulled out my phone. "Or maybe I should write a piece for the *Havencrest Express* about officious bouncers and their short-lived careers when the girlfriend of a bass player who has attracted some big-name producers to the show tonight is denied his good luck kiss."

Brad lifted the velvet rope and ushered us through.

"A wise decision," I called back over my shoulder. "Although Isla's ass is something to behold."

The back door to the alley had been propped open, and we walked outside, where the new Dante's Inferno was unloading their gear for what we hoped would be the gig that landed Dante a sessional contract with a mega-famous band.

I leaned against the brick wall to take the pressure off my leg and drew in a deep breath of fresh spring air. "Before the night gets crazy, I have to tell you something."

Isla brightened. "You got another tattoo?"

"No."

"If you made a new playlist, I can pretend to be excited, but just don't make me listen to a long explanation about what all the songs mean."

"I did make a new playlist for Dante, but that's not my big surprise." I took a deep breath. "I got the summer internship at the *Chicago Tribune*!"

After my big story had broken, I'd been invited to interview at all the major media outlets in the city, but the *Chicago Tribune*, with their formidable investigative reporting team, was where I wanted to be.

"Oh my God." Isla wrapped me in a hug. "That's amazing! Does that mean you won't be going back to Denver for the summer?"

"It means you have a roommate for as long as you can stand me."

"I told you I had a sixth sense about these things," Isla said. "Do you remember that?"

I remembered everything about the night I met Dante. "You said my dreams would come true. I thought you meant I'd get on the basketball team, but it was my real dream you were talking about."

"You can thank me with an endless supply of coffee so I can get through summer session." Isla pulled out a package of jellybeans and tapped one into her hand. She'd developed a candy addiction after giving up vaping, much to her dentist's dismay. Two cavities later, she'd begged me to help her quit.

"Iz . . ." I shook my head. "You promised me you were going to switch to something healthy. Where are your sunflower seeds?"

"I just need one," she said. "It gives me the kind of buzz I can't get from seeds. I'm not a bird."

"Give me the jellybeans." I reached for the package and she backed away.

"This is the last one. I promise."

I lunged for her, and she backed away just as Dante emerged from the van carrying a large amp. Isla stumbled just as my hand clasped around her wrist. We went down hard, falling on the amp and knocking it to the ground. I rolled off Isla and snaked up beside her to grab the jellybean from her hand.

"I think we really need to talk about your inability to stay on your feet when I'm around," Dante said, helping us both up with a wry grin.

Out of the corner of my eye, I saw Nick heading over to Isla. My gaze slid back to Dante, who was wearing his Inferno T-shirt and his favorite worn black jeans. His hair was a sexy mess like he'd just rolled out of bed—which, in fact, he had, because I'd insisted on good luck sex before the gig.

"Don't let it go to your head." Even after almost eight months together, sometimes his sheer gorgeousness took my breath away. "Your ego is already so big I have to step around it."

His lips quirked at the corners. "Is that why you made me a new playlist?"

"It was supposed to be a surprise," I grumbled. "It's a playlist about us."

"I want my surprise now." He backed me up against the van and placed one hand beside my head, leaning forward in a seemingly casual manner that sent a wave of liquid heat through my veins. "Tell me the songs, Skye. I want to know our story."

I couldn't deny him anything, not when he was looking at me as if I were the most beautiful woman in the world. "First meeting, 'You Really Got Me' by The Kinks since you instantly captured my attention."

Dante cupped my jaw in one hand and tipped my head back, his breath whispering over my lips. "What was next?"

"'Crazy Little Thing Called Love' by Queen."

"It was a crazy time." He feathered kisses along my jaw. "I felt like you'd cast some kind of spell on me."

"Then 'Love Hurts' by Nazareth," I whispered. "That was a bad time when we were hating on each other."

"I never hated you," he whispered in my ear. "I was hurt but I'd take any pain for you."

"Then you'll like that my next song is 'Don't Stop Believin' by Journey."

"Journey?" He pulled away, his brow creasing in a frown. "I don't want Journey on our playlist."

"I created the list, and the song is perfect. Stop grumbling."

Dante huffed and went back to tormenting me with little butterfly kisses. "I want to choose the last song."

"I already chose a last song."

"It's not going to be as good as mine."

"Seriously?"

"When it comes to you, I'm very serious." He slid one arm around my waist and pulled me close. "I pick 'Everlong' by Foo Fighters."

"Why that song?"

Dante kissed me, his lips soft and sweet. "Because that's how long I'll love you."

CHAPTER FORTY-ONE

"Sweet Caroline" by Neil Diamond

DANTE

I found the envelope on my desk two months into my tenure as station manager. No stamp. No postmark. Just my name in Noah's familiar scrawl. For the briefest moment, I wished I had accepted the university's offer to install cameras when I finally got them to do the basement upgrades. But Noah would never have wanted cameras, and Siobhan and I were trying to run the station in a way that would honor his legacy—open and honest and free.

At first, I couldn't bring myself to open it. I didn't want to know if Noah was finally gone. I liked the idea of him out in the world, playing in dive bars or busking on street corners, on his quest to find Caroline. It had made the grief bearable, the days of carefully packing up Noah's treasured albums a chance to relive memories instead of dwell on the pain of loss.

I finally gave in after I finished my show. *Dante's Darkness* was now the number one late-night show in Chicago and there were talks of syndication. I'd even received an offer to DJ at one of the top radio stations in the city, but I was committed to developing my career playing bass, and if I was going to do any radio, WJPK would always be my home.

I poured myself a drink and sat in Noah's office, bracing myself for bad news as I sliced open the envelope.

Dear Dante,

I am not dead. I wanted to write that on the front of the envelope because I knew that's what you'd think when you received it, but I couldn't take the risk that someone else might see it and spread the good news. I don't know how long I have left but I'm making the most of each and every day. I've been traveling around the country saying goodbye to all the people who made a difference in my life. It's how I started my musical journey and I can't think of a better way for it to end.

But I couldn't say goodbye to you.

You weren't just a friend to me; you were my son in every sense of that word, and the day you came into my life was the day I started living again. You said I saved you, but you saved me. You gave me a purpose. You showed me that the past did not define me, and when I saw you with Skye, you made me believe in love again. You made me want to find my Caroline and tell her what I should have told her all those years ago.

And I will find her. I know it in my bones.

Since these are my last words to you, I have to make a confession. From the moment I met Skye, I knew she was the one for you. She spoke our language. She shared our passion for music. She was fierce, brave, compassionate, and determined and I knew that if anyone could drag you out of the darkness, it was her. I knew I had to do everything I could to keep her in your life. She may not have been the best candidate, but as I told her, she was the right candidate, and she proved herself to be that and much more over and over again.

Hold Skye tight. Love her with all your heart. Nothing is more important than the people we care about. Not even Bob Dylan's Highway 61 Revisited, *which is probably the greatest album ever made.*

Before I left, I asked my lawyer to transfer the house and everything I own into your name. My family disowned me a long time ago and Bella has always understood how I felt about you. I hope one day you can do what I couldn't—fill those rooms with laughter, music, joy, and life.

When you think of me—and you'd better think of me—imagine me forever on the road. I'll be in the roughest dive bars and on the grittiest street corners. I'll be playing my guitar until my fingers bleed and kissing my Caroline until I can't breathe. And I'll be there for every gig you play, if not in body, then in spirit. Look for me in the audience. I'll be the one shouting "That's my boy!"

You have my music so you will always have me. Put on my favorite records and listen to my songs. I am always in your heart. And remember, no matter how hard life gets, you just have to rock on.

ACKNOWLEDGMENTS

I've held many positions over the years, from bouncer to librarian and from lawyer to storyteller, but none captured my imagination as much as my job in independent radio. From the moment I walked in the door, I felt like I'd found my people and I've always wanted to tell their story (fictitious, of course!).

Thank you to Monique Patterson for giving me the opportunity to bring the world of college radio to life, and to Erika Tsang for your enthusiasm and expert editorial guidance. Thank you to my longtime agent, Laura Bradford, for your endless patience and advice. A huge thank-you to the Bramble art team for the beautiful cover and to the production team for polishing the book and making it shine.

I was fortunate to have two music experts to help me find the perfect songs and create my playlists. Thank you, Jamie and Hannah. I hope you didn't have too many heated discussions about your recommendations. I am forever grateful for all the new music you shared with me.

To John for the endless acts of service. You are loved more than you know. And to my medium and small ones, thank you for being so excited about this book. You're still too young to read it. Maybe in twenty years . . .

And finally, thank you to the boy with the blue metal-flake bass . . . in a terms-of-endearment kind of way.

ABOUT THE AUTHOR

Linda Mackie Photography

SARAH CASTILLE is the *New York Times* and *USA Today* bestselling author of over twenty romance novels featuring sexy fighters, rugged bikers, dangerously seductive mafia bosses, and tattooed bad boys. She is known for her steamy love scenes, heart-wrenching stories, and swoon-worthy happy endings.

A former bouncer, radio DJ, librarian, historian, and lawyer, Castille lives on Vancouver Island with her lively and energetic family. When she's not tormenting imaginary alpha heroes or wrangling kids, she's probably in her little red kayak, paddling out to sea.

For more information about Castille and her books, visit sarahcastille.com.